MISTRESS'S

MASTER

JAYNE RYLON

eBook ISBN: 978-1-941785-25-6
Print ISBN: 978-1-941785-59-1

Ebook Cover Art By Angela Waters
Print Book Cover Art By Jayne Rylon
Interior Print Book Design By Jayne Rylon

Sign Up For The Naughty News!
Contests, sneak peeks, appearance info, and more.
www.jaynerylon.com/newsletter

Shop
Autographed books, reading-themed apparel,
notebooks, totes, and more.
www.jaynerylon.com/shop

Contact Jayne
Email: contact@jaynerylon.com
Website: www.jaynerylon.com
Facebook: Facebook.com/JayneRylon
Twitter: @JayneRylon

OTHER BOOKS BY JAYNE RYLON

DIVEMASTERS
Going Down
Going Deep
Going Hard

MEN IN BLUE
Night is Darkest
Razor's Edge
Mistress's Master
Spread Your Wings
Wounded Hearts
Bound For You

POWERTOOLS
Kate's Crew
Morgan's Surprise
Kayla's Gift
Devon's Pair
Nailed to the Wall
Hammer it Home

HOTRODS
King Cobra
Mustang Sally
Super Nova
Rebel on the Run
Swinger Style
Barracuda's Heart

Touch of Amber
Long Time Coming

COMPASS BROTHERS
Northern Exposure
Southern Comfort
Eastern Ambitions
Western Ties

COMPASS GIRLS
Winter's Thaw
Hope Springs
Summer Fling
Falling Softly

PLAY DOCTOR
Dream Machine
Healing Touch

STANDALONES
4-Ever Theirs
Nice & Naughty
Where There's Smoke
Report For Booty

RACING FOR LOVE
Driven
Shifting Gears

RED LIGHT
Through My Window
Star

Can't Buy Love
Free For All

PARANORMALS
Picture Perfect
Reborn

PICK YOUR PLEASURES
Pick Your Pleasure
Pick Your Pleasure 2

DEDICATION

For the special fans I've gotten to know including Zina, Drea, Gigi, Kitty Kelly, Ive, Dawn, Suz C and all the rest I can't begin to name. Also to all of you I haven't met yet online or in person. Thank you for reading!

CHAPTER ONE

The crack of the whip rent the air. Strips of oiled leather painted bright crimson streaks across pale skin. Shock waves originated from the impact site then radiated through the rapt audience. Jeremy wouldn't have been surprised if the wooden bleachers they sat on tipped over since nearly all the members in attendance leaned forward in their seats. Relaxed, he reclined, slowly spinning the stem of his wineglass between his fingers.

He closed his eyes.

Not to avoid the scene before him. Rather to savor the crisp whistle of the expertly wielded tool. It sounded again and again. Pregnant anticipation overflowed the instant before the braided cat-o'-nine connected with its target—a fit male slave's taut buttocks. Even Jeremy could appreciate the man's form, as if he were a marble statue in the Smithsonian.

Except this art lived. It breathed, groaned and...screamed.

The slave on the receiving end of Mistress Lily's strike jerked in the wide leather cuffs shackling him, spread eagle, facing the dungeon wall. His fists clenched, and his toes curled where they hung six inches or so off the concrete floor. The man tolerated pain well. He responded beautifully, evidence of the quality of his training.

Another precisely placed contact blasted the audience with reverberations of the energy sparking between the slave and his Mistress. The woman—so tiny, so elegant, so gorgeous and so damn strong—could deliver extreme punishment and still seem like an avenging angel or a violent fairy. She overwhelmed Jeremy with admiration. And lust.

The only thing better than observing her work would be to have her at his mercy.

He placed his drink on a silver tray beside his premium seat, which she had reserved at his last-minute request. Suddenly, he feared he'd grip the delicate crystal goblet too tightly and crush the dazzling vessel. A true Master understood his strength and protected the things he valued at all times. At all costs. Even if it meant denying himself something he'd like—no, needed—to have.

With his free hand, he adjusted his rock-hard cock. One thought of Lily ruined his ironclad control. Yet another reason he should leave her the hell alone.

Three months had passed since he'd cornered the manager of Black Lily, an underground bondage club. He chuckled to himself. The fetish label seemed frivolous, fun and light compared to all that had gone on there. Jeremy recalled trapping Lily in her office to probe for information on his last—current, really—case.

He'd stolen a taste of her succulent lips while they'd wrestled for dominance.

Witnesses to her skills would have laughed him out of the dungeon if he expressed his suspicions, but he swore he'd sensed a hairline crack in her armor. That miniscule hint of surrender had driven his imagination mad every night since. He'd replayed the encounter in his mind so many times he might have worn out those brain cells.

Tonight he didn't have to rely on the vivid memory. Despite explicit orders from his boss—the head of the

2

DEA task force tracking The Scientist and his designer drug—to avoid Lily's domain, he hadn't been able to comply with the directive. He'd sat on his hands long enough. Twelve fucking weeks worth of idleness had compelled him to take a risk when he'd caught wind of tonight's extravaganza in Lily's honor.

He wouldn't miss her *going away* party.

Where the fuck did she plan to run to anyway? When would she come home?

Something was happening. He could sense it in every fiber of his being. So why hadn't she reached out? She wouldn't disappear without warning. Wouldn't abandon the legitimate submissives who begged for her mastery and relied on her to provide a safe outlet for their desires. Would she?

All attempts to contact her had failed. She'd obviously received his veiled messages and saved him a spot. Still, she hadn't had the guts to pick up his call or accost him in one of the shadowy recesses he'd lurked in before the show began. Son of a bitch. Had she lingered nearby, had the roles been reversed, he couldn't have prevented himself from initiating contact.

Damn her.

Despite his frustration, he appraised the star of his fantasies. Her waist-length braid would make a great tether, wrapped around his wrist. Thick and shiny, it snaked down her vinyl-coated spine. The rope tapered off near the swell of her pert ass, which made his palm itch to smack it. He'd give his last month's pay to observe it jiggle and flush red. Spanking her—inspiring a sting across his skin even as he shared the burn—ranked high on his bucket list.

High-gloss, obsidian fabric might as well have been painted onto her skin. It couldn't get more form fitting. Every curve of her toned calves and thighs along with her lush hips and breasts tantalized him—visible yet hidden. Catwoman couldn't hold a flame to her.

His obsession released her prey temporarily, enlisting the help of two additional slaves to reposition the focus of her attention. Her devotees scrambled to obey. If they behaved, exceeding her lofty expectations, they might be next. This could be their last chance to suffer for her. To shine for her. The beauty of the voluntary power exchange playing out before him stole his breath.

It'd been *so* fucking long.

The glorious oblation of her admirers underscored the horror wrought by those who would pervert the sacred relationship, forcing others to submit. As had happened here so recently. Hell, maybe still did in the unmonitored corners of the dungeon.

Had Lily decided to abandon her haven because evil continued to infiltrate the club?

Why wouldn't his superiors turn him loose? Let him help.

Maybe they figured he'd be recognized. After all, he *had* assisted Lily in freeing the victims of her psychotic, drug-addicted father and the chemical for which the asshole had sacrificed his life.

Jeremy doubted he would ever enter this place without remembering the day he'd stood by Lily's side as she personally apologized to each woman she'd unshackled and escorted to safety. He'd tried to comfort her silent anguish and convince her the victims' misery hadn't been her fault.

Yet, the Dom in him understood the burden of her suffering. The injury, or worse, of a submissive entrusted to your care and protection left a soul-deep scar that never healed.

He carried one of his own.

Jeremy resisted the urge to scratch the new growth prickling his jaw and cheeks when a sheen of perspiration developed on his skin. The neat beard suited him surprisingly well, considering he'd never worn one before. It rocketed him from geeky computer detective to badass Master. Then again, his leather pants, shiny black boots and bare, ripped chest—which revealed the barbells in his nipples and the string of tattoos low on his abdomen—didn't hurt either.

For once, his appearance matched his soul. None of the potential enemies in attendance would suspect his affiliation with law enforcement or worry about him infiltrating their inner sanctum. At least he had to believe so. Otherwise, his presence might jeopardize Lily.

Unacceptable.

Jeremy licked his lips as his mole circled her oh-so-willing charge.

The man whimpered when she ran her delicate fingers through his damp hair, combing it off his brow. He arched his neck and strained toward her touch. She hardly had to stoop to reach his head despite his position—kneeling on all fours over a black metal contraption—even considering the mile-high platform stiletto boots gracing her dainty feet.

The David-and-Goliath-factor added to the mesmerizing show unfolding before the mixed audience. The majority of the attendees had no ulterior motives. They enjoyed the scene with their partners for a night of extreme pleasure or came solo in the hopes of meeting someone who shared their kinks. Others...

"Too eager." One of the bastards who didn't comprehend the gift of surrender grumbled from Jeremy's right in the VIP section. Strict background checks and membership controls must have ensured the man's comfort in running his mouth to a stranger. *Fool.* "She needs fresh meat—a toy who hasn't had all the fight beaten out of him yet. I've heard there's a new batch about to hit the market."

The asshole peeked in Jeremy's direction.

If he expected a grin, or any other affirmation of his blatant disregard of the fundamental tenants of humanity, which Jeremy upheld, he'd be sorely disappointed.

Trouble was Jeremy and his squad had filtered the same message about an impending auction. *God damn it.*

They'd thought they had eliminated the source of the human trafficking in their city when they freed the pool of women who'd been test subjects for The Scientist and the new sex drug he'd synthesized. Although the men in blue had squashed The Scientist's large-scale production facility, the monster had escaped with an optimized formula. They weren't foolish enough to hope he wouldn't try again, although they hadn't heard a peep about it yet. However, even if he had already constructed another lab, no further studies would be needed.

So why were there more slaves to auction?

The DEA task force Jeremy had been assigned to, along with fellow officers Matt Ludwig and Clint Griggs, had picked up rumblings. Hints sprinkled through the noise that'd shrouded this case from the start. Still, Agent Sterns had refused to allow them to pursue the rumors through regular channels.

Time to bring cash and play big. He'd gone rogue, undercover without authorization, unleashing more than they could have understood into this dark world of dangerous games. If he sought answers, he'd have to dig deep and immerse himself in a culture he'd forsaken.

Jeremy swallowed his disgust, indignation and fury. He smirked at the pompous loser to his right, who tainted a sacred bond. The guy pretended to be something Jeremy simply was. Suddenly, he wouldn't change his nature if he could. His innate aptitude for mind fucking was about to come in handy.

"Didn't expect you to know about the good stuff." Jeremy raised a disdainful eyebrow at the slightly overweight man. Nothing worked better than insults to force an arrogant player to show his hand.

"Excuse me?" The man tightened his fist on the collar of the broken woman kneeling at his feet, wringing a choke from her bowed neck. Her dull eyes lacked the sparkle of devotion illuminating the men onstage. Poor girl hadn't gifted this trash with her obedience. "I'm Tony Morselli. Perhaps you've fucking heard of me?"

Of course Jeremy recognized the bastard from his files. Lily must have selected his seat accordingly. He forced himself to stay relaxed instead of teaching the dirtbag a lesson, introducing him to a fraction of the pain he'd inflicted on his unwilling pet.

"Ah, Morselli..." He antagonized the creep. "Sounds familiar. The West Coast network is so much more robust than your local operation. Sometimes we catch small news from out here."

"And who the hell are *you*?"

"Master Jeremy Radisson." He extended his hand. Tony contaminated Jeremy's skin with the malevolence clinging to him like a slime coating. As though his touch weren't distasteful enough, Tony gripped Jeremy's fingers with excessive force.

Jeremy obliged the petty power play by returning the scum's crushing clutch with interest. His lip curved up in a half-smile-half-snarl when Morselli's knuckles ground between his thumb and forefinger.

Tony relented in record time.

Jeremy didn't worry for one instant about revealing his identity to the suspected criminal. His legendary hacking skills guaranteed he'd wiped all traces of the cop and left for discovery only those deep, dark secrets that would promote his cause. Who'd have thought ancient history could someday prove useful? Previously, he'd buried those facts and highlighted others—more wholesome and dignified—along with a smattering of falsehoods.

Suddenly, the reverse proved useful. His entire life turned inside out.

"It's quality not quantity that counts. Here." Tony threw Jeremy the leather loop at the end of his prisoner's leash. "Enjoy the show. Hell, why don't you keep her? Welcome."

"Ah, a lovely gift... *Friend.*" Good thing Tony couldn't read the sarcasm in Jeremy's heart. At least his smile was genuine. If he could make it through the rest of the evening without blowing his cover, he could grant this woman freedom from a nightmare.

"She's not worth much. I planned to eliminate her anyway. She fought like a mustang at first. Now, nothing. A waste of time. Not worth the price I paid."

The slack features of the slave broke Jeremy's heart. She crawled toward him without question, coming to rest on her haunches between his spread knees. No telling how many other men she'd had to service to preserve her life. To persist in such circumstances, she had to be brave, worthy of his respect. He couldn't stop himself from brushing his thumb over her chapped and cracked mouth. When she flinched at even the softest of touches, he resigned himself to what he'd have to do to ensure her safety.

No, what he'd have to let her do to him.

Jeremy reached for his wine and drained all but a few sips. Then he held the glass toward the abused woman. She licked her lips, staring at him from lowered lids as though wondering if it were a trick. He wrapped his fingers gently around the nape of her neck then tilted the glass until she had no choice other than to swallow or wear the burgundy liquid on her bruised, naked skin.

She gulped the remaining alcohol. Considering the outline of her ribs, which fluttered beneath the force of her rapid, shallow respiration, he figured it wouldn't take much to numb her.

Hang on. You're tough. You've lasted so long. Just a little more. I promise.

8

Jeremy prayed she could read a smidge of his encouragement in his gaze.

He tried to place her from the mile-long list of women who'd gone missing in the past six months. The task force suspected hundreds, if not more, had been destroyed by The Scientist, his drug and the slavery ring flushing the operation's human byproducts.

Jeremy's gut cramped.

The woman shuffled closer on her knees, resting her head on his thigh with a sigh. Her fingers squeezed his left ankle, out of sight of the man who'd stolen her pride.

"Son of a bitch." Tony growled when he noticed her compliance. "I suppose my hard work finally paid off. Six months of delicious rebellion then utter disinterest and *now* she decides to behave."

"Too late." Jeremy would tear the place apart to keep her from returning to Tony's clutches. "She belongs to me."

The ominous tone of his warning did the trick. Tony flushed. Jeremy couldn't say if it was because of the heat building in the dungeon, fury over losing in general or embarrassment for underestimating the true worth of his *toy*.

"Plenty more where that one came from." Tony swiped his finger over the screen of his smartphone, jabbing more harshly than required to communicate. In less than thirty seconds, a burly man delivered a new slave to take the first's place.

She would suffer for the damage Jeremy had wrought tonight. *Fuck!*

No matter how many scenarios flashed through his mind, none allowed him to save both women or the steady stream of innocents who would fill in their places. Like a man digging out of a sand pit with his bare hands, every scoop led to more grains tumbling into the void left behind by those evacuated.

"When is the sale?" Jeremy absently petted the woman trembling against his leg, trying to infuse a glimmer of warmth or reassurance into the gesture as best he could considering the circumstances. He imagined her dressed, well fed, happy. She might have been lovely not so long ago, though it probably seemed like a million lifetimes to her.

"Sunday. If we start early we might finish by midnight. We like to display and test the goods appropriately before opening the bidding. Some end up damaged. The best ones command top dollar. Satisfaction guaranteed." Tony unbuttoned his designer slacks then ripped apart the zipper. He yanked the new arrival toward him. When she refused to comply with his obvious intent, he gouged the tender hinge of her jaw until tears overflowed and streaked her cheeks.

Her lips parted.

The terrified woman between Jeremy's knees quaked. He angled her face so she didn't have to watch the torment of her replacement.

Tony withdrew an oral spreader from his pocket and inserted it in his slave's mouth, preventing her from snapping her teeth closed. His flawless execution, despite his victim's struggles, spoke of practice.

For an instant, Jeremy doubted he had the willpower to continue his charade despite the long-term benefits. He shifted in his seat, edging toward the heinous trampling of the slave's rights. The woman sheltered between his legs increased the pressure of her grip on his ankle, her torn fingernails creating crescent impressions on his skin.

He glanced down at her and nodded subtly. If he acted, he'd doom them all.

Tony fastened the gag's straps tight behind his captive's head. He depressed the lever on the side of the metal contraption lodged in the woman's mouth. A grotesque click accompanied every ratcheting of the device until her mouth gaped open. Tony tangled her hair in his fist. He used the painful grip to position her face in his crotch. The devil inserted his unimpressive yet erect cock between her spread lips and ground her forward until her nose pressed to his abdomen. He didn't stop when she gagged.

Jeremy willed his gaze from the horror. If he witnessed a single millisecond more he'd fly across the gap separating them and beat Tony to a pulp. He'd destroy the immoral fuckwad and blow every opportunity they'd crafted to save *all* the people in danger, instead of just one or two.

It ranked in the top three most difficult moments of his life along with watching Izzy take a bullet and...

He shivered.

"If you're interested, I could arrange an interview for you at my estate. Some simple questions, appropriate background checks, the usual. Mistress Lily will be joining us for the first time as well. She's agreed to work for my institute, where we can put her skills to better use." Tony spoke as though he weren't violating the woman before him—as though his transgressions didn't matter.

Jeremy trembled with barely suppressed rage. His fingers squeezed the seat cushion until the woman cradled between his legs covered his hands with hers and urged him to relax. She understood. Her courage humbled him. He rotated his palms until she could lay hers on top, bonding them in that instant.

Neither one could escape. Both would sacrifice to survive and continue the fight.

"I'm not sure I'm in the market for any additions. But, maybe... There isn't much else to do around here on a Sunday afternoon." Acid seared Jeremy's esophagus as he spun a web of lies. Though some universal truths held constant. "Mistress Lily *is* spectacular. I'd enjoy watching her work...unhindered."

"I can't fucking wait." Tony grunted. "So many possibilities. I intend to test her commitment to our cause. And if she fails to please, we can always take out our disappointment on her."

The world turned red.

The woman whose leash he held nuzzled her cheek against his knee, breaking him from the fury threatening to overpower his common sense. He clamped his eyes closed and fought the urge to go ballistic.

Jeremy ignored the slick smacks and plaintive whimpers zinging from the seat beside him. He opened his eyes and stared straight ahead—into a compassionate face. Lily only held his gaze for a moment. The brief contact settled him enough to continue.

He took a slow, shaky, gigantic breath.

Lily proceeded with her welcome manipulation of the man on display. His begging for more contrasted sharply with the protests of Tony's victim.

"Watch me," she commanded. Her subs probably hadn't blinked all evening. They hadn't been the true object of her orders.

Jeremy focused on the action. While he'd been distracted, Lily had secured her volunteer to a contraption constructed of steel pipes welded into an unusual shape. It resembled a small-scale, ultra-ominous picnic table. The scaffolding supported her partner with padded benches, one each for his hands and knees to balance on. A series of long bars jutted up in the center— parallel to the floor—for the man to settle his torso on, converting his back into the tabletop.

Lily checked his bindings. When satisfied the cuffs at his ankles, knees, waist, elbows and wrists were secure yet safe, she guided the man's head lower, pressing his Adam's apple to a wide fur-lined steel semi-circle. Though he'd waited patiently for his previous bondage, he balked the instant his neck skimmed the rest.

Jeremy sympathized. Nothing quite matched the ultimate surrender of pressure on your windpipe. It could be terrifying or thrilling. Always extreme. The act was only suitable for the most skilled and knowledgeable of Doms. Or Dommes.

Lily bent low, whispering into the ear of her subject. She praised the man when he relaxed into her complete hold. She snapped a second semi-circle above the man's neck, completing his generous restraint. Though his Mistress's fist could easily have slipped inside the hoop ringing him, he could not withdraw his head.

"Thank you, Mistress." He earned a pet along his flank and a press on the glowing marks lingering there. The tap transformed into a caress between his spread legs. Black latex, which gloved Lily's porcelain hands, slipped across the man's puckered asshole, on prominent display. When he attempted to rock deeper into her grasp, the cuffs stopped him short. His cock jerked beneath him and a dribble of pre-come landed on the padded bench that supported his knees.

"Clean that." Her tone brooked no argument.

One of her assistants dropped to his knees behind the captive man and lapped the growing puddle from the leather pad. Lily cupped her trainee's heavy balls before roaming along the length of his cock. She manipulated his erection, squeezing more proof of his arousal onto the cheek of the man below.

The helper reached for the sticky line. Lily halted him with a glare. "Did I instruct you to remove my present?"

"No, Mistress."

"Ted, share with David." She angled her chin at the third slave eagerly awaiting a chance to participate.

The two free men approached each other, eyeing their competition with such trepidation Jeremy would swear neither had a bisexual bone in his body. Still, they didn't hesitate to obey Lily's wish. She bent their

13

inhibitions into taboo pleasure. Ted closed his eyes and tilted his head. David cupped Ted's chin and the back of his skull in broad fingers. He steadied his target as he devoured another man's come.

If their raging hard-ons, which tested the limits of their leather cock-and-ball harnesses, were any indication, neither one found the task distasteful.

"Very good." Lily studied them up close then smiled.

Who wouldn't be awed by her delight?

"I think you've all earned a reward. My pets are truly the best."

The men grinned.

"Who would like to fuck?" Her innocent question should have advertised her wicked intent as clearly as an enormous neon sign on a highway diner at two in the morning. Neither man had enough blood left in his brain to anticipate the extent of her sadistic streak.

When David answered at the speed of light, edging out Ted, he doomed himself. "I would, Mistress."

"Ah, perfect." She tapped him on the cheek then spun toward her stash of equipment, leaving him standing in the open. "Use this."

David's shoulders dropped, his muscles flexing beneath the leather straps crisscrossing his broad back. He accepted the long pole. Similar to a broomstick, a large dildo capped the end in place of bristles. The fake cock had been encased in a condom and generously lubed.

"I...don't understand."

"Or choose not to do as I've asked?" Lily slapped his ass. The resulting crack made several people in the audience jump. Jeremy noted most had accessed their genitals by now, shoving skirts high, opening pants to stroke cocks, or removing breasts from leather bustiers to share the heightened sexuality Lily engineered. Several couples engaged in full intercourse, adding to the array of visual treats encouraging others to join the show.

Jeremy checked on Tony's target. It annoyed him when relief flooded his veins. He shouldn't accept the status quo. Still, he had no choice. Tony kept the woman close, refraining from fucking her helpless face. Probably afraid he'd erupt in half a second and ruin his fun.

Bastard.

Tension rippled through Jeremy's body once more. The woman between his thighs—holy hell how had Lily made him forget her?—massaged his knotted muscles. He smiled then attempted to brush her fingers aside. No way would he force her to service him. It was bad enough he sported wood despite the atrocity nearby.

Fuck, it had been a lifetime since he mingled with like-minded friends, reveling in the surrender of a *willing* submissive. And Lily did things to him no woman had managed before.

His charge stared at him so long, Jeremy worried she might speak up. Then she reached forward, cupping the bulge his monster erection created in his leather pants.

No hiding there.

He stilled her hands, swallowing a groan when the extra pressure inspired plans other than retreat in his cock. Again, she slipped from his gentle hold to continue her expert handling. Jeremy swallowed bile when he thought of how she'd learned those skills.

Once more, he attempted to dislodge her. She gripped him tight enough to edge into discomfort. He couldn't help it. The Dom inside him roared to life. He shot her an intense stare without thinking. Instead of cringing in fear, she winked.

He blinked. Twice.

Then he glanced up. Lily focused on Jeremy as she let awkward silence persuade her slave to grip the fuck pole she'd offered. Their gazes collided. She nodded almost imperceptibly.

Shit. She wasn't the only person stealing glimpses in his direction. If he sought a place in the ranks of Black Lily's patrons, he had to prove his commitment to the pursuit of dark passion. This could be a golden opportunity.

He cupped the woman's chin in his palm and nudged her face until she looked at him.

Be sure. Please. I won't hurt you.

He had never prayed for psychic abilities before. The woman peeking up at him, with more life than he'd glimpsed in the short time he'd known her, hesitated.

Then she tucked her fingers in the waistband of his pants and ripped.

CHAPTER TWO

Three quick snaps accompanied the unfastening of Jeremy's pants. His cock sprang from its confines and thudded onto his taut belly. He hummed at the relieved pressure.

His instincts took control. They urged him to place his ass on the edge of his seat and sink low. He spread his legs wider, inviting the lady between his knees to attempt to please him or not, as she chose. She snuggled up to the trunk of his body and wrapped her fingers around his shaft. Her petite hand couldn't quite encompass his full erection, but she did her best.

Tony nearly ruined the moment when he cheered, "Yeah, that's right. Show her who's boss."

Asshole.

The woman licked Jeremy's cock from base to tip, shoring up the wiltage caused by their neighbor.

God knew Jeremy had done a ton of kinky, outrageous and extreme things in his sex life. The consequences of those early indulgences had convinced him to trap his urges in a vault deep in his heart. Now they tore free, filling him with elation and a high so powerful he swore the faction of people who considered sex a drug had nailed the truth.

Still, nothing in his prior experience could top observing Lily perform while another woman, one whose name he hadn't yet learned, chose to blow him in front of anyone who wished to watch. Denial flew out the window. He couldn't commit himself to self-flagellation over fundamental needs.

Not tonight. Not with a storm of emotions assaulting him.

Instead, he chose to relish his return. Because he would never be able to stuff all this exhilaration back into a self-manufactured box.

He felt whole.

Alive.

For the first time in years.

"Yes." Jeremy hissed when his gift alternated working the oozing head of his cock with lapping at his painfully tight sac. He refused to order her to take more as he might have under different circumstances. "Good girl."

In the limelight, Lily thrust David toward the slave waiting patiently on the apparatus. "He loves to be fucked. Since I doubt you'd relish using your own equipment, I've provided an alternative. Although, if I'm wrong about your orientation, feel free to speak up now."

David shook his head.

"That's what I thought. A shame. I do enjoy watching my slaves play together." Her gentle touch on his shoulder made it clear she accepted his boundaries and wouldn't push them—not the hard and fast variety. Her undeniable instinct impressed Jeremy.

Lily stood beside her bound slave's hips. She withdrew a bottle of lube from a utility belt slung around the waist of her latex catsuit. A stream of gel cascaded over the man's asshole. His gasp morphed into a grunt when Lily probed his back passage. The slave took three of her fingers easily. He thanked her over and over, begging for more.

Lily crooked her finger. David neared in a flash. He positioned himself so that he stood a few feet away then aimed the tip of the dildo at the slave's ass. It almost seemed as though he engaged in some obscene type of fishing.

"Right there." Lily notched the blunt head of the instrument at the entrance to her subject's body. "Steady. Slow at first. Grant him what he likes. But not too hard, even if he insists."

David nodded. "Yes, Mistress."

Jeremy noted the man's cock stood at attention despite his initial uncertainty. Even Jeremy couldn't deny the arousal plumping his hard-on to the max as the large dildo gradually disappeared inside the bound slave's stretched hole. Lily grabbed one of his ass cheeks in each palm and spread him wide, easing the penetration of her tool. When satisfied with their progress, she smiled at David. "Very nice. Keep going. If you make him come, I'll treat you to my pussy. I'll ride you as hard as you like. *If* you do a good job."

Several groans echoed through the dungeon. Patrons surrendered to the rapture of her promise alone. Jeremy's cock jerked in his temporary partner's warm mouth. She sucked him deeper, harder.

"Now, you..." Lily marched to Ted and threaded her fingers through a ring in his collar. "I have a use for your sexy muscles."

The giant man shivered beneath the light scrape of Lily's nails over his pecs. When she flicked the nipple ring decorating the right side of his chest with the tip of her tongue, Jeremy gripped the arms of his chair. He could picture trapping her head to his chest, indulging in hours of her skilled teasing around his similar adornments.

Would it be so bad to grant her control if they needed the same things?

The stray thought jolted him from his daydream. He submitted for no one.

Lily positioned Ted at the head of her shackled slave. The man released a steady stream of moans as

David plundered his ass with long, deep strokes. She stepped into the tight space between Ted's groin and the slave's face.

"Lift me." She instructed Ted in a no-nonsense tone that had pre-come bursting from the tip of Jeremy's cock before he could warn the woman devouring him.

The near stranger didn't seem to mind. In fact, she hummed her appreciation, drawing more fluid from his body.

"Support me while he eats me. I don't have to tell you how upset I'd be if you dropped me before I came, right?" Lily's adorable smile somehow didn't detract from her authority.

Ted cradled her as if she'd hung the stars in the sky. He cushioned his Mistress against his chest without a tremble in his biceps. Jeremy could attest her slight weight posed no challenge for a man in shape. He'd held Lily in his arms once, sheltered her as she grieved for the loss of one of her submissives.

She placed her wicked heels on her trapped slave's shoulders.

Jeremy noted how the prick of pain caused by the point of her stilettos seemed to drive her boy wild. No wonder she'd insisted on the neck restraint. If she hadn't, he could very well have bucked hard enough to dislodge his body from the pipe framework, potentially injuring himself or one of his playmates.

Lily spread her legs, bent her knees, unzipped the access panel in the crotch of her specialty apparel and tucked her pussy immediately before her slave's lips. He devoured her without instruction, burying his face as deep as possible in the moist heat of her sex. She sighed and ruffled his hair.

Jeremy silently thanked David for having the presence of mind—or more likely, the proper training—to stand to the side as he reamed the bound slave, leaving the view of Lily free and clear.

She didn't shy from Jeremy's bold stare. No, she returned his heat with interest.

The woman between his legs increased the swirl of her tongue along the underside of his shaft, occasionally tracing the defined ridge of the head before taking him into her throat. Lily grinned, her eyelids drooping a little as her slave treated her clit and pussy to similar pleasure.

Jeremy and Lily gazed at each other, sharing the moment despite the physical distance between them. The appreciative moans, curses and grunts of the spectators faded into the background as they indulged their kinky sides.

Come, Lily. Show me your pretty blue eyes darken with lust. You love his tongue strumming your clit. You can't resist the men who do your bidding because you've earned their trust. Give us what we want. Take your enjoyment as payment. Do it. Come.

Lily lauded the man devouring her with urgent yet clear praise as she came on his face.

The woman between Jeremy's legs encircled the base of his cock and squeezed just as he suspected he would join Lily. The pressure alleviated the danger of an early orgasm. He laid his fingers on her shoulder as he witnessed Lily wring every drop of rapture from her pet's gift.

Jeremy hummed when Lily's eyes opened, revealing her hunger. The explosion, though impressive, hadn't fully satisfied her.

Ted lowered her to her feet, continuing to band his arms around her frame until she whispered something to him and nodded. He placed his hand beneath her elbow when she wobbled, but she stood tall.

She swiped some of her juice from her slave's lips then turned, feeding it to Ted. He groaned. Jeremy would have killed for a taste of her sweetness.

21

"I knew you wouldn't disappoint me, Ted." He flushed beneath her approval. "I have an offer for you."

"Yes, Mistress?"

"David is working hard, plowing this slave's ass. Isn't he?"

Ted squirmed a little as he peeked at the toy stretching the other man's hole. "Yes, Mistress."

"But he won't earn my pussy if he doesn't make our friend here erupt."

Ted retreated a miniscule step, unsure of where she led him.

"Don't you want to help, Ted?" She arched an eyebrow when he hesitated.

"If it pleases you."

"It does." She beamed at him. "And I have a feeling you'll like it too. This slave loves to be used. The more people who fill his holes, the better. Isn't that right?"

The man's cries escalated.

"Would you like to try feeding him?" Lily grabbed Ted's crotch and rubbed his hard cock. She unsnapped the leather decorating the long shaft along with the ring stretching his balls, and rubbed out a few of the impressions the material had made over the past hour or so he'd probably worn it.

"W-what do you mean, Mistress?"

"Let him suck your cock, Ted. He's quite good at it. Or so I hear."

"Yes!" the slave pleaded for the treat.

Ted didn't withdraw farther. Instead, he inched closer to the bound man before him.

"That's right. Go ahead. Slip inside his warm, wet mouth. You know you'd like his velvety tongue rubbing on you. He's a come slut. His cheeks will hollow as he draws every last bit of seed from your balls. His mouth is larger than a female's. He'll probably take all of your shaft. Something you must not experience often." Lily measured Ted's long, thick cock with her hand.

The woman working over Jeremy's hard-on mimicked Lily's promises. He gritted his teeth.

Ted surrendered with a strangled groan. He inserted his erection between the open lips of the bound slave.

"Nice and easy." Lily wrapped her fist around the base of Ted's cock, preventing him from jamming his tool fully into the slave's throat on the initial pass, too eager to revel in his first male-to-male blow job. "That's right, good boys."

Both men cried out, her sanction enhancing their passion. She peeled her fingers off Ted's cock one by one until the slave swallowed Ted's entire length at the height of each stroke.

"You may come as soon as you're able. Both of you." The men tensed, primed for release. How long had they battled the sizzling arousal boiling their blood? "Faster, David. Fuck him a little harder now."

Both men impaled the slave, working in tandem to stuff him full. Lily crouched near his strapped hips, providing Jeremy with another glimpse of her spread, glistening pussy. She traced the ring of her slave's anus around the inserted fuckpole with her gloved finger then tickled the seam decorating his sac. Finally, her index finger brushed the tip of his cock.

The slave shuddered. His toes curled tight, and his back arched.

"If you don't come soon, I'll think you don't appreciate Ted and David's hard work. That would make me unhap—"

Lily never finished her sentence.

Thick blasts of cum shot from the slave's cock. She encircled his pulsing erection with her fingers and milked it dry. Jet after jet of pearly fluid spilled onto the apparatus. As the stream of his release began to ebb, Ted threw back his head and roared.

Lily halted David's motion with the fuckpole, easing it from her slave while he still lingered in a sensual haze. She glided to Ted's side, rubbing his shoulders and kneading his ass as he poured the last traces of his release into the bound slave's mouth. She played each man with precision, providing exactly what they required.

When Ted quieted, she tugged him lower, kissed him on the cheek then whispered in his ear.

He hugged her tight then nodded. "Yes, Mistress."

The pure affection radiating from her subjects made Jeremy jealous. Until the steady sucking of the woman who treated him to a world-class blowjob declared him a hypocrite.

Ted liberated the slave, tending to him as Lily had obviously instructed.

"You, David." She pointed to an inclined platform less than ten feet away. The black leather surface tipped toward the audience, which had thinned a bit when the lightweight spectators succumbed to their own arousal then headed for the bar. The remaining hardcore witnesses fucked in the aisles or simply enjoyed the thrill of the complete mastery Lily wielded as surely as a knight with a broadsword.

She escorted David to the furniture she'd selected then shoved with one palm on his chest. He stumbled, falling backward with an *oomph* when his shoulders landed on the lightly padded surface. In less than five seconds, she'd clamped him in place at wrists and ankles.

Lily teased his cock with light strokes until David thrashed in his bindings. Soon both of them had no doubt he was well and truly held. She removed the cock harness he stretched and rolled a condom over the man's straining erection.

"Tell me what you desire."

"I need you to fuck me. Please, let me inside your pussy. Use me. Come on me. Please. *Please.*"

"Very nice, David." Lily climbed two stairs built into the side of the slab. She swung one leg over her captive, her boot landing on the top of the stair on the opposite side. Towering over the man, she granted him an unhindered view of her crotch as she posed, hands on hips, facing the onlookers. "You like to watch my ass as I ride you, don't you?"

"God, yes."

She bent at the waist to smack the inside of his thigh. "What did you say?"

"Yes, Mistress. I love your ass. So sexy."

"That's better." Lily crouched, making a show of wiggling her buttocks as she reached for David's cock. She held him perpendicular to his body as she lowered herself onto his solid length. She had to raise and lower herself several times, working his shaft into her bit by bit.

Jeremy groaned. If Lily had to stretch to take this man, Jeremy would overflow her pussy.

He put one hand on his charge's elbow, warning her. He couldn't stand much more torture. She didn't stop her delicious treatment.

Lily braced herself behind her back with one palm, splaying her fingers on David's six-pack abs. She worked her pelvis like a stripper intent on retiring early through proceeds from epic lap dances. The fluid motion mesmerized Jeremy. He imagined flipping her to her hands and knees, pounding into her while she tried to fuck him from below.

His nostrils flared and his balls drew tight to his body.

She smiled at him and licked her lips.

Fuck!

Lily slipped one finger between her bright red lips, showing him how she'd suck his cock if it were her between his thighs. Then she trailed the digit over the

25

outline of her diamond-tipped breasts, evident through the latex hugging her form.

She mouthed something that looked a hell of a lot like, "Ready?"

Was he ever.

He nodded then whispered, "If you are."

She touched the slick tip of her index finger to her clit and drew wet circles over the swollen bundle of nerves while she ground on the cock buried inside her.

A rush of exhilaration and pleasure flowed over Jeremy.

He couldn't swear who surrendered first. In the end, it didn't matter. Cries of completion filled the space as many of the members exploded with them. Lily fucked David hard enough to shake the table he laid on. The full length of his cock plunged in and out of her as she increased the amplitude of her strokes.

Come boiled from Jeremy's balls while Lily quaked on top of David. The man bellowed her name and emptied himself into the condom sheathing his cock. Jeremy tried to withdraw from the mouth of the woman sucking him off, but she knocked his hand away and slid down his length until the head of his dick slipped into her throat. She swallowed again and again as he overflowed her orifice.

Still, he couldn't peel his stare from Lily, who gazed at him in return.

Time suspended. The distance between them shrank. Jeremy swore he could hear her pleas, begging him to make her his.

Or maybe that was just wishful thinking.

Lily smiled. He sighed.

A ragged groan snapped Jeremy's attention to his right, to Morselli. A hired thug, the dude who'd led in the new slave, pinned his captive's thrashing legs to the concrete floor beneath their cushy seats at the base of the bleachers. Tony's knuckles went white as he anchored the girl's head to his groin and shot his load down her opened throat.

Tony tarnished what could have been a sublime moment—one Jeremy had ached for. Lusted after. Gone half-mad abstaining from.

The bastard reminded him of how easily this lifestyle could spiral out of control.

Satisfied, Morselli released his prisoner. She crumpled onto the floor. Tears streaked her cheeks. Jeremy had to sit on his hands to keep from comforting her or annihilating her abuser. Honor screamed for him to act. Immediately.

Before he could finish battling the urges, the slave wrenched from the goon's hands and clambered to her feet with a strength and resilience that awed Jeremy. Morselli must have been equally surprised because he didn't manage to cover his face fast enough. The young girl spit the remnants of his come through the open-mouthed gag, into his eyes. Sticky globs landed on his cheeks and in his hair.

No!

Jeremy lunged for her. Too late. Tony's bodyguard backhanded her, knocking her unconscious. A trickle of blood dibbled from her cut lip as the dirtbag tossed her over his shoulder.

"You'll pay for that, Bruno." Morselli snarled as he mopped his face with a silk handkerchief. "After I throw her to the rest of my men, maybe I'll let them have a go at you too. With a drop or two of our *medicine* they won't stop until you're begging to die."

Holy fuck. The drug. Tony had some. And he wasn't lying. Jeremy had suffered its effects himself a few months earlier. One spritz into the enclosed space of a van had knocked him, Lily, fellow cop Razor and the rookie's girl, Izzy, for a loop and a half.

Despite a trip to the hospital, the effects had lingered for days.

Jeremy had nearly rubbed himself raw searching for satisfaction.

Before he could process all that had happened, or figure out how to rescue the woman being carted from the dungeon, Morselli stood. He sneered. "Enjoy my leftovers."

"I will, Tony. Don't worry. I'll repay you. Someday *very* soon." The slave between Jeremy's legs refastened his pants. She broke protocol as she rose of her own volition, interrupting his line of sight with the monster, who pivoted to leave.

They'd come too far for rash wrath to ruin the plan. He accepted the leather loop the woman held between her teeth then guided her from the room in the opposite direction, pausing to shoot a backward glance at Lily. Her slaves tended to her—cleaned her, straightened her hair, daubed sweat from what little flesh she bared.

Abandoning her in a hedonistic den where foxes lurked—corrupting her pure pursuit of fantasy—didn't sit well, though she could fend for herself. She'd battled The Scientist and the human traffickers from inside their network for so long, she had to be pushing her luck.

Be careful. Watch your back. I'm coming for you. Soon.

She blew him a kiss.

CHAPTER THREE

Jeremy paced the hardwood floor outside the guest bedroom in Mason, Tyler and Lacey's new house. He didn't pause to admire the soothing color Lacey had bribed the men in blue—with pizza and beer—to paint the walls.

"JRad." Razor climbed the stairs. "Give it a rest. That squeak in the floor you're nailing at the end of your run is driving us bananas down there."

"James!" Isabella slapped the rookie's ass as she trailed him. She squeezed past her boyfriend on the landing and trotted toward Jeremy.

Without thought he opened his arms, welcoming her into his gentle embrace. Despite recent events, she remained innocent, affectionate and sweet. Everything he wasn't.

"Don't pay attention to him, Jeremy."

"When did you two show up?" He tucked a strand of hair behind her ear, reluctant to release her. For so long he'd relied on the happiness of his friends to banish his loneliness. Their bliss acted like balm on his open wounds.

"About five minutes ago. Clint and Matt are in the living room too." She rubbed his lower back, which sat at the right height for the sprite, as she filled him in.

Jeremy closed his eyes. His breathing slowed. He bundled her close then pretended the diminutive woman he held wasn't Izzy, but instead, her half-sister. Lily.

When his cock inflated, he rejected Isabella's comfort, separating them a little more forcefully than he intended. Razor caught her, shooting Jeremy a glare over her platinum-blond hair. The women were so much the same and yet so different. Even if *his* midnight beauty hadn't admitted it yet, fate or some other force of nature kept drawing them together—circumstances and their incompatible sexual preferences be damned.

"You saw her." Izzy chewed her bottom lip.

"What makes you so sure?" No use in pretending he didn't understand who *her* was.

"Your eyes. Your restlessness. Your..." She peeked at his crotch. A blush heated her cheeks despite the months she'd spent discovering intimacy with Razor.

"You can say cock." He chuckled. "Hell, it's not like I haven't watched you suck one before, sweetheart."

Damn. Another tick in the Cons column for a relationship with Lily. Coached her sister through her first BJ. Check. Followed closely by manually-inspected-her-sister's-virginity. Double check.

Razor growled and tugged Izzy beneath his arm.

"Is Lily okay?" Isabella glanced up from her spot against her lover's chest. She fit so well with him. Not like Lily, whom Jeremy would tower over.

Lost in thought, he didn't answer immediately.

"Oh no. She's not?"

Razor stroked her hair. "He didn't say that, Izzy. Don't jump to conclusions."

"Shit. Sorry." Jeremy spun on his heel and strode to the end of the hallway, dodging the loose floorboard, before returning once more. He scrubbed his hand through his hair, sure it stuck out on end after repeated passes. "Lily's fine. Great, actually. She was fucking *amazing.*"

Razor's lifted brows asked for details he wasn't about to get. Not with Izzy in the room. She probably wouldn't care to hear the gritty details about her sister.

The photographs they'd uncovered last winter had freaked her out enough.

They'd turned Jeremy on.

He might have appropriated copies off the station's evidence storage server.

Oops.

"So what has you this upset?" Isabella reached out and snagged his wrist. She prevented him from spinning off for another circuit of the passageway with the softest of touches.

"It's confirmed. There's another auction on Sunday. I'm afraid she'll risk too much. Eventually someone will realize she's smuggling women out of that hellhole. We have to shut it down before they do. Otherwise..." He couldn't finish.

"We'll figure something out, JRad."

"Last time I looked you guys weren't all on the DEA team." He didn't intend to insult the kid. Facts were facts. "Besides, I'm likely to be canned or arrested—maybe both—as soon as Agent Sterns discovers I went to Black Lily. Then I'll be no help to her at all."

"We may not be part of your fancy task force, but we're still your friends. Asshole." Razor settled when Isabella murmured his name. She nuzzled the rookie's jaw then rested her cheek over the scars on his chest.

Jeremy would be lying if he said the sight of her utter trust and devotion didn't propagate envy in his soul. He suspected constant exposure to the radiation emitted by Mason, Tyler, Lacey, Razor and Izzy's scorching love had caused a malignant lesion to start festering on his heart. Could he ever have something as brilliant? Would Lily grant him the right to protect her? To lean on her?

He shook his head to clear the bitterness.

"Razor, after the stunt you pulled with Izzy at the clean side of the club last year, you would blow my cover in a flash. Mason and Tyler too." Jeremy cursed. He could use some backup that didn't mind bending a rule or two. The DEA guys had a real stick up their ass about protocol. Something he'd never succeeded at enforcing.

"Matt and Clint kept their distance." Razor sowed the seed of a plan in his mind.

"That's true—"

The door to the guest bedroom cracked open before Lacey slipped into the hall. Tyler shadowed her. Figured her men would refuse to leave their soul mate alone with a stranger. Still, it was probably best they hadn't assigned Mason to watchdog duty. His hulking frame would remind the woman Jeremy had rescued too much of the muscle-bound bullies Morselli employed.

"How is she?"

The woman hadn't uttered a peep during the entire ride to his friends' home. Jeremy couldn't risk admitting her to a hospital in case Morselli found out. But she hadn't seemed to believe him when he assured her he'd brought her to a nurse. That Lacey would help.

He guessed she'd been too scared to hope for the impossible—terrified the prospect of escape might be another cruel deception used to break her spirit. God only knew what she had endured.

"She's hanging in there." Lacey ran her hand down his arm, lending him strength. He loved how unafraid of him she was. Same as Izzy. If they had learned his secrets, they never would have relaxed like this around him. "Dehydrated, malnourished, exhausted, exhibiting shock symptoms and bruised all over. Somehow, still optimistic. And so very grateful for your help."

His disbelief must have shown through his attempted mask.

"Truly. You saved her life, Jeremy."

He would have objected but Ty cut him off. "She asked to speak to you. After her shower and dinner, Lacey gave her some strong shit. She's checking out quick. Go ahead before she's asleep. We can settle stuff afterward. Meet us in the living room when you're done."

Jeremy nodded then strode past his friends.

Lacey had plugged a nightlight in the outlet near the bed. In the dim glow, the shadows beneath the woman's eyes seemed enormous. He approached her cautiously, unwilling to wake her if she'd conked out or frighten her if she hadn't.

"You really took me away from there?" She winced. "It's over? I never have to serve *him* or his friends again?"

"Christ. I'm so sorry. Please forgive—"

"Not necessary." She waved her fingers at his apology as if she lacked the energy to move her entire hand.

"The hell it isn't. I used you. I had no right."

"You did what you had to. Same as I have." She grimaced. "Better actually, since you tried to stop me."

"I didn't fight very hard." He sank into the chair beside her bed, ridiculously pleased when she reached out to touch his knee.

"You get off on BDSM." She sighed. "So do I."

"How'd you end up..."

"A slave? I chose to submit." She huffed then sniffled when her eyes filled for what he'd bet was the first time in months.

Jeremy scooted closer, rocking her against his chest. Once the flow began it didn't stop for long minutes. Eventually her sobs quieted to soft hiccups. He didn't ask for more, but she elected to give it.

"My M-master used to be kind—stern though attentive. Like you..."

He cringed.

She enfolded his hand between her chilled fingers and kissed his knuckles. "That was a compliment."

"If he's so damn great, how could he abandon you? Why didn't he protect you?" Jeremy sneered as he considered his own failures.

"He got s-sick." She shook her head slowly. "No. Hooked on drugs. I had to remind myself it was a disease, something killing my Master as surely as if he'd contracted AIDS or had cancer. The chemical ate him from the inside. It attacked the man I loved and destroyed him cell by cell. There's a substance. If it has an official name, I've never heard it. Morselli's staff and his prisoners call it Sex Offender. It's supposed to be some kind of libido-enhancer. It's potent. Unimaginably addictive. I think it makes you crazy if you do too much."

"I know." Jeremy winced.

"You've taken it?" She would have scooted to the opposite edge of the bed—or hobbled from the room—if he hadn't stopped her.

"Not willingly." He cursed. "It's a long story. I got dosed by accident."

"Did you hurt anyone?" Her lips trembled. "It wouldn't have been your fault under the influence. My Master didn't mean the things he did to me. I *have* to believe that."

"We were in the middle of a big case. When it wrapped, I locked myself in my apartment for a few days. Called in sick to work until I felt normal again." He rubbed his temples as he remembered the dreams, the voices urging him to find a partner, any woman, to slake his desire with. He'd like to believe he could have controlled himself. Like Razor and Izzy must have. But he couldn't be sure.

"You're strong. A good man. A good Master." The woman linked her fingers with his. He met her gaze when she squeezed his knuckles lightly. "Mine was too. Except for his weakness. He couldn't fight it. In the end, he traded me to Morselli for a stash of Sex Offender he could never have afforded. He overdosed the same night, within hours. I never said goodbye. Morselli confiscated the rest of the drugs and refused to let me leave."

"Shit. I'm so sorry." Jeremy knuckled another tear from the corner of one of her soft gray eyes.

"Almost all the other women in the private holding cells had similar stories. Morselli is smart. He doesn't touch the stuff. Unless it's to use it for leverage. Power—from money, women or men—that's what he's after. Nothing matters to him but the rush from what I could tell."

"He made you suffer for resisting him." Jeremy didn't have to ask.

"Nothing he did hurt as much as it would have to kneel for a man who didn't deserve it." She cringed. "I thought he'd destroyed my life. Everything I knew about myself, my Master, my nature felt like a lie. I was so lost. Ready to surrender. When you took charge of me, everything clicked into place. Apparently even months of torture couldn't alter my wiring. You helped me rediscover myself. Does that mean I deserved what...happened to me? Am I responsible for the things I did to stay alive?"

The hitch accompanying her genuine curiosity had him stroking her cheek in an instant. "Never. That's bullshit."

"So why is it any different for you? You're a worthy Master." She covered his hand with hers. The drugs Lacey had administered in the drip bag began to kick in. Her speech slurred, and her lids drooped as he considered her wisdom.

"I suppose it's not. Thanks. I still wish I hadn't added to your burdens." He scrubbed his beard. "Can I ask you something?"

"Yes, sir." Her response came softer as she faded out.

"What's your name?"

Her bright smile gave him hope she'd recover with time and care. After the horrors she'd borne, he respected her resilience.

"I'm Zina."

"Nice." He nodded. "Sounds like the warrior princess."

"Everyone says that." She giggled. "I guess now it's sort of true."

"It is. I'm Master Jeremy. If you ever need anything—"

"Are you looking for a sub?" Her cheeks flushed a delightful pink.

His aspirations lay within arm's reach. He could care for this generous woman so easily. All he had to do was collar her. A Master without a slave was a pitiful thing. And still...

Fuck him. Fuck his stubborn heart.

"I'm sorry, no." He petted her damp hair. "There's someone..."

"The woman from the club? The switch?"

"What!" Thank God for the dim light. His pupils couldn't have dilated much more.

"The woman who performed tonight. I think her name is Lily." Zina yawned before continuing. "I've met her a couple times. She's nice. She snuck me food and medicine. Tried to help."

"Why did you call her a switch?" Jeremy's heart pounded so hard he nearly missed her dwindling whisper.

"Because you're a Dom, through and through. If you're interested... Plus, there's something about her. She anticipates her slaves too well. She perceives too much." Zina closed her eyes and murmured, "She's one of us. But not."

"Yes, yes. That's exactly it." Jeremy acted on instinct. He brushed a kiss over her parted lips. "I can't tell you how thankful I am we met tonight, even if I hate the circumstances that led us to each other. I'm here for you, Z. No matter what."

"Thank you." She tipped her face into the pillow. "For now it's enough to sleep without worrying."

"You're safe here. Sweet dreams." He sat beside her, monitoring the subtle rise and fall of her quilt-covered chest as though he could ward off any negative energy that might plague her. Eventually satisfied she rested comfortably, he tucked her in, bussed her cheek then headed for his comrades.

They had to make this right.

***

Jeremy stalked down the rear staircase into the kitchen. He could use a beer or three before joining the crowd strategizing in low, urgent exchanges next door. Their consideration for the refugee he'd entrusted to their care didn't surprise him.

Light spilled across the slate flooring when he cracked the stainless-steel fridge and reached for a bottle of microbrew from the six-pack on the second shelf. Clean white illumination from the bulb hanging above a leftover pizza box highlighted a bulky man at the kitchen table.

Jeremy nearly gave himself whiplash when his head swiveled.

"Jesus, Clark." The door shut harder than he intended. His free hand instinctively fisted. "What are you doing sitting in the dark?"

"Waiting for you." Mason Clark, the third angle in Lacey and Tyler's triad, chuckled. "Take a seat for a second, would you?"

"Sure, dickhead." He glared as he straddled a chair at the butcher-block table. "But you could have asked like a normal human being instead of lurking in the shadows like a serial killer."

"I suppose." Mason shrugged. "Where would be the fun in that?"

"Did you have a point?" Unease settled in his gut. He had to figure out how to stop Lily from putting herself in danger. If she joined Morselli's staff, Jeremy couldn't possibly provide a sliver of protection. Every minute he spent spinning his wheels was a moment she might not have to waste.

"I do." Mason, the unofficial leader of their squad, rocked his chair onto two legs. His massive arms crossed over his chest. "Before you head in there and start making a bunch of plans you intend to throw out the window at the first opportunity, I thought I'd tell you I get it."

"Huh?" Jeremy checked his watch. *Fuck.* It was nearly two in the morning already. Would Lily still be at the club?

"Focus, JRad," Mason barked. "This is *exactly* the shit I'm talking about. You need to pull your head out of your ass and remember, for once, that you're not the Lone-fucking-Ranger. Yeah, you're a geek. You don't have a partner like Ty and me. You don't do patrols like Matt, Clint or Razor. But you're one of us. A part of *our* team."

"I... Uh, right." Jeremy deserved the lecture. He'd blazed past procedure, rules and better judgment on a whim dozens of times in the past. When he saw a solution, he snatched it even if it meant venturing out alone, beyond boundaries. Paperwork came later.

"You and I have more in common than you might think. When it comes to what's ours, we might have some control *issues.* At least, that's what Ty and Lacey tell me." He snarled. "And that's why I'm sure this assignment is going to suck donkey dick for you."

When Jeremy would have denied it, Mason spoke over him.

"Last year...with the threats to Lacey, I didn't always keep my shit under control. You were there to set me straight. I'll never forget you took her call *that* night, pieced the last of the puzzle together and organized the cavalry. Now you need to let us return the favor. Objectivity is impossible when you're this close to the action."

"What are you saying?" If Mason attempted to prevent him from aiding Lily however he saw fit, the cop wasted his breath.

"Only this... You won't be able to help yourself from diving into the deep end of the shitstorm pool. Before you do anything crazy, tell me." Mason's chair clunked to the floor as he leaned forward to grip Jeremy's tense upper arm. "We'll cover your ass and haul you out if you start to flounder. Lily too. No matter what, JRad."

Jeremy cleared his throat. He nodded. "In that case, there's something you should know."

"Oh, son of a bitch. Already?" Mason grinned. "I'm glad I didn't wait for you to sneak out the back door."

He didn't dare deny he'd considered the option. "Things are different these days. I won't do anything to put you, Ty or Razor in danger. Lacey and Isabella need you."

"There's always Matt and Clint to help in the field. The rest of us can work behind the scenes. We all contribute in our own way. How many times has Lacey sewn one of us up? Think about all the research you've done, legitimate or otherwise."

"Fair enough." Some of the pressure building behind Jeremy's eyes evaporated. He hadn't realized how tense he'd been. "Maybe we should take this into the living room. No need to repeat myself."

"I'm glad you see it that way too. First..." Mason smirked then swiped Jeremy's brew. "You might want to grab another bottle."

"That really wasn't a win, Clark. It's your house, your beer."

"Good point." He scowled as he headed for his lovers and the rest of their friends.

"Mason?"

"Yeah?"

"Thanks."

"Anytime, JRad."

He took a second to compose himself as he plucked not one, but two, of the brown glass bottles from the fridge. It'd be foolish to dismiss help if it improved his odds of ending this cycle of destruction and removing Lily from the line of fire.

A hush descended over the ever-growing assortment of their eclectic yet tight family. Lacey curled up with Tyler while Mason towered over them from his place at the back of the oversized leather recliner they shared. Razor lounged on the floor with his shoulders propped against the coffee table and Izzy snugged against his chest, between his thighs. There should have been plenty of room for Jeremy to plop between Matt and Clint on the comfy couch except the duo sprawled, even more than usual.

It all clicked into place when he noticed the shy woman squeezed between them. She huddled in her cute sci-fi themed scrubs, trying to make herself as small as possible.

"Hello, Jambrea." He smiled at her obvious discomfort. When would Lacey's co-worker realize Matt and Clint were ready to fight each other to the death for a date with her? The partners' constant bickering had driven them all insane for months. Starting when they'd met the sassy nurse, after Razor had been shot. Their initial interest had escalated by degrees into a full-on crush. Too bad neither would grant the other a fair chance.

Why couldn't the wrinkles in Jeremy's relationship be so easy to iron out? No reason the cops couldn't share and leave them all happy. Hell, ménage seemed pretty fantastic for Lacey, Mason and Ty.

"Jeremy." She waved, squeaking when her fingers brushed the tribal tattoo encircling Matt's encroaching bicep. "Here, take my spot. I brought over some supplies for your...guest. I heard she's sleeping now so I should probably skedaddle."

"Did you forget your car wouldn't start the last time you tried to leave?" Clint snagged her, banding his forearm around her waist. He dragged her onto his lap.

"I'll take you home. As soon as we're finished," Matt promised.

"Don't you have to drop your sister off at the airport at five?" Clint feigned casual interest. "No worries, I'll drive Jambi so you don't have to rush."

Jambrea was too busy gawking and squirming in an attempt to evade Clint to notice Matt flip his partner the bird. She didn't miss the effect of her struggles for long though. When her hip brushed Clint's crotch, she froze. Her stare flitted around the room as though panicked they might notice their friend's arousal.

Matt glared.

Jeremy did them all a favor by sinking between the men before their petty one-upping could deteriorate into a fistfight sure to smash at least one of Lacey's upgraded furnishings and wake Zina. Clint grinned and Matt pouted.

Both objected when Jambrea protested, "Let me up. I'm going to squash you."

"Shush." She quieted beneath the intensity of Jeremy's stare. "Don't be ridiculous, Jambi. You'll cause a riot. I need them to pay attention for a little bit."

Both Matt and Clint blinked at him when Jambrea responded to his subtle authority. Maybe they'd figure out to take the reins sooner or later.

"What's up, JRad?" Tyler rubbed his thumb in broad arcs across Lacey's knee.

"An email from Black Lily showed up in my inbox this afternoon. One of their promos for a special event."

"Don't you have to be a member to receive those notices?" Izzy tilted her head.

41

"Uh…" he stalled.

"Never mind." She rolled her eyes. "Dumb question. So you've been hacking into their systems to spy on my sister. What did you find out?"

He didn't tell her about the security camera feeds and the nights he'd spent watching Lily in action while she amused herself and her guests in the common areas of the club. It'd taken all his willpower not to invade her privacy by streaming the sessions she conducted behind closed doors.

"The invite was for a party in Lily's honor. A send-off."

"What?" Tyler squinted. "You stopped her from leaving, right?"

"Not exactly." Jeremy ran his hand through his hair.

Jambrea surprised him when she laid a hand on his shoulder. "I'm sorry."

Did everyone know he craved the infamous Mistress? Probably. He was no more subtle than Matt or Clint dogging their cute nurse when it came to Lily. "I tried to call her. Email. Text. Everything except freaking smoke signals. She ignored me. I left a message, told her I'd be at the show. Asked her to save me a seat."

"You went to the club? Alone?" Mason cursed. "I should have given you my speech yesterday."

"Wouldn't have hurt." Jeremy nodded. "There were some tense moments tonight. I could have used backup. In the end, I didn't talk to Lily. I saw her. She…performed."

"Do I want to hear this?" Isabella winced even as Matt and Clint leaned closer.

"Not so much." He slumped in his seat. "Hell, I don't really care to rehash it myself. I mean Lily was *spectacular*. But…I'm afraid she's in too deep. Things are evolving. She reserved a place for me, beside Tony Morselli. Not a chance in hell that was an accident."

"God damn, JRad." Razor bundled his girl closer. "He's no joke."

"I got that, kid." He related the important facts—about Lily, Zina and his new buddy, Morselli—while skirting the darker flavors of his evening out. His friends didn't need his proclivity for bondage spelled out. His aptitude for dominance wasn't relevant. Well, not any more than they already guessed at.

"So now you have to fill Agent Sterns in." Clint referred to their DEA handler.

"Convince him to allow you to take Morselli up on his offer. Better if you could rope us in too. If we can work this from the inside..."

"It's dangerous, JRad." Worry lined Matt's normally jovial face.

"What about our job isn't?" Jeremy stood and resumed his pacing. No one bothered to stop him this time.

"This has nothing to do with your career, does it?" Isabella peered up at him from the shelter of Razor's arms, which banded around her chest, keeping her close.

"Of course not." He crouched beside her. "I'm desperate. Lily's sticking her neck out too far. She can't avoid disaster forever. There are so many land mines surrounding her, I can't believe she's made it this far."

"Then I'm glad you went tonight. Even if you should have told us first." Such a tiny thing shouldn't be able to cow a man three times her size. In that regard, she and her sister were a matched set.

"I promise to keep you all in the loop from now on." He looked from person to person, his gaze landing last on Mason, who smiled. "As long as you're aware I *will* do this. Nothing can stop me from following her."

"Then you better decide quick if you want me to answer this, JRad." Clint held up his vibrating phone. "I have a feeling Sterns is about to rip you a new one."

43

"Fuck." No sense in putting off the inevitable. "I'll take it."

CHAPTER FOUR

If Jeremy had to say, "Yes, sir," one more time, he might crack a molar.

Somehow, Sterns had discovered his foray into Black Lily. To say the news displeased his superior officer might have been the understatement of the century. Like claiming he was attracted to Lily when his craving was more on the order of magnitude of the gravitational force of the sun.

Ten billion suns.

"As long as we understand each other, Radisson."

"Yes, sir." He'd stopped listening to the man's rebukes.

"Then I have to admit, an inside line could be the break we've been waiting for."

"What?" Jeremy held the phone away from his ear and squinted at it. Had he imagined the go-ahead?

"I'm not a complete moron, you know." Sterns coughed up a gruff chuckle. "You're uniquely qualified for this task. I've heard rumors. Seen some history in your government files."

Stuff Jeremy had dusted off and planted in plain sight in preparation for this exact moment. Still, having that info become common knowledge after so long in the shadows made his skin crawl. Exposing himself didn't come naturally.

If that's what it took to protect Lily, he'd do it a hundred times over.

"Right. I'm glad we're on the same page, sir." He barely kept himself from growling. "How do you feel about Ludwig and Griggs working with me on this?"

"Well... Huh. Not sure they're the type to do what it takes, no matter the cost." Sterns's veiled implications sat a little funny in Jeremy's gut. "I know *you* won't let us down, JRad. You'll get the job done, whatever perverted shit might be required. Hell, I suppose it ain't so disgusting to some. Like us. There are worse things than forcing a woman to obey, I say."

The agent's twisted tone spiked the hair on Jeremy's forearm. He bit his tongue to prevent himself from informing the jackass of the true nature of a Dom/sub relationship. It had nothing to do with the filthy innuendo loading his boss's contempt.

In some regards, the man had it right. Jeremy would do just about anything for Lily's safety. Even if it meant playing along with the dumbass's misconceptions. He focused on achieving his goal and forced an empathetic chuckle.

"I'm glad you agree, Agent." He infused his request with the steel he used when commanding a reticent partner to do what they yearned for but feared. "So trust my judgment on this. Having the two of them around will give me more chances to take down The Scientist and track the drug. Morselli will lead us to the source."

"It'll be difficult enough for you to convince him to allow you into his network, never mind two other strangers." Sterns's confidence made Jeremy wonder what he hadn't shared. What did he know? "He's not the gullible sort, and he likes to be in charge. Three of you might be too big of a threat to his ridiculous ego."

"Trust me. I have it covered. We'll prove our worth if we have to." Jeremy sighed. "I've laid the groundwork. He can check me out. He'll find what he needs to be satisfied of my genuine interest."

"Agreed." The agent whistled. "I can't believe your squad has never questioned your suitability for your position. Then again, the locals probably never unearthed what we have."

Clint's phone creaked when Jeremy nearly crushed the device. How dare this fucker insult his division?

Deep breath.

"You don't seem to mind my...talents." Jeremy couldn't resist slipping in one itsy dig.

"Sometimes an instrument presents itself when you least expect it." Sterns took on an edge Jeremy had never noticed before. "I've learned not to underestimate men. That doesn't mean shit for when we're through here. You got that?"

"Yes, *sir*."

"Good. Don't forget to write home. I expect progress reports daily." Sterns sneered. "And don't leave out any juicy details to cover your ass."

More like the agent wanted to jerk off to the debauchery occurring inside Morselli's stronghold. Fuck.

Sterns saved him from doing anything stupid when he ended the conversation. "Don't fuck this up. Bury yourself in their organization. Take the two locals with you if you can. Blow your cover trying to get too fancy and I'll have your badge faster than the snap of a whip. And, Radisson?"

"What?" He couldn't bear to placate the man with his title any more.

"Don't choke."

Jeremy stared at the darkened phone, grateful for the severed connection. Otherwise he might have gone postal. Could Sterns know? Had he connected the dots between the few puzzle pieces Jeremy had scattered in the dark? Or had it been a harmless coincidence?

Son of a bitch.

A soft touch on his heaving shoulder had him rounding in a flash.

Isabella stumbled backward a step or two. Moisture made her eyes shine even in the dim kitchen. He hadn't bothered to turn the lights on. His conversation seemed better suited to darkness.

"Shit. I didn't mean to frighten you, Izzy."

"I'm not scared for me." Her whisper cracked. "It's Lily I'm worried about. And you. God, look at you."

Isabella set the tray she carried on the counter then crept closer until barely an inch remained between his flexing abdomen and her breasts. She reached upward as she rose onto her tiptoes. He bent forward into her embrace, allowing the warmth of her arms to dissolve the knot at the base of his neck.

"We're going to end this once and for all." He whispered into her hair. "I'll get her back. Make her safe."

"Thank you." She kissed his cheek. "Promise me you won't sacrifice yourself in trade. I'm greedy. I want you both. From what I saw at Malcolm's funeral, and after, I doubt my sister could be truly happy without you. Something happens when you two are together, when you touch. Something powerful. Special. The past year has taught me to believe in fate. You're meant for each other. I know it to the bottom of my soul."

Jeremy couldn't bear to hope the universe had his back. It never had before. No, he made his own destiny. Try as he might, sometimes he crashed and burned, no matter his intent. "I hope you're right, Izzy."

***

"Ah, Jeremy. Come in." Morselli rose from behind his polished desk, crafted of some exotic wood Jeremy had never seen before, when a servant showed them into Morselli's office. "I'd started to think you wouldn't show."

More like Jeremy hadn't granted the fucker excess time to pepper him with inquiries about his past or to stir up trouble. He strode toward the scum, repressing a grin when the supposedly fearless proprietor of the private establishment avoided offering another handshake.

"I'm a busy man." Jeremy didn't announce his companions, dressed entirely in black. Instead he pretended not to notice Matt—with his arms crossed over his massive chest—take up his post by the door or Clint sliding discreetly into the space to his left.

"What exactly is it that you do?" Morselli settled into his slick, modern chair, folding his fingers over his not-quite-flat belly.

"I'm an independent trainer. I fulfill requests from women who wish to seek a Master but need experience first or those who aren't sure if the lifestyle is meant for them. Sometimes I instruct other Doms or Dommes. Occasionally, a Master will hire me to take their slave beyond boundaries they're comfortable exploring without expert guidance."

"I see."

"Why ask me questions you already know the answer to? I'm sure you've done your homework by now. If not, perhaps I should be going. I only work with the most reputable enterprises."

"There's surprisingly little information available about you, Master Radisson. I did, however, speak to Gunther Spadius."

Despite the lurch in his chest, he couldn't stop his smile. The notorious trainer would have Jeremy's back. His mentor had begged Jeremy to return after the accident. The legendary Dom hadn't held the tragedy against Jeremy.

He wished he could say the same of himself.

"An impressive recommendation. He assured me you're an asset to any organization with a flair for...our specialties." Morselli leaned forward, resting his elbows on the gleaming surface of his desk. "I invited you here today as my guest. However, if you're interested in a new position, I'm sure I can find a use for you."

"I wasn't aware you offered services. I thought you invited friends to indulge their common ground and potentially make a new acquisition for their collection."

"For the most part, yes. Some, like Mistress Lily, will have their stable of paying slave-clients hosted here as well. An audience for other menu items I plan to market." Morselli paused, weighing his options. "There are special cases. Sometimes a prospective customer can't afford to pay cash. I think we're generous, allowing them to work off their bills. Lately, we've also taken a few shipments in trade. They need a touch of cleaning up before I can offer them to the more discerning buyers in good faith."

Jeremy gritted his teeth. He had no method for separating legitimate participants from the rest except by monitoring their reactions closely. Then again, how many of those who volunteered did so for access to Sex Offender? Bad enough to prey on people's addictions. How could Morselli assume anything he did to unwilling women, and probably some men, was in *good faith*?

"There are times, like today, we require a special set of skills."

"By that you mean..." Jeremy clenched his jaw.

"I hope you'll understand. When we bring new members into our circle, we have to be certain they share our values and will uphold our traditions." Morselli grinned. "I think having you and Lily joining us on the same day lends us some interesting opportunities."

Jeremy didn't trust himself to speak. He waited.

"Don't tell me you didn't enjoy her show the other night. I saw how hard you came while admiring her scene."

"She's talented."

"Wicked and gorgeous as sin too." Morselli's leer set Jeremy on the cusp of rational thought. "I had planned to test her myself, a delicious opening act before tonight's main events. Now I think I have a better idea. Why don't you come with me?"

Jeremy stood. Matt and Clint flanked him.

Morselli nodded toward the bulky men. "I hope one day you'll find precautions unnecessary."

"We'll see. I'm a conservative sort of man." He allowed a shred of reality to shine through, enhancing the believability of his story. Subtle shifts melded honesty into something twisted beyond recognition. "Truth be told, they're more friend than protection most times. Today, a little of both."

"Never can be too careful." Morselli clapped him on the back.

Jeremy wished he could show the jackass they were anything but pals.

"Let's see how tonight goes before we indulge in the full facilities tour. We're transferring a bunch of Lily's bootlickers to our campus. They're all rich, kept men, willing to pay for room and board and...whatever else it is they desire. She insisted I pamper them before she would abandon her playground despite my assurance we were state of the art compared to her joke of a shop. Still, things are a bit chaotic in her wing just now."

"I'll look forward to checking it out. It's been a while. I'm not sure anything can top Gunther's setup. I'm curious to inspect your attempt."

"Don't worry, I guarantee you'll be impressed."

They strolled along a marble hallway. Ostentatious and cold, it could never approach Jeremy's dream home. No matter how much money he had, he would never choose to live somewhere so lifeless. So uncomfortable.

"We don't have much time. I was hoping to meet with you earlier today. Our guests will arrive within the hour. If all remains on schedule, Lily's preparations have already begun."

"What is she arranging?" They descended a wide spiral staircase, the echo of their footsteps reverberating along the corridor.

"Oh, you misunderstood. It's *her* we're getting ready. See for yourself." Tony stopped before a heavy wooden door covered in intricate scrollwork. He punched in a code on a pinpad beside the portal. When the panel swung open, a balcony loomed before them. They approached the curved banister.

The wide room below reminded Jeremy of a pit at the coliseum where gladiators would wait for battle, some fired up and some resigned to their fate. Staff members adorned with uniforms made of slender chrome chains and black leather—tan, oiled skin peeking between—swarmed at least a dozen women and a handful of men. Each slave was held at a station where several attendants fussed with their hair and applied elaborate makeup to hide any marks from prior events. Bright red lipstick, vivid eye shadow and lots of rouge painted life into the victims who'd ceased to fight.

Matt cleared his throat as an inspector approached the team closest to them. The man chuckled as he worked through an extensive checklist, verifying the smoothness of the woman's waxing and breathing deep against her skin to test her fresh scent before finally signing off on his clipboard.

His nod to one of the attendants incited a flurry of activity. The woman who'd passed muster was unstrapped from the chair confining her. A brute squashed her weak attempt at rebellion without putting a hair out of place. He toted her to the next staging area while the original team plucked another shivering woman from the holding zone and tossed her toward the tiled wall in the corner. Fine mist filled the air when they blasted her with a strong spray of water from several hoses. Her shrieks and chattering gasps testified to the chill of the liquid.

Tony adjusted the bulge at his crotch when the prisoner danced in an attempt to evade the cruel shower.

Clint hissed a curse beneath his breath, low enough only Jeremy could hear. He followed his friend's gaze to the original subject, who was forced to conform to the outline of a contraption along with the rest of the slaves who'd already met physical standards.

The wrangler pressed his charge to her back on a small square platform a few inches below waist height. The supporting surface ended at her ass. Her captor locked the top half of a thick wooden stockade board around her neck and wrists, which were pinned beside her face. Several chains and clips secured the board with half-moon carve outs to the matching side bolted to the platform.

The woman's back arched at an extreme angle. Her abdomen rose as her thighs dangled and she sought to relieve some of the pressure by balancing on her tiptoes, which barely reached the floor. Her fingers clawed at the binding on her neck though she stood no chance of freeing herself. Hoarse shouts along with her struggles earned her a bright red ball gag between her matching lips.

Before she could cause herself damage or muss the carefully crafted illusion of glamour the prior team had cast, her attendant lifted two thick supports and tightened the bolts so they remained parallel to her legs at a forty-five degree angle to the platform surface, pointing backward at her body.

He grasped another plank—this one sported two larger holes—from a shelf under the main surface of the unit then knelt to guide her feet into the openings. He lifted the board until it hovered just above her knees. The leather-hooded man pressed the restraint toward her torso, bending the woman in half until the board rested on the two supports at her hips. He hammered the wood into place.

The woman reclined, her arms and neck pinned to the platform, her body folded as though stuck in an obscene crunch. Her legs spread wide, kept in place by the stockade engulfing her thighs. The position left her stretched, opened, her pussy and ass on display.

She released a keening cry when the man attempted to plunge two long fingers into her pussy. He shook his head then called over his shoulder, "Spreader plugs."

Before he'd finished his request, someone wheeled a cart to his side. He rummaged through various supplies before finding what he sought. He lifted a moderate plug from a box and dunked the plastic object in a pail filled with thin lubrication before aligning it with the opening of the woman's pussy. He slipped the insert between her puffy lips then held it in place with one hand while he repeated the act on her tight ass with a bit more difficulty.

When the objects were embedded, he attached a thin, clear hose to the base of each. The other end of the hose he attached to a nozzle on the shelf of the platform, which presented his slave. Once satisfied with the connection, he flipped a switch. The woman writhed to the extent her confinement allowed.

"What is he doing to her?" Jeremy wondered.

"They're inflatable with tiny holes. One of our latest inventions." Tony hummed. "He's filling them with warmed lubricating jelly. They'll stretch her and leave her moist...hot...for our guests. When they bury their cocks in her, she'll be eager and welcoming."

"Or at least it will seem that way." Jeremy hid his disgust. This woman hadn't chosen her fate. He'd bet his life on it.

Tony grinned.

The attendant patted the prisoner's flank then released the brake on wheels at the bottom of the platform, which Jeremy hadn't noticed. The rig became mobile. "Station seventeen, ready for placement."

Another chain-and-leather-liveried servant approached. He wrapped his hands around a bar above the woman's head, hidden by the fall of her hair. He steered the platform from the room, ignoring the squeals of the bound woman as cool air wafted across her tender, exposed skin.

Jeremy scanned the rest of the room. Each of the night's entertainers occupied an original apparatus, making them each into a unique work of erotic art.

"Impressive, yes?" Tony's thick question betrayed his arousal.

"The staff seems very...dedicated." Jeremy stopped himself from hurling insults. While the activity below would have turned him on if he could be sure all participants had selected their roles, their false submission destroyed any measure of arousal he might have felt. His cock shriveled as drastically as if he'd joined the polar bear club.

"Thank you." The dumbass didn't realize it wasn't a compliment. "They were hand selected. It's amazing what some of our guests are capable of turning into when offered a chance to improve their station."

"You mean some of them were slaves once?" Jeremy couldn't believe the horrors they must have suffered. Choosing to torment a fellow human in order to escape a life of degradation and pain sounded like a coward's bargain, but he couldn't blame them. He guessed many had sacrificed their ethics to evade a fate they couldn't stomach and remain sane.

"Yes. Reformed now." He smiled. "The handlers accept various forms of payment."

"Like what?" He didn't truly want to know. He could guess enough.

"Some prefer topping but can't afford their own slaves. Some are working off debts incurred by their former owners. Some.... Well, let's just say there are many reasons."

Sex Offender.

Jeremy couldn't deny his gaze skimmed the helpless fodder for tonight's feast. He searched for one sexy woman, sure she would hook his glance during his sweep of the floor.

His stare roved from end to end. Nothing.

"Ah, my friend. You're hungry to meet her again."

Shit, he'd have to disguise his interest better.

"You said it yourself, Mistress Lily is impressive." Allowing Tony to detect even a fraction of his craving for Lily would only lead to disaster. He couldn't allow the man any leverage.

Tony crooked his finger then strolled toward the far end of the observation deck. "You're right about one thing. She's not a common prize. I have her in a private holding room. Even tonight, she deserves respect. She's earned that at least, maybe more. Don't you agree?"

Tony led them to a niche, unapparent in the odd angles and shadows of the room. He lifted a subtle handle, crafted to match the hardware embellishing the decorative paneling of the rest of the loft. They slipped through the doorway one by one, Tony leading their pack with Matt bringing up the rear.

"I suppose." Jeremy shrugged. "But what use would I have for a Domme?"

When his eyes adjusted to the dim interior of the room they now occupied, he came face to face with Lily's accusing glare. It seemed to shout, *You liked it the other night.*

He couldn't respond—couldn't move or even breathe. If he blinked, rage would overpower his good sense. When Clint subtly tapped his elbow, he jumped. Thank God they'd come with him. Otherwise he might have blown his cover when he saw what Morselli had done to Lily.

CHAPTER FIVE

L ily smiled as she permitted the five men ringing her to assist in removing her skimpy clothes. Tony Morselli had welcomed her in style. No fruit basket cluttered the ebony inlaid desk in her quarters. Instead, he'd gifted her with the use of his submissives to help her clear her mind and prepare for tonight's festivities. She glanced around the meditation room in the main section of the house, dismissing the opulence of her surroundings in favor of concentrating on the priceless men at her feet.

Eagerness to obey enhanced the sparkle of their eyes, which ranged the full spectrum from chestnut brown to the lightest green imaginable. The stud by her side licked his lips and thanked her for selecting him as part of her entourage when she propped her boot on his folded leg. He untied the laces and slipped first one then the other from her aching feet.

The location of her suite in Morselli's mansion, her temporary home, meant a longer trip to the dungeon. Ridiculous when she considered on a typical day she traversed three and a half blocks from her apartment to Black Lily yet today she hadn't even left the building. Despite her graveyard hours, which left her walking alone in the middle of the night, she'd never looked over her shoulder as often as she had while wandering toward the main hall and the lovely presents awaiting her arrival.

The slaves' grateful servitude alleviated her fear of abuse.

Tony wouldn't risk offending her ideals before she'd entangled herself in his organization. He wouldn't expose his dirty secrets until he'd gained some leverage. She regulated her deep breaths as she contemplated granting him any measure of power over her. Especially after only recently breaking free of her father's tyranny, putting herself under anyone's thumb rankled.

It had to be done.

For now she would enjoy the treat he'd bestowed. There would be plenty of time for worrying later. She lifted her arms and basked in the appreciative murmurs of her temporary pets when they unwrapped her torso from the racy satin and lace corset that had hugged her all afternoon. She adored severe lingerie—bustiers, corsets, merry widows. Nothing could compare to the sweet pressure, which reinforced her controlled posture and respiration, squeezing her when she donned the garments.

Lily prided herself on how strong she'd grown despite a childhood rough enough to crush someone weaker. She'd never broken. Never quit fighting until she ruled her world.

The hungry glances the attendants shot toward her assets filled her with a powerful thrill. She plumped her breasts, enhancing her cleavage, then tipped forward until she nearly smothered one of the men with her chest. A happy death. A chuckle escaped her when he groaned and proceeded to nuzzle the mounds with his smooth cheek.

Lily slung one arm to each side, curving them around the shoulders of the two closest men. On their knees, the slaves were the proper height for her to use them as supports. The dark-haired sweetheart beneath her right elbow smiled then angled his head to kiss the soft skin of her upper arm without asking for her permission. She allowed the transgression to pass. Unlike some Mistresses, she preferred the affection of her trainees to flow unfettered.

"Unzip my skirt. Take it off." She hadn't finished issuing the command before her matching panties and garter were revealed. Her restrictive pencil skirt didn't have time to pool at her ankles. One of the men encircled her waist in his broad hands and lifted her so another of his brothers in bondage could remove the discarded silk.

"Come closer." She crooked her finger at the tall blond, who hovered in the background. When he did as she instructed, she smiled. "Don't be shy. Why don't you roll my stockings down?"

"Yes, Mistress." He crouched, displaying the ripple of honed muscle across his bare back as he engulfed her thigh easily in his palms. The brush of his trembling grip had her suppressing the urge to squirm.

It wouldn't do to show even a hint of weakness. Not to these men, or any slave.

But what about a Master? The *right* Master. She would be able to release her moans beneath his caring. Let go for once. Take instead of give.

Jeremy Radisson's intense stare flashed through her mind. The continual stroking of the men surrounding her inspired a purr. How would Jeremy's touch differ? When he'd caught her in her office, his firm grip had coaxed and molded rather than worshipping. It had jellied her knees. She could still feel the impression of his fingertips though it had been months since their skin-to-skin contact.

Lily shook her head, clearing the wayward thoughts that had encroached on her waking hours after running rampant through her dreams. Now was not the time for distractions.

"May we offer a massage, Lady?"

"That sounds lovely. Thank you." Lily opened her arms to the lucky man who'd suggested the treatment.

She savored the floating sensation when he lifted her to the padded table occupying one wall in the luxurious room.

A sigh escaped her parted lips as she burrowed her cheek in the soft microfiber that covered the pillowed surface. Low tones of a soothing chant emanated from inset speakers behind a modern fountain. Tranquility washed over her. Completely at ease with her nudity and that of the slaves around her, she basked in their attention.

Lavender oil perfumed the air, encouraging her nostrils to flare as she inhaled deeply. Generous lubrication caused the familiar slap of slick flesh as each man coated his hands then passed the bottle to the slave beside him. The cap *snicked* closed moments before fifty warm fingers splayed across her torso.

Multiple pairs of hands worked every inch of her body, starting with her toes, palms and scalp then spiraling inward. The swirl of fingertips soothed her shoulders, rose above her wrists and ankles, concentrated on her back and calves before climbing her thighs and sinking over her buttocks until they pressed near the entrance to her pussy.

Still, their training held. None of the men crossed her boundaries or whined for what their stiffening cocks proclaimed they desired. She would grant them some of what they craved.

"Who would like to make me come?" She rolled to her back, spreading her legs until her heels dangled off the edges of the table.

"I would, Mistress." The shy blond volunteered in a flash, beating out the rest of his comrades by a split second. "Please, may I taste you?"

"Greedy." She laughed softly. "You would be lucky if I allowed you to touch me, never mind drink my juices as I came on your face."

The slave bowed his head, whispering an apology as though she would punish him harshly for his honesty.

How could she refuse such sweet surrender? Granting wishes, making dreams come true—as no one had ever done for her—remained the driving force behind her role. Situations like these were win-win.

"What's your name?" The strong submissive met her gaze when asked a direct question. The shocking sparkle of his eyes reminded her of Jeremy and the potent stare he'd leveled on her two nights before. She could drown in the attention.

"I'm Ryan. At your service, Mistress Lily."

"Good boy." She shifted to her right. The other four men understood her intent. They rotated her ninety degrees until she was perpendicular to her starting point and her legs draped over Ryan's shoulders. The man who'd been at her left supported her shoulders against his buff chest, never missing a beat as he massaged her forehead, cheeks and temples.

Divine.

The three unburdened slaves continued to stroke her body, cupping her breasts, petting her belly and chaffing her arms. Puffs of Ryan's elevated respiration dusted the lips of her bare pussy.

"Go ahead, sweetheart." She guided his tongue to her clit with a firm grip on his too-long hair. "That's nice. Suck my clit. A little harder. Yes, perfect."

Lily relaxed, allowing her eyes to flutter closed as Ryan demonstrated impressive skill.

After long minutes of reveling in the pressure building inside, she tapped the long fingers making a circuit from her knee to her hip. "Inside me. Feel how hot my pussy is. For you. All of you."

The man groaned as he kneeled beside Ryan. The slaves pressed close in order to fulfill her wishes. She enjoyed the manscape as their defined pectoral muscles gleamed with a light sheen of sweat.

The second slave notched two digits at the entrance of her pussy and began to work them inside. "Yes, like that."

"You're delicious, Mistress." Ryan redoubled his licking at the moisture coating her pussy. His tongue flickered over the other man's knuckles.

"Would you like a taste?" She tilted her head toward the second slave as she observed the man tunneling deeper within her sheath on every pass.

"May I?" He looked as if afraid to hope. Who had treated these men so poorly? She made a mental note to offer to incorporate them into her personal stable.

"Of course." She interjected as his fingers neared his mouth. "But I'd prefer you to take your sample from Ryan's lips."

He hesitated, debating.

"That's not an order." She wouldn't force either of the men to violate their boundaries. "Merely a statement of my preference."

Ryan lifted his head from her drenched folds. He nodded at the man studying his glistening lips and chin. "If you want to, Ben..."

Ben eroded the distance between them, tentatively extending his tongue. He touched the tip of the thick muscle to Ryan's parted lips and licked. A teeny taste. His lashes fluttered, and he groaned. He returned for seconds, this time sealing their mouths firmly.

Lily studied the men as they devoured each other, battling for supremacy. Few things ranked as high as witnessing two hard, sexy men kiss, especially when they did it to please her.

She shivered.

"Very nice." She regulated the breathy quality of her praise. "Now, finish what you've started. Make me come then you can play with each other if you're interested."

Their instant enthusiasm brought a grin to her lips. The men massaging her drove her insane with gentle swipes across her belly and breasts. "Suck my nipples."

The men not holding her head or perched between her knees dipped down and teased the hard tips of her breasts. They licked, nibbled and suckled until her toes curled.

She couldn't hold on to the whirlwind of desire. She opened her eyes and met the adoring gaze of the man supporting her neck. "Kiss me."

He obeyed her passionate hiss, allowing her to part his lips with her tongue. She coaxed him to explore the recesses of her mouth, enjoying the minty taste she sucked from his mouth when pleasure expanded, radiating outward from her pussy.

"Mistress Lily is coming." The man burrowing his fingers beneath Ryan's oral manipulation informed his brothers. "She's squeezing me tight. So tight."

She rode his hand and Ryan's face until every last drop of satisfaction had been wrung from her body. Their cocks must have ached from the persistent pressure in them. None of the five asked for relief.

Lily hummed as she scooted toward the wall, bracing her back on the cool surface. She patted the space between her thighs. "Hop up here, Ryan."

He leapt onto the table with the grace of a jungle cat. She nudged his shoulder until he understood what she had in mind. He spun, lying between her thighs, his shoulders dwarfing her abdomen where they rested against her heated skin.

The slave cuddled into her embrace. She brushed the hair from his brow and petted his face as he leaned into her touch. "Very nice, sweetheart. Would you like some help with your pretty hard-on?"

"Yes, please." His ass flexed, thrusting his pelvis upward. "Let me come for you, Mistress."

"Oh, you will." She smiled at the men ringing them. "All of you."

When Ryan reached for his cock, she stopped him with a curt, "No."

His hand dropped to his hip instantly.

"Ben, stroke him." The other man bit his lip but reached out tentatively, surrounding his fellow submissive's dick with thick fingers. "Very nice. Now, you..."

She tipped her chin at the man beside Ben. "He shouldn't be left out of the fun, should he?"

"No, ma'am." His southern accent amplified her grin. Adorable.

"Help Ben."

The slave didn't pretend to balk. He wrapped his supple, lotioned hand around Ben's impressive shaft and began to glide it up and down. Two sets of male grunts floated through the room. She nodded at the other three men. They moved in unison, each gripping the cock of the man beside him.

"Close the circle, Ryan." She nibbled his ear, momentarily drawing his attention from the pleasure Ben gifted him with. The long, slow glide of the slave's hand from root to tip on his erection had to feel phenomenal. No one knew better than another man how to stroke dick.

When Ben concentrated his undulating fingers on the oozing head of Ryan's cock, Ryan latched on to the stiff, waving shaft of the man to his right. He linked them all in a ring of pleasure.

Lily sighed and rubbed her spread pussy on Ryan's flexing back. His knotted muscles made a nice pad for stroking her clit. The sight of five impressive male specimens surrendering to their lust at her command did more to rocket her toward orgasm than the squirming of Ryan's velvety tongue had.

Their cocks strained, growing more rigid and defined, darker as blood pumped between their legs. Pre-come bubbled from their balls, adding to the slippery sounds interspersed with grunts and soft curses from the cohorts.

"Who will be first?" Lily panted when the pace of their strokes sped up as though by mutual agreement. Each man communicated his rising need through his attention to his neighbor.

Ryan shuddered in her hold.

She clutched his chest as it bellowed with his pants.

"Maybe me. Close. So close. Please, Mistress. Please, Ben."

Lily smiled at the man stroking Ryan's cock when he looked to her for guidance.

"Whenever you're ready. All of you." She struggled to appear calm when their surrender to her wishes set her ablaze. "Make sure you come on Ryan. I want to see your pleasure spilling over him."

As though they found the idea as appealing as she did, the men lost all reserve. One by one they tipped their heads back and roared. The first man to surrender to orgasm shuffled closer, as tight as he could get to the table. His partner aimed the purple head of his cock at Ryan, who looked like a very unvirginal human sacrifice.

Come dribbled from the tip of his cock. The meager display disappointed her insatiable libido a tiny bit. Until she realized it was just the warm up. Blast after blast of thick white come shot from his cock, coating Ryan's defined abs and Ben's pumping fist.

His pleasure unlocked the rest. All of the men erupted in near unison. Ben's motion turned jerky as he emptied his load across Ryan's chest. The pearly white fluid meandered down the man's abdomen. When it pooled near his belly button, mingling with the fluid from the other slaves, Ryan froze in her hold, locked in an endless orgasm.

She came with him, grinding her pussy against his taut muscles as the final spurt of his come launched from his cock. He came so hard and so long she feared he might have a heart attack. At least she would have worried if he hadn't been the picture of physical fitness.

Possessing the power to do this to such strong, vibrant creatures filled her with satisfaction. Nothing could please her more than bestowing ecstasy.

Lily allowed them all to soak in the positive energy zinging around the room for a minute or two. Then she nodded to one of the men leaning heavily on locked arms against the massage table. "When you're steady, grab one of the towels from the pile by the sink and clean Ryan off."

"Yes, ma'am."

Ryan groaned as his buddy swiped come from the ridges of his abdomen with hasty strokes.

"In a hurry?" Lily raised an eyebrow at the man, noting the sweat beading on his forehead.

"There's a lot to do and not much time, Mistress." He forced himself to slow, but she noted the tension creeping into the slaves she'd managed to relax so recently. All of them averted their gazes.

Morselli had a lot to answer to. Their nervousness outraged her.

"Let me worry about our punctuality. I'm the one responsible for any delays caused by our impromptu session, not you. It will be no reflection on your service—unless it is an exceptionally positive one—that you pleased me enough to linger. I assure you, I'll see to that."

The halfhearted acknowledgement of her statement burned in her stomach as though she'd eaten pepperoni pizza too close to bedtime. It would take more than a single assurance to rewire beliefs honed by mistreatment.

She sighed. "We'll keep moving. I need to wash the massage oil out of my hair before I can put on makeup and get dressed. I'm a simple woman when it comes to those things so we should have plenty of time."

Ryan carried her as though she were a priceless vase when she waved her hand toward the sink in the corner of the room. He situated her in the reclining chair before moving aside so one of the other men could fulfill his duties.

"Can any of you paint my nails without making me look like a serial killer who works with her bare hands?" She didn't expect them to own up to such a skill.

"I can." Ben blushed when the rest of the slaves turned to stare. "I practically raised my little sister. And my niece. Julie's seven. She gets a kick out of the glittery kind."

Lily wished they were alone, somewhere private, so she could dig into the root cause of the lines etching his face and release some of his stress. She admired the strength it must have taken him to step into a leadership role so young. Hell, he couldn't be more than twenty-five now.

What would it have been like to have a protector? Someone who would have indulged her girlish whims and shouldered the burdens of reality when she was a child? Suddenly, his need to submit, to turn over the reins and be cared for, made perfect sense. Every once in a while she wished...

But hoping was a waste of time.

"I'd like something a bit more serious. How about the dark burgundy on the top left of that rack." She tilted her chin toward the shade she desired.

"Yes, Mistress."

Lily closed her eyes and allowed the men to showcase their expertise. The slave at her head completed the massage of her scalp as he shampooed and conditioned her thick mane. One of Ben's broad hands cupped her fingers as the other began applying polish. She imagined the tiny brush dwarfed by his digits. He'd learned a delicate touch for the sake of his family.

Why hadn't her relatives ever been compelled to do the same? She considered her mother's addictions and her father's cruelty. Evaporating shellac tipped her hands and feet with coolness. Goose bumps rose on her arms.

She had barely registered the chill when soft sponges, damp with steamy, soapy water, swiped over her torso and between her legs. Warmth pumped through her as she admitted she'd created her own family from the men who'd sought her care and attention, giving it a hundred times in return.

The pampering of her attendants befitted the respect due to a visiting Mistress, especially the guest of honor. No one could blame her for letting her guard down, relaxing in the company of the well-trained submissives. True, they didn't owe their allegiance to her. No one in this hellhole did except the men she'd arranged to house in the private wing of the mansion and a few members of her covert coalition, who wouldn't arrive until later in the evening.

Still, they had bonded. Shared ecstasy. The bliss they'd generated had derailed her from the laser-like focus she'd maintained since accepting Morselli's offer of employment. She hadn't had much choice other than taking him up on it. He reigned over the heart of the trouble resurfacing after several months lurking beneath deceptively calm waters. Though she hadn't yet discovered his link to The Scientist, she'd pinpointed his estate as the primary distribution channel flooding the market with the latest batch of Sex Offender after a half dozen Black Lily patrons had developed the telltale gleam in their eyes and an obsession for visiting the previously unknown fetish house.

Turning the tide meant breaching his defenses, worming inside to eat out the core.

As the slaves groomed her body, Lily cemented her resolve. Morselli would test her. Tonight. Somehow. Anticipating all the trials she might have to endure to prove her loyalty, she devised countermeasures for preserving her values. Most likely, she'd be made to top one of his victims. She grinned as she considered how she'd managed to plant one of her ally's pets in the lineup of slaves supposedly here involuntarily.

Just in case.

Having met Ben, Ryan and the other submissives tending her, she would be comfortable drawing on them to satisfy any required demonstrations. If Morselli offered the drug, she'd cite her father's very public untimely demise as reason to abstain.

If—no, when—he tried to sell victims, she'd trust her instructions to her alliance would hold. They'd outbid the crowd. She'd repay them out of the enormous account Isabella had insisted she accept from their father's estate. Thank God. She'd drained her own hefty savings over the past year, bailing out as many unwilling captives as she could. The ones she hadn't been able to save ate at her soul. Their faces flashed through her nightmares like a parade of ghosts.

Lily had run through about a thousand scenarios by the time the man at her head began to squeegee excess moisture from her waist-length tresses. He wrapped the damp mass in a towel. She quieted her mind using some of the techniques she'd developed as a child during the long, terrifying nights.

When she opened her eyes, she caught Ryan gesturing frantically to Ben. The bloodshot tinge to his stare hadn't been there minutes ago. He shook his head and waved his hands before stepping between her and his fellow slave. His shoulders heaved as he planted his feet shoulder-width apart.

"Ryan. Look at me."

His hands shook as he turned to face her. Slowly.

"What's the matter?" She reached for his arm, but he retreated.

"It's not right." Ryan snarled when the other men ringed her tighter. "This is bullshit! How much will we let him take? When will it stop? He's not going to release your family, Ben. They're probably already dead."

Lily sat bolt upright. Her gaze whipped between the two men.

"I'm sorry, Mistress." Ben bowed his head, his explanation rushing from him in one breath that sounded as though it wheezed from the pit of hell instead of his magnificent chest. "They have Julie. And April. If I don't do it, Morselli will hurt them. Jesus. Julie's so little. I can't think about what they'd do to her."

"Calm down, tell me the whole story."

"I can't, Mistress."

Ryan shook his head and held his ground as Ben approached. "You will not touch her."

"I don't have a choice. None of us do. Move, Ry. Please. Don't make me hurt you. We've suffered enough already." The two slaves who'd kissed each other as if they couldn't stand to stop for a breath balled their fists and prepared to settle their differences.

"Stop. Right now." Lily didn't have to raise her voice. They obeyed instantly, the reaction hardwired into their systems. She rose, yearning for her boots when her stare landed well below their defined pecs. Before she could command them to reveal the source of their friction, the hair on the back of her nape lifted.

"Morselli has us all by the balls, Ben." The gentle southerner spoke up. He looked her straight in the eye and whispered, "I'm sorry. This is a tragedy. Another time where I violate all I believe in. Someday I'll beg you to punish me for this."

His hand latched on to her ankle.

Lily tried to kick off his hold. He pinned her tighter. Three other slaves, including Ben, snagged her remaining limbs. They constricted their grips around her wrists and ankles in synch. She thrashed in their unbreakable grasp—teeth snapping at anything within reach—for a split second, unable to squash the instinct until she saw the sick horror and dread on Ryan's face.

She went slack instantly, refusing to amplify his torment. It wasn't like she had any hope of escape against their hefty muscles. As strong as her willpower was, she stood no chance in a physical matchup.

Tony's staff worked as a single unit, carting her toward a covered object in the opposite corner of the room. Ben whipped a sheet off the fixture as Ryan scrambled to hold it in place.

"Ryan." She commanded his attention. "Stop fighting them. It's okay. I'll be fine. Do what you have to."

"But—"

"Argue with me and I *will* be offended." She smiled. "Help them."

He stood to the side and allowed the others to deposit her on the stand they'd revealed.

"Forgive me, Mistress," one of the slaves whispered as he manipulated the angle of her leg, bending her knee. When she realized what they intended, she assumed the position required, kneeling with her thighs spread wide and her arms outstretched. Her pride remained whole as heavy chains lashed her ankles and knees to a gleaming, polished granite pedestal with thick links of freezing, inescapable steel.

Lily's arms reached wide, as though prepared to welcome an old friend into a grotesque embrace. Ryan wept as he locked first one wrist than the other into unforgiving shackles. They adorned a metal framework that resembled a T, the base of which was bolted behind her back, between her legs. A lightly padded bump protruded from the trunk of the macabre tree, inflicting a severe arch to her spine.

Mirrors on the ceiling and walls reflected her predicament. She noted how the position highlighted the ridges of her ribs and her svelte abdominal muscles, earned through endless hours riding her slaves. Fucking toned better than any gym workout. Bowed, she seemed to present her firm breasts like a pair of gifts on top of her chest. Her ultra-petite stature made the mounds appear larger than they were.

The men cared for her like a carefully synchronized watch, all the moving parts of their assemblage keeping impeccable time. They apologized, seeking absolution she granted freely as they held her immobile and called for a stylist over the room's intercom.

Her time was running short.

"Gather around me. All of you." She infused her request with kindness.

They flocked to her side in an instant.

"Closer. Huddle up."

The men draped their arms over the slaves to either side until they resembled a football team more than a collection of high-quality submissives. Lily checked the gaps between them, finding none. She pitched her voice low enough not to carry. "Good boys. I'm certain this room is filled with cameras and microphones. So, I'm only going to say this once. Believe me."

She met each of their eyes, assuring them of her honesty.

"None of this is your fault. You're not responsible for what you've been forced to do here today or what might occur this evening. I came here fully aware of the risks. If you think this erases one shred of my dignity or authority then you've underestimated my strength. Promise me, no matter what you see tonight, you will *not* intervene. I'm fully capable of surviving—thriving even—despite Tony Morselli's petty display of phony sovereignty. I've endured far worse. This will be nothing."

Maybe not *nothing*. Still, she would brazen through. Just like old times.

"But—"

"No, Ryan." She cut him off. "In this I won't accept disobedience. If you violate my wishes then I'll consider you to have disgraced your station and the lifestyle you value as much as I do."

"Yes, Mistress." The corded tendons in his neck relaxed.

"Very good." She smiled then stretched to the limits of her confinement in order to sip the lingering moisture from his cheek. "Be careful. All of you. When this storm has passed, I'll search you out. You have an open invitation to join me."

The click of the door unlatching terminated their conversation. The men nodded as a pair of beautiful women dressed only in slender silver chains and tiny leather panels entered the space.

Despite Lily's command otherwise, one beautician slathered her face with drastic yet flattering makeup, including blood-red lipstick. The other blow-dried her hair, glamming it up with unnecessary product and enhancing the gentle waves Lily usually forced into absolutely straight, austere lines. To make it worse, the attendant left the fall of her mane loose. The sultry curtain brushed the upper curve of her ass with softness as foreign to her as the bite of the metal trapping her ankles and calves to the hard block, which gouged her knees.

When Lily had resigned herself to the bondage and her frou-frou appearance, they imposed one final restraint. The women braided a thin section of her hair, originating at the crown of her skull. They worked a long black ribbon into the tresses. Once interwoven, it held as tightly as if they'd super glued it to her skull. They tugged experimentally, yanking her head back until Ben growled from his place by her side.

The women chuckled as they secured the end of the tie to a formidable steel ring affixed to the pedestal between Lily's pointed feet. The too-short cord guaranteed she continued the elegant curve of her body through her neck, which ached instantly in the awkward position. Even worse, she couldn't watch her surroundings directly. Instead she relied on the mirrored ceiling to track the movement of the players in the space.

"Mr. Morselli instructed us to place her in the center of the room, facing the north entrance," one of the women barked at Ryan. He ignored her shrill command, looking instead to Lily. She smiled, about all she could do.

Four of the men surrounded her, each gripping a chrome handle on his side of the cube she knelt upon. They carefully lifted her, their muscles straining beneath the weight of the stone, while Ben slid a dolly beneath the structure. They wheeled her into position.

"It's time to arrange the main hall. We can't keep our guests waiting. They'll begin arriving soon." The women marched toward the exit. The five men moved slower, sharing glances with each other.

"Thank you for your service." Lily tried again to alleviate their concern.

"Enough," one of the women tossed over her shoulder. "Don't forget the gag."

"Go ahead," Lily whispered to Ryan, who approached her with minced steps so unfitting to his size and strength she almost laughed. "I'll be fine. Do it."

She watched in the mirror as he lifted the black ball gag and opened her mouth before he touched it to her lips. He fed her the soft foam then buckled it on the loosest setting, though even that left no wiggle room.

"The pleasure was ours, Mistress." Ryan inclined his shoulders in a tiny bow the rest of the men mimicked before trundling through the door, which seemed smaller when their bulk passed through the opening.

As soon as they were gone, the pleasant harmony she'd enjoyed during her massage disappeared. Even the trickle of water in the fountain ceased. Absolute silence in the insulated chamber left her ears ringing with a high-pitched buzz. A moment later, the lights flicked off. Either the controls were located on a panel outside the room, or her suspicions had been confirmed.

Someone was watching.

They knew she'd been abandoned.

Lily closed her eyes and imagined she'd caused the darkness—controlled her surroundings. She consciously relaxed each muscle in her body, starting with her toes. The awkwardness of her pose melted into insignificance as she focused on generating an accurate accounting of the slow, steady beats of her heart.

Her mind freed itself from her environment, relying on the techniques she'd honed as a child to ignore Buchanan abusing her mother all through the night just so her only true parent could drink away the pocket change he tossed her afterward.

Lily's control slipped as memories haunted her. Until she reminded herself they were gone. Both of her lousy excuses for parents. Forever.

She smiled into the pitch black, hoping Morselli had infrared cameras. Instead of the castle haven she'd imagined her sister-princess inviting her to live in as a child, she drew the happiest moments of her life around her like the most effective security blanket in the universe.

Topping the list was Lily's recollection of Isabella's welcoming grace at the discovery of her bastard half-sister. The generosity and instant affection her sister had lavished brought tears of joy to her eyes. Not far behind, the brilliant flames of true love she'd witnessed sparking between her sister and Razor, the young cop Izzy had fallen for, had rekindled dreams Lily thought long dead. Heat infused her chilled body as she recalled the peace she'd found in the strong arms of Jeremy Radisson. Her sister's friend had singed her with his intense stare. He'd comforted her at the funeral of a prized submissive.

God, Malcolm. Even months later it hurt to think of that tragedy.

Jeremy had understood something she could never have explained. A level of grief you had to feel to know. How could they be so much the same? How could he make her wish she could be someone different, someone he needed, for the first time in her life?

After more than three thousand beats of Lily's heart, a cramp threatened to wring a groan from her stuffed lips. She drove it off with a vision of Jeremy. No matter how hard she tried to force the illusion of him, she couldn't imagine him kneeling when he offered to relax her. The icy heat in his eyes alone would melt the tension from every molecule of her body, if she let it.

Damn that look and the natural dominance oozing from him whether he wore leathers, as he had the night in her office, or the casual jeans and T-shirt she'd spotted him in most often. He didn't need the trappings to scream his intent loud and clear. It was simply a part of him. A part that had her gulping for air. His wolf-in-sheep's-clothing act may have fooled his friends, but she saw straight through the disguise.

Her mind wandered to a recurring fantasy. A dream she hadn't been able to laugh off on waking. So many nights in a row. At first, she'd thought their accidental inhalation of Sex Offender had caused the irrational riot of her hormones. Months of recurrence had taught her better. His effect on her hadn't faded over the months since the last time she'd allowed herself to share space with him.

The time he'd kissed her, promising to do so again soon, then disappeared for months.

A stab of pain raced through her overextended shoulder when she tensed. Deep breaths in and out returned her calm. Maybe he had a reason for walking away. If she hadn't been so damn stubborn, she might have discussed it with him the other night. When he'd finally called—more like unleashed a torrent of texts, emails and voicemails really.

Stubborn and annoyed, she'd refused to answer him after months of silence.

Lily sighed as she remembered the extravaganza at Black Lily and the scene they'd shared despite the distance between them. They'd lived every moment together. If he were here now, she wouldn't be surprised to learn his heart beat three thousand four hundred and twenty-seven times. Exactly in tune with hers.

Just the thought of him illuminated her world of darkness.

She rolled her eyes at such foolish thoughts. But the tiny sliver of brightness grew. It became impossible to deny the blackness-birthed fuzzy shadows.

A familiar voice rang in her ears.

"What use would I have for a Domme?" Jeremy Radisson crushed the bubble of bliss that had sustained her spirit for nearly an hour in her contortionist prison.

CHAPTER SIX

"Ah, Lily. Don't mind my guest. You remember Master Jeremy from the other night, yes? You look gorgeous." Tony dragged one fingertip from Lily's chin down her neck along the dip of her collarbone between her breasts over her taut belly to her pussy.

Jeremy drew up short when pressure on his neck made him aware of Matt or Clint tugging on this shirttail, urging him not to rip Tony's filthy paw from the flawless porcelain skin on display.

Where another woman would certainly have flinched, Lily held her ground. With no possibility of escape, attempting to evade the taunting examination would only have wasted energy and fueled Morselli's sadistic streak.

Jeremy scrunched his eyes closed and hoped for a fraction of her fortitude. He would sure as hell need it.

"I trust you were treated well."

Again Lily refused to utter a peep, which they wouldn't have been able to decipher considering the gag buried between her lush red lips. Her chest rose and fell in deep, even breaths. Her pulse remained steady in the exposed curve of her neck.

Jeremy would kill to devour the sensitive column. He'd leave a bright purple mark, claiming her as his property. His responsibility.

Only the daggers flashing from Lily's eyes, colder than he'd ever seen them, hinted at how badly they'd pissed her off. If he hadn't fumed along with her, he might have admired the attention to detail Tony's staff had paid to their charge.

Morselli enjoyed the fruits of their labor laid out on top of a stone pedestal like a rare artifact in a museum. Lily would be a one-of-a-kind addition to any collection.

Taller than a step stool but short enough to ensure its occupant remained below eye level for Morselli's average-at-best height, the furnishing presented her for their approval. The bastard hummed as his manicured fingernails lingered near the entrance to Lily's nude sex.

Spread-eagle, no part of her body remained sheltered, private.

Jeremy's fingers curled into fists by his side as he prepared to loosen some of his host's bright-white teeth. Nothing would stop him from landing a blow or twenty if Morselli attempted to force any part of himself inside her unwelcoming body. At the last instant, the asshole flashed a gold-capped grin and shied away.

But he couldn't leave well enough alone.

When he grazed the swell of Lily's hipbone, where a freshly healed tattoo swirled, her calm evaporated. She hurled several garbled insults in their direction. Jeremy couldn't prevent Morselli from tainting the memorial piece with his filthy touch. He poked the artfully arranged tails of a cat-o'-nine where they splayed across elegant cursive spelling out Malcolm's name.

Somehow Jeremy doubted Lily's sister Isabella, who'd been married to the man, would hold a similar regard. And yet he understood. Perfectly. His own inked reminder of tragedy occupied a similar spot on his trunk.

Jesus. Lily had survived so much pain. Everything she'd ever loved or hoped for had been stolen from her. He swore then and there to stop the cycle—to grant her a chance at happiness if he could.

The intent of the muffled stream of her curses slipped clearly enough past the ball gag spreading her jaw. Jeremy's gaze fixated on the crimson O of her lips as he devised a plan.

"Is that any way to talk to your new boss?" Tony's ire held none of the charm or class he pretended to possess in public. He tweaked Lily's pink nipple, puckered from the chill of the room.

Jeremy would bet the zing of light pain awoke nerves long gone numb from Morselli's indiscriminate posing of her figure. Instead of whimpering or attempting to shy away, her pupils dilated and she arched further, daring the fucker to do it again.

He'd bet she harnessed the spark, used it to help her concentrate.

That's my girl.

To survive tonight intact, she'd need all her wits and every bit of the mental fortitude she'd developed at the hands of her dead father and the minions he'd employed to instruct her. Tony Morselli had no idea what she'd lived through. No one could be better prepared to outlast his malice.

Maybe even enjoy it.

Jeremy would bet she'd learned long ago to swap the pain for pleasure—to feed off the energy and use it to grow stronger, not weaker. His own training had granted him such focus. He'd trade places with her in an instant. Gladly accept the flare of agony and arousal to shield her from the sting, despite her ability to own it.

In fact... Yes, it could work.

Tony snarled as he kept rambling. "Be nice, Lily. Or I won't limit your use tonight to our new friend Master Jeremy and the rest of my guests. There are plenty of others in the complex who would gladly ruin you."

She froze when she realized what Morselli intended.

Jeremy stepped closer, pretending to conduct his own assessment of her form. He towered over her, caressing the knotted muscles of her back until she could meet his stare despite the extreme angle of her neck. He hoped she could read his conviction.

I'm here. I won't let anyone hurt you.

She blinked three times in rapid succession.

He prayed he hadn't lied.

Jeremy scanned her from head to toe and back before cradling her head in one palm and licking the stretched ring of her lips. She trembled when he tasted her.

"You're right, Tony," he growled. "She's exquisite. A rare treasure, not a common bauble."

Morselli chuckled, completely oblivious to the ominous tone of his praise.

Far more observant, Lily looked from side to side since she couldn't shake her head, but their course had already been charted. He followed where fate had led them.

"She's a dark fantasy come to life." Morselli shifted the hard-on disrupting the lay of his slacks. "I've always wondered how she would look, bound, her eyes begging for something only I could give."

"Me too." His honest hunger surprised Lily as much as it had him if her trembling fingers and escalating respiration were any indication. He couldn't prevent the soothing caress he placed on her cheek.

She shocked him when every muscle in her body went lax beneath his attentions and her lids fluttered closed. Onyx lashes stood out against her pale skin.

"Yes. Yes." Morselli huffed beside her, toying with the buckle of his belt. "Maybe I've changed my mind. No reason we both can't have her tonight."

Matt shifted subtly, blocking their suspect's access to Lily.

Her eyes popped open, her gaze flicking toward the man in the mirror.

"I do appreciate the gesture, Tony." Jeremy spun lazily on his heel, as though the current of electricity arcing between them hadn't jolted him like a live wire. "But, I think I'll pass."

"Is this some kind of joke?" Though Morselli squawked the question, even Matt and Clint raised eyebrows at their teammate.

Jeremy reached around Morselli to disengage one of the manacles pinning Lily's delicate wrist to the harsh support. "Nope. It's not sporting. I don't need a handicap or some false head start. If I take Lily... No, *when* I take her, she'll ask me for it. She'll kneel and beg me to ravish her because she admits who owns her. This is...artificial."

"You don't approve? This isn't the time to wax philosophical, my *friend*." Tony sneered. "Any number of Doms already on the premises would kill for the once-in-a-lifetime chance to top her. Any idiot can see she doesn't have a single submissive bone in her body. Or is that it? You don't care to be embarrassed by fucking a woman who won't bend to you? Do this tonight. Both of you. Prove your loyalty and I'll share my kingdom with you. Neither of you grasps how much profit there is to be made. If I can trust you. I need partners to expand my network. Show me what you're willing to sacrifice. A tiny bit of your pride isn't a lot to ask."

"No." Jeremy tested his luck by exacerbating Tony's temper, hoping to throw the man out of the realm of rationality. If he could manipulate the bastard a little more, he could secure agreement for his plan.

Lily's tiny, almost inaudible sigh whipped his head around. Could the puff of air have been caused by a shard of disappointment slicing her deep inside? Since when did she long to surrender?

Jeremy wondered if she could trust someone with her soul despite all the scar tissue she'd developed around her heart. He'd thought the fantasy unattainable. Not that he'd let that stop him from trying.

"Fine, I'll appoint someone else. I'm sure there'll be no shortage of volunteers."

Matt and Clint turned to Jeremy with wide eyes, as though he'd permit another man to exercise Lily. She could accept punishment, would survive pain easily. Still, something inside her—something delicate and frail—sputtered on the verge of being extinguished. An emotional flame he yearned to fan to life. A glow he wouldn't risk snuffing out.

"Tony, you were willing to give me this opportunity because you're sure I'm the best. If one of your peons believes in this...." Jeremy waved at her bogus supplication. "Then they're no kind of professional. Certainly not someone you want as your right-hand man. A real Master would earn her submission, not force it. A worthy challenge."

"You think you're capable of that? In one evening? Hell, less than an hour?" The maniacal laugh Morselli released inspired a shiver in Lily. Her chains jingled with the tremor.

Sadly, though, Tony could be right. She might never bow for another.

"I'd rather try than take her like this."

"Your vanity is astounding. Flat-out stupid. But, what the hell..." Tony paused, scratching his chin. "I'll turn her loose if you insist."

"Excellent." Jeremy reached for the key to her shackles, which dangled from the pedestal, on a hook beside her knee.

"Not so fast. I'll set her free. But...*one* of you will be my centerpiece. If you can't bend her knees then you'll take her place. Plenty of my guests prefer male slaves and their higher pain thresholds." Morselli smirked. "I'll leave you alone to work things out. Decide amongst yourselves who'll entertain my guests. Either way, it should be fun."

With one hand on the gleaming, gold doorknob, he spun. Clint and Matt tensed where they flanked Lily when Tony reached into the breast pocket of his suit coat. "In the spirit of our future partnership, take this. On the house."

He tossed a capsule onto a long table holding supplies.

"It'll overcome any lingering distaste when you cave, Jeremy. A little insurance to guarantee you'll put on a killer show. Sorry, Lily. At least it'll be a wild ride. No more than an hour, children. Don't be late to your own party." He raised his fingers to his brow in a mock salute then slipped from the room.

Matt followed, pressing his ear to the panel to monitor Morselli's receding footsteps. He stayed, one giant foot wedged in front of the portal to assure it didn't reopen before they were ready. Clint took up a similar post at the other entrance. Both men averted their wide-eyed stares, affording Lily as much privacy as possible in the miniscule area.

She yelled behind her gag, something that could have been, "Get me the fuck out of here."

"Hush." Jeremy kissed the tip of her nose as he unbuttoned his pants and ripped the zipper open.

Instead of quieting, she thrashed in her bindings, rattling her chains and shrieking demands. He'd bet his life she'd have accepted her situation without a peep had it been anyone but him in the room. She reacted so differently to him, he wondered if she realized it.

"Calm down." His quiet insistence didn't dent her objections.

She shook her head from side to side hard enough he worried she might injure her neck.

"Lily, stop. Now." The iron in his command caused the men in blue to stand up straighter where they manned their posts. They'd never witnessed his true nature before. At least not outside of a police operation. Then they'd probably been too caught up in their own adrenaline and keen instincts to notice.

"That's right." He crooned when she stilled, resting his left palm on the side of her neck, brushing it with his thumb. His other hand reached into his boxer briefs.

"What the fuck are you doing, JRad?" Clint took a stride forward, as though to stop him.

Matt joined in the chorus. "Have you lost your mind? We didn't bust in here so you could turn into one of those freaks."

"All of you. Shut up." Jeremy sidled closer to Lily, suppressing a groan when his hard abs brushed her taut belly. He used her form to shield his fingers as they removed a tiny gadget from beneath his sac.

Not exactly suave or debonair. Bond had never had to work in reality. If Jeremy hadn't taken the precaution, he would have lost the jammer to the pat down that had gotten more intimate than the first time he'd made it to third base with Drea Becraft under the bleachers of his high-school football field.

He depressed the button and waited for the confirmation beep before relaxing.

"All clear." He shot his friends a glare before sharing his ire with Lily. "You dumbasses. I would *never* attack her. I thought you knew me better than that. You have to be more careful. I'd bet my right nut, which will bear a permanent dent from this fucking thing by the way, every inch of this place is wired. Don't forget for one instant that they're watching."

"Shit." Matt grumbled beneath his breath, something Jeremy probably didn't care to hear anyway. "Sorry, bro. This place has me on edge. Those women downstairs..."

"I know." Jeremy didn't waste another second. He unhooked Lily's gag without fumbling with the tricky catch. His training returned in a rush as though he hadn't been absent from the lifestyle for a single day, never mind ten years.

"Go slowly." He worked Lily's jaw from side to side, wincing at the crunchiness beneath his thumb and the soft pops he heard before allowing her to open wider and eject the foam plug.

"Mother fucker."

"I missed you too." Jeremy brushed a soft kiss over those glossy crimson lips, which still parted as though they'd forgotten how to close entirely. "What hurts the worst?"

"My back." She didn't even grimace as she relayed the facts. "I've been in here about an hour. Unattended. Other than the cameras. Those bastards have no regard for safety."

Jeremy let her vent as he refastened his slacks and circled the pedestal. He picked apart the complex knot anchoring the bow tied neatly in the black ribbon. When it flowed free, he took his place in front of her once more.

"It's gonna hurt like a bitch. I'm ready." She braced herself then met his concerned gaze. "Do it, quick. We need time to figure out...God *damn!*"

Jeremy held his breath and supported her neck as he tipped her head forward. The numbness and deadened receptors would roar to life as Lily's vertebrae realigned. He pressed his thumbs against the base of her neck then dragged them upward, releasing the tension. His hands made quick work of the knob controlling the protrusion of the bumper, which disfigured her spine.

She sagged in the restraints, her head lolling forward, looking more like a crucifixion victim with every modification he made. Next he mauled the chains pinching the bare flesh of her legs. Bruises dotted the tender curve of her calves, ringing them with pretty purple bands. He admired her flexibility when she drew herself up far enough to tuck her sexy legs under then unfold them so they dangled in front of her.

Pins and needles probably jabbed her joints like a thousand white-hot bee stings. Still, she didn't complain. Jeremy wrapped one arm around her waist, lifting her, bearing her slight weight, relieving the pressure on her shoulders. They had to come a close second to the agony in her back. He turned the key in her manacles, catching her when she flopped forward and would have collapsed onto the ground.

"I can stand on my own," she snarled and tried to shove him. Rubbery arms led to futile efforts.

He cradled her against his chest, trying not to jostle her as he transported her the few feet to the padded table, intending to rub her down. The instant he settled her onto the surface, she popped upright.

"I'm fine." Lily shook her arms and kicked her feet, returning circulation to her limbs.

Jeremy stared. Dom or not, he was still a man.

"Eyes up here, Radisson."

"You jiggle nice." Clint barked out a laugh at Matt.

Jeremy expected Lily to castrate the enormous man. Instead, she sneered. "Guys are so easy to lead. A flash of boobies and they're hypnotized."

"I'm glad you're feeling better." He reached out to touch her shoulder. She slapped his hand with a precise chop that hurt a hell of a lot worse than he'd ever let on. Son of a bitch.

"I've had enough groping for one day."

"You sure?" He leaned in, determined to turn serious. "Are you going to pretend a part of you didn't wonder what it would be like to surrender?"

"Damn straight. Wouldn't you?" She sneered. "I know all about Gunther's shop, *Master Jeremy*."

"Shit...are we the only ones who have no idea what that means?" Clint asked Matt in the background. "Who the fuck is Gunther?"

"I'm starting to think our computer geek has another side." Matt frowned. "You could have told us the truth, JRad. We wouldn't have judged you. Hell, Mason and Tyler are into some freaky shit. I'm sure they would have had your back. Probably joined in."

"That's not me anymore." Jeremy couldn't explain why the lie persisted.

"Are you sure, lover boy?" Lily slithered from the table like an anaconda stalking its prey. She circled him, twisting his insides into knots when she ran her fingers low on his abs, around his hips, over his ass then overflowed her dainty fist with his package. "This nice, stiff cock tells me otherwise."

If she expected him to run from her brazen touch, she had another thing coming. He leaned into the rough caress and considered the spell she wove effortlessly. How many men had thrown themselves, prostrate, at her feet? He could almost understand why.

Then his instincts rebelled, launching a counterstrike. His hand snapped out, locking hers to his crotch. "I'm glad you approve of your effect on me. I've dreamed of you tied, your eyes begging like they were when I entered this room. Tonight I'll show you how damn good I can make it for you."

"Like hell." She snarled and altered her grip, lacing her fondle with a bite of pain from her razor-sharp claws. The enhanced sensation only made him stiffer.

"Wildcat. I like your spirit." He swooped down and bit her lip before she could retreat, tethered to his body by her shorter arms. "You can fight all you want. I promise I won't take your rote objections seriously."

"If I tell you no, it's not a reflex. It's because I don't approve of your bossy mitts on me, asshole." She dropped her hand from his crotch and strode behind his back.

Not giving her the satisfaction of preaching from his rear, he rotated. They spiraled around each other in the tiled space. His shoes clicked in the dead silence while her bare soles padded on the hard surface. Like two wrestlers facing off, they searched for the best angle of attack.

"It's too warm in here to blame the temperature for your hard nipples, Lily." He licked his lips. "Why not let me taste them. Let me treat you to a night off. Maintaining an intense scene is draining. How many things run through your mind simultaneously? The safety of your submissive, ensuring their pleasure while crafting your own, teaching lessons, performing for others...all of it is exhausting."

"So don't stress yourself. I'll coddle you." She grinned. "Lie back and relax. I'll be gentle. Mostly."

Jeremy growled. "I don't think so."

"Matt and Clint will be there to protect you from any of Morselli's guests who try to swerve into realms too extreme." Lily's gait smoothed out as she recovered from her stiffness.

Too bad his got choppier as his dick swelled to epic proportions.

"I'm glad you trust them." Jeremy shook his head, concentrating on their battle. Nothing would keep him from ruling her tonight—sharing the experience he could build for them both, salvaging the wreckage Morselli caused. Together they could make bittersweet lemonade. "You're right. They'll keep things in control and leave me to focus on you alone. If you're a good girl, maybe they'll frisk you a little too. I've seen how much you enjoy fucking multiple men. I can give you that, Lily."

"I take whatever I need." She rolled her eyes. "I don't need you to pimp me out. But...if you'd like to try being the center of some male attention, I'm sure there are plenty of attendees who'd be glad to fuck you. Have you ever been used by another man, Jeremy? Maybe as part of your training?"

He didn't answer her as he squashed the flashes of memory rising to the surface.

"I thought so. Care for a replay?"

"Enough, Lily." Jeremy grabbed for her. She dodged, quick despite her atrophied muscles. "We need some ground rules. Limits."

"Okay, fine. I won't permit any guys to fuck you."

"A safe word for *you*, sweetheart." He smiled at her disdain. "Simple, okay? Yes is no and no is yes. The best way to make the bark worse than the bite for Morselli's guests."

"So when you scream protests I should whip you harder?" She tilted her head. The corners of her decadent mouth tipped up. "You've got it, *baby*."

"Lily—" His exasperated sigh was cut short when the door slammed into Matt's foot. The giant's bulk didn't budge.

"Should I open this, JRad?"

He stepped in front of Lily, shielding her from whoever might enter their temporary haven. When he nodded to Matt, she took advantage of the diversion and came to stand by his side, shoulder to shoulder. Or shoulder to rib cage at least.

How could one tiny, naked woman seem so imposing?

Matt yanked the handle, and a sparsely dressed man tumbled into the space. "Mr. Morselli requires your attendance in the main hall. You're to wear this." He thrust a fist full of black leather straps, studded with metal brads at each of them.

"We have at least forty-five minutes before the event." Jeremy refused to accept the delivery.

"Not anymore." The messenger shook his head. "Mr. Morselli ordered me to evacuate this space. He thinks there may be a *maintenance* issue making it unsafe. If we're not there in ten minutes, he's coming up."

Lily planted her fists on her hips.

"Please, don't make him seek you out." The man dipped his head and pleaded with Lily. "It will be me who pays, not you ma'am."

91

"Damn it." Lily hissed worse curses under her breath. Rationality rose to the surface in an instant. She packed away their differences and turned to him. "We can settle this downstairs."

She spun, seeking her boots and corset, ignoring the standard costume their attendant had offered.

Jeremy nearly swallowed his tongue when she bent over to snatch the scrap of her black lace thong off the bench then wiggled into it. She had her boots on and nearly laced before he'd recovered. The wheeze of Clint's appreciative breaths echoed in the space.

When she came to the corset, her arms reached behind her but couldn't quite secure the catch. He ambled closer and whispered into the nape of her neck, "Don't strain your shoulders any more than they already are, Lily. Let me."

He grasped her wrists in one hand, pinning them in the small of her back for a heartbeat. Long enough to savor the catch of her breath. Then he released them in favor of drawing the panels of her fine-boned garment closed. He secured the delicate hooks, so many of them lending unimaginable strength.

The smooth glide of her skin brushed his knuckles, tempting his fingertips to roam over her shoulders and down her arms. When he closed the final clasp, he couldn't resist. His hand caressed her spine above the fabric then circled her neck. He cupped Lily's delicate throat in his palm, keeping her from escaping when he brushed her hair aside and placed a gentle kiss between her bared shoulder blades.

"I'll be with you." Their last private exchange slipped from his lips, a hairsbreadth from her ear. "No matter what. You'll be protected. Trust us. Trust me. I'll take you where you need to go and deliver you safely through the night."

He grinned when she melted. Until the moment her elbow drove into his gut.

"Quit fucking around and change." She snatched the leather harness and pants from the slave watching with wide eyes. "If you make this man suffer for your indulgences I'll take it out on your ass tonight."

She strode into the hallway, leaving him to don the apparel. Despite the circumstances, he had to admit he felt better wearing the supple material, which heated to match the scorching surface of his flesh. Thank God or his raging erection would never have fit inside.

Finally, he snatched the packet off the table and tucked it inside the pocket intended to be more for design than function. Luckily the tiny paper wrapper didn't make much of an impression.

Matt had tailed Lily, never abandoning her. Clint clapped a hand on his shoulder, the gesture making a loud slap as bare skin met bare skin. "You have your work cut out, JRad."

"She's worth it."

"All the best ones are. Lucky bastard."

CHAPTER SEVEN

The rumble of mingled discussions increased as they approached the black curtain. Crystalline clinks interspersed with soft laughter and the occasional crack of a paddle on bare ass, composing a familiar soundtrack. Lily had attended many exclusive kink parties.

Never one with stakes as high as this.

The man beside her threw off her A game. Her nerves jangled where usually they lay dormant. Her pussy heated at the thought of what the night had in store. Uncertain victory affected her system, tilting it out of whack. The outcome of her usual liaisons were never in doubt.

Tonight, anything could happen.

She almost regretted the possibility of striping Jeremy's skin with the kiss of her whip. The golden bronze of his strong back seemed perfect as it was made. No enhancement necessary beyond the ink and leather he'd adorned it with.

Lily would be lying to herself if she denied her urge to bond with him by burying his cock inside her. Her pussy clenched at the thought. She visualized riding him, working them into a frenzy to release the delicious tension coiling them both tighter than springs. The anticipation glowing around them tasted sweeter than any she'd experienced before.

Somehow, her mental motion picture morphed. Jeremy pressed her face to the floor as he fucked her from behind. He possessed her, protected her and satisfied her—freed her from inhibitions so she could experience without calculating the effects of every action. Constant risk evaluation and monitoring of the image she projected could detract from her experience.

What would it be like to simply react and trust her partner to provide for her needs?

She must have sighed aloud.

The arrogant jerk turned to her with a grin. "Feeling all right?"

"I wouldn't gloat if I were you." She stared at the bulge in his pants, refusing to allow her tongue to peek out and lick her lips. "It'll only make your surrender more difficult."

A frown dimmed his smirk. "You don't have to pretend with me, Lily. Don't always have to be so tough. I've got your back. No matter what."

Shivers tingled up her spine like the effervescent bubbles in the champagne being consumed nearby. She blinked to clear the moisture threatening to prickle. "Promises are meant to be broken. It's better if you don't offer what you can't guarantee."

She studied the setup of the space, anything to avoid the temptation of his gaze.

His hand enveloped hers.

Lily should have wrenched her fingers away. She couldn't.

Though he didn't comment, he didn't persist in his argument either. The simple connection would be enough for now. She took a deep breath, threaded her fingers through his and squeezed.

She might have imagined the tiny tremor that ran through him, but she didn't think so. Hopefully she could return the favor and grant him some reassurance. After all, he hadn't played hardball in a *very* long time.

Lily still couldn't believe it. Master Jeremy had emerged from retirement. The man was something of a legend. A myth, more like it. Someone she'd never imagined being real. An exaggerated urban fantasy. His story was a fable you told dominants in training to stress the importance of comprehending the depths of your submissive's needs. She'd been young when the accident had happened. Too far away to learn the details, like his full name or the girl's.

Yet she remembered. The horror had been used as a part of her own instruction. True dominants accepted their responsibility and the pain caused by failing one of their charges. Sometimes you had to make tough choices for the good of a slave, escort them to a place more extreme than you would have chosen for them. Because in the end, you were guiding them along the path of their desires, not yours.

Turning squeamish could result in a slave seeking relief elsewhere—somewhere outside the safe harbor of their Master's domain—with someone who wouldn't treasure their supplication as their caretaker would. When deep-rooted need drove a true submissive, they could so easily fall in to hands that would abuse their pure faith, placing them in grave danger. She'd seen ghosts of that knowledge in Jeremy's stare when it had landed on her tattoo in honor of Malcolm.

Could they be any more alike? And yet, so very different.

How could two equal and opposite forces mingle without destroying one another?

They were about to find out. Before they could seek out Morselli or finalize their game plan, someone shoved them both toward the curtain. Matt and Clint stepped forward. Furious gestures, pointing and puffed up chests followed.

"It's okay, guys." Jeremy called off his friends. "Keep your eyes open and stay on the sidelines unless we need you."

They grumbled but followed his curt instructions, crossing thick arms over their chests as they took posts on the outskirts of the space. Lily couldn't quite distinguish the shadows lurking in the recesses. She thought they might be on a stage. Racks of undefined equipment occupied the far reaches of her vision in the dim area. As her eyes adjusted to the darkness, she picked out details.

An impressive selection of whips, paddles, floggers, canes and other spanking implements lined one wall. The other held more unusual fare. Shock sticks, a cattle prod, low voltage TASERs and electrostimulation units completed the spark section. Candles, needles and clamps gleamed ominously below them. Lily had never enjoyed inflicting excessive pain though she'd accepted some clients who required it. Her hands were steady as she satisfied their urges. They trusted her to take them to their limits and a tiny bit beyond.

She'd become an excellent judge of human reactions. Hell, she'd hurt plenty of times. Enough to know that sometimes the ache of her flesh could distract from gaping wounds in her heart and soul.

A welcome balm.

Intense stimulation forced adrenaline to rush through a slave's system, replacing agony with elation, driving them to a zone where they were reduced to the fundamentals of survival—living every instant to the fullest as they became aware of each heartbeat, breath or blink.

"Is that what you want?" Jeremy studied her as she recalled history. He traced her stare to the wicked implements.

"No." She answered honestly. Though there might have been a period in her life where she had needed it, the point had long since passed.

"I'm glad."

She bit her lip when his thumb brushed the back of her hand.

"I could give it to you." He lifted their hands to his lips and kissed her knuckles. "But I'd rather please you. I think bondage would better suit. Drive you insane with your willingness to submit to me. Steal your ability to do anything except soak up every morsel of attention I'd pay your gorgeous body. Show you to accept the cravings, revel in the luxury of trust and honest affection."

"Not going to happen."

"It will. Tonight."

Lily refused to be dragged into a juvenile display of will-not-will-so. Totally unbecoming of her station. Though damn him, now she imagined what it would be like to grant someone privileges and never have them abuse their rights.

She barely contained a snort. It was a fairy-tale less believable than the prophecy of the man beside her. They shared the silence, breathing in and out in unison. Until a wedge of light appeared in the center of the velvety fabric before them. It expanded as the two panels of the curtain were raised.

Lily shook her hand, attempting to escape Jeremy's grasp. He clung as long as possible until she slipped her fingers from between his knuckles before the congregation could catch a glimpse of their connection.

She ignored his glare, studying the gathering instead. Counting the individuals she could distinguish in the glow spilling from the chandeliers overhead, she estimated over fifty people mingled in the ballroom. Sparkles danced over the guests wolfing lavish *hors d'oeuvres* and the slaves stationed throughout the room on pedestals like the one she'd been imprisoned on, if somewhat less elaborate.

Men and women clustered around the pieces, admiring them. Some touched, poked and prodded as if they were testing a melon in the grocery store. Lily tensed when Jeremy growled beside her.

She followed his line of sight to one woman, imprisoned on her back inside a wooden restraint, her legs captured in some kind of stockade that left her completely exposed, vulnerable. The woman stared at the ceiling, her eyes glazed, as a man dipped his fingers in her pussy, taunting her for not responding. When he slapped her mound and shook his head, seeming bored before abandoning her, Jeremy took a giant step in that direction.

Lily snagged the harness decorating his back. His forward momentum nearly ripped her arm off before he realized what caused the pressure on his lean yet powerful chest. *Christ.* She'd seen a shit-ton of naked men in her life. None of them had seemed as fine to her as this one.

The jolt of pain radiating through her shoulder surprised her. She refused to make a sound. Jeremy stopped on a dime. He pivoted slowly, giving her time to release him so he didn't tug her limb further out of joint.

"Shit." He cursed when he examined her pupils, which were probably dilated. She would have used the same gauge on a slave who enjoyed pain to decide when their body had taken enough despite their willingness to proceed. Some things couldn't be controlled. Certain reactions didn't lie.

"You can't save her."

When lines marred the corners of his mouth, she could no longer stand still. Lily banded her arms around his waist and laid her cheek on his sternum. She ignored the prick of the metal studs decorating his gear. "I'm sorry, Jeremy. It'll be hard, but—"

She would have whispered reassurance if his hand hadn't trapped her confession about her league and the benefactors who'd arranged to attend. The funds she'd provided should cover the hostages she'd scanned.

He nuzzled the hair at her temples then murmured. "I know. Thank God. No more risks. Don't mention it here."

"Well, isn't this sweet? It seems my new friends are getting along just fine." The crowd clapped as Morselli climbed a set of stairs to join Jeremy and Lily on the elevated stage. He snaked between them, slinging a flabby arm—concealed by a designer suit—around each of their shoulders. "Dear guests, welcome to tonight's event. Thank you for all the lovely compliments on our offerings. I realize you're eager to commence the examinations and bid on our fine prizes. Perhaps find some *magic* in the meantime. However, I have a special treat for you all."

The low-level drone of the attendees diminished as they halted their sidebar conversations.

"Many of you will recognize the illustrious Mistress Lily. As promised, tonight she joins our fine establishment."

A quick nod bobbed her head when she acknowledged the whistles and cheers from both the legitimate submissives and their owners, ignoring the gleam of others in the crowd. Several men near the stage exhibited the odd, excessive blinking she'd come to associate with users of Sex Offender. No doubt they played Morselli's games to secure more of the drug. Black magic.

"However," he continued, "this man is not one of her slaves."

Jeremy outright laughed. Several of her plants in the audience joined him. Damn them. Just because the man emitted pride and control from every pore didn't mean she couldn't tame him tonight.

She tried to visualize him kneeling for her, begging. The fantasy refused to coalesce.

"No, friends, this is truly a rare occasion." Morselli continued to drag out the anticipation. "It's my pleasure to present to you a long-lost pillar of our community. Please welcome, Master Jeremy Radisson."

A smattering of gasps fractured the dead silence of the room. Then a cheer raced through the hall. Men turned to their neighbors, filling in the few who hadn't heard the rumors.

"Yes, yes." Morselli held his hands, palms down and quieted the throng. "So you're in for an amazing show. To prove their dedication to our causes, they've agreed...well, what have you decided?"

Tony looked from Jeremy to her and back. "Who will broaden their horizons tonight? Which of you will bow to the other?"

The audible turbulence of speculation bubbled through the crowd.

"Neither." Jeremy turned inward. "If you respect us, you'll withdraw your request. We'd be glad to team up and demonstrate on someone who will appreciate our skills."

No less than a dozen hands were immediately thrust high into the air.

"I'm afraid not." Tony turned a bit purple. "One of you will break the other. I thought you understood when we parted earlier."

Lily faced Jeremy. Neither backed down. The force of his compelling stare nearly melted her knees yet she resisted the urge to bend.

"Since our deliberation ended much sooner than anticipated, we had not yet reached an agreement," Jeremy stalled again.

"Then, by all means, continue to convince each other. Don't let us bother you." Morselli strode toward the edge of the stage. "Maybe this will help."

He reached out and snagged a wicked, braided cat-o'-nine. He tossed the implement in their direction. Lily had the advantage as Jeremy's stare remained glued to her face. She gave no outward indication of the object's impending arrival, maintaining her mask.

At the last second, she launched herself toward the whip, snagging the handle out of midair. The crowd cheered for her though their approval was short-lived.

Jeremy may have missed the implement, but he grabbed her. His hands spanned her waist, preventing her from escaping his grasp.

"Put me down," she commanded.

With his back to the rest of the room he whispered, "Yes."

She blinked. When he didn't move, she realized he'd initiated their code.

Yes is no and no is yes.

"Don't make me do this." She offered one last chance. "Surrender now and I'll go easy on you."

He only grinned.

Lily pulled back her arm and swung the whip. Knots tied in the ends of the leather stung his back, their impact enhanced as the tips gained speed when they folded over the curve of his shoulder.

He shook his head like a wet dog and his grin spread wider. "You swing like a girl."

Oh, fuck him.

All consideration for his lack of recent conditioning flew out the window. If she came out strong, they could finish quickly—move on. She landed a second blow, this one several times harder. When he still didn't budge, she continued to build the intensity, working in an uneven rhythm designed to throw him off balance.

Jeremy held her still, never dropping her, never flinching. His pain endurance impressed her jaded sensibilities. He waited until she reached a little too far before attempting a grab for the implement.

Lily twisted out of his reach.

The cheers of the assembly broke through her concentration when Jeremy put his back to her, heading for the stash of tools on the wall. She couldn't allow him to reach them. She took advantage of the wide-open target. She flailed his shoulders, ass and thighs, careful to avoid his spine and kidneys.

A well-placed blow would drop him, without doubt.

She would never stoop so low and risk injuring him permanently.

Lily chased him in slow motion, since he didn't actually run. She lashed him over and over. He strode across the stage as though he hadn't noticed the crimson lines latticing his exposed hide. Matt edged toward her as they neared his side of the stage.

"Stay out of it." Jeremy called him off. "This is between Lily and me."

Damn him, his voice didn't hold a hint of strain. Clear command halted his friend.

She landed several more strikes, the warmed leather snapping against his skin. This time she layered the knots over the brightest of his rising welts. He flinched but didn't utter a peep.

"Enough." He growled as he looked over his shoulder. Instead of the anger, pain or disgust she feared, desire loosed his features. Delicious heat colored his cheeks between the scruff of his beard.

God damn, did he have to be so fucking sexy?

"If you stop now, I'll pretend this didn't happen. I'll go gentle on you. I'll make sure you enjoy your subjugation."

She stuck out her tongue at him then placed a harder strike on his ass. The leather absorbed some of the impact. It seemed a shame to ruin a garment that fit to perfection, cupping his tight butt as though it'd molded to the solid muscle. A frayed rip slashed diagonally across his left cheek.

"Have it your way." He selected a long bullwhip from the pegboard. He tested the grip in his right hand as she continued to pepper him with a barrage of short, light, unrelenting blows. When she paused, expecting him to turn, cautious over striking him in an unsafe location, he surprised her by plucking a soft, doeskin flogger from the rack.

The thick mass of wide strips would have almost no sting yet tons of thud. She lost her balance as she considered the contrast he could paint with both implements.

"Good news." He smiled. "I'm a righty by nature, but I practiced until I could use my left hand even more accurately. It took years to be comfortable double fisting."

Her eyebrows rose.

Jeremy took advantage of her temporary distraction. He led with the bullwhip, not granting her any quarter. The tip sliced across the upper swell of her right breast, where it plumped above the line of her corset.

Fire spread through her chest, igniting her instincts. She traded impacts with him, feeling less like a boxer counteracting a punch than a lover alternating caresses. The same desire infusing her with raging arousal radiated from his hungry stare.

He'd sacrificed for so long. She accepted the force of the flogger over the more severe marks he'd left, dulling the sting, replacing it with soothing pressure. The longer she held out the more she could allow him to indulge his lost pleasure before making him hers for the night.

She owed him that at least.

Lily lifted her chin, accepting the kiss of his whip on her inner thigh.

The crowd roared when Jeremy stepped forward, forcing her to retreat to stay out of his long-armed reach. He twirled the whip in his palm.

"Show-off." She snatched the opening to land a blow to his bicep, twisting her wrist at the last instant to splay the knotted ends of her implement across a wider swatch of his body.

"Are you impressed yet?" He snarled as he shook off the zing caused by the knot that had landed on the sensitive underside of his arm. "When you beg me to take you, you'll know you're requesting the best."

She snorted, ladylike or not, then treated his other arm to similar strikes. Maybe a little harder since his hand holding the bullwhip started to drive beyond her comfort zone. Fuck, that thing hurt. "Arrogant bastard. More likely I'll know how valuable my new slave is."

Patches of heat seared her legs from her calves to her hips. At least her skirt and corset protected her most sensitive regions. The thought of the whip landing directly on her crotch inspired a curl of dread in her gut. She'd be lying if she denied the tingle of wonder that accompanied her trepidation.

Lily continued to inch backward, driven by his assault. She cursed herself when her eyes closed for a moment after the soft strips of the flogger danced over her chest.

"You liked that?" It wasn't really a question.

"Hell no."

He grinned at her use of their yes-is-no edict.

Why deny it? She didn't have to lie. If she did, he wouldn't take her seriously when she ended this ridiculous game.

"Good girl," he murmured then repeated the action a dozen times at least.

Whistles from the audience shook her from the trance he'd initiated. When had her shoulders come to rest on the opposite wall?

Jeremy closed in for the kill. He crowded her, preventing her use of the whip as she could no longer swing her arm to gain enough momentum.

"Too bad, Lily." He groaned as he buried his face in the crook of her neck, sucking until the tightness on her throat guaranteed he'd marked her. "Maybe next time you'll put up a better fight."

He dusted a kiss over her lips. She indulged in the sweet taste of him for a second or two before dropping the whip and raking her nails down his back. When they passed over the ridges she'd left on him, he jerked.

Clint called out a warning too late.

She'd snatched a device off the board behind her. Her fingers had frantically inspected the handle while she lulled him with tenderness. When he recoiled, she flipped the switch, hoping she held what she thought and not one of the more extreme implements she'd spied earlier.

Lily whipped her arm in between their bodies. She touched the tip of the neon green stick she held to Jeremy's abdomen and pressed the trigger. He flinched then stumbled backward, allowing her to escape his grasp.

A chorus of *ohhs* rose from beyond the stage.

"Sorry." She nibbled her lip, ingesting the last of his lingering flavor. "That had to hurt. Especially without warning."

"*No.*" He grunted. "Fuck."

She couldn't help it. She laughed.

When had she ever had this much fun?

"I see it didn't bother you that much." She cocked her head as she measured the hard length of his erection, which reached toward his hipbone despite the constriction of his pants.

"I've never needed to fuck someone as badly as I do right now." He wiped his forearm across the beads of sweat beginning to dot his forehead.

"I'm sure there are plenty of women here tonight who'd beg for the chance to serve you." Her stomach lurched at the thought even as delighted shrieks filled the air.

"Only you." He encroached on her space again. "Tonight, only you will do."

The coercion of his tone, his bearing, his innate dominance had her frozen as he approached. At the last second, she dug her willpower from the clutches of her libido. She shocked him again, this time on his arm.

Lily had tested this exact brand of slave prod on herself. She owned two or three of the popular devices. The jolt it caused would have brought her to her knees. Jeremy's tall, solid-though-not-bulky frame shouldn't have withstood the blast of electricity. Still, he kept coming.

Coming for her.

"Do it again and I'll punish you, Lily." He strengthened rather than wilting beneath the pain. It seemed as though he harnessed the energy and used it to his advantage. "I'll put you over my knee in front of all our friends. I'll make you come as you squirm in my hold until you can't deny to anyone here, including yourself, that you need what only I can give you."

She stumbled beneath the ferocity of his conviction. Still she held the neon green shock stick before her like a vampire hunter with a cross. "Stay back."

"*Yes.*" He spoke softly, for her ears only despite his use of their reverse denial. "Nothing could take me away from you now. Surrender. Let me have you."

Was he pleading with her?

Her sense of up and down, right and wrong, good and bad all jumbled. Was it submission if the person you knelt to needed you so badly? Didn't it give her control of him to grant his wishes? Who was more powerful when they both craved the same thing?

They would be equals, wouldn't they?

"*Yes.*" She couldn't do it.

She pressed the button once more, electrifying his hip.

"That's it." He snapped his wrist, slinging the tail of the bullwhip he still clutched along the floor. The end of the lash spiraled around her ankle, stinging as it ensnared her.

Jeremy yanked her feet from beneath her. Wind rushed from her chest as her back slammed the ground. Before she bounced, he was there, cradling her head to keep it from smacking the floor. He knelt over her supine form.

The gathering cheered his name over and over. Rowdy shouts and clapping rolled past them.

Until her hand lifted—somehow she'd maintained her grip on the stick—and shocked him directly on the balls.

He rolled on the floor in agony, his tools abandoned.

Lily flung the device far enough away that his flailing hands wouldn't land on it then scrambled to her knees. She settled his head on her lap and cradled him close. The string of soothing nonsense pouring from her lips as she rocked him surprised them both. He quieted as she stroked numb fingers through his hair, horrified at the destruction she'd wrought.

"Mistress Lily." He cleared his throat before trying again, louder this time. "You've earned a privilege I've never before granted another."

She looked up into the audience and caught sight of Ben and Ryan watching the spectacle side by side. Suddenly, she knew exactly how they'd felt earlier.

This was the Twilight Zone.

Not at all how things should be. A tiny piece of her convictions wavered. She glanced from the expectant crowd to the gentle eyes peering up at her. She could survive one night under his domination. But maybe he wasn't strong enough to tolerate the same from her. Not one single submissive molecule belonged in his constitution. She stared into his eyes and whispered, "*Yes.*"

"What?" He blinked. When she didn't answer he continued, "Mistress, will you please—"

Lily clamped her fingers over his mouth to prevent him from sealing their fate. She needed a second. Maybe a couple of them. She couldn't think.

Everyone held their breath as they witnessed the impending power exchange.

Was she strong enough? Could she do it?

Her gaze roamed over the magnificent man in her arms. Suddenly, she couldn't imagine topping him. Didn't want to. This wasn't the person who thrilled her. Impressed her. Turned her on. Her stare landed on the tiny bump in his pocket. At first, she thought she might have singed him when she shocked his hip.

Her free hand wandered to the anomaly, afraid of what she might find.

When her fingers latched on to the capsule he'd tucked there, her eyes widened.

Jeremy tried to sit up straighter. She pinned him with one knee on his shoulder then withdrew the packet containing a dose of Sex Offender.

"Lily!" He thrashed, but his legs didn't work quite right. "Yes! Yes! Yes!"

"That's right. Give him something to ease his pain. He'll love every minute of your attention. He'll grovel and thank you a million times over." Morselli made up her mind. She could never do that to the Master who'd captured her imagination.

The paper ripped easily when she gripped it with one hand and trapped the top between her teeth. She released Jeremy long enough to separate the halves of the capsule and inhale deeply, holding the mist it contained in her lungs long enough she thought she might pass out.

Nothing happened.

Could the new formula be less potent than the blast she'd breathed in the day of Malcolm's funeral?

Jeremy's brow furrowed. He coordinated his limbs and rose beside her. Matt and Clint rushed to their sides. All three men shouted questions, asking if she was okay. It was Jeremy who caught her when a blinding wave of mingled passion and burning agony blazed through her every nerve ending.

"Master Jeremy." She mewled as she rubbed herself against his hard body, trying to ease the ache in her nipples or the throbbing of her clit. "You *have* to take me. Please. Hurry. Tonight, I'm yours. Oh God. Please, help me."

The crowd went wild.

CHAPTER EIGHT

Jeremy barked orders as he toted Lily to a station that had caught his attention earlier. "Matt, lower the sling. Clint, find restraints. Thick but soft. Nothing that will cut her. She won't be able to keep still."

Hell, even now she squirmed in his hold, pressing the lush softness of her breasts to his chest, wriggling like a fish out of water in a desperate attempt to slake the white-hot need raging through her veins. He spun when fast-approaching footsteps vibrated the surface of the stage.

Two men ran toward him.

Jeremy angled Lily away from the servants, dressed in the leather and silver chains of Morselli's house submissives.

"Master, we'd like to help." The first to arrive held his empty hands up, slowing as he neared.

"I'm Ryan. This is Ben. We...served Mistress Lily this afternoon."

Jeremy flushed as his anger found a place to vent. "You! The two of you are responsible for leaving her trussed, alone?"

"We didn't have a choice." Ryan spoke softly. "Please, let us make it up to her. To you."

"Fine." He didn't have time to waste on them. Lily began to shudder in his arms.

"Hang on, wildcat."

"You, help Matt with the sling. He has no clue what he's doing." The cables verged on tangling beyond repair.

This was not the time for on-the-job training. Not when safety counted on the rig's proper setup.

"Ben, is it?" He drew the other man's horrified stare from the tears pouring down Lily's cheeks. She would hate for anyone to witness her so overwhelmed.

The slave nodded.

"Focus. Grab condoms. A bunch of them."

"Yes, sir."

Lily's heart pounded, the reverberations palpable where their chests fused. A standard dosage of any drug would affect her more than the average person. Considering Jeremy had watched her father commit suicide by injecting a massive amount of the substance, her immediate and overwhelming response to the chemical terrified him.

He ignored the chaos around them and centered all his attention on her.

"Lily, listen to me." He tried speaking gently, attempting to calm her as she had done to him minutes ago. The throb in his balls had nothing on the terror gripping his soul. She didn't respond. Instead she gurgled and clawed at her clothes, succeeding in ripping the hem of her skirt with the enhanced strength ruling her system.

If he let her, she'd tear all her nails off in her haste to undress.

He knelt less than two feet to the side of the contraption Matt and Ryan worked to lower to the stage. "Stop."

The two men froze at the insistence in his tone.

"Not you." He never glanced away from Lily, observing their progress in his peripheral vision. "*Lily.* Stop."

She blinked.

"That's right." He smiled when she looked at him as though surfacing from a long, deep sleep. Even now her blue eyes amazed him. Gorgeous. "Concentrate on me. Hear my voice."

"H-help me."

"Shh. I will." He hoped he could keep his promise. "Stay strong. You can do this. We'll work through it together. Okay?"

"*No.*"

He recoiled before he realized she'd gained lucidity. Her inverse response relieved him. After the initial shock, she fought to the surface. Tough, confident...

"Fuck me."

Still on fire.

"Soon. I promise." Jeremy deposited her onto the floor as though she were fragile despite his certainty otherwise. Her hands instinctively drifted toward her clothes again.

He covered her with his frame, pinning her wrists above her head.

Her legs locked around his waist, or would have if not for the tight ring of her pencil skirt. Damn, her ass looked fine in it, but now he wished she'd worn something else. Anything that would have allowed him to feel the heat of her pussy on the front of his pants.

"You're not hard anymore." She whimpered as she humped the trunk of his body.

"Darling, you zapped my nuts with a fucking TASER. Give me a minute here."

"Or is it because I surrendered?" Lily averted her gaze.

He tapped her cheek with three fingers. "Didn't I tell you to look at me? I'm not going to say it again."

The summer sky of her eyes greeted him once more. "Yes, sir."

He dropped closer, whispering against her lips, "Having you beneath me is a dream come true. Believe me, it's not going to take long for my cock to recover. And when it does, I plan to fuck the shit out of you. Maybe more than once."

"*No.*" She struggled to grind harder against him.

He bit the lobe of her ear, hiding his lips from the onlookers when he asked, "Do you want other guys to fuck you? To ease your suffering? It might kill me, but I'll let them touch you. I'll protect you. Whatever you need."

"*No!*" She thrashed in his hold.

"It will take some of the pressure off the other slaves bound in the audience too. You can handle it, Lily. You love to fuck. I promise to stand by your side. I have you. You're safe."

"*Nooooooo!*"

"Very nice, Jeremy." Morselli blessed their performance from his spot near the edge of the stage. "No more secrets. What are you threatening her with? I'm sure the ache in your junk won't improve her fate."

"I've told her my plans to share her. With you all."

Several audience members encroached on the stairs.

"When I tell you." He glanced to his left. A soft leather sling in the shape of an inverted Y landed beside them.

"Ready, Lily?"

"*No!*" She drummed her heels.

"Too bad." Jeremy grinned into her raven tresses as he lifted her. He wove her petite form between the nylon webbing that attached the leather rest to pulleys. "Make sure she's centered. Put her ass right on the edge."

He counted on Matt and Ryan to assist him. They aligned Lily despite the unconscious movement of her muscles, which ached for relief.

"Soon." He crooned to her as he double-checked the fit. Once satisfied, he nodded, accepting a roll of foam tape from Clint. "Perfect."

He'd used the material before. It was some sort of sport injury support when not ensuring the immobility of his slaves.

116

"Lift the top a few inches." Ryan hoisted the cord, raising the tail of the Y. It didn't take much material to wind around the sling and Lily's dainty wrists, pinning them together above her head. He tore the material from the roll with his teeth. "A little more."

When the incline increased, he fit his hands beneath the leather cradling Lily. Next, he wrapped a wider loop halfway between her shoulders and elbows. He kept it loose enough that her aching shoulders weren't pressed too far beyond comfortable. All the while, she held her head upright, her stare locked on him.

"Go ahead and watch." He caressed her, running a fingertip from her nose through the furrow of her upper lip, across her parted mouth to her chin. "When your neck gets tired, you'll have a nice pillow, okay?"

"*No.*" She kicked his shin. "Faster. Or let me loose so I can take care of myself."

Jeremy was sure she hadn't intended the command to emerge as a whine. He recalled the burning pressure that had haunted him for days after inhaling far less Sex Offender than she had. He hustled. No time to waste on fancy clasps and extra buttons.

"Clint. Scissors."

His fellow officer handed him a pair. Clearly he'd never used the foam tape before if he hadn't realized how easy it was to tear.

Jeremy didn't complain. "Keep her still."

Matt, Clint, Ryan and Ben all chipped in, arresting Lily despite her increased struggles. Jeremy snipped her skirt in half then yanked it from her body. He tossed the scraps over his shoulder before starting on her corset. He hacked through the satin, shaking his head. A shame to destroy something so elegant. Please, please let it be just her trappings and not the woman herself who would bear irrevocable damage after tonight.

His astonishment at her actions began to wear off along with the tingling between his legs. *Holy shit.* Was this really happening?

As soon as her bare flesh was exposed to the air, Lily tested the four men trapping her diminutive form. The breeze in the open room buffeted her sultry flesh, triggering a response in her drug-enhanced sensory receptors.

"Hang on."

"*Yes!*" She screamed as he worked, unwilling to sacrifice her safety for instant gratification.

"Clint." Jeremy nodded to his friend, hoping like hell the man didn't choose then to balk. "Take your cock out. Give her something to suck on. Fill her mouth and keep her quiet."

He feared she might blow their cover if she didn't find relief soon.

"Uh...JRad," Clint whispered, his stare whipping up to Matt's. "Are you sure?"

"I think you'd better do what he says." The man's partner spoke softly, though not low enough to prevent Jeremy from hearing their exchange.

"Go ahead." Jeremy nodded. "I'm pretty sure she won't bite your dick off."

Clint unzipped his cargo pants. He'd shoved his tighty-whiteys down far enough to withdraw a fairly long hard-on when Lily lunged for him. She licked the drop of pre-come from his tip before swallowing him to the root in one gulp.

"God damn." Matt moaned.

Jeremy grinned when Clint's head tipped back and his hands fisted at his sides. He'd bet that felt fucking great. His cock stirred in his pants, pumping up as the blood flow returned. "Almost there, Lily."

He handed the scissors to Ben then tugged the remainder of her tattered clothing from beneath her slender ribcage. Stopping himself from teasing the diamond tips of her breasts with tiny pinches before swiping his palms over her waist and hips—dragging her thong down and off—would have proved impossible.

Aromatic arousal greeted him as her pussy was exposed. Could the potent drug be passed through her body? The smell of her intoxicated him, driving him deeper into the insanity caused by his overwhelming lust for her.

Jeremy sat on his heels, admiring her nude form for a handful of seconds. It could never be long enough. Clint had begun a steady stream of curses and groans that seemed to match up with the flex of Lily's throat.

"Best blow job of my life." Clint opened his eyes, sharing the moment with his partner. "Oh my God, she's amazing."

"Lift her higher." Jeremy ordered Matt and Ryan. They tugged the cords attached to the section supporting Lily's torso. Her shoulders rose up, slamming her mouth farther down Clint's shaft. Lucky bastard.

Jeremy wrapped Lily's chest, just above her breasts, securing her to the sling. He wouldn't chance her slipping off, getting hurt while she abandoned herself to ecstasy. The band squished her chest. He checked that there was no pressure on her windpipe from the material. He revisited the site of the contact no less than three times before certainty allowed him to move on.

Next he applied another band around her ribs, just below her magnificent tits. The mounds squished between the two fastenings, standing taller, urging him to suckle them. So he did.

Lily cooed around Clint's cock, attempting to shimmy despite her bindings, with limited success. Jeremy rewarded her eagerness, slapping his tongue on the tight peaks of her nipple, drawing the other away from her body between his thumb and forefinger. Her hips bucked against him.

119

"Higher." They heaved again, and her hips left the ground. She swung in gentle arcs, knocking into Clint's thighs. Jeremy mummified her hips, securing them before moving on to her thighs. On his way, he paused at her pussy. The puffy, pink lips called to him. They lured his fingers into exploring their moist folds.

"Ahh!" she shouted when he traced the valley of her slit, pressing into the slippery tissue as he neared the entrance to her pussy. His cock stiffened, fully recovered from her earlier abuse.

Jeremy inserted his index finger in her, fusing their bodies for the first time, burying the digit to his second knuckle. Despite the copious amounts of lubrication slicking her channel, her tiny body made for a tight fit. "I can't wait to introduce my cock to you. I'll stretch you. Ride you hard. Make you scream. Will you come for me? Will you love every second?"

She pulled off Clint's cock with a slurp. "*No!*"

He chuckled when his fellow officer fed his cock to the spitfire as though he couldn't stand to be outside her mouth for more than an instant.

"Is she doing a good job?" Jeremy arched an eyebrow at his friend.

"Fuck, yes." Clint panted. "I might need to tag Matt here soon if you don't want me to blow in her mouth."

"Swap." Jeremy needed them hard. Lily would require more than he could give her to be satisfied.

Matt hesitated when Clint's cock drew across Lily's cheek, painting it with their mingled fluids.

"Go ahead." Clint reassured his partner. "She wants it. Trust me. A woman doesn't suck like that if she's forced."

"It's not her talking. It's the drugs." Matt gripped the nylon cord, pushing her away from nuzzling his crotch.

"Either way, she's desperate." Clint continued to persuade Matt as Jeremy swirled his fingers through the soft flesh between Lily's legs. He traced the ridge of her lips to her clit. When he drew a spiral around the hard knot of nerves, she broke free of the restraining hands on her arms and legs. She swung softly, bumping into the five men surrounding her.

Every time she made contact with someone, something, she cried out. Ultrasensitive, her skin drove her need, painful if not dampened by continuous action.

"Do it, Matt." Jeremy sighed as he removed his hand and finished binding her. "She needs you to."

Ben reached out to unfasten Matt's fly.

"Whoa! I got this." Matt ripped the button loose, yanked the front of his pants apart and sighed when a cock proportional to his refrigerator build flopped free.

"Damn." Ryan's eyes widened. "I'm not sure she's going to be able to take more than the tip."

Lily seemed up to the challenge. She strained her neck, opened her mouth wide and drew him in. Jaw spread, she stretched her lips around his girth. *Son of a bitch.*

Still, it stuck Jeremy that she remained the aggressor despite her bonds and the absolute helplessness of her position. Lily acted of her own free will. She called the shots and took the lead. Not for long.

He removed her boots then tucked her ankles into the cuffs, which acted as stirrups, suspended from independent wires. Thighs spread wide, she displayed her pussy for him. It clenched, kissing the air as though it already hugged his cock.

"Everyone stand back."

Matt groaned when he removed his cock from her lips with a pop.

Lily screamed. "*Yes!*"

Jeremy motioned to Matt and Ryan. Each of them worked the pulley system on their side of Lily. They hoisted her with strong jerks that set her breasts bouncing. A series of cables, one at her fists and each ankle, two near her shoulders, her hips and a pair on either side of her knees balanced the light load. When she came level with his pelvis, Jeremy instructed them to tie off the ropes.

He supervised their knot work. Ben assisted Matt when he needed it.

Satisfied she was securely held, Jeremy approached Lily. He took his place between her spread legs, shoving lightly on the cables to initiate an arc. As she swung, he leaned into her approach, grinding their crotches at the pinnacle of each of her journeys.

When she tried to lift up and meet him, he stepped back.

Lily gawked at him as though he'd started speaking in tongues.

"You're not in control here." He spanked her pussy lightly, granting her some reprieve from the pressure building in her core.

"Shut up and fuck me. If you're not man enough, someone else out there will." She acknowledged the crowd for the first time. A sea of whistles confirmed her declaration.

"I don't think so. I'll take you first. And last. No doubt about that." He groaned as he tortured them both by prolonging the inevitable. Because it wasn't enough to fuck her. No, he had to claim her. Show her that she could trust him to see to her pleasure. They'd balanced on the razor's edge when she held his fate in her hands. Yet she'd chosen to give him this chance—one opportunity to prove she belonged to him, body, mind and heart.

She may have been a born Mistress, but he was the Mistress's Master.

He knew it straight to his soul.

"Besides, I promised you I'd punish you if you shocked me again." He grimaced. "Remember that?"

She smirked. "I might have heard something like blah blah don't do it again or else."

Every dominant instinct he possessed stood up and took notice of her smarmy tone and the twinkle in her eye. It dared him to respond out of hand. A pathetic test.

"You can't upset me so easily, Lily." He shook his head. "I'm not angry with you."

"You should be," someone from the crowd shouted. "She shocked your nuts."

"I cornered her." He pivoted toward the shortsighted visitor. "I left her no choice, and worse, I underestimated her."

Jeremy turned back to Lily. "I'm sorry for that. It won't happen again."

She nodded.

"Neither will I ignore your disobedience." He stared deep into her eyes, hoping she understood. "I refuse to demean you by acting like you aren't strong enough to take what you deserve."

Her lip trembled.

"You agree, you've earned it?"

She shook her head and gasped, "*No!*"

"JRad..." Clint ceased his objection when he spied the determination in Jeremy's stare.

He would never dishonor Lily by taking the easy way out. She deserved so much better than that. Clint and Matt may not fathom all the intricacies of the scene unfolding before them, but they trusted him.

Just as Lily would come to do. Someday. Somehow.

He spun, searching the stage until the green glow of the shock stick caught his attention. The instrument had rolled beneath a machine he couldn't decipher the intent of. In any case it looked wicked...or delicious, if in the right hands.

Jeremy prayed he had the golden touch for Lily.

Rusty reflexes sprang to life as though the chemistry between them acted like the best oil in the universe, greasing connections long since seized from disuse. He approached Lily and the four men who petted her, quieting the effects of the drug. The fall of her raven hair, which almost dragged the ground, drew his admiration.

What had he done in his life to deserve a gift so exquisite?

When he resumed his position, he held the slave goad for her to consider. He dragged the uncharged tip down the center of her body from her neck, between her breasts to her pussy. When he hovered over the apex of her thighs, she couldn't repress her pleas.

"I'm sorry, Master. Please, not there. Don't—" She cut off mid-beg as though realizing what she'd done. He almost considered her bruised ego punishment enough.

"Why don't you offer a sacrifice, Lily?" Forcing her to ask for it would hurt twice as bad as any selection he might make. "Be sure it's somewhere suitably painful or I won't think you're truly sorry. You can't claim you're ignorant to how delicate a man's balls are. I've watched you work. You're fantastic. Someone I'd be proud to top with."

She closed her eyes for a moment then surprised him. "The sole of my foot."

Jeremy should have had a plan B. Although, it was the site he would have chosen himself. Her tender arches would ache almost as much as his balls yet leave her pussy unscathed for the usage she required. Soon. Her fingers trembled above her head, her body shaking as she battled the onslaught of Sex Offender.

The kindest thing he could do was be quick about her penance and move on to soothing her, hoping she'd turn pliant in the aftermath of their clash.

"Ask me for it."

"Master Jeremy," she paused before croaking, "Please punish me for disobeying you."

Before anyone could interject, his hand flashed to the side and touched the device to her left foot. He met her stare as he depressed the button.

Lily shrieked then writhed in the harness. She bit her lip and slammed her eyes closed as she fought the radiating pain. Jeremy switched the tool off then handed it to Ben. "Put this away."

He cupped Lily's pretty foot in his hands and placed a series of kisses from her heel to her toes. He massaged the site of the shock, easing the sting and the uncomfortable tingles whose counterparts lingered across his belly, arm, side and crotch.

If he never saw another of those sadistic toys it'd be too soon.

Ryan, Matt and Clint glared at him as he snugged himself between her thighs. He didn't expect the cops to understand—one of the reasons he'd never shared his past with the men in blue despite considering them closer than brothers.

Lily...she got it.

She opened her eyes and spared him a watery smile. "Thank you, Master."

Jeremy couldn't wait another moment. He forced himself to slow down as he opened the front of his leathers, drawing out her anticipation. This was the moment. The one they would remember forever. The instant their bodies joined for the first time.

It would be so sweet. He could hardly stand to savor it.

He withdrew his cock, not bothering to remove his pants. It would be impossible to wait that long to tunnel inside her. He stroked the full length of his hard-on, rubbing out the last of his discomfort.

Lily watched the progress of his fingers through each of the three or four circuits he made. When he aimed the swollen purple head at her opening, it wasn't his prisoner that objected.

Ben shoved a bag of condoms at him. "Wear one."

Despite his craving to possess her bare, he wouldn't set such a risky precedent with the nearby horde of men who chomped at the bit for a chance to fill his sub.

Jeremy snatched a foil packet from the pile. He had it open and rolled on in a flash.

Lily opened her mouth as though to urge him to hurry. Instead, she closed it again, relaxing into the comforting support of her restraints. Nothing could have thrilled him more.

"Magnificent. You're stunning. Mine, Lily. You were meant to be mine." He prodded her slit with his cock, sliding into position on the first pass. His ass clenched, tipping his hips forward. The motion burrowed his tip inside the tight ring of muscle guarding her entrance.

They both moaned.

He wrapped his fingers in the line of tape around her hips and used it to draw her onto his hard-on. The sling began to swing and he capitalized on the motion, settling into a rhythm designed to fuck him deeper into her clinging sheath on every arc. Lily stared at the juncture of their bodies, witnessing her pussy swallow him whole.

Jeremy raked his gaze from the tips of her pinned hands to the seductive haze turning her eyes glassy. He relished the flush rising over her chest and neck to her cheeks. The presentation of her breasts and the dusky rose nipples on top had him twitching within her.

Orders for the others to touch her, bring her higher, hovered on the tip of his tongue. He swallowed them. He couldn't issue the command. This once he needed to be selfish. Just the first time. To isolate their effect on each other without interference from anyone else. He couldn't stand to give her reason to doubt this connection tomorrow. The effects of the drug would be hard enough to overcome.

Ben and Ryan joined Matt and Clint in stroking their cocks as they watched Lily and Jeremy's union. Their attraction expanded outward—undeniable, irresistible. The guests toed closer and closer until they hopped up onto the edge of the stage. As more men and women joined them, the audience closed in, forming a circle around the main attraction.

Jeremy paid them no attention. Matt and Clint would make sure the newcomers kept their distance. For now. His laser beam stare locked on Lily and every ripple of her pleasure that increased the vise of her pussy, squeezing his cock, making him work to penetrate the rings of her muscles.

"*No, no,*" she shouted, her voice breaking. Morselli cackled in the background, completely unaware of the sham of her denial. For God's sake, how could anyone think Lily didn't welcome his advance into her body, heart and mind?

Jeremy stroked her belly and her chest. He dipped a finger into her mouth, letting her suck on it as he began to fuck her faster, with long gliding strokes that took him to the far reaches of her depths and receding to the very entrance of her pussy. He pulled out entirely before sinking into her heat once more.

She whimpered and tried to change the angle of her hips, impossible in the sling.

He granted her wish.

Using the saliva she'd left on his fingertip, he slid the digit around the top of her nude slit, seeking the bump of her clit. When he stroked the right spot, she keened. The motion of the swing was easy to maintain with one hand and the pressure of his hips colliding with hers, shoving back. It allowed her to slam onto his cock faster and faster while he manipulated her pussy.

Her slick heat felt like paradise. He'd never had sex this powerful, this all-encompassing in his life. He worried he might break something—like a blood vessel or maybe his heart—when he finally surrendered to his orgasm. Which wouldn't be long.

A quivering pressure initiated deep in Lily's pussy. It massaged the end of his cock where it prodded the soft tissue of her inner walls. "Yes. That's the way. Hug my shaft. Come on me. Shatter for me. I'll be here to catch you. Don't hold anything back. Give me everything."

He fucked her harder, trying to extend their rapture. Something this superior couldn't last forever.

"*No!*" She hooked her gaze on his as though all that mattered was that look. The pleasure surrounding them both had more to do with that exchange than the friction of his cock, which pummeled her pussy. Nothing to do with the drug rampaging through her veins. "*No*, please. Don't do this to me."

She cried as she shattered, breaking his heart. Still their emotions couldn't stop the freight train of endorphins, hormones and base physical need railroading them both.

Jeremy poured his release into the reservoir of his condom, damning the situation that stole the opportunity for his seed to pump deep inside her and stain her with the indelible mark of his possession. She came in violent waves around his embedded flesh, milking every last drop of come from his sore balls.

When the world dimmed beneath the heavy consequences of the moment—one that had changed the course of his life forever—a hungry demand burst from Lily's chest.

"More. Please. I need more." Desperate, she forgot to play their semantics game.

But he had nothing left to give.

CHAPTER NINE

"Clint, Matt." Jeremy glanced between his friends. "Suit up. Give it to her."

Lily mourned the loss when he slipped from between her legs. A trickle of her arousal chased him down her thigh. She'd come hard enough to rattle her molars, and still she burned. Though she'd always enjoyed sex with multiple partners, she would have given what remained of her life savings to have this man topping her and teaching her to love it again and again.

She must have closed her eyes as she took stock of the internal devastation he'd left in the wake of his passing, as damaging as an F5 tornado. What had happened to her carefully constructed defenses? How had he razed them with one simple fuck?

Nothing about Jeremy could be uncomplicated. If she were honest, months of slow erosion had weakened the foundation of her convictions. Nights filled with seductive dreams had piqued her curiosity.

Now she knew. One taste of him would never suffice.

So where had he gone? She searched the limited field of her vision. Had he slaked his craving? Would his interest persist after taming Mistress Lily?

There could be no doubt between them. She'd crumbled in the face of his mastery.

Sex Offender amplified her lingering arousal until it became painful and insistent. She needed to fuck. The one man she wanted was nowhere to be found.

"Don't worry."

She moaned when he crouched beside her shoulder, tipping her face toward his.

Jeremy rained kisses over her cheeks, her forehead and her lips. He leaned in close to murmur in her ear. "I don't need drugs to addict me to you. We're going to talk about that stunt later. It's not your right to harm my property."

She groaned as she pictured herself bound to his bed with smooth silk ties. Candlelight flickered over her bare body before splashes of fragrant wax transformed her into a canvas, primed to display his Pollock-esque art. The altered chemistry of her brain advocated the idea. Her abdomen flexed as her pussy squeezed, hugging only air.

Damn it, she needed him. However she had to buy his touch.

"That's right. I might have to dole out some discipline before I feed my cock to your hungry pussy. Soon."

"Promise?" She couldn't believe the wistful rasp shading her question.

"Yeah." His rare full-on smile stole her breath. "Watching you take these men will have me hard. Fast. It won't be long before we're joined again. And next time it'll be even better."

"I'm not sure that's possible."

"Flattery won't save you, slave." He raised his voice for all to hear as he regained his feet. "You're nowhere near finished. In fact, you've only begun."

Lily cast her gaze around the stage. Spectators encroached, shrinking the diameter of free space buffering her from the swarming masses. Several of the men in the front row rubbed their crotches through their fetish gear. A few extracted their cocks, rubbing slow and long or fast and furious over the tips of their dicks as they observed Clint inch between her legs.

A cramp gripped her, forcing her to groan despite her gritted teeth. The relaxation of her orgasm faded as the temporary reprieve Jeremy had granted disintegrated and the scalding urge to procreate returned, stealing her sanity.

"Come on, Clint." Jeremy gripped her tethered wrists in one hand. She stared up at where he stood—legs spread, one hand on his hip—and encouraged his colleague to fuck her. Not because he got off on watching, though he might, but because he correctly interpreted her cravings. "If you can't do it, move aside. She's getting worse. I won't stand for anyone to hurt her."

A few of the guests took a step back.

The authority in Jeremy's tone might have given her pause too if she hadn't been the recipient of his protection. Another blast of desire ripped through her, this time knotting her muscles until she swore a charley horse wrung her uterus.

"Breathe." Jeremy covered her mouth with his warm lips and infused her with a taste of peach candy. Who would guess a man like him would have a sweet tooth?

She inhaled, if only to draw the scent of him into her lungs.

"That's it." He shared several puffs of air with her, establishing a pattern. "Keep it up."

She focused on obeying as he monitored her implementation of his feedback. After a handful of breaths, he nodded.

"What are you waiting for?" he growled at Clint.

The officer drew a triangle between her, Jeremy and Matt. When his stare clashed with his partner's, he shrugged. "Is this insane?"

"Yes." Matt scrubbed his hands through his exceptionally short hair. "Totally."

Lily cried out when a spasm clenched her toes. From breasts to pussy, her nerves screamed. Her nails scraped

Jeremy's forearm when her fingers curled into fists. Why wouldn't someone touch her?

"Get out of my way. I'll fuck her if you won't."

Ryan deflected the man who attempted to breach the shrinking gap between her and the throng of Morselli's acquaintances.

"It's crazy. But she needs it. You." Matt placed his hand on Clint's shoulder then nudged his partner closer to her. "Do it."

"Are you sure, Lily?"

He didn't hear her whimpered, "*No.*"

"She's not calling the shots." Jeremy diverted attention from her as she mouthed a thank you in Matt's direction. "Her fate is in *my* hands. And I say fuck her."

Clint cursed as he surrounded his hard-on with his thick fingers. He glanced in her direction. "I can't resist."

She wrestled with the raw passion singeing her guts until something warm and smooth nudged her pussy. A shriek ripped past her lips before she could stop it.

If he'd pulled back any faster, Clint would have busted his ass.

Ben prevented him from retreating another step. The slave wasn't timid. He put his hands on Clint's waist and guided the other man into place.

Encouragement bubbled up then crescendoed as bystanders joined the chant. "Do it. Do it. Do it."

This time, when Clint touched the tip of his erection to her soaked folds, he didn't hesitate. Lily trembled as he worked his length inside her. She soaked in the pressure of Jeremy's hands, which cupped her shoulders, planting her in place. He braced her for his friend to plow into.

"Oh, shit." Clint's erection throbbed where it lodged partially inside her. "She's on fire. That stuff she took..."

"It's more than that." Jeremy's declaration brimmed with pride. "She's flawless. Adventurous. Dying to please me, and you because I've expressed my wish. Give it to her, Clint."

The fun-loving cop turned serious. He clutched the cords suspending her. Level with his solid chest, his fists closed around the pair attached in the crease between her spread thighs and her hips. She sighed as he soothed some of the intensity inside her, turning it into ecstasy.

"Good girl." Jeremy petted her hair, wrapping the long length around his hands. "Does he feel nice inside that steamy pussy?"

"*No.*" She squirmed in an attempt to lock them together more solidly. Instead, her motion squeezed Clint from her depths as he began to thrust, still edging deeper inside the inferno of her body.

"Little liar." Jeremy grinned as he bent slightly, reaching for her breasts.

She choked when he palmed the mounds. Under the influence of Sex Offender, it felt like he'd draped a cool, damp cloth over massive sunburn.

"You three, put your hands on her. Touch her. Everywhere." Jeremy jerked his chin at Ben, Ryan and Matt.

"I can help." A familiar man navigated the crowd surrounding them.

"Josh." Lily squeezed Jeremy's thigh where it rested beside her tethered hands.

He paused his manipulation to study her reaction to the newcomer. "You're a greedy thing, aren't you? You'd like him to join us?"

"*No.*" She could have denied it for years, and Jeremy would have refused to believe her pathetic misdirection, regardless of the ridiculous safe words they'd arranged. Anyone familiar with the Domme—including her allies in attendance tonight—would see it too.

"Too bad you aren't calling the shots." Jeremy laughed then nodded to Matt, who stepped aside to allow the older, still fit gentleman to join them. No less than ten others approached. Ben and Ryan would have stopped them if Matt hadn't pulled them aside and whispered discreetly in their ears.

Soon Lily couldn't separate the myriad caresses. Individuals didn't matter. Only the havoc they wreaked on her as one unit counted. Through it all she clutched Jeremy, using him to ground her in the surreal experience.

Clint grunted as he began to pump inside her. "Shit. That's so sexy. They all want you, Lily. But I have you."

"For now. On loan." Jeremy's rumble caught Clint's attention. The cop's stride hitched, leaving her yearning for his return.

Even the slight pause had her tensing. She whimpered.

Didn't he understand? She belonged to Jeremy. Though it wasn't his cock inside her—stretching her, massaging her—he still fucked her. His ultimate control shaped the experience. He granted all her wishes and sated her needs.

Lily couldn't hold back. She exploded around Clint.

The orgasm paled in comparison to the one Jeremy had delivered personally. The pleasure blossomed then faded in time for her to catch the last of his friend's shouts as he filled the condom he wore. Before he'd finished shuddering between her thighs, Ryan nudged the cop aside.

"Yes." Jeremy became her voice, her will. He choreographed the scene when all she could manage was accepting the outcome. "Don't hold back. She needs it rougher. Faster. Go."

"Ah, damn." Ryan took direction a hell of a lot better than Clint had. He permitted Jeremy to mold him into a precise instrument. The Master wielded it as expertly as a fine craftsman to shape the exchange into something original and spectacular.

The gentle man who'd licked her earlier—soft and sweet—pounded her now. The motion drove her away and the sea of hands holding the fire at bay guided her home. The sway and the constant caresses lulled her into some sort of sexual trance.

All her senses elevated.

Harsh breaths, groans and the slick slapping of hands on cocks reverberated in her ears. Touches dotted every inch of her exposed skin from her toes to her belly to her breasts and her arms. When one of Ryan's lunges shoved her higher, her hand glanced off Jeremy's firming cock.

She extended her fingers, stealing a touch on him at the apex of every arc. Though the overload of sensations felt divine, it still wasn't enough.

Lily opened her eyes and took stock of the dozen or so adoring gazes engulfing her in their spotlight. "Please."

"More?" Jeremy's cock seemed harder the next time she managed to touch it.

"No." She panted, unable to catch her breath beneath the force of Ryan's shuttling impacts. "No. No. No."

"Shh." Jeremy cupped her chin then inserted his fingers between her lips. "You'll take what we have to give and love every minute."

She sucked greedily on his hand, wishing she could taste the salty tang of his hard-on.

"You two, put your mouths on her breasts. Suck those nipples. Bite them. Gently." Two faceless men devoured her chest eagerly. She didn't care who they were anymore. Friend or foe. She suspected her five protectors had weeded out those who clearly had no respect for her or the enchantment they wove.

Their lips followed the motion of her body as they tongued her aching breasts.

Lily's back arched, her neck curving until she met Jeremy's intense stare.

"That's right. Come again for me." He smiled as she shattered, destroying Ryan's persistent motion.

The submissive-turned-fuck-toy slammed to the hilt. He held still as he pumped his release deep inside her.

The flex of his cock seemed blatant to her altered senses. The pulsing meshed with her own contractions, each twitch inciting another round of reflexive clenching in her pussy. They fed off each other, prolonging the pleasure.

And still, she had barely caught her breath when the ache returned. Small and distant, the spark in her belly sputtered to life like a trick candle on a birthday cake.

Never fully extinguished.

Matt groaned, rubbing the head of his thick cock on her ribs.

"Not you." Jeremy waved off his partner when the cop angled his torso toward her legs. "Not yet. You're too big. We don't have time to take things slow."

Matt nodded, settling instead for dragging his balls over her tummy when Ryan withdrew, letting her swing in his wake.

Ben took his turn at the plate, embedding his thicker cock between her slick folds. This time as she rocked, she deflected off the men tightening the ring around her. She licked her lips as she caught glimpses of them jerking off above her.

"Not all of them will make it." Jeremy withdrew his fingers from her mouth, painting moisture over her lips. "Some are too close to wait for that pussy. They won't last."

Her eyes rolled backward as Ben took up where Ryan had left off. Each man had his own patterns, his own stride. His unique cock rubbed her in a way expressly his own. The differences and similarities had her lost in a whirlwind of desire. A storm of passion made it difficult to focus, even on Jeremy and his directions.

A tiny part of her mind recalled her training. For the first time she really understood the necessity of asking questions and demanding a response. Did she cause her submissives to float away from the earth and leave all their worries behind like this?

She sure hoped so.

"Answer me, Lily." Jeremy's stern demand reached her wandering mind through the fog of arousal limiting her attention on anything but the dense blanket of rapture surrounding her. "Do you want them to come on you? They'll show you how much they appreciate your beauty and your surrender."

She barely remembered to switch her answer when another orgasm crashed through her. "*Nooo.*"

Jeremy kissed the tear of pure joy that trickled along her temple. "You're more than I imagined. More than I could have hoped."

Ben must have come with her. No sooner had he retracted his softening erection than another replaced it. Thank God. She'd reached a place where she could no longer detect the beginning or ending of her rapture. She came again and again, each orgasm leading into the next. Never truly stopping, the pleasure waned before rising again like bubbles in the champagne her partners had consumed. Each orb popped as it reached the surface, relieving tension until the next seed of passion sprouted within her.

The hands on her body were joined by warmer, harder flesh. She opened her eyes long enough to count no fewer than five men rubbing their shafts over whatever part of her they could access. Someone bent her leg, fucking the crease between the underside of her calf and the back of her thigh.

Another climax squeezed her lids shut again. She struggled to breathe, fought to maintain consciousness through the battery of pleasure. Cries leaked from her parted lips with every wave crashing over her body. Stopping the plaintive sounds was no longer an option.

The exhibition of her complete capitulation must have affected the men surrounding her. They joined her vocalization of rapture, some spilling their come over her breasts or belly, easing the glide of others across her skin. Someone smacked the solid length of his cock on her nipples, spreading the slippery moisture falling there as constantly as rain drops in a warm summer shower.

The pressure between her legs changed again. She groaned as her well-used pussy stretched to accommodate the newcomer.

"That's right, Lily." Jeremy guided her when she reached out, finding him right where she expected the moment she needed his reassurance. "You're doing great. Relax and let Matt in. If you can take him, I'll let you have my cock again. You've earned a reward."

"Not helping." Matt cursed. "Making her tighter. She's tiny, JRad. I'm hurting her."

"*Yes!*" Lily shrieked and though it might have looked as though she tried to evade Matt's invasion, she squirmed to help him bury deeper. The burn as he spread her pussy wider than ever before eclipsed her reasoning.

"Don't believe her for one second." Jeremy laughed. "She loves your cock. Don't you?"

"*No.*" The objection might have been discredited somewhat by her next orgasm, which distorted the cry.

"That's right." Jeremy crooned as he shooed the man near her shoulder so he could come closer. "Suck on my cock, Lily. It'll keep you from screaming something you might regret."

Like how much she craved what they were doing to her? Like how she needed the man she devoured to set her free?

He was probably right. Again.

Damn him.

She scraped her teeth over his shaft, rebelling one last time.

"Hell, yes." He groaned. "I like it a little rough, wildcat. Do your worst. It'll only make me fuck you that much harder."

When Matt began to move between her legs, she nearly choked. How had he impaled her on that mammoth cock? Somehow, Jeremy had distracted her through the worst of the insertion. Now that her body adjusted, gloving his thick hard-on, the pressure felt divine.

"You should see how your pretty pussy is stretched around his dick." Jeremy's dirty talk triggered several of the guests to tip over the edge. Another wash of warm come decorated her skin. Each line of heat scorching her proved the power she held despite her position. One of the men reached out, using his broad palm to rub the evidence of her glory into her skin.

Her tummy fluttered beneath the reverent touch.

Matt growled and cursed again. He began to fuck her with fast twitches of his hips that tapped her clit without making her uncomfortable. "Shit. Not going to take much. Too tight. Waited too long. It's too good."

Lily agreed. She couldn't endure a ton of the overstimulation.

She lapped at the underside of Jeremy's shaft, stealing as much of his flavor as she could. She attempted to communicate with every flick of her tongue, suck of her lips and hollow of her cheeks how much she appreciated the experience he'd made possible. He'd altered her life in a single hour.

Everything crashed around her.

Matt's hoarse shouts triggered another pinnacle. It felt so good it hurt. And still, she needed one more thing. One more man.

She opened her eyes and stared straight into Jeremy's intense gaze. He measured her visual plea since her mouth was too full of his cock to beg.

He didn't make her suffer.

CHAPTER TEN

The moment Matt abandoned her pussy, Lily noticed a difference. The frantic insanity caused by the drug had begun to fade. It lingered, causing occasional spikes of mingled agony and desire. But it had subsided. Jeremy had seen her through the worst of the high.

Lily glanced around the room. Most of the men lounged, exhausted, observing the show through heavy-lidded eyes as slaves brought them drinks and attended to their comfort. Matt, Clint, Ryan and Ben hovered around her, a pillar of support at each of the main cables stringing her up. Ryan accepted a towel from a female slave, who wore Morselli's uniform, and began to clean Lily with tender passes of the soft cloth while Jeremy took his rightful place between her legs.

"Do you want me, Lily?"

"*No.*" She sobbed the false denial.

"Same here." He shook his head as he slipped on a condom then tucked his cock into the entrance of her pussy. "I didn't intend to need you like this. I don't see how it's possible. But it is. I have to have you."

Jeremy plunged into her. His absolute possession had more to do with the fierce determination in his gaze than the insertion of his delicious cock. Lily felt like Goldilocks—not too big, not too small. He fit her just right, as though cosmically designed as her counterpart.

He buried himself to the root, slow and steady, as though savoring the meshing of their bodies. The small

141

touches of his fingers over her ribs, his thumb caressing the insides of her knees and his broad palms gliding over her hips did more to influence her than the steady advance and retreat he initiated.

The gleam in his eyes when he observed her response to his presence drove her insane. Still, the glut of the evening combined with the crashing of her system after the fervor of her Sex Offender high. Tears blurred her vision when she wondered if she would be able to come again. Just once more. She needed to share this moment with him.

Doubt chased the sparkles of her arousal to the dim reaches of her psyche. Elusive, they evaded her attempts to rekindle them. The harder she tried, the farther they slipped away.

"You're doing fine, Lily," he murmured. "Allow it to happen. Don't fight so hard. I could fuck you all night and never tire of this feeling. We don't have to rush."

His gentle reassurance brought her need flooding back. How could he assess her so well? No one ever had before. They'd thought her cold. Tough. No one had seen the girl inside, praying for someone—anyone—to trust.

"That's right." He smiled, honing in on the motion that triggered the highest response in her overworked pussy. "I'll take care of you. Give yourself to me. I can worry for us both. All you have to do is enjoy. Obey and I'll handle the rest."

The room went dead silent as Jeremy entranced everyone in attendance.

Lily shivered as he seduced her.

"Ryan, Ben, come closer."

The submissives inched forward until their thighs brushed her hips, one on each side of her. "Lick her. Gently. Help her come for me."

Neither slave hesitated. Ben squatted while Ryan bent at the waist. Their tongues reached out, tentative as the firmed tips made contact with either side of her clit.

142

Trapped between the two wet, warm muscles, which wriggled around her sensitive flesh, she could no longer resist.

Her pussy clenched on Jeremy's cock as it glided from the very entrance of her pussy to the farthest depths he could reach. He worked over her. Patient, calm and steady, he mixed a combination of qualities as potent and unstoppable as gravity.

Lily visualized a ripple in a pond originating in the pit of her belly. As it expanded outward, she relaxed each part of her it touched. Her fists fell open. Her toes uncurled. Appreciative murmurs ran through the dominants in attendance when she went slack, accepting all Jeremy had to give.

"Ah, yes. Just like that." He put a hand on the back of Ryan's head, urging the man closer before doing the same to Ben. "Feel how much deeper you can take me now?"

The garble that flew from her lips couldn't be deciphered, but he nodded.

"It feels amazing to me too." He smiled as he ground deep then picked up his pace.

Ben and Ryan grew more adventurous. Their tongues lashed over each other as they played with her pussy. One of them nipped her swollen lips when the other sealed his mouth over her clit and sucked.

"Nice." Jeremy's praise mesmerized her. The smoky timbre of his voice did as much to arouse her as the two mouths working her exterior while Jeremy caressed her deep inside. "You've got this. Feel me taking you to the edge. Soar, Lily. Leap."

The idea terrified her. He'd lifted her higher than she'd ever ventured before. What if she crashed? What if she couldn't survive the impact?

One tiny moment of hesitation was obliterated when he promised, "I'll catch you. Always."

How could she not take the risk? In all her life she'd never met another man who read her so perfectly.

Jeremy stared deep into her eyes as she lost control. Her body seized. Her heart stopped beating for one prime moment. He didn't speed up or hammer her tender flesh. Instead, he remained solid as a rock, pumping every last bit of rapture from her with consistent glides of his cock.

Even when he came, with a fierce growl she'd dream of the rest of her life, he kept his gaze locked on hers. A wry smile elicited a dimple in his chiseled cheeks. He rocked against her, filling the barrier between them with his release. She wished she could have felt him pouring, molten, inside her.

His strokes slowed. They didn't stop until she whimpered. Gingerly, he withdrew from her swollen pussy, leaving her wrecked.

Suddenly she couldn't catch her breath. What had she done?

She'd given him everything.

Jeremy dismissed Ryan and Ben, waving them aside so he could bend over her immobile form. He stared into her eyes as he cupped her cheeks in his palms. The press of his lips on hers startled her, causing an aftershock to wring her pussy. His tongue snuck out to swipe across her smile. It stole inside her mouth and licked her with tender strokes.

The very last remaining shred of her independence began to slip away. He left her no choice. *"Yes."*

The pressure of his kiss obliterated her objection.

She chanted it over and over until he caught her reverse meaning.

He stopped dead. Sixty to zero as though he'd slammed into a brick wall.

A cool breeze buffeted her skin when he stood abruptly, honoring their pact.

Some part of her, deep within, cried out for him to return. To overrule her fear.

Before he could, Morselli called out, "Very nice, kids. Too nice. You've ruined my party."

Lily glanced around. No one seemed interested in the abandoned slaves occupying the main section of the hall.

"All bids submitted on arrival will be honored," Morselli addressed the crowd. Thank God Lily had instructed her allies to show their interest up front. Many of the other buyers would have waited for demonstrations.

Jeremy snarled when their host approached, his stubby hand flashing over his modest hard-on. Purple splotches dotted his cheeks and forehead. Maybe he'd keel over and save them some trouble. Lily braced herself for his seed, mourning the taint he'd layer on top of the pure passion melting her bones.

Everything happened so fast.

Exhaustion prevented her from reacting when Morselli slapped her breast with his cock.

"Clint, hand me a robe for Lily." The urgency in Jeremy's instruction caught the attention of her fuzzy brain. "She'll need it as soon as we're finished. She's cooling off."

The undercover cop rummaged around in the supplies out of Lily's line of sight as Morselli began to huff and puff, on the verge of exploding. She flinched when he grunted, preparing for the splash of his meager load.

It never came.

Clint spun around, knocking into Morselli's shoulder as he transferred a bundle of terrycloth to Jeremy. A strangled combination moan-turned-curse accompanied Tony's graceless sprawl. His whole body jerked as he spilled his come onto the stage, crashing onto one knee to avoid a full-out face-plant.

A few guests chuckled at the sight of the man's graceless tumble and the desperate spasms jerking his hips as he erupted all over himself.

"You careless fucker!" He glared at Clint as he regained his feet, slowly, shakily. Giant pants bled steam from Morselli's continued rant.

Lily was too tired to be amused. She battled the oblivion swallowing her consciousness.

"Excuse me." Clint offered a hand up, but Morselli knocked it away. Jeremy's friend shrugged then returned to her side.

"Unhook her." Jeremy ignored the commotion. His focus never strayed from her.

Her eyes drifted closed as the lines were released and she drooped onto the stage. Hands worked over her, freeing her arms, legs and torso from her bonds. Still she couldn't move.

"Get up, Lily." Jeremy didn't lift her. He didn't humiliate her by assuming she couldn't take care of herself.

She smiled and cracked open her lids, which seemed to weigh ten tons.

Damn Sex Offender.

Damn the most powerful orgasms of her life.

Damn the dozen men who'd fed the flames until they consumed every bit of her energy.

Lily rolled to her front, shoving onto wobbly arms and legs. They collapsed beneath her as if she were Bambi. Heat rose in her cheeks. Lucidity returned in the wake of the drug's potent effects. What would the crowd think of Mistress Lily now?

Despite her reaction to Jeremy, she couldn't deny the life she'd built. It boggled her mind, too zoned now to comprehend the ramifications of this indulgent evening. Could she be both the woman who ruled her slaves with unwavering command and the willing submissive of one undeniable Master?

Not if she didn't shape people's expectations. Right then. She channeled every ounce of her remaining strength and tried again. Desperation drove her to regulate the quivering of her elbows and knees for longer than she should have been able. Still, she crumpled to the floor once more.

Dread weakened her limbs further as she considered all she had riding on the line. She curled into a ball and shivered on the floor.

Ryan stepped forward at the same time Matt held his arms out to her. Their forms distorted as moisture filled her eyes. Temptation to accept Matt's offer—huddle in his embrace and be toted away—poisoned her sense of self.

"Leave her." Jeremy's steely tone brooked no arguments.

"JRad—" Clint would have had more luck bargaining with a suicide bomber.

"No. She'll walk out on her own or she'll lie here all night. Alone."

"What the fuck?" Matt whipped around, glaring at his friend and supposed boss.

Shit. If Morselli suspected their ruse, the men, including Jeremy, would find themselves quickly destroyed. For making a fool of Tony, they'd suffer before he had them killed.

She wouldn't allow them to be hurt because of her.

Lily bit her lip to keep from crying out when her muscles protested her third attempt at rising. Her knees gave out, banging into the unforgiving surface of the stage. The bruising force cleared her mind some. She managed to stay upright, kneeling. She stared into the warm depths of Jeremy's eyes as she forced her limp body to obey through sheer determination.

Planting her right foot on the floor, she never broke the connection between her gaze and Jeremy's stare. He nodded when she transferred her weight and lurched

147

upward, swaying. She waved off all of the helping hands extended in her direction. The slap of her left sole on the floor sounded like a gunshot in her mind. Every cell of her brain concentrated on battling the flashes of light threatening her balance.

If she fell, she'd never recover.

She leaned forward, shifting her weight then staggering onto her extended leg.

The first step was the hardest.

By the fourth and fifth, a smile formed on her lips. Her shoulders spread back and wide, at least as far as her frame would allow. She may have given her physical form to these men to enjoy for an hour or two. None of them affected her soul.

Well, maybe one.

Jeremy nodded when she drew up in front of him. Toe to toe, she had to incur a drastic bend in her neck to maintain their line of sight. It was worth the crick to catch a glimpse of his approval and admiration.

"That's right." He held out his hand to her. "We'll walk together."

"Let me carry—"

Jeremy cut Ben off. "No."

She smiled. "Thank you, sir."

He nodded. "Any time."

Ryan steadied her while Clint slipped the robe on her shaky body. He bundled her in the soft fabric then cinched the belt. The tie clasping her waist drew a shimmer of pleasure from her belly. Son of a bitch, no wonder people got so addicted to this garbage.

Jeremy linked their fingers as he turned. He tempered his long strides, moderating his pace so she had a chance of making it at least out of the public venue. Whistles, claps and cheers filled the enormous space like thunder on a sultry summer night as the entourage retreated. They'd nearly reached the passage leading to the main hallway when Jeremy glanced at Morselli over his shoulder, not pausing.

"I'm taking these two with us." He motioned with his chin to Ryan and Ben. "They belong to Lily now. She's earned their loyalty. Have their belongings transferred to the wing housing her subs and her things delivered to my suites while we're touring the facilities tomorrow afternoon."

Morselli didn't dare object. Arguing in front of so many would have tarnished his already battered reputation. "Of course. Consider them my gift to you both in honor of our *partnership*. I'm sure many would love to try a little of the magic behind Mistress Lily's performance tonight. If it can do that for her, imagine what it could do for them."

The slimy bastard twisted their priceless experience into an infomercial.

Jeremy's thumb rubbed the scalloped ridge of her knuckles when she tensed, squeezing his fingers. The pressure of her front teeth on her lip would probably leave indentations. At least she prevented herself from ruining everything for the fleeting satisfaction it would bring to call the bastard out.

As soon as they crossed through the grand archway and angled toward their living space, the noise and activity died down. All of the staff attended to the guests and ensured Morselli's party concluded to his satisfaction.

"Clint, take the lead. You remember the way back?"

"Yeah. I've got it, JRad." He passed easily by the couple, who walked side by side in the wide thoroughfare. If he'd so much as brushed Lily, she might have tipped.

Ryan drew near, staying close to her side. He lagged a step behind her and Jeremy. Ben mirrored him off Jeremy's opposite shoulder. Matt trailed them all, bringing up the rear.

"You're doing great." Jeremy draped his arm around her waist, bearing nearly all of her weight now that they were alone. Mostly. "Keep going. Force some more of that crap out of your bloodstream."

"Feel better." She couldn't manage more through her gritted teeth. Absorbed with maintaining her balance, she banished the lure of his skin pressed so close to hers. Friction rubbed the tops of her thighs together, threatening to reignite the embers glowing there.

She refused to indulge the lingering symptoms.

"Liar."

The walk to their quarters lasted at least triple the time it'd taken her to march into Morselli's clutches this afternoon, bold yet ignorant of what he had in store for her. Though the day had taken its toll, she wouldn't change a single thing.

"So many saved." Lily didn't realize she'd whispered aloud until Jeremy swooped in and kissed her. If he hadn't braced her, she would have fallen flat on her ass. The succulence of his parted lips drove everything but the taste of him from her mind.

After several nibbles he glided over to tease the lobe of her ear. "Not out here. Almost home, okay?"

She blinked up at him.

"I can see the lobby of JRad's apartment," Clint called out.

"A few more steps." He encouraged her when she thought she had nothing left to give. "You have it now. Count them out. Focus."

"One..." She channeled her energy into naming each motion. Before they hit double digits, he unlocked the door to his private space.

"Ryan, Ben, are you able to stay out here tonight?"

"Whatever she needs, we'll do," Ryan spoke for them both.

"Good. Take turns on guard. Switch every two hours so you stay alert. Make sure I know if anyone comes snooping around. I don't want to be interrupted without notice." He stroked her hair all the way along her spine, leaving his hand on her ass. "She's going to need me. Need to sleep this off too."

The men nodded.

"Matt, Clint, head out." Jeremy's direction to the cops seemed vague compared to his instructions to Ryan and Ben.

She didn't have the capacity to wonder why at the moment.

"Visit your girlfriend. See if she has any of the extra strong coffee she gave me that time I needed to wake up. Come back in the morning, after you've taken care of stuff."

"On it." Matt smiled at Lily. "I can't believe you made it on your own. You're a freak. In every awesome way. Thanks for tonight."

"Impressive." Clint braved Jeremy's wrath long enough to buss her cheek. "See you tomorrow."

The heavy door had only just *snicked* closed when Lily's knees gave out. She pitched forward, prepared for impact with the marble flooring.

Jeremy caught her before she came anywhere close to cracking her skull. He cradled her in his arms and carried her across the room. A detour took them past a panel of flashing lights and a jumble of electronics, which occupied the surface of the desk littered with not one but three laptops.

She couldn't do more than stare at the chaos while he used his right hand to hunt and peck a series of commands.

"There. Nice and secure. Private." He nodded before regripping her legs and continuing on to the bathroom. "Jesus, Lily. You did so well. It was beautiful. I couldn't be more proud of you."

151

He lavished praise along with a steady waterfall of kisses. With him she didn't have to fight. She allowed herself to remain pliant, savoring the oddity of someone else's care for her.

Water gushed from several ornate gold faucets into a gargantuan bathtub, more like a small swimming pool than the garden tub in her decent apartment. Steam swirled around them.

"Stay right there. Your balance is still jacked up." Jeremy set her on the tiled ledge surrounding the tub. He kept one hand on her shoulder as he kicked off his shoes and bent one leg then the other to peel off his socks. She stared at his long, tan feet wondering how even his toes could be so fucking sexy.

A moan escaped her lips when Sex Offender amplified her natural ripple of pleasure.

"I know, Lily." He made short work of the clasp on his leathers, shoving them off one hip then the other. "It hurts. I'm so sorry. I'll try to fix it. Try to help. Matt and Clint should be able to procure some of the antidote from the hospital. Jambrea has been working on the test team. You remember her, right?"

She appreciated his attempt at distraction. "The sweet-looking nurse hiding her naughty side?"

"Pretty unsuccessfully, but yeah." Jeremy beamed at her. "Matt and Clint have been about to duke it out for a chance with her since you saw her last."

When he yanked the end of the harness crisscrossing his magnificent chest and unfastened the straps, she swore she drooled.

"Why don't they share?" Lily tilted her head as she recalled the blushes coupled with no-so-discreet glances in the cops' direction. "She'd go for it."

Jeremy swiped the robe from her with a coordinated motion too fast for her sluggish mind to completely register. She craned her neck to keep his sleek body in sight when he climbed into the tub. Always, he maintained their contact, bracing her.

"I said the same thing. They weren't ready to listen. Maybe after tonight..." Jeremy straddled the wall separating the elaborate spa from the rest of the bathroom. He planted his feet, making sure he was steady before plucking her from her perch. "I'm serious. You were spectacular. The way you responded to all those men. Well, it might change their minds about ménage."

They settled into the rising water. He sat with his shoulders resting against the side of the basin, his form lounging in the contoured seat built into the structure. Waves glided from her belly to her breasts in the wake they caused by sliding partially below the surface.

The balmy fluid arrowed straight toward her aching muscles. She couldn't suppress a decadent sigh. Between the soothing heat of the water and the scorching impression of Jeremy's chest on her back, she could have been in heaven.

"I think you proved tonight that sharing sex with more than one man can take a woman to new heights. Who wouldn't want that for someone they cared for?"

"No reason to fuck around. I can't handle mind games tonight." Too tired to do more than rest against his scrumptious body, she cut to the chase. "What are you digging for?"

Jeremy laughed. "You know all my tricks. This is going to be interesting."

"I'm pretty sure you showed me some new ones tonight."

Jeremy washed her. He lathered his hands with sweet-smelling soap then massaged away the dirt, grime and some of the ache permeating her body. He stayed silent so long she thought he might not continue his train of thought.

He worked his way up her torso, cupping her chin lightly in his hand and tipping her face until they could share a long, heated stare. "There could have been a thousand men there tonight. *I* was the only one that mattered. You pleased them because it pleased me. That's what got you off. Again and again. I lost count of how many times you came."

She didn't want to look away from his brilliant eyes, but her sore neck couldn't maintain the severe angle. As though he could read her mind, Jeremy adjusted her position. He turned her sideways. Her ass rested on the bottom of the tub between his legs, her knees bent over his thigh. Layers of sinew in his biceps made a remarkably comfortable pillow for her to recline on. The bulk of his full erection branded her hip.

A yelp escaped her when a spear of need ripped through her guts. "Fuck if I understand how that happened. I guess Sex Offender really is all they say. Even now, it's making my reactions go haywire."

"Don't." His entire body went rigid around her. "Don't you dare lie to me. Or yourself. You used the drug as a crutch to take what you wanted. It was the only moment of weakness you showed tonight. And sometime soon I'll paddle your ass for choosing the easy way out."

"You wouldn't dare." Her sneer probably would have held more weight if she'd been able to sit up and separate herself from his loose embrace. Nothing she did could make her leeched strength return. She rested in his hold, completely at his mercy.

"Not tonight. You're not up for what I'll give you for taking such a risk with my property." For a moment, harsh lines slashed the corners of his mouth and eyes. He moved his arm to scrub them away.

Left unsupported, she descended close to the rising waterline.

A whimper forced through her clenched windpipe.

"You're completely done, aren't you?" Jeremy studied her reactions. "I have no idea how you're still awake."

"Me either." Deep inside she knew how. She'd dreamed of spending time with him for months. Considered seeking him out to relay information about the case just to see him again.

A wicked bend to his lips transformed his soft smile into something more sinister. "You push all my buttons, Lily. I may not be able to punish you tonight, but I think I can make my point quite nicely."

"Oh really?" She couldn't say why she baited him except that the gnawing ache in her tummy began to rev to full speed once more.

"Yeah."

CHAPTER ELEVEN

Jeremy shifted his hands, moving one between her shoulder blade and the other to her ass. He lifted her until she bobbed on the surface of the water. She floated, not difficult considering her boneless state. He propped her lower body on his bent knee, then used the hand that had been supporting her to dribble water from his fingertips over the beaded tips of her breasts, down her stomach and finally to her bare mound.

She mewled as her legs drifted open of their own volition.

Jeremy chuckled.

"It's not funny." She grimaced. "It aches. The drug is still kicking around. Let it die. Let me rest. I can block it out if you leave me alone."

"The pressure is nowhere close to how bad it was before, right? You were a live wire out there on that stage. Screaming for more. Taking all you could get." He dipped lower and sucked on her breast. "Bet I can make you come harder than you did at the height of the frenzy without even fucking you."

"Not possible." She closed her eyes. Not preferable either.

"Don't worry, Lily." He kissed her eyelids. "I won't make you suffer. I remember the dull throbbing and the endless cycles of need. Tell me when it flares up. I'll soothe it. You don't have to pretend or hide. Your poor pussy is going to be sore tomorrow, though. I won't add to your pain. Don't need to right now. I can teach you a lesson. Something we both need to confirm."

Damn his persuasive velvet speech. He turned her on, promised relief.

"Do you want to learn about us?"

She trembled in his hold, sloshing droplets onto her breasts where they emerged from the depths. "Yes."

"Yes what?"

She'd never given the title Master to anyone. Certainly not her trainers. Even after tonight, she wasn't ready. The best she could do escaped instead. "Yes, sir."

He frowned but didn't object.

"If all you want is an orgasm, I can give it to you with thirty seconds of feasting on your clit." He growled. "You need more, don't you? Would you like to play?"

"Yes." She amended her insistence. "Please, sir."

"That's better." He smiled. "I won't go easy on you, Lily. Not tonight. Not ever. You know the rules. Hell, you've made up a few of your own I'd imagine. I'll never disrespect you. If anything, I'll push you harder. Take you farther than you suspect possible."

"Thank you, sir." Gratitude rolled off her tongue, surprising her with how right it sounded.

"Nice." He shoved off the bottom of the tub, water now lapping at his pierced nipples.

Had she rested on the floor, her mouth and nose would have been underwater. She shivered.

Cool tile shocked her calf when he propped it on the wall of the tub. She blinked at where it rested beside the taps. The long ornate spigot extended well into the huge tub, maintaining proper scale.

When Jeremy grabbed her other ankle and lifted it, she deciphered his intent.

A giant moan flew from her chest when the laminar flow splashed over her mound.

"That's right." He supported her shoulders and sat so that his head was directly over hers as he monitored her breathing. "I bet it feels nice on that naughty pussy."

Her eyes rolled back as he adjusted her position. He reached between her legs, spreading the lips of her pussy with two fingers. Water poured over her clit, gentle yet insistent.

"Ah!" She couldn't manage anything more coherent.

Jeremy's mouth descended, kissing her tenderly. She dipped a little lower, the roar of the water changing, deepening as her ears submerged below the waterline. Her eyes popped open, locked on his.

"Shh. I have you." He nuzzled their noses. "You trust me, yes?"

She nodded.

"Let me hear it, Lily."

"Yes, sir. I trust you." And somehow it was true. She'd seen his ultimate *goodness* during Malcolm's funeral and their fight to rescue her sister. Nothing had ever attracted her to a man so much as his integrity. Someone that noble would never break a promise.

"Are you sure?" He stared deep into her eyes.

She whispered, "Positive."

"I know. And that's why you gave yourself to me tonight. *That's* why you climbed so high earlier. It had nothing to do with Sex Offender. Not at all. It was the faith you had in me to guide the experience that drove you to the edge."

"Arrogant much? Maybe it was the dozen men who fucked me."

"I think it might have been closer to fifteen." He shook his head. "Would you like a demonstration?"

"How?"

"Does the water feel good?" He infuriated her by diverting her curiosity. At least, she thought he had.

159

"Yes, sir." She would have squirmed if her muscles took any direction from her brain. If she could align her clit a little better she'd come within five seconds.

"Really great, even?" He taunted her by shifting her the fraction of an inch she required for direct stimulation. Spasms began deep in her pussy.

"God, yes."

He chuckled. "Okay. You think about that for a minute, alright. Enjoy while I wash your hair. Feel free to come as much as you want."

Confusion set in. He'd been on the verge of a revelation. Then he retreated. Docile. Generous. The ease of the moment disappointed her a little. How sick was that?

Still, it didn't keep her clamoring nerves from soaking up the pleasure. She had to feed the growing hunger.

Jeremy poured a dollop of shampoo into his hands then massaged it into her scalp. The pressure of his broad fingertips became the only thing keeping her afloat beside her heels, hooked on the ledge. The delicious weight of his hands easing the tension from her head combined with the consistent flow of the water. Pleasure ramped up the delight suffusing her until his thumbs, climbing the nape of her neck to the base of her skull, triggered her orgasm.

She panted as a pleasant release throbbed in her pussy. Nothing like the intensity of her earlier adventure. If this is what he'd planned to show her...

Lily sighed as she settled from the meager peak, afraid to open her eyes and let him see that he'd failed.

"Very pretty." He didn't seem too worried. "Sweet. Gentle."

She tried to wring more from the last vestiges of her pleasure. No use.

"Now, let me rinse your hair then I'll put you to bed." He purred near her cheek. "Take a deep breath, Lily."

She did as instructed. Anything to finish this exchange and make it to bed where she could bury her face in the pillow and hide her disappointment in sleep.

Jeremy let go.

Lily plummeted beneath the surface of the tub. Her heels kept her legs elevated while her head sank and sank. She attempted to thrash, to kick to the surface. Her drained body wouldn't respond. Nothing happened.

Giant bubbles glugged to the surface as she shouted for help.

No sooner had she opened her mouth then Jeremy responded. He whisked her into the delicious air, wiping her eyes, tilting her head to make sure no water ran up her nose as she sputtered.

"That's what I thought," he murmured, "You've got nothing left physically to fight with. Your body has disappointed you. You're complete at my mercy, Lily."

The pulses between her legs amplified as she accepted the truth. She lay in his hands, completely reliant on him for not just her pleasure but also her safety. Her life depended on him. What greater trust could there be than that?

Another wave of ecstasy crashed over her without warning. Apparently her pussy hadn't heard the news. Sex Offender may have made the reaction possible. It didn't account for why her first climax had been ordinary, meek, when this one wrung her dry.

"Feel how it changes everything?" Jeremy rained kisses over her cheeks, her lips, her chin and her forehead. "The power I wield makes all the difference. It's the same on my side. Watching you come like this will tear me apart. I swear I could shoot from watching you surrender."

"Yes, sir." She groaned. "More. I need more."

161

"Are you sure?" He kissed her cheek. "Are you ready?"

"Are you?" She raised an eyebrow. Surely he hadn't experimented like this in years. Not since...

"How can I disgrace you? If you trust me, I think it's fucking time I believe in myself."

"Do it."

He stared at her and shook his head. His hands trembled where they supported her neck.

"Please." She panted as she relished the water surrounding her limp arms, which floated on the surface. "Jeremy, I have faith in you. Do it. Sir."

They inhaled in unison.

Then he lowered her by degrees, controlling her descent.

Sound distorted. The crash of water over her clit thrilled her before it smashed into the tub, creating a dull roar in the alternate universe surrounding her. She opened her eyes, observing her mane drifting in the tub. It entangled both her and Jeremy in the mass of wet strands, binding them.

The throb in her clit built in tandem with the burn of her lungs. Long before she could panic, Jeremy brought her to the surface.

"More," she whined. The ball of passion pulsing inside her had grown brighter and brighter with every fraction of a second she lingered underwater. "Longer."

"I won't risk your safety. Ever. I'm holding my breath with you Lily. When it becomes the tiniest bit difficult you're coming up."

"No." She would have stomped her feet if she could have, screw her reputation. She had to have more. "Longer."

The rush of the water didn't seem to soothe her or build her closer to the elusive orgasm she'd seemed so certain of moments ago. She had to have relief—had to come.

He lowered her again. This time the pleasure was instant. It swamped her the moment her lips descended into the depths.

Jeremy's stare pierced the surface. It clashed with hers, locking on her eyes for any hint of distress. She wondered if he could read the rapture there instead. She chased the building desire as it blossomed. The idea of surrendering to it frightened her a little.

It had the potential to level her. She blinked a few times in rapid succession.

Water sluiced off her body as she crested the surface.

"No, no, no," she cried out, robbed of her orgasm. "So close. More. Please."

Jeremy growled as he bit her shoulder. "Once more, that's it. This is a dangerous game. Only one more try. Show me how much you trust me. Show me how much it matters."

He dunked her.

Ripples raced through her abdomen like a shock wave. The liquid pouring over her pussy, still at the waterline, enhanced the mind fuck he delivered. She exploded, thankful for the liquid cooling her off so she didn't spontaneously combust. Somewhere in the far reaches of her mind she noted the silvery strands of Jeremy's come swirling around her an instant before he fished her from the tub.

Lily continued to climax, her body racked with contractions potent enough to jerk her limbs. She flopped on the deep pile of the bathmat—as big as an area rug in most homes—like a fish out of water. Jeremy followed her down, blanketing her, echoing her moans and gasps as he ground against her slippery skin.

"Oh God," she cried out as the relief knocked her toward unconsciousness. "Better. So much better. Than anything. Anyone. Thank you...*Master*."

Jeremy stared at the woman out cold on the bathroom floor. He reached for a towel, using the corner to dab a tear from his eye. Thank God she'd missed that.

Hearing the title had always thrilled him. But earning it from her...

Jesus.

He took extra care in drying her, worshiping every curve and plane of her flawless form. His fingers shook when he gathered her hair and wrapped it in another wide cloth. He swiped himself off with a few hurried passes of the damp terrycloth then bundled Lily into his arms.

Rocking her as he walked, he wasn't surprised she didn't rouse even a bit from her unnatural slumber. Today had tested them both. He tucked her into the center of the enormous, canopied bed, drawing the luxurious sheets over her porcelain skin. The bruises on her body called to him, urging him to place a gentle kiss on each before they were obscured by the down comforter.

He craved nothing more than to crawl in beside her and wrap her in his arms, promising to shelter her from anyone who would dare to hurt her. Before he could, he had one more thing to do. Yes, he'd satisfied her temporarily.

Tamed her.

Quenched the need driving her.

But it wouldn't last.

Until the men in blue returned with the antidote, Lily would suffer periodic relapses. He had to be ready. As much as he would love to fuck her—long and slow—through the worst of the storm, his attention wouldn't be enough.

He scrubbed his hands through his hair then strode to the door naked. Fuck it. Not like the two men in the lobby hadn't seen an exposed dude before. Hell, they weren't wearing much more than him at the moment. They wouldn't blink at his display.

Well, maybe.

Ben studied him as he relayed the list of supplies he required. He'd spotted several of the items on the stage and the remainder in the holding pen where the captives had been prepped. Lily had found a way to spare all of the victims the horrors the evening could have brought. It seemed only fitting that the tools intended to break them should provide his slave relief.

His slave?

He paused his instructions.

"Is that all?" Ryan tilted his head when the hesitation stretched too long.

Shit, when had he claimed her? In his heart, he admitted he hadn't. She'd branded him the very first moment he'd laid eyes on her strutting through Black Lily in the best disguise he'd ever seen. No, that wasn't true. Her Mistress side wasn't a front. It was another part of her. One he would have to support or risk destroying the woman he was coming to...

"Master Jeremy?" Ben tapped his elbow, startling him. "Are you alright?"

"Yeah. Shit. Sorry." He raked his fingers through his hair. "Tired. She'll also need one of the fucking machines. You can leave everything inside the door. I'll see to the setup myself."

"I'll be back in thirty minutes tops."

"Thank you. With any luck, she'll sleep a few hours through at first. After that, it could get rough."

Jeremy returned to her. He angled the screen of one of his laptops, which occupied the surface of the nightstand, toward the bed. The abstract screensaver cast a soft glow over their resting place. Hopefully, she wouldn't be afraid if she woke up disoriented. Not that Lily would panic. She'd assess the situation and react accordingly, as life had trained her to do.

He crawled beside her in the nest of plush covers then tucked her to his chest. One day he hoped her instinctive defenses dulled. They would if he did his job right.

The split second of indecision she'd demonstrated—when she held his fate in her hands yet chose to submit—had convinced him. Her scars stopped short of her soul. Maybe his did too. Because every time he looked at her, something inside him, something long dormant, stretched before rattling the bars of its cage.

Damn. So brilliant.

Jeremy played with her hair. Damp strands ensnared his fingers. He twisted the end of a lock and painted moisture across her slightly parted lips. Shiny, flushed, soft. They called to him, begging him to steal a tiny taste.

"Sweet dreams, Lily." He kissed her good night, allowing himself to stare a minute more at her nestled there like an angel on a cloud.

Electrocuting his balls would be the least she'd do if she could read his thoughts.

Grinning, he situated her in the curve of his body.

A soft sigh drifted from her when she settled into his embrace.

Jeremy buried his nose in her raven tresses, wound his arm around her waist and scissored their legs. His hand naturally palmed her breast. He relaxed for the first time in months, resting during the eye of the storm.

CHAPTER TWELVE

L ily squirmed. Discomfort prodded her to shift despite the haze of half-sleep muddling her brain. She dipped into unconsciousness and back a dozen times before the simmering longing in her center refused to allow her to rest a moment longer.

She blinked as she ran through everything she could remember, starting with leaving her room, zooming past her pampering to the captivity that had followed and the epic session on stage. As soon as her mind caught up, slowing to relish the recollection of her aquatic adventure, she relaxed.

Broad male fingers painted a tender line across her cheek. Her pupils dilated in the dead of night. Focus returned bit by bit, no matter how long she wished to savor her memories.

A soft light in the corner created an unnatural dusk from somewhere over Jeremy's shoulder.

Jeremy.

"Four hours," he murmured, "You slept longer than I would have thought."

"Guess you wore me out." Holy shit, what had happened to her voice? It sounded like she'd eaten a bag of broken glass.

Lily whimpered when the bed rocked though he didn't leave her for more than an instant. His arm slithered beneath her shoulders and elevated her torso before he touched an ornate crystal glass to her lips.

She would have glugged the cool liquid. Instead, he canted the glass so only a trickle at a time ran over her parched tongue. After a few swallows, her throat seemed to function better and he increased the refreshing stream until she'd drained every last drop.

"There, better?"

"Yes, thank you." She yawned and scrubbed her eyes with the back of her hand, trying to ignore the urge to climb on top of him and ride. Had he been any other man, the thrill of using him to satisfy her urges would have appealed.

Jeremy granted other opportunities. The luxury of entrusting someone to tend to her didn't appear very often—as in *never* before. She didn't care to waste the chance.

Especially not after the gluttony of the prior evening.

"I won't take all the credit, but I did my best." A grin crossed his full lips. Then it was erased, a slight frown in its place. "How do you feel?"

She turned her head, increasing the pressure of his hand on her cheek. "Okay."

"More specific." He cataloged her answers as he lay on his side, hovering over her.

"Sleepy. Achy. Horny."

"About what I expected." The caress of his lips over hers had her sighing. "On a scale of one to ten, how bad is the horny part?"

She considered lying then dismissed the folly. He would cut through her bullshit like a knife through butter. "Seven point five two."

He laughed. "Thanks for being specific."

"Planning on fixing it?"

"Not if you address me with that sassy attitude." He nipped her lip, making her hips thrust in his direction. His hand dipped a little more, his fingertips resting on the base of her throat. An embarrassing gurgle left her at the hint of pressure. "Shh. Just taking your pulse. I wouldn't..."

Before she could assure him she didn't fear his touch, he nodded and moved on.

This time he pinched her hardening nipple between his finger and thumb.

"Don't think you can read my vitals there." It'd be worth earning a spanking to make him smile again.

He increased the force behind his grip.

Reward or a punishment? Maybe both, it hurt so good. And there it was. The drug activated the dregs of her arousal, shoving them to the forefront as bright and shiny as if they hadn't spent hours taking the edge off earlier.

No wonder the feeling suckered people into making Sex Offender a habit.

Jeremy lowered his head and consumed her other breast while his hand strummed the mound he held captive. A lava flow of need flared inside her.

"Help me." She panted as another stream of longing poured over her, amplifying instead of diminishing as she emerged more fully from unconsciousness. "Please. Sir."

"Ah, I can never resist begging." He rolled on top of her.

A gasp rattled from her chest.

His heat and toned weight settled over her, dwarfing her with his defined muscles. She couldn't stop herself from stroking his back, grabbing his ass.

The instant she yanked him tighter to the cradle of her thighs, he wrenched away.

"No, Lily." The narrow ring of his irises gleamed despite the dimness. "That isn't how we fit. Remember the bath? Remember tonight? Don't steal that experience from yourself. Or from me. I need it as much as you do. It's been so fucking long."

Memories assaulted her as her mind screamed for her to obey, to embrace the ultimate ecstasy only he could supply. With anyone else she'd have considered how she looked, how every move she made affected her partner.

Jeremy insured she couldn't assume the director role. All she could do was go along for the ride. He freed her to experience, granted her the right to soak up his attention like a bone-dry sponge. She melted into the mattress, allowing him to compress her ribs and pin her to the bed.

"There you go." He mitigated the sting of surrender with a kiss. Experienced lips caressed hers, nudging them apart so he could lick the ridges of her gums and tease the tip of her tongue with his. Sometime during the exchange, his hips returned, rubbing his erection over her slick pussy. The ache lingering from the evening's activities fed her arousal. She purred as he stroked the thick length of his cock across her mound, prodding her clit.

Need him closer. Deeper.

When he separated them, she froze. "Did I grab you again? Tie me up. I can't think when—"

"Shh." He dipped lower to sample her lips again before reaching toward the nightstand. He rummaged around the computer equipment, cursing beneath his breath. "You're doing great. It's me who's lacking practice. Damn it. I could have sworn I put a handful of condoms over here. I must be more out of the swing of things than I realized. I'll be right back."

"Wait. Don't." He froze when she bracketed as much of his rib cage as she could with her splayed fingers. "Please."

He braced himself on one elbow, returning his scrutiny to her face.

"Do you understand what you're asking for? Look at what this fucking drug has done to your eyes. You're not yourself. Not thinking...I promise I'll take care of you. Thirty seconds. You may touch yourself while I'm gone."

"God." She blinked, half-tempted to take him up on it. Anything to ease the arousal edging into unpleasantness as it danced along her sensory receptors. No, not without settling this first. "Nothing between us. Please. You know the club's rules. I'm tested every two weeks. I'm clean. It's been years since I had unprotected sex."

"Let me guess. Your father's trainers?"

"They tried everything—pain, humiliation, isolation." She swallowed hard. "Nothing broke me. My father gave them the key. Promised them I'd cave. If nothing else, he had genius when it came to people, their motivations and how to use their weaknesses against them. He knew I'd freak. Considering my mom and all the guys she slept with and how careful I was...how determined I was to be different."

"Ah, Lily." He rained butterfly kisses over her upturned face.

"I didn't find out until I burned his files after—"

"After he killed himself." Jeremy didn't judge her. He surrounded her with his heat, absorbing her pain and lending his strength.

"Yeah. He'd only chosen men who had vasectomies to fuck me." She shook her head. "In his own insane way, I think it was the nicest thing he ever did for me. He thought he was protecting me. Making me stronger. They created Mistress Lily."

"You took what they started and molded it into your own thing. You've helped so many submissives. Legitimately, as their handler. Their safe harbor to express themselves when others would have taken advantage. Not to mention the slaves you've freed. God, Lily, how many have there been? Dozens?"

"Maybe a hundred." She shivered in his arms. "It's been so long, Jeremy. So hard. Too many I couldn't protect. I'm afraid I can't last much longer. Will it ever end?"

"I promise it will." He sipped the single tear trickling along her temple.

She wasn't crying. It was the drug. Making her eyes water. That was it.

"We're going to finish this."

"I believe you." And she did. "You have no idea how attractive that is, do you?"

"What?" He tilted his head.

"Your commitment to justice. It's unreal. Rare. Such a part of you. You wear it so easily, I'm shocked Tony didn't kick you out on your ass in a heartbeat."

"Nothing could keep me from you. I'd have clawed a tunnel into this place with my bare hands if I had to. I won't be separated from you again. The last three months have killed me."

"Then don't stop now. Please, take me. Naked." She set the back of her hands on the pillow, almost as though motioning for surrender while horizontal.

He groaned. "It's such a precious gift. I don't deserve it. It's too much—too important for tonight. Let's wait until you're clearer. Until we can take other precautions or discuss the consequences."

"I get birth control shots as part of my regular health screenings. There's nothing else to consider if it pleases you. I mean...unless..."

"Unless nothing." Jeremy's hips rocked, nudging his stiff cock into the folds of her pussy. "I'm dying to mark you. No one else may see it. They may never know. But we will. You'll never be able to erase me from inside you."

"I'm not sure I could now. Maybe not since the moment I met you." Her head tossed on the fine sheets as he tortured her. So close and yet so far from where he belonged. "Damn you. What have you done to me?"

"Easy, Lily. I've loved you."

The simplicity of his statement shocked her into silence. She'd cared for many of her submissives. All of them to some degree. Others, like Malcolm, as deeply as love. She had to in order to grant their wishes. Dare she hope for more? There was a big difference between loving someone and being in love with them.

Later.

Worry about it later.

Her fingers formed a fist. Nails left impressions on the heel of her palm.

Jeremy reached between them to align himself better. Two fingers forced his erection, aimed straight for her swollen pussy, to comply with gravity despite a lust that defied all forces of nature.

She sighed when he pushed the slightest bit inside her, soothing the fingers of chemical fire gripping her in their clutches. Every place they made skin-on-skin contact, the drug's effect paled beside the impact his honest affection had on her system.

Shallow, gentle strokes of his wide, plum-shaped head through her sensitive opening had her moaning. His sensual advance terrified her even as it filled an emptiness she'd refused to acknowledge.

"That's right, let me in." He delved deeper, still with relentless tenderness.

She clenched around his cock, savoring the hiss of his breath and the plunge of his stiff flesh that followed.

"Enough of that. You can't force me to lose control." Jeremy stared into her eyes. "Uncurl your fists. Relax."

He fucked her a little harder when she complied.

"Good girl. Don't move them unless I tell you to."

"Yes, sir." Using the appellation thrilled her. She'd never dreamed of granting it to a man until she'd met Jeremy. Now she couldn't fathom living without this. Lucky. How had she gotten so damn lucky in the shitstorm of her life as to find the one human being capable of liberating her?

Lily laughed, unable to contain her joy, as he spread her moist tissue.

"What's that for?" He screwed his hips, nudging his cock against a particularly sensitive spot inside her as he devoured her smile.

Her chuckle morphed into a moan as she hugged him tight, welcoming him within her without boundaries or constraints. "You know how I like to make my subs touch each other?"

He paused, angling his head. "Yes, but I don't play like that."

"No, no. Not what I meant." Her pelvis lifted, presenting herself for his continued fucking. He resumed, making her explanation take twice as long. "So many say they've never wanted to explore until I ordered it. I've never believed their bi-for-you claims."

"Lily." He growled. "If you have a point, make it. Otherwise, save your story for the morning and savor what I'm giving you."

"I'm sub-for-you, Jeremy." She beamed up at him. "No one else. Ever. Only you."

"Hell, yes." Tendons bulged, highlighting the thick stretch of his neck. He thrust, hard, embedding himself to the root in her body. "For me. For this. For us."

His fingers meshed with hers as he clasped their hands. Pressure built on her forearms when he leaned on her, caging her in. Claustrophobia never entered the picture. With him on top of her, no one could reach her. Nothing could threaten their joining.

Jeremy trapped her ankles with his shins, completing her imprisonment.

"I'm going to come." She tried to resist. "Please, let me."

"Won't let you." He captured her lips, nipping the bottom one before roaming along her jaw to nuzzle her neck. "I'll *make* you."

174

When he clamped his mouth over the tender spot and sucked, she lost every hint of self-control. The purple badge he left on her pale skin couldn't compare to the brand he stamped on her soul. He jerked between her thighs, pumping her full of his come. The throb of his cock enhanced every spasm of her pussy until she wondered if the symbiotic duet could last eternally.

All too soon, they crashed toward reality from the heaven he'd fashioned for her.

Good thing the bed was soft.

***

The next time Lily woke—with hunger gnawing at her guts—she reached for him. Her arms didn't budge. She rested on her stomach with her head turned sideways against the mattress so her cheek lay flush. Her eyes remained closed as she wriggled, or tried. Something firm and cool trapped her ankles, probably tethered to her thighs since she couldn't straighten the right angles of her bent knees or close her spread-wide thighs.

"No faking." Jeremy slapped her ass hard enough to sting.

She would have jerked but the bondage he'd imposed kept her stationary.

"Nice job." She appreciated his handiwork, testing the figure eight brackets locking her wrists to her thighs. "Comfortable yet effective."

"Glad you approve." His chuckle rumbled from behind her a moment before his fingertip drew a line from her heel over her arch to her toes, which curled in the air. "Is your foot sore?"

"No." She couldn't resist. "How about your balls?"

"They're nowhere near as painful as your ass will be if you keep up the backtalk."

175

"Cross your heart?" She enjoyed the searing energy of pain on occasion.

"Fuck yes." He wrapped his fist in her hair and tugged until her neck bowed, bending her body into an uneven U. "I've missed the weight of my flogger in my grip as I make my prize dance. The yelps that turn into cries and moans then begging for more are my favorite. Someday, not long from now, I'll remind us both what we've sacrificed."

She glanced over her shoulder, curious about his arrangement.

Another spank heated her cheeks.

"No peeking either." He rubbed out the heat flushing her bottom then spread her cheeks wide.

The arousal saturating her turned chilly in the night air. She tried to grind her clit on the bed, seeking any measure of relief. None was granted. The slight incline produced by her elevated legs ensured she couldn't force contact. Devious bastard.

"Tell me, Lily. How bad is it now?"

"Better."

"That's not what I asked." He tsked. "How bad?"

"A six."

"Ah, damn." He paused to gather his thoughts. "I was afraid of that. It's been less than an hour, darling. I need more time."

"I'm okay."

"Don't ever lie to me." This time he spanked her harder. Beyond playful. "I can see the sheen of sweat your skin. I can hear the catch in your breathing. You need it."

"Yes, sir." No use in pretending. Their bond would require an adjustment period.

"No worries. I have you covered."

Metallic clanks piqued both professional and very, very personal curiosity. She refused to disappoint him by looking. Something blunt, cool and slightly squishy brushed her spread pussy then vanished. She tensed, unable to evade the device he must have aligned.

The unmistakable snick of a tube of lube being uncapped elevated her respiration. Jeremy coached her, "Just my fingers. Nice and wet. Ready?"

"Yes." She cried out when he penetrated her pussy, impaling her on his long digits. He slathered her with jelly, the compound slicking her already moist interior.

"So lovely." He kissed the small of her back as he withdrew his fingers. "Would you like to see my Lily arrangement?"

"I bet no one's requested that bouquet from a florist before."

"A shame, really." He petted her flank as he observed the product of his labor. "You're even more stunning than usual."

Jeremy paced as he spoke. At least that's what she thought until he commanded, "Look."

She turned her head to the other side, observing herself in the stand mirror he framed with his hands. Attempting to view the world through his lens took effort when all she craved was to fuck.

"What do you see?"

"Someone powerless."

"Try again." He shook his head and gritted his teeth. "You know better."

"Someone on the edge of discovery."

"That's better." He nodded.

"How do you know I was talking about me?" She grinned. "Maybe I meant you."

"You'd be right in either case. Every time I touch you I learn more about myself and the depth of emotion I'm capable of experiencing. Every time you entrust yourself to me, the extent of your generosity is explored."

He propped the mirror against the wall, parallel with her torso. "Keep watching."

She shuddered when he retrieved a heavy object from the foot of the bed. The attachment locked on to a metal plate, which bolted to the bar between her knees. It would have been impossible to mistake the intent of the motor leading to an aluminum pole tipped with a medium-sized, bright blue dildo.

"It's filled with gel." He answered the question in her mind before she could vocalize it. "Chilled. Not too much. The coolness won't last long, but it should counteract some of your soreness. Pleasure alone. That's all I hope for you tonight."

He fit the toy to her pussy.

Lily cried out, need and relief mingling.

A remote landed beside her on the mattress, bouncing against her shoulder. "I'll look into your eyes as it fucks you for me. As long and often as you need it."

He climbed into the bed, resting his broad shoulders on the headboard, framing her body with his powerful legs, guiding her head to rest on his lap. The reflection of their intimate embrace had her pussy kissing the tip of the refreshing dildo parked at her entrance.

She whimpered.

"What do you want? All you have to do is ask and I'll give you the world."

As bad as she needed to hold his implement within her, she needed something else more. "Let me suck your cock, please."

"Ah, damn." He tensed beneath her cheek. "As amazing as you are, it's not going to work just yet. I promise. I'll make this good for you."

"I didn't say anything about bringing you to orgasm." She nuzzled his crotch. "Or even getting you hard. I want to taste you again, feel you in my mouth. Please, sir."

His skull *thunked* against the headboard. She could have sworn she detected his lips moving in silent prayer. Then he struck in a flash, using her hair to angle her face toward his soft cock. He fed it into her greedy, open mouth.

When she hummed around him, suckling softly on the treat, he snatched the remote from the bed and triggered the forward motion of his creation. The greased probe slipped easily inside her.

"Watch your teeth." He tapped her hollowed cheek with one finger.

Lily lifted her eyes to stare into his briefly. The golden flare there fueled her desire more than any amount of decadent foreplay ever could. She shivered when she tightened on the revitalizing surface of the malleable dildo. It drilled into her steadily, consistently, undeniably.

Contentment stole over her. He'd freed her to experience, unable to do more than revel in his offering. Her lids fluttered closed as she sighed, still sucking on his flesh like a baby with a pacifier.

"That's right." He massaged the back of her head. "Relax. Settle in. Come when you need to. Rest when you don't. I'll be here. All night. I've got you."

CHAPTER THIRTEEN

"**T**his is nice." Lily breathed deeply of Jeremy's spice. The strong blend of their mingled scents couldn't erase the clean smell of him. She'd never forget it. Anytime she remembered the night before—how he'd held her, coddled her, granted her relief, taken over for the machine once he had recovered, fucked her soft and slow then fast and rough—she'd recall the unique flavor of him.

"It's just my soap. Nothing fancy."

"I like that too. But that's not what I meant. I've never slept with a man before. Never woken up with one." She traced the heated metal of his nipple piercing then several of the black and gray lines decorating his abdomen. "Do you feel okay?"

"Are you joking? I'm not the one who got high as a kite and entertained a dozen men last night. And now I'm cuddling with the woman I've been obsessed with for months after finding out reality is better than everything I've imagined. Doesn't get much better. Why?"

"You're burning up." The bottom of her stomach dropped out. "You didn't catch any Sex Offender when I opened the capsule did you?"

"Nah, I held my breath. I'm pretty sure this is how I always am."

"Mmm. Like my own personal sun."

"Snuggle up, Lily." He drew her closer. "We have a lot to discuss."

She burrowed into the furnace of his chest, allowing her lids to drift closed when comfort saturated her pores. In the heart of enemy territory, she felt safer than at any other time in her life.

Jeremy stroked her hair from the crown of her head to the swell of her ass. He petted her with lulling swirls of his fingertips as though he memorized the topography of her body's landscape.

"You're right," he whispered. "This *is* nice. I could stay here, with you, forever."

She hummed.

They lay on their sides, facing each other. Though he didn't loom over her, she gladly relinquished control, allowing him to caress every inch he could reach. She smiled when he traced the shell of her ear.

Their legs entwined as they strained closer. One of her feet rubbed his furry calf, impressed by the muscles there. She'd never grow tired of him surrounding her. Finally, she understood women who'd dedicated their lives to one man—like Isabella with Razor.

Izzy. "How's my sister?"

"She misses you."

"She hardly knows me."

"Enough to love you." He nuzzled his lips into the crook of her neck and nibbled beneath her jaw. His light beard abraded her with a fuzzy scratch. "Once Izzy makes up her mind about someone, she's loyal to a fault. She'll always care for you. Welcome you into her life."

"What about you, Jeremy?" The steady vibration of his chest against her lips soothed her, encouraging her to take a risk.

"You're part of our family. An honorary member of the men in blue. Twice over. Because even if you had no tie to Izzy, you'd still belong to me."

Lily shivered.

He hugged her tighter.

"All my life, I didn't really give a shit about being poor. I sort of learned to like the rhythm of our street and the diversity of the people who drifted in and out of the neighborhood. Only one thing had the potential to make me bitter. My father used it against me. He knew what I needed. A real family. I used to watch sitcoms on the TV in the pawnshop window across the street. I couldn't hear them or anything. I would imagine the actors were my relatives. That I could trust them to look out for me."

"We'll always be here for you, Lily. No matter what." He smoothed her carefully arched brow. "If something happens to me, they'll still have your back. If things go bad on this assignment—"

"Don't say that." She tensed in his hold.

He nodded. "Just remember. They care for you too. You know that right?"

"I'm starting to believe." She kissed the side of his neck, as far up as she could reach without shifting her boneless body.

"You'll never be alone again. I promise."

With one oath, the damage caused by at least a handful of years she'd spend scrounging to survive scabbed over and began to heal. "You help me forget everything that's come before. None of it matters when I'm with you."

"Same goes, Lily." He traced her smile, first with his fingertip then with his lips.

But did it? Or had she surfaced his long-buried pain?

Afraid to shatter the moment, she still couldn't keep herself from wondering aloud. "Last night, in the tub... I wanted to say thank you. That had to be difficult for you."

"It was what you needed." He swallowed hard.

"Tell me what you were thinking. Tell me how it made you feel when you watched me panic the first time I went below the water. I'm familiar with the sacrifices a good top sometimes makes for their charges." She grimaced. "Shit, sorry. It's habit. I mean, I'm here...if you choose to share."

He scooped his arms beneath her then rolled to his back, pillowing her on his chest. "No, don't apologize. You're free to ask me anything you like. I may not answer. Even if I don't, I'll explain why. There's a big difference between a submissive lover and a mindless robot. You know that. Maybe that was my problem all along. I needed someone who could endure the full extent of what I have to share. Someone who comprehends what it's like. Someone who can handle all of me. Someone who's not too delicate. Someone exactly like you."

They shared the silence for so long Lily assumed he'd chosen to abandon the conversation. She focused on comforting him, letting him smother her with trembling arms while she rubbed his broad chest and counted the racing beats of his heart.

"How much do you know of the accident?" His gulp rang in her ears.

"Not a lot." She bit her lip. "Probably almost nothing of the truth. By the time the story reached me it was passed through a bunch of people, an anecdote for what not to do."

"Shit." He scrunched his eyes closed.

"Sorry." Lily propped herself on her hands, which didn't come close to spanning his pecs. "I never believed the gory details. Honestly, I didn't even think you were a real person."

"I wished I wasn't for a long time after that." He clenched his hands on her ass, probably unaware of the bruises he'd leave there. "I'll never forget how she looked when I found her. Surprised. Her fingers wrapped around the scarf at her throat. So...blue."

"Jeremy—"

"No, I want to tell you, Lily. Please. I haven't said this out loud to anyone. You're right. In the past ten years it's been like she didn't exist. Me either. Not the old me. I've been hiding under some ridiculous computer whiz disguise as though I could make myself something I wasn't."

"I'm pretty sure you really are a geek at heart." She tossed a pointed stare at the equipment scattered around the room, glad to see a faint smile dusting his full lips when she returned her focus. "A sexy, dominant nerd. I saw through your Clark Kent routine the first moment I met you."

"You remind me of Karen in some ways." He relaxed his grip on her, sliding his hands to her upper thighs. "She had an impeccable sense of timing. She could make me laugh even in the middle of an intense session. I guess I always assumed she'd gotten into BDSM because of me."

"What do you mean? You can tell when a sub isn't a natural fit."

"I know. I analyzed it to death. We were young. Dated since middle school. No way could I have gotten that lucky—to find the right girl from the start. I convinced myself I was taking advantage of her." He shook his head. "Gunther tried to explain I was being a moron. Like you said...he kept assuring me she could never have gone as far as we did just to stay together. I doubted her. I tried to send her away."

"Oh Jeremy." She kissed his cheek.

"Yeah." He grimaced. "I told her to go to college, find a decent guy to settle down with, someone who wouldn't dream of hurting her like I did. When she flipped out, screaming and throwing things, I lost it. I pinned her to the wall and snarled my darkest fantasy right in her face. I told her I was a gasper. Into strangulation."

"You tried to scare her off." Lily could tell the lie had haunted him for a decade.

"Yeah."

185

She rode the rise and fall of his bellowing chest, allowing him to vent the poison he'd held so long. She dug deep into her training and forced herself to push him through the worst of the exorcism. "Finish it. Tell me."

"Karen begged me to use her. To stop underestimating her devotion." His eyes were bugged when they met hers. "I didn't even tell her I loved her when I left. She crumpled onto the floor and cried. I heard her wails from outside her apartment building until I shut the door to my car."

"Every couple fights, Jeremy."

"Not like that." He clutched her to his chest. "She swore she'd ask another Dom at Guther's to train her. I forbade it. I gave her no choice. I stole any safe outlet for her curiosity. I drove her to experiment on her own and practically dared her to prove herself worthy of my command."

"You didn't intend to. Not if you really believed she submitted only for you."

"How fucking arrogant was I?"

"You've paid a high enough price for one mistake, don't you think?" She couldn't stop herself from kissing him, showing him through her gentle caresses how much she wished she could absorb his pain.

"I'm not sure it'll ever be enough." His story turned raspy. "I went straight to Gunther, who talked me off the ledge not only as my mentor but also as my friend. He told me to bring Karen to the club so he could moderate a session for us. Whatever she needed. I spent the whole night getting my shit straight and planning out my apology when I should have raced to her, the hell with fancy promises and proposals. I went to see her the next morning with three dozen roses."

"Oh God." No wonder he'd cut himself off for so long. An honorable man like him could never condone failing someone they'd sworn to protect.

"I'll always remember the petals scattered over her pale, stiff body. I didn't know what to do. I called Gunther. I tried CPR. He had to rip me off her when he arrived on the scene. I think I might have still had those fucking flowers in my hand. I don't know. I've tried so hard to forget."

"No more, Jeremy." She clung to him as tight as he did to her. "She doesn't have to live in the shadows of your memory anymore. And neither do you. Don't disrespect her. Don't make the lesson be learned for nothing. Stay true to yourself. Your needs and mine. I'll know if you take things light on me. I can handle anything you have to give."

"I know you can." He stared straight into her eyes. "I won't let you down."

She leaned into the hand cupping her cheek. "I have one little problem..."

"What's that?" He held his breath.

"I think your old boss is kind of pissed at me."

"You know Gunther?"

"Yeah, sort of. He scouted me from Black Lily. For a new club he's opening in the city." She chuckled at his wide eyes. "You hadn't heard?"

"I don't keep my ear to the ground on the kink front much anymore."

"More like you avoided it so you weren't tempted."

He smacked her ass with a glancing swing that resulted in more sound than sting.

"Gunther attended several of my sessions, offering me a slot in his organization after every one. He's pretty convincing. I accepted a position at his club to escape my father, the whole situation, once I realized the bastard had used me. And then I discovered the women being sold. I had to renege on my contract. I couldn't walk away from that. If we could settle this once and for all... Well, will you smooth things over?"

"Even though Black Lily is all yours? You'd still leave?"

"I'm considering a merger. Combined, we'd rock the market. To be honest, the Lily holds too many ghosts these days."

His fingers clenched on her waist.

Jeremy grinned. "That old softie is going to love you. He sends me a birthday card every year. I think I'll use you to shield me from a serious beating. He'll be so happy to have you maybe he'll forget about all I've fucked up. Especially if I tell him about how much you enjoy sex with more than one guy at once. Would you like me to share you with the boss man?"

Lily shivered. "There's something about him. I might be willing to sacrifice for you."

"Yeah, he kicks ass." Jeremy sighed. "I miss him."

"I'm sure he'll be glad to have you home. Even if for a visit."

"I hope you're right." Jeremy flipped them, settling between her thighs. "It's time to reclaim what's mine. Time to be the man I was destined to be."

"Show me," she begged.

And he did.

***

Matt banged on the door at the top of the open-backed staircase. He grimaced when the cracked wood bowed and paint flakes fluttered to the ground, two stories below. Hell, the railing rattled with each of his blows. Probably the piece of shit would give. He and Clint would land on the potholed blacktop below, impaled on the rusty metal.

"Easy," Clint growled. "Are you trying to scare the shit out of Jambi? It's the dead of the night. Normal people are sleeping."

"We can't hang out up here. Anyone could see us, completely exposed." He snarled at his partner. "Besides, you know her schedule as well as I do. She probably got off shift less than an hour ago."

Sure enough, the warm orange glow of a dying incandescent bulb spilled from the corner of the window nearby as Jambrea peeked from behind her frilly curtains. The rattle of chains and locks flipping came a moment later. At least she took precautions.

Too bad the shitty door would disintegrate with one swift kick.

"We'll put in a steel one next day off." Clint must have caught his mumbled curses.

He nodded.

"Uh..." Jambrea tugged down the thin cotton of her oversized nightshirt, which featured some ridiculous cartoon character. Her close-cropped hair was damp as though she'd finished showering not long ago. She pressed her glasses higher up her nose with one finger on the crossbar above her bridge. "Hi."

"Can we come in?" Clint asked over his partner's shoulder when it became apparent Matt couldn't yank his tongue inside his mouth fast enough to do the job.

"Yeah, sure. It's kind of a mess in here, though. I've been getting organized. Haven't made it to the kitchen yet."

"Couldn't be worse than Clint's apartment." Matt swallowed hard as he willed himself to stop staring at the outline of her hard nipples. Clint's fist to the middle of his back aided his efforts. Matt flung a glare over his shoulder. Clint smiled sweetly as though he hadn't left a bruise the size of an orange.

"Shut up, asshole," Clint hissed between his curved lips.

When Jambrea turned and led them inside her home, both of them hurried after her. Matt felt like a giant in her cozy living room. He easily occupied half of the free space. Hunching his shoulders helped a little. Not a heck of a lot.

"Cute." Clint surveyed the eclectic mix of line drawings, trinkets and military paraphernalia dotted around the room. "It suits you. What's with the Air Force stuff?"

"I was in the service for a few years right out of school. I trained as a medic before deciding to pursue nursing."

"No shit."

Matt let his partner do the talking. He merely observed, cataloging every detail of the woman who'd intrigued him with her disparate shy and saucy sides.

"Who's this little guy?" Clint wiggled his finger on the glass of a ten-gallon aquarium filled with neon pink rocks and a silly plastic scuba diver blowing bubbles. A googly-eyed goldfish swam over to investigate.

"Guys, meet Parker." Jambrea laughed when the fish smacked the surface, splashing Clint through the crack in the glass top. "He's a fatty. Give him some flakes and he'll be your pal for life."

"Cool." Clint shook some of the red, green and yellow food into the tank. Parker gobbled it up then retreated to his outrageous ceramic castle.

"So, not that I mind you stopping by before the ass-crack of dawn or anything..."

"Ah, shit." Matt scrubbed his hand over his face. How could he have forgotten about their assignment so fast? "Sorry, we're here on business."

Did he imagine the flicker of disappointment in her pretty hazel eyes?

"Of course. I figured." She wandered toward the kitchen. "Let me put some coffee on."

"Don't go to any trouble for us." Clint waved her off.

"It's for me, not you." Jambrea stifled a yawn behind her hand. "I worked a double. Was about to crash."

"Shit. Sorry, Jambi." Clint deflected her toward the couch. "Take a load off. Matt will make you something to drink."

Bastard. Matt ignored his partner's arm around Jambrea's lush curves as the jerk steered her onto the comfy-looking sofa. As if Matt had a clue how to brew coffee. Though he drank about a gallon of the stuff on their late-night duties, it always came from the station's crusty pot or some gas station along their patrol route.

How hard could it be?

Matt rummaged around on the counter until he came up with a stainless-steel container of grounds and a box of filters. He dumped a pile of the black granules straight from the tin then flipped on the faucet a little too hard.

The handle popped off.

"Oh, shit!" He jammed it back on before anyone noticed. Once the pot filled with tap water, he tipped it over the coffee. It ran out onto the counter.

"Are you finding everything okay?" He looked up from mopping the spillage with a wad of paper towels in time to catch Clint tugging her down to the microfiber cushion once more.

"Yeah, yeah. Fine." Matt poked around the back of the coffee pot until he found a flap on the top. Hopefully putting the water in there wouldn't break the machine. He crossed his fingers and poured.

Nothing happened.

Nice. He hit the on switch and stared long enough to be satisfied the hisses and pops sounded normal before rejoining the duo—he refused to think of them as a couple—in the other room. When Jambi tasted his coffee she'd forget all about the way Clint's hand massaged the back of her neck while they waited for him to finish.

His partner sprawled on the couch, pushing Jambrea past the middle of the sofa. He refused to surrender so easily. Awkward and not giving a damn, Matt squeezed into the space remaining. Not his problem the move left Jambrea practically sitting in his lap.

He grinned over her head at Clint.

The other man flipped him off, trying to turn his blatant middle finger into an innocent jaw scratch when Jambrea turned her attention in that direction.

"Oh my God." She slapped one hand on each of their thighs. "Enough. I can't take another second of this."

Both men retreated to opposite corners of the couch.

Matt hadn't meant to crowd her.

"What's wrong? You're scaring me." Her nails dug into his knee as the pitch of her request rose. "Who is it this time? Please tell me no one's dead at least."

"Ah, fuck." Matt tugged her to his side, smothering her fears. "Sorry, we're idiots. Didn't mean to keep you in suspense. It's Lily—"

"Oh my God." Jambrea's face went white.

"No, no..." Clint jumped in to save Matt's mangled attempt at comfort. "She's okay. Mostly. She took Sex Offender."

"Why would she do that?" Jambrea would have launched to her feet if Matt had let her. Her strength was no match for his arms, which looked enormous wrapped around her. "Doesn't she realize how dangerous it is? The test results are insane. I've never seen anything like it. Especially after her dad and Izzy's ex-husband—"

"It's a long story." Matt shook his head. He couldn't describe what they'd witnessed anyway. The battle between her and Jeremy culminating in her graceful surrender still rocked him. "It came down to her or JRad."

Jambrea nodded. "Of course. She wouldn't do that to him. There's something between them, isn't there?"

"If there wasn't before there sure as hell is now." Clint sounded as reverent as Matt felt. Sharing in the glow their friends generated had ranked high on his list of life experiences.

"You need some of the anecdote the hospital's been developing." She sighed. "If you'd called me while I was still there we could've saved some time. How much SO did she take? Is she suffering badly? Is anyone monitoring her blood pressure? Her pulse? Her temperature?"

"I'm not sure how big the dosage was. It fit in a capsule like this." Clint held his thumb and forefinger a half inch apart.

"Shit." Jambrea pushed until Matt let her escape from his arms.

He missed the pressure of her breasts on his ribs. Damn, what was wrong with him? He'd already gotten laid once tonight in one of the most intense fucks of his life.

Matt shifted the bulge of his hardening cock. Not now.

"Actually," she glanced at the clock. "I bet Lacey is still at the hospital. A three-car accident called in to the ER as I was making my last rounds. I'll give her my codes. She can swing by on the way home."

"I'm not sure that's a good idea." Clint glanced up, seeking Matt's opinion.

"Do Ty and Mason still insist on picking her up?" Matt asked Jambrea.

"Yeah." She smiled. "Lacey complains, but she likes it or she wouldn't allow it. All the nurses tease her about her cops."

"That's what I'm worried about." Matt held her hand. He noticed Clint took the other. "We have to be careful not to blow our cover. We can't be hanging out with other cops in public."

"Stay inside. Lacey can run the stuff up quick. Tyler and Mason don't have to get out of the car. Everyone knows we're friends. They've dropped me off loads of times when my car's been in the garage."

"You need something more reliable," Clint scolded her.

She shrugged. "I like my little junker. Never have to worry about door dings or whether or not someone's going to steal it. Bessie gets the job done."

"Do you really call your car Bessie?" Matt laughed.

"No. You get the point though."

The force of her full grin stole his breath.

"You should do that more, Jambi." He brushed his free thumb over the corner of her lips. "So pretty when you smile."

She swallowed hard, causing his stare to migrate to the flex of her pale neck.

Clint cleared his throat. "I think the coffee's ready."

Jambrea hummed, and Matt cursed. He headed to the kitchen.

"Mugs are in the cabinet to the left of the sink." Jambrea left him to pour three helpings while she dialed Lacey on her cell. The short exchange concluded as Clint took one of the cups Matt balanced. For once it came in handy to be giant-sized.

"Okay, we'll see you in ten." Jambrea disconnected then accepted a chipped vessel from him.

"Thank you." She inhaled the aromatic steam before testing a sip. Her eyes widened before she whispered. "Mmm. Good."

Matt's shoulders spread wide. Damn straight.

Until Clint ruined the effect by spraying his coffee into a mist across the living room. "Oh Jesus. That's a fucking health and safety hazard if I ever saw one. What are you trying to do, poison us?"

"That bad?" He glanced at Jambrea, who shrugged.

He chugged a little, the burn on his tongue disguising the taste for an instant. "Nasty! Shit. Sorry."

Matt barely resisted wiping his palm over his tongue.

Jambrea giggled. "It's the thought that counts. We all know things could be worse."

That sobered them pretty damn quick.

"How is Lily?" She blushed. "I've heard it can hurt really bad if you're exposed to Sex Offender and you don't..."

Matt looked to Clint. Clint stared right back, unwilling to bail him out of the sticky situation. They let the silence linger too long.

"Oh." Jambrea blinked. "Right then."

"Morselli had a party. He used her as the main attraction." Matt couldn't think of a polite way to phrase it. "There were a lot of guys there."

"They gang raped her?" Tears pooled in Jambrea's eyes, making them shine.

Matt framed her face with his hands. She looked tiny compared to his thick fingers. "I promise you they didn't."

Clint edged nearer. He rubbed her back, soothing her terror. "I can't explain it, Jambi. It was like she gave herself to JRad and let him use her. Not in a bad way."

"It was amazing." Matt tried to rescue Clint. "He directed the action, selecting the guys who could be what she needed, when she needed it, even when she was completely out of control and couldn't fend for herself. He knew exactly what to do. She loved every minute."

Jambrea worried her bottom lip between her teeth.

"I promise. She wanted it. Every guy she fucked, she screamed for more. She came over and over. They all worshiped her."

"I believe you." She wilted a little, sagging against the cushions.

Matt noticed she crossed her legs one direction then the other, fidgeting between him and Clint. Did they make her uncomfortable?

"Then what's this about?" He brushed his fingertip over the swollen patch on her lip.

She sucked in a breath.

"I wondered... Did you?" Her brows lifted as she turned to Clint. "And you?"

Honor refused to allow them to lie, despite the damage it might do to their prospects with this sweet girl. "Yeah. I did. We both did."

She scrunched her eyes closed. "I see."

"Does that bother you?" Clint chafed the goose bumps rising on her forearm.

"A bit." She winced. "If I'm honest, I'm a little jealous."

"Only a little?" Matt could have decked Clint for making light of her feelings.

Still, she smiled in return. Damn.

"Yeah, I mean I'm used to guys passing me over for women like her."

"What the fuck is *that* supposed to mean?" Matt's hackles rose.

"You know, skinny, sexy, petite..."

"Fuck that bullshit." Clint angled her jaw toward him, refusing to allow her to evade the rare frustration etched onto his face. "You're adorable exactly as you are."

"I'm not saying I disagree." She shut him right up. "But other guys have."

"Neither of us would." Matt couldn't believe men would be that blind or stupid.

"Thanks." She snorted as if she didn't think he was dead serious.

Jambrea might as well have triple-dog dared them.

Matt leaned in while Clint scooted closer, trapping her between them. "You like the idea of Lily with all those guys? Have you ever had sex with more than one man at once?"

He cupped her jaw in his hand to prevent her from giving herself whiplash, which she would if she continued to glance back and forth between them so much.

"It sounds pretty hot. A crazy thing to dream about. You know, like Lacey with Ty and Mason. That's got to rock." A light blush spread up her neck to her cheeks. "Not that I've really thought about it or anything."

"I gotta say, I have. About a million times." Clint surprised the hell out of Matt with that revelation. "Nothing I pictured compared to what I witnessed tonight. The intensity blew me away."

Matt cleared his throat when they waited for him to respond. "I wouldn't have expected to enjoy sharing my partner with someone else."

"That phone pole in your shorts didn't seem to have any trouble with it in the heat of the moment." Clint dropped his stare to where Matt's half-hard dick inflated rapidly toward full-on erection.

"All I know is how much better it could be with someone I was already attracted to." He dropped his face close to Jambrea's, lowering his voice along with his lips. "With you."

Matt groaned when his lips encountered her pliant, parted mouth. He exposed his curiosity and pent-up desire. She consumed every scrap and begged for more with plaintive whimpers. When the rasp of Clint's encouragement broke through the haze in Matt's mind, he hesitated for an instant.

"Cold feet?" Clint took smarmy to a whole new level.

Matt refused to be dissuaded that easily. He stared at his partner as he redoubled his assault on Jambrea's better sense. She relented by degrees, surprising him with an aggressive attack on his crotch.

Clint's yelp seemed to indicate she'd taken them both in hand. Hell, maybe this could be a lot more fun than he'd assumed. Truth be told, the weeks of feeling at odds with his partner had taken their toll. He hated arguing with the fucker. Not that he'd ever admit it.

"My turn." Masculine fingers prodded Matt's jaw, separating him from his treat. Somehow the touch didn't wilt his hard-on.

Watching up close and personal as Jambrea and Clint made out certainly didn't affect him either. Unless it was to make him hornier. Could that even be possible?

His fingers toyed with the hem of Jambi's nighty. About to make a break for her free breasts, craving the weight of them in his palm, he jumped when a crash from the doorway shattered the moment.

Clint rocketed to his feet, a little unsteady. He stepped in front of Jambrea, sheltering her from the intruders.

"What the...?" Mason glowered from beside the splintered wood that used to be Jambrea's door. "Are you fucking kidding me? You three are so busy fooling around you couldn't hear Lacey knocking or shouting out to you?"

"You could have called before going Rambo on the fucking door." Matt admitted to himself he was more pissed off about the ache in his groin.

"We did, dumbass." Tyler bustled Lacey in out of the night. "No one answered. We got worried."

"I felt something moving in my pants but I, uh, didn't think it was my phone." Clint scowled. "Sorry."

"Yeah, yeah." Mason grinned as Lacey rushed over to Jambrea and smothered her in a hug. "We know all about that. Sorry to crash the party. We've got your stuff here."

He tossed an insulated bag to Matt. "You better hit the road. It has to stay cold or it loses its effectiveness. Right, Jambrea?"

She blinked, dazed and overwhelmed. Matt wished he could tuck her into bed. Preferably one with him in it. And maybe Clint too. Maybe.

"Yes." She waved her hands toward the mess on the floor. "I'll take care of this. You need to give that to Lily

198

within the hour. I'd feel better if I could examine her myself."

"No." All four men barked in unison.

"Don't bother arguing." Lacey rolled her eyes. "Save your breath."

"Trust me." Matt placed one hand on her shoulder. "She's fine. I swear. JRad stayed with her. He'll take care of her."

"Oh, I bet he will." Tyler singsonged.

Mason slapped the slighter man in the gut with the back of his hand. "Quit that."

Clint spun toward the wreckage of the door after one last heated look in Jambrea's direction. "This isn't finished."

"No, it's hardly even begun." Matt licked his lips, savoring the taste of her.

"We'll board up the door and take Jambi to our house tonight." Mason crossed his arms over his chest and planted his feet.

"Fine." She grumbled. "As long as I can put Parker in his travel bowl. I'm not leaving him here alone."

"Deal." Tyler grinned. "This should be fun."

CHAPTER FOURTEEN

Jeremy leaned his hip against a marble-topped vanity as he surveyed their haven. The rumpled bed couldn't arrest his attention for long when Lily wriggled into a skin-tight, red leather outfit. A high collar covered every inch of her below her jaw. It didn't diminish the plump mounds of her breasts, which the strategic squish of material over her ribs enhanced and showcased.

Ebony rope fashioned from her hair slithered along her spine, dusting her ass as she squirmed into the matching pants. Shit, he would have thought he'd never sport another boner after last night. Or this morning. Wrong.

"Would you like a hand?" He focused on relaxing his muscles. Out of sight he gripped the edge of the ornate fixture supporting him.

"Nope. I have a lot of practice at this." Her dazzling smile punched him in the gut.

She sucked in her svelte stomach and yanked the laces holding the bodice on the suit before buckling the cinch straps that transformed her into a living, breathing—if shallowly—BDSM action figure. *Jesus Christ.*

Tight globes reflected light off the shiny surface of her coated ass when she bent to retrieve her matching thigh-high boots with wicked six-inch stiletto heels.

A muffled gasp reached his ears when the material pulled tight between her legs.

"Still?"

"Only a three and a half now." She winced over her shoulder.

"You promised to tell me when you need to come." He tensed until the sharp edge of the table dug into his bunched thigh. "If you suffer, it'll be because I decide to torture you, not because you're depriving yourself without properly informing me of your condition."

Strong enough to bury any discomfort, she could undermine his control whether on purpose or by force of habit. He refused to allow her the opportunity. She'd endured enough senseless pain before meeting him.

"I will." She concentrated on fastening the dozens of metal clasps laddering her boots like an exaggerated zipper. The closures transformed the gentle curve of her cut calves into something formidable and undeniably sexy.

Lily inspected the flogger she lifted from a case beside the rest of her belongings. Her tools had to be immaculate before she'd use them on her stable. Jeremy respected her attention to detail and her commitment to serving the needs of those entrusted to her care.

No doubt about it. She was a consummate professional.

"I'm dying to watch your sessions." His nostrils flared as she strapped a belt around her waist and stabbed the handle of the flogger into its holster. Wide strips of the fringe splayed across her leg like a plume of feathers on an exotic bird.

"I'm glad." She drew on crimson leather gloves, flexing her fingers until they worked into the supple leather, which molded to conform to her figure as it warmed with the heat radiating from her.

Not many other people would have noticed her infinitesimal hesitation.

Jeremy abandoned his perch and flew to her side. He used her hair to position her face where required to stare into her gorgeous eyes. "What?"

"Nothing."

"Not acceptable, Lily." He tugged a little harder. "Everything is something when it pertains to you. You'll share it all with me and leave it to me to decide what's important and what's not."

"Yes, sir," she whispered. "That's going to take some getting used to."

"I can be patient." He kissed her maroon lips softly, uncaring about the transfer of the pigment to his own mouth. She tasted too good to stop after a nibble. "I won't punish you. This time. Now spill."

"Things will be different." She dropped her guard. A curtain fell, revealing all the inner workings of her mind. Faint lines crinkled the edges of her heavily lined eyes. "By now rumors will have spread. Everyone in the complex will know about last night. They'll talk."

"Damn straight." He couldn't suppress his shit-eating grin. "You're mine. No one can deny it."

"So, how will that work?" Her bottom lip quivered for a moment before she bit it. "Will my slaves obey, or will they look to you instead? I can't stand the thought of all their training evaporating. I may kneel for you, but they belong to me. That part of me isn't changing. It's who I am."

"Hush." Jeremy nuzzled her temple. "What happens in this room is between us. I won't deny I crave you at my mercy. Part of what makes your deference so special is how strong you are. It's the difference between domesticating a stray alley cat and taming a tiger—how naturally you could turn the tables and wield control. I adore the woman you are. All of you. I would never undermine your authority with your subs, though I would enjoy observing your handiwork."

"Of course." She nodded. "I'd like you to attend. I can't think of any of my stable who would object. If anything, the boys will enjoy it."

"That's where it ends, Lily." He fingered the seams of the outfit she wore, a modern marvel of fashion engineering. "Me. Watching. Looking after your safety. Hell, even my paperboy is bigger than you."

"Hey." Her chin rose. "I can take care of myself."

"True, but it's my job now. My pleasure."

"Who the hell reads a newspaper anymore anyway?" She glanced at the pile of computer equipment in the corner before scoffing, "Don't you have live feeds from at least fifty countries piped into your brain via some wireless connection you MacGyvered?"

"Misdirection?" He laughed. "A lame, entry-level trick. Don't waste our time detracting from what's important. I won't stand for you to be harmed if things spiral out of control, but I won't interfere unless you really need me. I promise."

"Fair enough." She smiled. "Thank you."

"You're welcome." He fingered the ridge of leather between her legs. "Later you can demonstrate your gratitude. I'd kill to fuck you in this outfit. The pants open here, don't they?"

"Yes, sir." She sighed when he pressed the access panel in the general region of her clit.

"When we return, you'll crawl into the bed. Wait for me on all fours. Better yet, put your face down and leave your ass up. Beg me to drive out all thought and replace it with pleasure. No one for you to look after. Only your feelings to consider when you obey me."

A knock startled them both.

Good thing or they might not have made it out of the room anytime soon and her slaves were used to routine. She and Jeremy had both agreed the location shift meant Lily had to regiment the rest of their training. Stick to their usual schedules. Calm them and assure them she hadn't forgotten about them. Guarantee they were protected and untouched by Morselli's taint.

Jeremy guided her toward the door by her elbow, placing her behind him when he cracked the entrance.

"JRad, let us in."

He admitted Matt and Clint.

"You're free to speak in here. I've got the room jammed." He nodded toward the partners. They were sweating and breathing hard, as though they'd sprinted an entire mile.

"The antidote." Matt huffed as he thrust a bag toward Jeremy. "Jambrea says Lily needs to take it soon, before it warms to room temperature. Morselli's asshole security team raked over our car with a fine-toothed comb. Wasted over a half an hour and this place is fucking huge."

Jeremy reached into the bag and tested the vial. Still chilly.

"I think you're in time." He uncapped the medicine and wrapped one arm around Lily's shoulders. "Drink."

She leaned into his embrace, tipping her head back, trusting him to hold her steady.

Fuck yes.

Jeremy poured the thick brown syrup into her mouth.

She gagged but kept the fluid in.

"Fuck, that's disgusting!" Lily coughed and sputtered.

Clint jogged to the bar in the corner and poured her a drink. Jeremy gave the man credit for hopping over the fucking machine without comment.

"Here."

She chugged the double shot of cola he returned with. "I could use something a little stiffer than that. What am I, a baby?"

"Hey, at least I didn't make you a Shirley Temple."

She smiled. "Thank you both. And Jambrea too."

"Hopefully we didn't get her in trouble." Jeremy squinted when Clint and Matt shuffled their feet.

"Did you two finally make a move on her?" Lily perked up, straining against Jeremy's forearm as she studied their reactions.

"Would have if supercops Mason and Ty hadn't kicked the fucking door down."

Jeremy laughed, imagining the look on their faces.

"Oh sure, real funny, JRad," Clint grumbled. "You have your girl right here."

"Amazing how that changes your perspective." He turned and brushed a wisp of loose hair off Lily's cheek. "Though right now, I would prefer you were somewhere safer."

"Oh hell no, you're not sending me away." She propped her hand on her hip.

"No. I don't think I could anymore." Jeremy stroked her face with his thumb.

"Agent Sterns wouldn't like that very much either. The dickhead was furious Lily took the drug. He said she should have faked it and kept the sample for the DEA to analyze."

Matt's disgust convinced Jeremy his boss had spouted more nonsense, which his friend filtered. Good thing Jeremy hadn't heard it personally or he wouldn't have held his tongue. "That bastard can go fuck himself."

"I agree." Matt sighed. "The only thing that shut him up was convincing him the two of you would find some more by telling Morselli she's craving another hit...or maybe that you're planning to dose her again whether she likes it or not."

Jeremy squeezed Lily a little too tight. She squeaked.

When he peeked at her, he noticed the flush in her cheeks had died down and the fury in her gaze burned through the crystal clear lenses of her eyes.

"Damn, how fast does that shit work? I can see a difference already."

"I thought it was my imagination." She sighed. "I still want you. I always do. But now it doesn't ache. The fire inside me is disappearing. I've got pins and needles all over. It's okay, Jeremy, let them think whatever it takes to keep us in the game. We need some time. Free rein to explore, ask questions, dig for answers."

"And evidence," Clint added.

"Are you ready for your rounds, or should you lie down for a minute and see what happens?" They both knew going back to bed meant delaying their exit by an hour at least. Drug or no drug, the chemistry between them would always boil over.

The three men stared at her as though waiting for her to collapse. They should have known better.

She sliced her hand through the air. "No way in hell am I giving people a reason to call me weak."

"They wouldn't dare..." Clint smiled. "Mistress Lily."

"And don't you forget it." She smacked his ass as she strutted from the room. Ben and Ryan grinned when they took in her cheery disposition.

"Clint, Matt, take over watch on our quarters. I'm guessing Lily will want these two with her?" He lifted his eyebrows at his partner.

"Damn straight. Let's go, boys." She strode away.

The men followed her, avoiding tripping over their tongues at the spectacular rear view she granted them.

Lily savored the reverberation of her heels snapping against the tile with staccato blasts. Somehow, having Jeremy by her side made her more confident. More adventurous. More proud of the physique she used to tame her men. She'd gotten so accustomed to presenting her body as a prop, she'd forgotten what it was like to enjoy living in her own skin.

Hell, maybe she'd never really known at all. She certainly hadn't experienced sex as exhilarating as what they'd shared last night. His hand landed in the small of her back when her stride hitched at the memory. A smile spread across her lips as the heat of his palm soaked through the thick hide she wore.

She refused to admit how much she craved his approval. More even than she had hoped for her father's, before he'd proved himself unworthy of her effort.

Lily headed straight for the facilities she'd designed to her specifications. She would never jeopardize her clients. They were so much more than customers to her. She hated thinking of them in those terms. Some had grown into deep friends. It was rare for her to accept a new man into her stable and all of them had chosen to accompany her to Morselli's facility despite her frank explanation of the inherent risks.

The men—bouncers she'd brought from Black Lily—who guarded the entrance to the area, stepped aside as she approached. "Good morning, Steve. Lucas."

They held the doors wide for her, glaring at Jeremy. "How are you, Mistress Lily?"

"I'm fine." She patted Lucas's forearm, which was tight enough she feared it might shatter.

Jeremy tensed. He didn't interfere. Instead he waited for her to handle the situation. Her heart soared.

"We heard…" Steve didn't look her in the eye. A vein in his neck bulged. "We would have kept you safe. This is exactly why we tried to convince you to allow us to shadow you yesterday."

"I don't need protection from Jeremy. Period. I'll be staying with him for the remainder of our time here. It should make you less jumpy to know he has friends nearly as tough as you two watching our rooms, keeping an eye on things while we're out. As for my guests, Ben and Ryan will be joining our group. Since they're familiar with the household, I'll keep them with me most of the time." She introduced the men to each other, careful not to mention Morselli. Her staff didn't need to know how close to ugly things had gotten. "You did as I asked, yes?"

"The area is secure. Other than the food deliveries last night and this morning, no one has come in or out." Lucas reassured her. "When you missed early check-in, we had the managers set your slaves in the milking room as you instructed."

"Thank you. It's vital I can rely on you to worry about the safety of my charges. If I think you might leave your posts, I'll be distracted."

"*We* won't let you down." Steve flung a nasty look at her trio of protectors.

"We'll cover her." Ryan spoke low to Lucas as they passed by. Lily couldn't help her smile.

"Used to having every man in the world wrapped around your little finger, aren't you?" Jeremy whispered in her ear.

"Planning to join them?"

"Not exactly." He nipped her lobe. "So what was that bruiser talking about?"

"Who, Steve? He's a pussycat." Lily smiled when Ben muttered something lewd about sharp claws under his breath. "If you behave, I'll consider letting him play with you later, sweetie. He enjoys a bonus now and then."

A chuckle escaped her at Ben's wide-eyed hope.

She turned to Jeremy. "Why don't I show you?"

Her fingers wrapped around the long brass handle leading to the holding room where her submissives awaited her, patiently or not.

"Please do." His pupils had dilated until only a sparse ring of gold edged the darkness.

"You're sure it won't change how you think of me?" She worried her lip.

"Only to make me crave you more. You'll suffer later for every minute you make me stand here with this fucking hard-on in my pants." He sidled close, rubbing the bulge over her ass. "You're sexy when you're in charge."

Ryan or Ben, she couldn't tell which, surrendered a little moan as confirmation.

"All right, but don't say I didn't warn you." She winked at them over her shoulder. "These men have been with me for months. Some as long as years. They accept everything I can give them, and I wouldn't disrespect them by walking on eggshells to soothe any squeamishness you develop once we're inside."

"Do it, Lily." Jeremy swatted her ass. "No more stalling."

"Yes, sir," she whispered before flinging the doors open wide and marching through them.

Every man in the space stopped breathing. Those who could whipped their gazes around to land on her. A chorus of, "Good morning, Mistress" filled the long hall and bounced off the vaulted ceilings. Candles cast warm light over the space. Area rugs unfurled in patches over the marble floor and plush pads bore dents from the men who'd recently lounged in them while Lily's assistants— Suz, Kitty, Dawn, Gigi and Ive—had executed her preparation instructions.

The men occupied a variety of stations, molded into the specific position she'd selected for each personally based on their individual desires and how she'd played with them recently. Detailed notes and recordings helped her zero in on maximizing their enjoyment and ensuring variety in their training. Though she conducted a group session today, no one would experience exactly the same method of torture or ecstasy.

In between scenes, this would be an inviting space for the men to relax and enjoy each other's company. Camaraderie between like-minded individuals was one integral factor in her pets electing to apply to her harem. Ultra-selective, she'd accepted the proposals of a dozen or so who meshed seamlessly.

Sure, they had occasional squabbles. She suspected at last half of those were a sham, agreed on by the participants to encourage her to punish them.

Lily obliged their needs, gave them everything she could. She'd never before wondered why she anticipated them so damn well. Not until she met Jeremy, and realized he could do the same for her, did she fully comprehend the magnitude of the courage necessary for them to accept her manipulations.

Her thoughts ran to Malcolm's funeral for a split second. The subtle comfort Jeremy had given her there and at the hospital afterward... Not to mention the day she'd freed victims from the dungeons of her own establishment. No one else could have reached her.

These men needed her to do the same for them.

"Good morning." She smiled into their warm expressions, meeting the gaze of each man who'd pledged himself to her. "I trust you've all settled in. If there's anything at all you need, you only have to ask."

She wandered between the stations, each one presenting a slave in some fashion or another. A hush descended over the men as she checked their bindings, tested equipment and approved of her assistants' workmanship.

Training had been her career for nearly a decade. It also satisfied her.

Someday her apprentices would be Mistresses themselves. If she did her job properly, they'd spread joy and fulfill wishes instead of wreaking physical or mental havoc on vulnerable, trusting submissives. After her surrender to Jeremy, she admitted the alluring prospect of ultimate trust had driven her for so long she hadn't realized she'd sought the same for herself.

"I'd like you all to meet some special guests," she projected so even Joseph and Leon, who occupied the far side of the room, could hear her introductions. "Today is a big day. We have two new playmates, Ben and Ryan.

I'm sure you'll welcome them later. I also think it's only fair for you all to know I've pledged myself to Master Jeremy."

A hush descended over the group who'd whispered to their neighbor about the rare additions. She petted Peter's clenched fist until he relaxed his grip, allowing his bindings to cradle him on an inclined table once more.

"Don't worry, boys." She allowed her happiness to shine through. "He's agreed not to interfere in our relationships. If you object to him observing our exchanges I'll consider your requests. Otherwise, I expect you to show him the proper respect he deserves."

Jeremy cupped her elbow when a tendril of doubt wormed through her heart.

"I swear to care for her as well as she tends to her charges," Jeremy addressed the gathering. "Nothing changes between you. The bond you share is sacred. I'll never tread over that line unless she invites me to participate and you consent. You have nothing to fear from me."

Peter drew her attention from the gladness expanding her insides near to bursting. "Lucky."

Simon nuzzled her other hand, which lingered near his cheek. "Congratulations, Mistress."

"Thank you." She winked at the men surrounding her. "I'm thrilled to show you all off. So don't expect me to go easy on you because I'm in a good mood."

"I hope not. I love it when you play hard." Peter groaned when she pinched his nipple. "Yes, like that. Please may I have more?"

"Kitty." She tilted her head at the newest of her assistants. "Where are the clamps I ordered for Peter?"

CHAPTER FIFTEEN

"**R**ight here." The efficient blond extended a silver platter with the shiny metal clips, connected by a thin chain, laid out nicely. "I thought you'd like to give him your gift in person."

"Very nice." Lily double-checked the tension. Not too tight for a beginner set. "You did well. Go ahead and apply them, Kitty. Carefully."

"Thank you, Mistress." She followed orders, monitoring Peter's whimpers and groans while she slowly released the grip between her fingers, which counteracted the springs. When they were fully in place, Lily gave the cord a quick tug.

Peter's cock jumped against his belly, leaving a wet trail in its wake.

"Very nice. Since you've all been so good, I won't make you wait any longer. I apologize for missing our evening session last night and appreciate your sacrifices in delaying until this morning." She stared pointedly at the two men not stripped fully or rigged for their own personal brand of pleasure. Both Daniel and Bruce hung from cuffs around their wrists. They were bared to the waist, tight jeans hugging their lower bodies. A shame. The exquisite musculature of their torsos gleamed as though they'd been oiled. Probably had.

Not all her slaves were bisexual. Some were straight as an arrow. These two enjoyed men almost to the exclusion of all else. They reveled in her dominance, but trusted her to grant them access to other males for pleasure. Her assistants enjoyed highlighting their gorgeous bodies and flaunting their assets, which the men spent hours honing in the gym each day.

If her suspicions held true...

"Mistress Lily," they pleaded in unison.

"Bruce." She stalked to the gap between them, refusing to allow their much greater height to have any impact on her authority. "Why aren't you among the others? I had special treats planned for both of you. Nice rewards. It makes me sad not to give them you."

"I'm sorry, Mistress. It's my fault." He hung his head. "Please don't punish Daniel."

"Were you naughty, Bruce?"

Before he could agree, Daniel intervened.

"No, Mistress." He braced himself as she turned, prepared to accept whatever punishment she deemed appropriate for their transgressions. "I was to blame. I—"

His rare hesitation triggered her protective instincts in a flash.

"Shush. Both of you." She trailed one fingertip down the center of each of their chests, admiring the ridges of their sculpted muscles. "We'll discuss this privately. Later. *I* will decide who's violated the rules and how you can atone."

Bruce gulped.

"There's nothing to worry about." She patted their flanks as she embraced them both in a one armed hug. "We'll fix it. Even if it hurts a little. Don't pretend. You both enjoy a heavy-handed spanking now and again."

"Ah." She laughed when Daniel squirmed, making his chains rattle in his reflexive attempt to follow her retreating form.

Lily paused alongside a narrow cot. A thin pad supported Cameron, who hated to lie on hard or cold surfaces. Unlike most of the other men, his arms and legs were completely unbound. He displayed his inner strength by never budging from where she placed him. Much more difficult than obeying when forced by metal or rope, but he couldn't stand physical restraints any more than he could tolerate kneeling on tile.

She suspected he'd been abused by a wannabe Master once, though he still hadn't given her all the details of the nightmares the other men claimed he suffered from. One day, she'd lose him. He needed a man to top him. Until he could recover enough to seek one out, he settled for her less intimidating brand of control. She would miss his gentle insight and loving devotion when the time came for him to fly from her nest. At least she would console herself with the fact she'd helped him heal.

Lily had spent enough nights on the floor to know how uncomfortable they could be and how the ache on your shoulders or ribs could trigger unwanted memories. An unfamiliar place, with new surroundings, could shatter the security she'd crafted for Cameron in the facilities at Black Lily.

The move would be most difficult on him. Hopefully, having his brothers in submission nearby would calm any of his unease.

"Good morning, Mistress."

"How are you, sweetheart?" She studied him, thrilled to find his breathing steady and his muscles relaxed as Ive—the most maternal of her assistants—slipped a pressurized cup over his cock and balls. The clear plastic hissed as air pumped out of the tube connected to it, sucking on his half-hard dick.

"Better now that you're here." He moaned. "May I come for you? I'd like to show your Master how kind you are to me. To us. Please."

"What if I'd rather show him how stern I can be?"

"Whatever pleases you, lady. I'll gladly suffer for your cause." His long lashes dusted his cheek as he fought against the rhythmic pull of the device she'd crafted. She couldn't manually manipulate all of her stable at once. Instead, they'd come to adore their milking sessions when she felt the need to share with all of them simultaneously. Small modifications made for each man couldn't erase the similarity of their bonding.

"No, Cam." She bent to place a soft kiss on his forehead. "You've done so well. I know this is hard for you. You make me proud."

Lily crooked her finger in Jeremy's direction, thrilled at how the slaves accepted him. If their open arms were only for her benefit, she would reject their rote agreement. She should have known they'd sense his innate decency and command. Just as she did. "Join me, Master Jeremy?"

He strode to her side with two long sweeps of his booted feet.

"Damn." He heated her side as he stood close. "I knew you were good, Lily. But this...the connection is *so* strong."

She nodded, afraid to speak and reveal the emotions choking her.

"You've built an empire out of mutual respect, generosity and love." He threaded his fingers through hers. "I'm impressed. Awed. Grateful you've shared this with me. All of you."

Gigi rushed to slip the milking machines over the last of her group, who writhed with longing, on this side of the room. They were spoiled, never having to wait too long for relief. Exactly how Lily liked them. The transfer to Morselli's mansion plus her adventure last night had kept her pets in suspense.

"Show me what you've created, Lily?" Jeremy whispered close to her ear so none of the men would mistake it as a command. "I'd love to see the design."

She squeezed Cameron's knee then crossed to Rob. He'd been strapped upright to a leather bondage chair. His orgasms always came strongest when he sat, facing out to the crowd, observing his brothers. The wide spread of his legs made him an ideal model.

Behind them, Paul knelt on a padded spanking bench. She nudged his hip when they crowded around her exhibition. He scooted over, attempting to make room for Jeremy. A clatter followed as the milker slipped from his cock, which hadn't grown fully erect yet.

"Oops." She ruffled his hair. "Don't worry, you're not getting off that easy. Dawn will fix you up again. That was my fault."

The head of Lily's training staff repositioned Paul so the gap widened, allowing them each ample space to work. "Ryan, Ben, you may come closer if you'd like a better view."

The pair of submissives zoomed in, standing shoulder to shoulder for front row seats.

"Wipe the drool off, buddies." Rob flaunted his smartass nature, which constantly landed him in trouble.

The bondage chair allowed her to slap his inner thigh hard enough to sting.

He only grinned wider. "I missed you too."

"Watch that mouth of yours or I'll put it to good use, greeting our new friends." The threat didn't hold much deterrent. Rob loved to suck cock. "Or better yet, I'll let everyone else have a taste and leave you out of it."

"Shit." His skull knocked against the high wooden back of the chair. "I'll be good. I promise, Mistress."

"That's better." She squatted between his legs, palming his heavy balls. Jeremy crouched beside her as Dawn worked to re-outfit Paul.

"You see." Lily lifted Rob's thickening cock. "We've taken a mold of each slave's hard-on then created a sheath, custom-fitted like this."

She rubbed the pliable material, which allowed some small gaps while the slave's cock was flaccid. It would accommodate, if tightly, the full swell of Rob's burgeoning erection. The man bucked to the limit of his restraints when Jeremy reached out to sample the texture for himself.

"Interesting." He hummed. "I can think of a few uses for this myself."

Lily shivered.

Another clatter from behind Jeremy stole her attention. She peeked up at Dawn, who stroked additional stiffness into Paul's cock and mouthed, "Sorry."

"We're still tailoring the sizing." Lily tested the gasket at the base of Rob's cock, making the man gasp and squirm. "We were more successful in this case than in Paul's. I think we'll also need to add a belt to hold the device in place until full erection is achieved."

Jeremy nodded. "Damn gravity."

The smile they exchanged warmed her heart. How many lovers could she have found on Earth who'd share her kinks, her need to please and her desire for control?

"The sheath tool is hooked to a mild vacuum through this tube." Lily traced the line leading from the tip of Rob's cock, which now stood straight up on its own. "Right now they're all on the lowest setting. When I give the signal, we'll crank them up."

She smiled at the mix of sighs and grunts falling from her subjects' lips.

"I've programmed several different patterns. Some are designed to draw out the pleasure, some to end rapidly, some to tease and edge a man for hours. A couple we set to music for the hell of it." She shrugged at Jeremy.

"Could I mess with the software later? I'd love to see what I could do with it." His eyes sparkled.

"Of course, I should have figured." She laughed. "Master Jeremy is a computer freak."

Rob joined in. His cock bobbed, the hose bouncing along with it. The motion highlighted an attachment.

"What's this?" Jeremy flicked a finger over the black cord running beneath Rob's balls. His proximity to the other man's genitals didn't seem to faze him.

Lily squirmed at the sight.

"For the guys who like a little something extra." She wiggled her eyebrows at Paul. "We've integrated electrostimulation units into the milking machine circuits. He's wearing a fairly sizable bi-polar probe in his ass right now. Aren't you, Rob?"

"Yes, Mistress." The man groaned, his breathing starting to grow rough, uneven.

"Good boy. We fluctuate the current until it feels like someone's massaging his prostate." She fondled his balls for a little while longer, relishing how they grew tighter, drew closer to his body. Then she repeated her circuit up the sheath and along the tube until she came to her favorite component. "And…since my subs can be a little competitive sometimes, they suggested a fantastic improvement."

Paul groaned behind them. Dawn must have succeeded in refastening his milker.

"What was their idea?" Jeremy's deep inquiry proved he wasn't unaffected by the energy in the room. Who could be?

"They wanted to prove who enjoyed my invention best. So Gigi designed this valve. When fluid travels up the tube, it diverts from the air path and into a collection vial. Handy for keeping the machines clean too."

"Bonus." Jeremy grinned. She didn't think about it. She angled her head for a kiss, grateful when he obliged with a quick nibble.

"So each time we play in the milking room, I have their releases measured. Due to natural variation from man to man, I rate each slave against his previous recordings. Whoever has the greatest percentage increase in volume wins a special prize." She pinched Rob's flat stomach. "The loser gets a spanking from the winner, or offers a blowjob instead, based on their preferences."

"Damn, woman, you're devious." Praise from her Master did more to thrill her than witnessing those delicious sessions had. That was saying something.

"Mmm. I love to watch them all strain to pump out huge loads, attempting to demonstrate how much they appreciate my treatment."

A strangled gurgle from behind Jeremy caught Lily off guard. The program hadn't kicked into high gear yet. None of the men should have been in jeopardy of losing control. Except…

Creamy white come splashed across Jeremy's right boot. Line after line decorated the shiny leather in time to Paul's groans.

"Oh shit." She scurried around Jeremy, quick to comfort the thrashing sub.

"I'm so sorry, Mistress." He nearly sobbed. "I didn't mean to steal your fun. I—"

"Shhh…" She rubbed his back even as it still twitched with the last vestiges of his orgasm. "Enjoy it, Paul. You're fine. You didn't do anything wrong."

The man huffed as he stopped fighting the inevitable and wrung pleasure from his impressive climax.

Lily stared up at Dawn, waiting for an explanation. "The device had trouble at first then he got too hard, too fast. I couldn't slip it on."

"I'm so—"

"Do not apologize again or I *will* disapprove." Lily covered Paul's lips with three fingers. "The flaw in the milker was not your fault. Even worse, I failed to anticipate just how much you like dirty talk."

Paul scrunched his eyes closed.

"You've been holding out on me, haven't you?" She tapped his cheek.

"Maybe a little." He sagged in her grip. "I should have told you it turns me on."

"Oh, don't worry. I've noticed." She nuzzled her nose against his. "I underestimated the effect, though. Not a mistake I'll make again. This afternoon you'll work with Dawn. She'll record your session for my review later. I want to test a few things, uncover the extent of your attraction. Sound like fun?"

"Yes, ma'am. Thank you, Mistress."

She soothed his heaving shoulders.

"And for making me come."

"You're welcome." She whispered a proposal in his ear.

He nodded. "Please."

"Ask him," she commanded.

"Master Jeremy." Paul took a deep breath. "May I clean your boot for hiding my desires from Mistress Lily?"

Jeremy shot her a curious glance. Neither of them could deny the bulge in his tight jeans. They slung low on his hips, allowing his bare torso to take center stage between the panels of his open, white-linen shirt.

"Let him make it up to you." She nodded. "He won't be satisfied until he's punished. Paul hates to break the rules."

Lily could sense the erotic tension radiating from the remainder of her harem. She announced to the attendants, "Please skip the program ahead to stage three. Turn the machines to their full capacity. Slaves, you may come whenever you like. Show Master Jeremy how much you love being milked. We'll have two winners today. The prize will be giving our new members a welcome home blowjob."

Ryan and Ben squirmed beside her.

"Don't you dare come in your pants. Either of you. You wouldn't want to steal their treat would you?"

The men shook their heads and scanned the lascivious sharing filling the room.

221

Even Daniel and Bruce were flushed and engaged with the interaction before them.

Jeremy crept closer. His soggy shoe rested directly below Paul's face.

"Go ahead, honey." She cupped the slave's cheek as his tongue peeked out.

The very tip traced one of the opalescent branches across the clean toe of Jeremy's boot until it tangled in the leather laces. He sipped a puddle of come from a crease in the toe.

"Very nice. You came so hard for us. Look at all that semen. I bet you would have won today if you had the chance."

More men joined in the rapture they all shared. Groans, curses and shouts overflowed the spacious room. Even a few of her trainers looked like they might like to do the same, though none of them diverted their attention from their charges. Satisfied, Lily rose.

Jeremy followed her into the middle of the space. Cocks twitched as they emptied loads into the collection bags. Only one man remained unsatisfied.

Ramone. An unhealthy purple flush covered his cheeks.

"Why are you straining so hard, slave?" She rushed to his side, checking in with his trainer.

Suz shrugged.

"Stop the machine. Unhook him."

Ramone objected, but she wouldn't allow him to risk his health. This wasn't like him.

"It's okay." She held his hand, uncurling his clenched fingers. "You're doing great."

"No, I'm not. I couldn't come for you." He shook his head. "It sounded so amazing, felt like a warm mouth sucking my cock. I should have been right there with Paul. What's wrong with me?"

The despair etching lines beside his eyes hurt her heart. "We'll find out, baby. Let Suz clean you up. She'll take your blood pressure and make sure nothing else is out of the ordinary. Then we'll talk, okay?"

"Yes, Mistress." He relaxed beneath the steady strokes of her hand along his arm.

"I promise. We'll take care of everything." She kissed his cheek.

Suz worked with swift motions, ensuring Ramone's safety while talking him off the ledge. In the meantime, Gigi waved two fingers from her post at the head of the main machine the milkers fed into.

"Who wins today, Gigi?"

"Rob and Cameron."

She beamed at her subjects. "Thank you. All of you. For welcoming our guests, for making the transition here and for showing me every day how lucky I am. I need to speak with our naughty boys and work with Ramone. Until I'm finished, feel free to enjoy the show and each other."

"Mistress?" Ryan took a step back as the slaves who had been released gathered around him.

"You did want them to suck your cock, yes?" She laughed at the slight note of panic in his tone. "Don't worry, Ryan. Rob will be gentle with you."

"Can I share my reward, Mistress?" The jokester was serious as he crawled toward the delicious treat he'd earned.

"Very generous of you to offer." She smiled at the men circling Ryan and Ben. "Of course. Make them feel at home. Show them how friendly you all are."

In a flash, Ryan's shirt had been whisked away. The trainers who'd finished freeing their charges moderated the action, making sure no one seemed overwhelmed.

The long moan coming from Ryan as they bore him to one of the cushions on the area rugs had her smiling as she headed for the room she'd claimed as her office. Ben's hissed, "Yessss" trailed after her.

CHAPTER SIXTEEN

L ily's ass had barely met the plush cushion of her ornate desk chair when Daniel and Bruce were led through the archway.

Jeremy took a post behind her, placing his hand on her shoulder. She squeezed his fingers when the attendants left. The door shut lightly behind them. How often did she counsel submissives alone?

He spread his feet wide and crossed his arms over his chest. Whether they worshipped her or not, they could pose some danger.

So much stronger.

At least physically. They could hurt her without trying. Still, his respect for her multiplied when she cut straight to the heart of the matter.

"When did you two realize you were in love with each other?"

Whoa. Jeremy blinked. Neither man objected or denied her claim.

"Bruce is smarter than me. He figured it out a while ago." Daniel shook his head. "I guess I never expected to be so fortunate. I had you. I couldn't hope for more."

Jeremy understood exactly what the man meant. He swore he'd thanked all the powers of the universe for introducing him to Lily.

"I'm happy for you both." Genuine warmth colored Lily's assurance. "But this does put us in a difficult position. It wouldn't be right for me to interfere in your relationship. I assume you were busted together last night?"

"Uh, yeah." Daniel looked to Bruce, who nodded. "I didn't want to sleep alone in this place. It's so big. Everything sounds funny. Echoes everywhere. Even whispers seem giant."

"It was my fault, Mistress." Bruce sighed. "I took advantage."

"Yeah, like I resisted." Daniel snorted.

"In any case, we came without your permission." Both men studied the carpet. "We're sorry."

"It doesn't sit right for you to apologize for something so beautiful. Something you share honestly." Lily surprised Jeremy with her empathy. Her brand of dominance seemed so similar and yet so foreign to his own. "Usually, I mandate no sexual intercourse unless we're in a monitored situation for the protection of all my subs. That's not a valid concern here."

All three men stared as she reasoned toward the inevitable conclusion.

"I'll be sorry to see you leave." She sighed.

"No!" Daniel dropped to his knees on the carpet. The violent surge had Bruce out of his chair too. He snugged his lover to his chest, comforting Daniel as he begged, "Please, don't kick us out."

"You wish to stay?" Lily's head tilted as she observed their reaction.

The men clasped hands then turned to her as one. "Yes. Please."

"Well, damn." She tugged on Jeremy's hand, angling her face toward his, seeking his opinion. "Have you ever seen that work? Lovers that submit?"

"Only once." His chest puffed up as he searched the dark corners of his mind. "Gunther used to top a married couple."

"Okay." She didn't take the decision lightly. "Let me think about this. I'm not banishing you. Never. You'll always have a home with me. But I have to learn how to make it work. I'll set up a meeting with Master Gunther—learn more about his experiences. We'll figure this out. Fair enough?"

"More than, Mistress." Daniel nodded as he and Bruce staggered to their feet. "Thank you."

"A few rules are probably in order." Lily regained her composure, impressing Jeremy with her fortitude and fast thinking. "First, you'll bunk in the same room, the same bed, from now on."

The men smiled into each other's eyes, lacing their fingers.

"Second, I promise I'll never pit you against each other. It would be cruel."

Jeremy swore Daniel swiped a tear from the corner of his eye, though the man could have been scratching an itch.

"Finally, if you want to be with each other...tell one of the trainers. They'll make sure you have privacy until I can figure out how to handle this." She smiled at their slack jaws. "Rejoin the group. You may share the good news if you decide it's the right thing for you. I'll respect your wishes either way."

Bruce tried to speak but couldn't.

"Go ahead. We'll discuss it more later."

Jeremy caught her wistful sigh as the couple embraced. Before they abandoned Lily's office, Daniel glanced over his shoulder. He nearly yanked Bruce's arm from the socket when he stopped short, staring straight into Lily's eyes.

"I'm happy for you too, Mistress." He grinned. "Your Master looks at you like Bruce looks at me. No one deserves that more than you."

Before she could respond, they'd slipped from the office.

Jeremy didn't doubt their lifelong loyalty to one special Mistress had been cemented.

On their heels, one of the pretty protégés escorted Ramone into the room. She ran down the report detailing the slave's vital signs, assuring Lily he had passed all physical examinations. She rose from the desk and circled the mammoth furnishing to stand by her slave's side when he refused to pry his gaze from the carpet. "Do you feel okay, Ramone?"

"Suz told you, I'm fine."

Jeremy had to bite his tongue to keep from insisting the slave address Lily with a more appropriate tone. The man's disrespect, not only of his Mistress but also of Jeremy's submissive, rankled. Christ, this would take some adjusting to. He forced himself into statue mode when Lily approached the nude man, who sat on his haunches in the middle of the floor.

"No, she said your measurable responses fell within the normal range. That's not at all what I'm asking about." Lily sank beside her charge. "I've never seen you so distressed. Allow me to shoulder your burdens. Keep me fully informed. I couldn't forgive myself if I hurt you by accident."

Ramone flung his arms around Lily's waist. The force of the impact tumbled her backward.

Jeremy lunged in their direction before he realized the man hadn't intended any harm.

She flung a warning stare in his direction before welcoming her submissive into her embrace.

Hands out, Jeremy retreated, allowing them to work through Ramone's issues without his interference.

"It's all your fault."

Lily jerked at Ramone's accusation.

Somehow, Jeremy restrained himself from dashing to her aid.

"What did I do?"

"You made me like it." He took her shoulders between his hands and shook her a little.

Jeremy growled despite his best intentions.

Ramone blinked then released Lily.

"Like what?"

"I'm not gay, Mistress." He scrunched his eyes closed. "I saw Bruce and Daniel as they walked by. I've watched you match up other slaves."

"I do enjoy observing them share pleasure when appropriate." She smiled. "Of course."

"Not me. I'm not gay!" He shook his head. "You can't change me."

"What? Ramone, calm down." She laid her fingers on his shoulder, preventing his cathartic rocking. "It's obvious you're straight. I've never encouraged you to take a male lover, have I?"

"Not yet."

"Not ever. I can sense it's outside your comfort zone. That's all right." She kissed the submissive.

Somehow the sight of their long, gentle exchange turned Jeremy on more. With every skilled response Lily demonstrated, he lost another piece of his heart to her compassionate nature. For years, his friends had relied on him to talk through their problems. Lacey had shared her secrets during some dark times. Razor had turned to him often.

Until Jeremy observed Lily at work, he hadn't realized how much of his training had bled through his attempt at a vanilla life. For him, like Lily, the very framework of his nature guaranteed his role. He couldn't change the man he was. How could he ever have wanted to?

Reason began to penetrate. Wild light drained from Ramone's gray eyes. Lily paused, allowing him to spill his guts unhindered.

"I used to think that, Mistress. I thought you understood. But last week—"

"Oh. Ramone." She smiled as she pressed him to her bosom, making Jeremy a little jealous of the man's comfy resting place on the pillow of her breasts. "Enjoying anal stimulation doesn't make you gay. Plenty of men find it pleasurable."

"Gay men." He shook his head, damn near motorboating Lily's encased chest. "Don't think I hold anything against the other slaves. How they seek their pleasure is their business. It's just...it's screwing with my mind to wonder if something I've felt sure about my entire life was a lie. It's hard enough to be a submissive guy. So many people have assumed I'm weak because I get off on surrender."

"Why join the ranks of people who would stereotype?" Lily caressed his face. "You know who you are and what attracts you, Ramone. That doesn't change with a string of beads or a vibrator penetrating you. Labels are ridiculous. I can take you somewhere new— someplace higher—above simple classifications. Don't deny yourself the indulgence because you're afraid."

Her slave shivered.

"I'd bet a handful of spanks even Master Jeremy has taken pleasure from ass play before."

"Him?" Ramone pointed. "No way."

"You don't think if I slipped a finger inside him while I sucked his cock, he'd shoot ten times harder?"

"Keeping talking like that and we'll find out right here and now." Jeremy grimaced as he adjusted his package. "It's not the easiest to admit for me either, especially not as a Dom. But...yeah...it can feel great when it's done right. Once you've experienced it, I'd guess the depth of sensation could become addictive."

"Is *that* the problem, Ramone?" Lily scooted closer. "It's not that you liked me fucking you, is it? It's that you're having trouble coming without the extra stimulation. Like this morning. That frightened you didn't it?"

He nodded, his fingers plucking at a swirly design in the carpet.

"Say it." She grasped the man's jaw, angling his face so he couldn't escape her stare.

"I need something in my ass so bad I can't come without it anymore." His pitch rose as anxiety returned. Yet the admission seemed to help. He took a long, deep breath.

"There you go." Lily kissed his cheek. "Remember, you never have to worry alone. You're not supposed to keep secrets from me, Ramone. Tell me everything and trust me to fix it. Did you forget the rules? Or have I done something to break your trust?"

"No, Mistress." Ramone scrambled to reassure her. "I was confused. I tried to tell you, but you were busy with the going-away party. Then the move. And there were unfamiliar people, places."

Lily quirked an eyebrow.

"And...those are no excuses, really. I should have shared how I felt. With Suz if you were unavailable. You'll always take care of me."

"That's better." She rocked Ramone, sheltering him through the adrenaline storm raging in his veins. "I would punish you except it seems like poetic justice that you missed out on the fun this morning."

"My own fault, I know." He grimaced. "But I'm sorry, Mistress."

"The truth is, Ramone..." She peeked over her shoulder, flashing a tiny smile at Jeremy. "I understand a little too well I think."

"Do you really kneel for him?" Honest curiosity had his head tilting and his eyes scrunched as if someone had told him unicorns were real.

Jeremy's palms itched to grab Lily and demonstrate.

"Mmm. Yes." She licked her lips. "Only for him. If I'd let myself resist on principle, I would have missed out on some of the most fantastic experiences of my entire life."

Mine too, wildcat. She'd probably emasculate him with her tiny, razor-sharp claws if she could hear his thoughts.

"Would you like to be brave with me, Ramone? Maybe earn another chance to come?" She drew hypnotic patterns on the man's rough cheek.

"How?" He speared Lily with a look so hopeful, Jeremy inched closer to the pair.

"Let me teach you a lesson." She crooned, speaking to him like she might a feral animal. Soft, low, insistent. "I'll show you how phenomenal it is when you ride the crest of your desires. So close to falling, without tumbling over your boundaries."

"Can I watch you first?"

"Practice what you preach, Lily." Jeremy stroked his beard as his devious side constructed wicked plans. "Be a brave little girl and make a good role model for Ramone."

Lily glanced back and forth between them.

As much as he yearned to order her to submit, Jeremy allowed her make the call.

"Please, Mistress." Ramone nudged her toward Jeremy. "You're the strongest person I know. If you can bend, so can I. For the right person. People. Under the right circumstances."

"Because I care for you." She stroked the hair at his temple. "I'll share this. I'll always give you what you need."

"Thank you."

Lily rose from her crouch then strode the three steps across the plush carpet to stand before him, toe to toe. They stayed locked in place for long seconds, appraising the intensity in each other's stares before she thrilled him again with sweet yielding.

"Master, I need you."

"Because of the drug?" He whispered to keep the inquiry from reaching Ramone.

"No, because of who you are. Who I am. What we become when we're merged." She assumed the fundamental submissive position—knees bent, her thighs spread, hands clasped in the small of her back. The slight bow of her graceful neck acted like an intravenous shot of adrenaline on Jeremy's whole body.

"*Madre de dios.*"

"You can say that again, Ramone." Jeremy groaned when the peerless woman before him laid her cheek on his thigh. "Her surrender is so pure."

"Neither of us could be mistaken for virgins," she scoffed.

"You were untouched before last night. Unmarked by me. That's all that matters, Lily. You're the only woman who counts to me."

She sighed as she nuzzled his hand, kissing the center of his palm. "I'll never submit for another Master."

"Damn straight you won't." Jeremy grasped her shoulders and spun her to face Ramone. He didn't waste time pretending he had an objective more important than burying himself in her tight, steaming pussy. "Don't break contact with him. Show him all that's in your heart and mind when I slide deep inside you. Stare into his eyes and guarantee the advice you gave him was valid."

"Mistress..." Ramone put out a hand when she yelped. Too far away, he couldn't prevent Jeremy from ripping open the crotch of her sleek, sexy gear.

"Shh..." She must have smiled because the reflection of her happiness showed in the slave's answering grin. "He startled me, that's all. I like it. He knows exactly how to touch me."

"No, Lily. More like we crave the same things. You're so in synch with me. Damn." Jeremy couldn't take things slow. He tore at his fly as he knelt behind her. One arm wrapped around her waist with plenty of extra reach to curl his palm around her ribs on her opposite side. He clasped her tight to his chest. Within heartbeats, he rode the furrow of her moist folds, caressing the sensitive flesh with his anxious cock.

"And it's not a matter of like. You *love* this." He laid a trail of bites down her neck as he canted his hips, poking the tip of his erection into the entrance of her pussy. "Don't you?"

"Yes, sir." She squirmed in his grip, trying to impale herself on the blunt head of his hard-on.

"Behave, Lily." He wrenched her away far enough to smack her ass. The crack of his bare hand on her leather-covered muscle reverberated through the elegant space she'd arranged for her duties. "Ask me nicely and I'll give you your prize."

"Please, let me have your cock."

The sugary begging did nothing for his restraint. He gritted his teeth.

"Fuck me, fill me, love me."

"I do, Lily," he rasped into the loosening wisps of her raven hair. "I'll dream of being inside you until the day I die. Watching you train this morning was the sexiest thing I've seen in years. So capable. So skilled. I respect your talents. Am thrilled by your surrender to me. For me."

"Only you." She sobbed when he plowed through the clasping rings of her muscles, joining them into one being.

He cradled her neck in his loose, open grasp, thrilling at the pounding of her pulse over his splayed fingers. Anchoring her right where she belonged, his other arm held her pelvis still as he drilled deeper and deeper into her welcoming grasp. Heat encompassed him, combating the chill caused by years of isolation.

"No condom?" Ramone stared at the juncture of their bodies. The man's cock plumped by the second.

"Nothing between us." Jeremy couldn't stand it.

"You know...if I fuck you with a strap-on...you don't need a rubber." Lily's broken phrases slipped between the lunges of Jeremy's cock, which shuttled from the cusp of her pussy to her core. "I can make sure it's for you alone."

"What if your Master doesn't want you to train us anymore?" Ramone didn't blink once as though transfixed by the sight of Jeremy's possession of her—mind and body. "What if you don't need us now that you have him?"

"Show him." Jeremy halted his thrusts, unwilling to leave the man a shred of uncertainty. He refused to jeopardize Lily's relationship with her slaves.

She tried to hump backward onto his stiff flesh. He swatted her ass again, harder. She wouldn't appreciate him caving to her demands when she left her sensual haze long enough to realize the implications. Jeremy accepted responsibility for the well-being of Lily's charges, considering the impact damage to them would have on her. He vowed to protect them in order to guard her heart.

All three of them sucked in a breath as electricity arced around the room. They shared the energy generated by their personal discoveries.

"Do it, Lily." Jeremy withdrew from her sopping channel, mourning the loss of her tight fist squeezing him, massaging his entire length.

She flung a hand out for support as she passed her desk, rounding on a tall armoire on the far wall of her office. The doors winged open without a hint of a squeak. Objects of every shape, size and color lined the cabinet. Organized and methodical, she didn't have to rummage for what she sought.

"Damn," Ramone cursed softly when her fingers skimmed past a variety of crops, paddles and even a short cane before sliding out a drawer. From inside she withdrew a thin, translucent purple dildo, still inside the package, along with a bottle of lube.

235

Jeremy nodded at her selection, the least realistic looking phallus in her stash.

Scissors trembled in her hand as she attempted to cut the toy loose. He feared she might slice herself in the process. Damn blister packs were more dangerous than a rogue Dom with a sadistic streak if you weren't careful.

"Bring it here, darling." Jeremy smiled when she blushed. "I'll get it out for you. You can't wait to play with Ramone can you?"

"Hurry." She bit her lip as she waited for him to free the contraption.

"You meant hurry, *please*. Right?" He held the implement over her head, even as he knelt in the same position he'd fucked her in less than a minute before. The sprite knew better than to grab for the dildo. Besides, her pride would never permit it.

"Yes, sir." She arched closer when he licked a spot above her mound. Though he couldn't taste her skin, she would have felt the pressure from the swipe of his tongue. "I need you inside me again. Please don't make me wait. Let me have you while I take Ramone. With you it can be perfect."

Jeremy grinned as he brought the suction cup base of the meager tool to his mouth, wetting the surface. He easily surrounded the thin probe with his fingers as he pressed it to the damp patch on Lily's leather-encased lower abdomen. It adhered, making her look like some kind of horny alien.

Neither man laughed. In fact, Ramone choked a bit.

She squeezed ample lubrication over her dainty hands then stroked the implement protruding from her torso. Desperate, needy and yet all business.

"What are you doing way over there, Ramone?"

236

CHAPTER SEVENTEEN

No sooner had Lily asked the question than her submissive transported to her side.

"On your back. Hold those knees up. Spread them wide. Give me lots of room to work while Master Jeremy—" Her instructions morphed into a wail as he crept up behind her and pressed inside once more.

"While I ride you hard?" He considered tempering his lunges but decided against it. The bob of her plastic dong *thwapped* on Ramone's belly along with the slave's flesh-and-blood cock.

Lily monitored the pleasure of her submissive even as she allowed Jeremy full access to her body. She slid two greased fingers around the man's hole, allowing the motion of their primal fuck to nudge her digits against the tight passage.

A harder than average thrust caused her to broach Ramone's resistance. Lily and her sub cried out simultaneously as her fingers danced along the ridge of the man's anus. She painted lubrication over his sensitive tissue despite the fact that he could probably have taken the thin column with no difficulties.

Lily would never risk sacrificing his pleasure. Especially not when the exchange held such significance for the man.

"Are you ready for me?" Her pussy clenched on Jeremy's cock as she aligned the tip of the dildo with her sub's asshole. "For us?"

Jeremy's fingers flexed where they cradled her across her breasts and at her hip. He guided her with the driving force of his pelvis, closer to her target with every pass. The grasp of her saturated tissue strangling his cock prevented him from hesitating while she completed her approach.

Ramone impressed Jeremy by taking the time to evaluate the situation before shouting his honest response. Lily earned true devotion, not mindless acceptance. She deserved it. "Yes. Please, Mistress. Show me what I've been missing."

"Keep breathing," she encouraged the man as Jeremy drove them both nearer. He watched over Lily's shoulder as Ramone's muscles stretched to admit the narrow girth of Lily's fake cock, which invaded his back passage.

The utter stillness accompanying the temporary hush of their trio erupted a moment later as an onslaught of undiluted pleasure attacked them all. Lily thrust her hips forward and back, wedging herself in Ramone's greedy sphincter then covering more of Jeremy's shaft with the glide of her slick pussy.

Her escalating whimpers alerted him to her erotic distress. She couldn't claim both of her desires simultaneously.

Jeremy would have to assist. He thrust deep then clamped her to his torso. "Shush. I've got you. I'll help."

He began to fuck, then ground against her ass to massage new depths inside his naughty little Mistress, bumping her cervix at the pinnacle of each circuit. His forward motion, when fully buried, inserted Lily's fake appendage into the waiting slave an inch at a time.

"Talk to me, Ramone." Lily's wheeze convinced Jeremy she could hardly issue the command.

"Oh, fuck. So good. Harder. More." The man's head thrashed from side to side. His cock flopped on his trim abdomen in the wake of the kinetic energy they generated. With his hands still holding his knees as instructed, his erection took on a life of its own.

Until Lily surrounded the distended flesh with her still-slick hand.

She controlled the motion, limiting it to the range benefiting Ramone's ecstasy the most. She maximized his pleasure. "Look how you respond to my touch. How eager you are *for me*. Not at all for another man. Are you strong enough to test that theory?"

Ramone gulped. He glanced at Jeremy then back to Lily. "Him?"

She nodded. "Trust me."

"I do."

"And I trust him. Completely. You can too. Let's find out together. However you feel is okay, Ramone. I'm here for you."

The submissive went slack. All the tension melted from his slight frame. Even on the smaller side of her slaves, he dwarfed Lily. Except she seemed to grow ten feet tall as she manipulated their experience.

Jeremy's stride hitched when she rotated her head, angling her face toward him. He stared into her wide, unblinking eyes. So, so blue. "You want me to touch him?"

"Just for a second. Show him the difference." She begged, "Please. I'll pay you back later. However you like."

"Have you forgotten I can take whatever I want at any time?"

"Never." She batted her midnight lashes. "Please, anyway."

"You don't have to beg for my help, Lily. I'm always here for you. Whatever you need."

Jeremy's hand snaked around her waist and hovered over Ramone's cock. Their gazes clashed. Lily let go, and Jeremy took hold. The unique feel of another man's shaft always startled him. Heavier than expected, hard yet soft, radiating warmth while lubrication cooled to the touch—the contrasts boggled his mind. Nuances had faded in the decade between his training and the instant he had to draw on his experience.

Bold ridges of the hard-on in his grip faded to a solid yet malleable erection within thirty seconds of gentle pumping.

Though Jeremy continued to ride Lily—because how could he ever stop when she felt so fucking good—Ramone's cries grew softer and less urgent. The man covered Jeremy's wrist and shoved lightly. "Sorry. It doesn't work for me."

"Of course not, Ramone." Lily tipped forward, blanketing the man on the floor. Her ass lifted as a result, spurring Jeremy to sink deeper. "Believe in your instincts. You know what you like. You know who you are and that man is special to me. Wonderful exactly as you are."

Somehow, Lily's tender offering to the other man didn't provoke Jeremy's jealousy in the least. In fact, it turned him on more. His woman was generous and loving. Strong and confident. Willing to bring all her fortitude to bear for others.

She would expect him to do the same for her.

Jeremy roared as he surged inside her, embedding her toy fully inside Ramone.

The submissive man grunted. His eyelids slammed shut and twitched as color burst across his cheekbones. "Yes, yes, yes."

The sweet indication of his pleasure affected Lily like another shot of Sex Offender. She flared, burning hot, around Jeremy. Her pussy gushed moisture, accompanying the increasing pace of his thrusts with wet slurps.

"Shit, yeah." Jeremy grabbed Lily's hips and began to hammer home.

"Is it me fucking you, Ramone?" Lily gasped as Jeremy impaled her with a frenzy of short, even thrusts, which shoved the dildo his woman wore deep within her slave's body. Over and over. "Or is it him?"

"It's—" The man cut off, a huge shudder racking his body. "It doesn't matter. It feels so good to share this with you. I love having you inside me, Mistress. I needed this...you."

Jeremy buried his face against the thick hair at Lily's temple. He whispered, "I need you too. God, how I've missed this."

Lily turned her face until they could share a long, lingering kiss. She lifted off Ramone far enough to grasp his cock. Her knuckles turned white as she stroked him. A mewl escaped her delicate throat. The pressure on Ramone's cock had the slave's eyes flying open. "Mistress, stop. Let go. I'm too close. Going to—"

Focus returned to the man in her clutches. Instead of releasing him, she shifted her grip to flick the pad of her thumb across the underside of the engorged head capping Ramone's erection.

The poor bastard didn't stand a chance.

A strangled cry erupted from his chest, which arched off the floor. The cords in his neck became prominent as his head tipped back, his chin rising as he strained closer to the woman who'd ensnared him. Streams of come blasted from the man's cock hard enough to launch seed over his shoulder. Some landed on his face before the next blast coated his chest with the proof of his enjoyment.

Lily trembled as she observed her successful treatment.

"Surrender." Jeremy didn't mean to growl. "He's satisfied. Your turn. You did so well. Deserve a reward. Come for me. With me."

Several lingering aftershocks formed a puddle of come near Ramone's belly button. She dipped her finger in it an instant before she exploded. Jeremy sprayed inside her quaking pussy, unable to resist the lure of her climaxing body. Her rapture infected him, making his heart light as he shot jet after jet.

Moisture trickled over his balls when he tugged her upright. His or hers or both, he couldn't say. He didn't care as long as she rested in his arms. The heated leather she wore adhered to his chest as he overflowed her, the spasms accompanied by several lingering twitches of his hips.

When the storm passed, he struggled to maintain balance in the whirlwind sweeping around them. Holding Lily secure, upright, he stole a kiss. He nudged her head with his chin until she responded, tipping her face toward his.

Their lips met and mingled, glided over each other, sharing gentle reassurance in the wake of the explosion of passion they'd crafted.

"So beautiful." Ramone's reverent whisper cut through their harsh breathing. "One day, that's what I want. If I'm lucky."

Lily smiled against Jeremy's mouth, the change in her plump lips inspiring a similar reaction in him. "So lucky."

He backed off to study the adoration in her eyes and hoped she could read the same in his. After one last sip of her lips he kissed her shoulder then nodded. "Ready?"

"Not really, but okay." She gripped the base of the toy she still wore.

Jeremy sat on his haunches, dragging Lily backward with him as slowly as he could manage. The long, low groan from Ramone confirmed she'd withdrawn from his depths. Reluctant to do the same, yet aware of the necessity, Jeremy braced Lily's hips as she climbed to her feet.

A long strand of moisture connected them, thinning impossibly before breaking. Regret stole a modicum of his enjoyment. He wished he never had to leave her. Thick droplets of his release dribbled from her pussy, down the leather hugging her thighs, as she tended to Ramone. She didn't wipe them away. Her attention fixated on caring for her submissive above all else.

Only when she'd satisfied herself Ramone had been cleaned and rested comfortably did she allow Jeremy to do the same for her.

They shared a deep stare, no words necessary, as he resealed the flap on her outfit.

For now.

Jeremy tucked himself into his jeans as Lily brought Ramone out of the sensual trance they'd induced. She spoke to him softly until a chuckle broke the intimate hush.

"Thank you, Mistress." The man bit his lip, something Jeremy wouldn't have expected in the lax aftermath they shared.

"Ramone, is there anything else you need to tell me?" She squinted at her charge. "If you hold back again, I won't be so lenient next time."

He grimaced.

"*Ramone...*" She drummed her bright red nails against her leather-coated forearm.

"I don't mean to spoil your fun. Seeing you this morning, so happy, I couldn't stand to ruin your glow. Now that's twice as true." He laid his cheek on her shoulder. "I'm sorry if this upsets you."

"What's wrong?" Lily sat up straighter, managing to maintain her aura of authority while looking thoroughly fucked.

"Last night, when they delivered our dinner, some of the guys were approached with offers..."

"Morselli's staff solicited sex?" Lily's face flushed.

"No, worse." Ramone winced. "Though there were plenty of snide comments. More like a chance to turn the tables. They spread lies about you. Of course none of the guys believed you came here for drugs or that you'd use them to make you a better Mistress. Such bullshit. They said they'd let us try some if we helped them sneak some dude out of the dungeon. A scientist."

"Fuck." Jeremy pounded his fist against his thigh, savoring the pain that radiated through his quadriceps.

"Mistress, I know you would never do that." Ramone grabbed her hand when she would have retreated. "We all heard the rumors back at Black Lily. About…"

"My father."

Jeremy steadied her with a hand on her back.

"Yeah." The sub looked like he would have spit on the ground had it been a little less opulent. "And Malcolm. Is…is it true?"

"Yes, Ramone." She nodded. "Buchanan overdosed on Sex Offender. Intentionally. The coward murdered Malcolm first. They were going to put him away for life."

"The fucker, sorry, had been killing that poor guy for years." Ramone shook his head. "I know you tried to protect him but… Maybe this was kinder. Faster."

"I doubt it."

Jeremy squeezed her shoulder though he would never dare to hint at the gory images he'd reviewed in the case file pertaining to Malcolm's brutal torture. The details would destroy her. She already agonized over the submissive's loss.

"Did anyone take them up on it?" Jeremy couldn't suppress his cop instincts, nearly as strong as his dominant tendencies. Hell, maybe they ran parallel in some respects. He'd seen his share of despicable cops, as abusive as rotten Doms.

"Hell, no." Ramone scrubbed his hand over his face. "Fuck. At least not yet. We kicked those losers out. I'm not gonna lie, though. A few of the guys looked like they wondered about it. At the club, it was only for the super elite. Buchanan, Malcolm, a handful of the other top dogs. Even from our group, none of us except maybe Cameron could afford it even if we wanted. Here, it seemed like the rules of the game are different. The drug easier to score."

Lily winced.

"Is it bad?" Ramone looked as though he would rise to comfort her.

"Stay." She didn't try to sugarcoat things or keep him in the shadows. Information would arm him against dangerous lies. "Listen carefully. Sex Offender is *highly* addictive. It will consume you, turn you crazy with desire if you let it."

"Then it must be true, it enhances your pleasure?"

"Yes." She planted her spike heels and met his stare head-on. "Those assholes weren't lying. I did use it last night."

"What?" Ramone braced one hand behind him as though to keep from tipping over. "Why would you do that?"

"She did it so I wouldn't have to take it." Jeremy glowered. "I'm sure I still owe her about five thousand spankings. Morselli trapped us. Set us against each other. It was her or me. It should have been me."

"Of course." Ramone sighed. "Is this why you moved us from Black Lily?"

Lily nodded. "Please believe I've taken every precaution I can think of to keep you all safe. Insulated. Still, I should have addressed the group. I would never forgive myself if something happened to you because of my decision."

"You think we don't know how many you've risked your life for already?" Ramone reached for her hand then stopped short of taking it.

She closed the gap, allowing him to kiss her knuckles.

"We adore you. For how many of us you've saved from ourselves and all the others we've caught rumors of in the darkness. You gave us all the option of leaving with no hard feelings. You offered to help us find another suitable Domme. No one took you up on it because there could never be another Mistress who would satisfy us like you do. No one we'd rather stand behind. How can we help?"

"By watching out for each other. Stick together and no one can harm you. I'll have Lucas and Steve tighten security. I'll bring in our own chef and supplies. They could easily slip some of that shit in the food. Damn it, I should have considered that."

"Mistress Lily." Ramone grew serious, his shoulders rolled back as he cleared his throat. "Use us. If they're hurting innocent people, we would be proud to stop it."

"Absolutely not." The strands of the flogger at her hip spread into a fan of leather as she pivoted on her wicked heels. "It's too risky."

"Okay. But don't have them cut off the delivery service. If you do, Mr. Morselli will know you suspect his staff. It all makes sense now. You're supposed to be helping him, right? He thinks you'll convince people to try the drug and get rid of the garbage after he hooks them. Is that it? We can dig for information. If that's all you'll allow, it's still something."

"He has a point, Lily." Jeremy reached out, snagging her wrist.

To her credit, she considered their arguments. "I don't like this one bit. It's too enticing. Even talking about it makes part of me crave another taste. It's a blur of color, passion and pleasure. All those men, surrounding me. The motion of the suspension rig. Your eyes. Always on me. To burn like that every night."

Lily shivered.

"I won't let you expose yourself to the chemical again." Jeremy groaned when a spark of the total abandon she'd harnessed entered her eyes. He tugged her close and smothered her in his grasp, blocking out the craving, replacing it with his heat. "Never again, Lily. We don't need to cheat."

"Damn it. Something that potent will tear through communities." Ramone clasped his hands, weaving his fingers. "My sister died of an overdose. Cocaine. I wouldn't wish that on anyone else's family. Please, it's just talk. I'll find out more. A location, something. I promise I'll keep an eye on the others and make sure no one slips up. Leave those two new guys. They have to know the score. Between all of us we can handle this."

When she still didn't respond, heat built in Ramone's entreaty. "Don't make the mistake so many others have. Our choice to submit does not mean we're weak."

"I've never believed that." She shook her head at the man at her feet.

"Prove it, Mistress."

"You can't keep fighting this alone, Lily." Jeremy murmured into her ear. "This is the break you were hoping for. If we pool our resources we might have a chance to shut it down. Keep it contained."

"Fine." Lily shoved from his chest. "You're right. Damn it. I don't fucking like it, but there's not a lot of choice left. If we don't cut this off soon it'll be too late. It's building, spreading."

He wished he could argue, give her some comfort. The hell of it was Jeremy heard the clock ticking as loud as a jet engine. They didn't have much time.

"Ramone, tell Suz to round up the rest of the boys as soon as they've enjoyed their rewards from this morning's session." Lily held her hands out, helping her charge to his feet. She tugged him closer, lifting to her tiptoes to place a gentle kiss on his cheek. "Have someone call when they're ready for me to address the group."

"Yes, Mistress." He hugged her tight. "Thank you. We'll make you proud."

"You always do."

Jeremy waited until the door had shut and Ramone's bare feet slapped down the marble hall before facing her. "We should split up."

"What? No." She evaded his grasp. "This won't take long. Then we can hunt Morselli. Find out what he has planned for us. You know as well as I, he wouldn't have asked us here if it were only about handling the fallout. I assumed he was working for The Scientist. Now, though...What Ramone said makes sense. Morselli's always been about power. He's trying to take over. He needs something to produce or distribute the drug and he thinks we can get it for him. That's the only thing that makes sense."

"Have you ever considered law enforcement?" Jeremy grinned. All through the night, he'd supervised her unnatural slumber between taming the bouts of drug-induced hunger ransacking her tiny body. While she'd dozed, he'd kept his tablet handy, typing in notes, building timelines, running probabilities, drafting reports on his theories for Agent Sterns.

By dawn, he'd come to the same conclusion.

Morselli had tried to usurp his partner. Maybe he'd acted too soon or underestimated The Scientist. The genius hadn't evaded police in a dozen countries by being stupid. Now he needed help to finish the job. Somehow he thought Jeremy or Lily would be able to secure what he needed.

"You had it right." She sat on the edge of her desk, distracting him with the graceful cross of one sleek thigh over the other. "Things are moving faster, running out of control. We should try to force his hand. I only need fifteen minutes tops to guarantee how key the safety of my subs and my staff is and how volatile the situation has become. I can't take off until that's done. I've earned the right to confront Morselli with you. Don't take that away from me."

"Shit." Jeremy scrubbed his knuckles over his eyes, trying to erase nightmare scenarios. They could break her so easily. Not because she was weak, but because they were ruthless. He forced his respiration into a steady rhythm. "This is hard, Lily."

"Like giving up control to you isn't?" She hopped up, slapping her hands on her hips. "No matter what happens when we're in bed, you have to trust me to take care of myself. Or was everything you said a lie? About needing someone strong enough..."

"No, never." Their whispered confessions rushed through his memory. How could she think what they'd shared could be false? He spun to face her head-on, cupping her cheeks in his hands, hoping she didn't notice the tiny tremble in his fingers. "I believe you're capable. It's just—"

"Yeah." She relaxed into his touch. "I know. It's freaky to trust someone after all this time. Hard to take another risk."

"I can't stand to lose again." He trailed his fingertips over her cheeks to her parted lips. "Not when I've finally found everything I want, everything I need. The stakes are too high."

"If you don't consider me your equal, and treat me the same, you'll lose me right now." The shimmer in her eyes promised it would rip them both to pieces. "I'll walk if I have to. I have my limits, Jeremy. I'll surrender to you in everything but this."

"Damn it." He smothered her upturned face with butterfly kisses. "I'm sorry. You're right. I'll wait. This is so new, Lily. So different. Phenomenal. You're going to have to bear with me, okay?"

"If you'll do the same for me." She wrapped her arms around his waist and buried her face against his tense pecs.

"Always."

"For so long I've worried about getting caught, not wondering *if* it would happen but *when* and how much of my father's damage I could fix before they stopped me. This is the first time in years, maybe ever, I believe things are going to be okay." Lily's whisper tore his heart. "I can handle anything when you stand with me."

"Same here, Lily. Together. We'll do this together."

CHAPTER EIGHTEEN

Jeremy observed from the hallway as Lily spoke to her intimate family, unwilling to infringe on their private moment or detract from her authority by hovering too close. He wished he'd seen them interact before he and the sultry switch had exchanged midnight confessions. Sitcom actors with false smiles and scripted, laugh-track reactions had nothing on the devout gazes of the men and women surrounding her.

Concern—not for themselves, but for the woman who formed the glue of their bond—wrinkled brows and had several holding hands with their friends and neighbors. The fierce loyalty she inspired in the group couldn't be forced. She'd earned their allegiance.

"Would you look at that?" Lucas leaned one shoulder against the doorjamb, kicking his foot across the other. "Every last dude wrapped around her little finger. You joining them?"

"None of your business, really." Jeremy studied the hired muscle.

"Agent Sterns seems to think it is, *Romeo.*"

Fuck. It hadn't been his imagination. Lily's help screamed military. He'd assumed they were the *ex* variety, earning a living with the skills they'd honed while enlisted. Should have guessed they were part of the special task force assembled from an alphabet soup of agencies to tackle what Sterns had codenamed Operation Romeo. "How long has he had you working from the inside?"

"About three months."

"No wonder that asshole wasn't in any hurry to put me in the game. Does she know?" Jeremy's gut burned at the thought of the men deceiving her. She deserved the truth.

"Hell, no." Steve joined their cluster. "She'd probably rip our balls off and make us eat 'em."

Lucas laughed. "No doubt. Besides, once we cleared her of any involvement, we couldn't risk her kicking us out. Manning this post keeps our ear to the ground and her fine ass covered."

"What you're saying is *you're* wrapped around her finger too." Jeremy raised an eyebrow at the men.

"Pretty much," Steve growled. "So you'd better convince us you're not fucking with her just to grab the inside line."

"Give me a little more credit than that." Jeremy glared at the overgrown goons. Reality was he would have issued the same challenge in their shoes. Hell, he probably wouldn't have been half as nice about it. "Fine. How's this? I'm glad she's had someone on her side. Enough that I'll make a case for keeping your jewels when I blow your cover to hell and back. I'm not about keeping secrets from her."

"Oh damn." Lucas's wry grin leeched the bitterness from his curse. "I hope she's as into you as she looked this morning."

"Me too." He clapped the man on the shoulder.

They might have swapped war stories and initiated the formation of a bond most safety and law officials found with other men of similar callings if pounding footfalls hadn't put them all on full alert. They stood three-wide across the main entrance to Lily's haven in the middle of the snake pit, braced for whomever was about to fly around the corner.

Jeremy sighed when Matt charged toward them.

"JRad." The beads of sweat on his brow contrasted with his hardly winded tone. The guy trained non-stop outside of his police duties. "You need to come check this out."

When Matt jerked his chin toward the wing housing their personal chambers, Jeremy waved him off. "Hold up a minute. What's going on? You can speak free in front of these guys. They're part of the team."

"What the fuck?"

Jeremy wouldn't have been surprised if a blood vessel burst in Matt's eye. He could relate. Why their superior had sent them into the situation without the full briefing they required, he couldn't say. True, he'd signed himself up for this particular duty, forced his involvement. Still, the DEA douche bag should have mentioned any onsite backup.

"Maybe he doesn't trust you two," Lucas challenged Matt. "How do we know you're not teaming up with Morselli for real?"

"Because the fucker is setting off alarms left and right in JRad's system."

"Screw that!" Jeremy wouldn't tolerate someone taking a virtual sneak and peak around his computers. His programming should hold to wipe the reports and other incriminating data clean if anyone attempted to tamper with his network, but the existence of such protocol alone would implicate him. Worse, suspicion would spread to Lily. Questions he couldn't afford to have asked would arise. Doubt would put her at risk.

"I'll take care of this." If he manned the terminal he could counter the attack, make things appear status quo by feeding the hacker what they hoped to see. The roadblocks he'd left should hold long enough for him to take control if he hustled. "I'll be back. No more than an hour. Make sure Lily doesn't leave your sight. This could go either way. If it's a disaster, smuggle her out of here however you have to. Please."

Not a word he used often.

"Between us and the guys in there, she'll be safe." Steve shoved Jeremy toward the door as he tried to steal one last glimpse of Lily through the open archway. He couldn't even make eye contact long enough to wave before Matt urged him to hurry.

He jogged backward for a few steps then pivoted. With a long look over his shoulder, he began to run.

***

Lily forced herself to stand still instead of gouging out her security team's eyes. Maybe she'd heard them wrong. "What the fuck did you just say?"

"Sorry, love." Lucas grimaced. "Your Master said you're not to leave until he returns for you personally."

"Since when do you work for him?" Lily swore she could feel the blood vessels in her eyes bursting. "And for the record, he's not my anything. Not after this bullshit."

"I'd want to protect you too if I were him—" Steve should have known better than to try and reason with her.

"Stop. And...you're fired."

"We're not going anywhere." Lucas and Steve refused to meet her furious stare.

"I figured he made sure of that. What'd he bribe you with? Did he promise you I'd suck your cocks? Tell you he'd let you fuck me too?" Heat flamed in her cheeks. After last night, they probably expected nothing less.

"Jesus." Matt stepped in. "It's nothing like that."

She growled. "They're still fired."

"Lily, wait..."

The plea fell on deaf ears. She refused to linger so they could see how deeply Jeremy's betrayal cut her. Anyone who knew her worth a damn would realize the crack in her composure that allowed her to flip them the bird as she stormed to her office was telling enough.

Her journey seemed ten times longer than the trek from the public stage to Jeremy's all-too-private quarters had been the night before though her furious stride ate up the hallway in a flash. She drew a wobbly breath as she approached what should have been her sanctuary. With her hand on the knob, she paused, afraid to step inside. Reminders of the lies Jeremy had fed her, and how greedily she'd gobbled them up, would surround her.

Fuck that. She swore to obliterate him from her soul. Somehow. The door crashed into the wall then rebounded, halfway closed. A well-placed shove of her boot took care of the rest.

Lily paced her chambers like a lioness trapped in a zoo. Apparently Jeremy had a different idea of *always* than she did. She could have whipped herself for imagining he'd meant forever-and-ever-until-death when he'd really meant until she turned her back and he could slink out of her realm.

Stupid motherfucker. Whether she referred to him or herself...well, either fit. More him if he thought she'd consent to act as an ornament for his collection, satisfied to be left idle. Locked away from the action. Screw that. She'd prepared herself to revolt if Morselli tried anything ridiculous. After all, he was a misogynistic dickhead if not worse.

But Jeremy.

How could he have sidelined her like this?

She punted a gleaming chrome garbage can halfway across the room, satisfied with the clang it made as it collided with a solid stone statue of a naked man in the corner. If only it had been the man she'd been foolish enough to call Master. His thick skull would have sounded like a gong when struck by the metal.

"Mistress." A soft knock came on the door a moment before it cracked open. Ryan peeked inside. "I...uh...heard a crash. Are you okay?"

"Fine." She put her back to him while she daubed a bit of moisture gathering at the corner of her eyes. Horrified, she slammed shut the floodgate of emotions Jeremy had pried open. Tears shed for someone undeserving only shamed her more.

"Can I talk to you for a minute?"

Lily forced herself to swallow the bitter taste of betrayal. If one of her submissives needed her attention, they came first. Before tending the ragged hole in her chest left behind when Jeremy had ripped her heart out. Why had she allowed herself to believe this time could be different? That the man she'd fallen for would live up to his promises? How had he convinced her to believe?

For months she'd dreamed about the aura of integrity he'd cast when they'd last met. Maybe she'd built him up to be more than humanly possible.

"I'll come back later." Ryan began to shut the door.

"No, please." She bit her lip then waved him to a chair. "Take a seat."

"What if I show you a way out instead?" A mischievous smile crimped his luscious lips. "Sorry, I didn't mean to pry. I overheard your doorstoppers. I was going to offer to diagram the servant quarters for you. There are passageways no one from the main house uses. You know, staff access routes. Morselli doesn't like the workers to be seen in his hallowed halls."

"Even here? In this wing?" Lily perked up. She crossed to Ryan and grasped his hands.

"Oh yeah, definitely here. Anywhere with a bedroom is likely to have access for twilight visitors. The passages are vast and intricate."

"You know how I can get to Morselli's office from here?" If she could search his desk, she was sure she'd find what she needed to locate The Scientist. Even if she didn't, the access would put her into contact with more of the servants. They had to know where the man was stashed if he was campaigning to turn them against their boss and break free.

"Yes, Mistress."

"Show me."

The slave studied the intricate pattern of the wallpaper over her shoulder. "He would call me there often. To make me watch while he threatened my sister. I should have told you this earlier, but there was no time. I didn't realize why it was important. Ellie...she worked in a laboratory. She didn't know what they were cooking up, I swear. Each tech had only a tiny piece of the total puzzle. The job paid well. I told her to take it. It's my fault."

His shoulders slumped.

"You couldn't have known." Lily crossed the space to wrap him in her arms.

"I got myself hired on here, did whatever he wanted. I thought I could snoop around and pull her out somehow. I hadn't managed more than glimpses before Morselli caught me. He made me do things. Bad things. Like yesterday. I'm so sorry we did that to you. But he said he would hurt my sister."

"Shh." She rubbed his broad shoulders. "It's going to be okay. I'll find Ellie. I'll help her if I'm able. I'll do what I can. Tell me how to get to his office and I'll try my best."

"It's dangerous. Take me with you?" He raised his brows, looking for all the world like a loveable puppy. No way would she drag him deeper into the shadows.

Jeremy had reminded her she worked best alone.

"Not this time." She silenced him with a finger over his lips. "If I can slip out, others can break in. I need you and Ben to stay. Lucas and Steve can't cover the whole area by themselves. Worrying about the group will be a distraction I can't afford. I'll be quick. In and out."

When he still didn't respond she let some of her simmering anger show.

"Jeremy already has Morselli distracted. They're probably somewhere in the holding cells. The safest time to go is now, while his attention is diverted." She hated to do it but she played her ace. "Whatever happens, this is not on you. I'm *ordering* you to tell me."

He scrunched his eyelids closed then gulped. "Yes, Mistress."

Lily stepped aside when he angled toward the curtains. A whoosh of silk followed his yank. If it hadn't been for the ornate pattern on the wall, she wouldn't have noticed the slight disruption caused by the tiny gap around the outside edge of the wallpapered door.

"Swipe along the bottom of the molding." Ryan took her hand and flipped it over. He cradled it in his larger palm as he demonstrated. "Feel that?"

"Yes." She smiled up at him. "I just press it like this…"

The panel swung inward. If she expected a shadowy, cobwebbed rathole, she would have been disappointed. Though not as elegant as the furnishings in the rest of the house, the passageway gleamed with diffuse white light and utilitarian linoleum. The space reminded her of a hospital.

If she descended the five or six steps dropping the passage below the windows, she'd then have to either go left or right. A small plaque had an arrow pointing toward kitchen and another aimed at residential. "Efficient."

"It takes a lot to run a place like this." Ryan sighed. "Despite what he'd have you think, there are people everywhere doing his dirty work. Head toward the residential section. When you come to the staircase go down three flights. His rooms are on the main floor. They take up the whole wing. His office is at the very end of the passage. If you see anyone along the way—"

"Don't worry." She grinned. "I'm used to playing games. I'll think of something."

Ryan nodded. "If you're not back in an hour, I'm coming after you."

"Fair enough." She tugged him lower for a gentle kiss. "Everything's going to be fine."

"I hope you're right."

But he didn't look certain when he disappeared behind the curtains.

***

Lily ignored the fine vibration of her fingers as she laid them on the brass handle at the top of the short flight of stairs. She hadn't had to use her mind-your-own-business glare even once on the trip to Morselli's office, though she'd passed several housekeeping carts at a brisk yet reasonable pace.

Bits of muffled conversations bulged then faded away, echoing through the hallway as she passed by. She wondered if anyone had heard her cries as she submitted to Jeremy last night or the gentle murmur of their hushed conversation this morning.

Damn him for conning her. He played the game like a pro—she'd give him that.

Shaking off the lingering blend of disgust and disappointment laying heavy in her gut, she pressed her ear to the door and held her breath. As she expected, she heard exactly nothing. Not even the rustling of someone dusting the mantle disturbed the absolute silence.

In and out, Lily. Get it done.

She shoved the panel far enough to slip behind the thick, blood-red curtains. The reek caused by overpowering cologne with a hint of expensive whiskey choked her. Morselli probably considered the stank attractive. Nasty.

Early afternoon sunshine sparkled through the window, casting her shadow across the desk and a trophy case on the opposite wall when she nudged the material aside. The pounding of her heart obscured the sound of birds swooping over the lush grounds or the splash of gentle waterfalls emptying into the nearby pond.

How could something so disgusting be nestled in the heart of such beauty? It would have seemed more fitting if the estate had looked like the wicked witch's tower or maybe the cracks of doom. Instead, she wondered where to begin her search. Skipping obvious spots like the notes on the desk blotter, she aimed for something a little subtler.

Without the security of locked doors and easy access to house staff, Morselli wouldn't dare leave crucial information in plain sight. Skimming the shelves of a barrister bookcase, she found nothing but antique volumes on hunting. After riffling through a chest in the corner, turning up nothing more damning than a bone-handled knife, which looked brand new, she wondered if the trip had been a bust.

Lily spun in a circle, scanning every surface for signs of recent use. Dust-free and pristine, the room provided no clues. The light glinted off a crystal decanter on the mantle. Sparkles danced off the surface and the mirror behind it.

A smudge marred the gleaming surface.

She snuck around a wing-backed chair and across the floor with a glance toward the open door. Something about the mark raised her suspicions. It didn't seem like a brush from someone reaching for a drink. Besides, who kept the good stuff here when a full mahogany bar graced the corner of the room?

Thankful for her gloves, Lily put her thumb on top of the larger print and gripped the edge of the mirror. It swung a few inches outward. Braced for a monumental crash, she was surprised by the glide of well-oiled hinges.

Holy shit.

If she'd discovered a safe, she could send someone to try and crack the code. Despite their personal differences, she would share the info with Jeremy and the rest of the men in blue. Nothing mattered more than putting Morselli out of business and eliminating the threat he posed.

The computer whiz had suffered a lot of trouble to break into the inner sanctum, even going as far as fucking her senseless to secure what he sought. He'd do the right thing. When it came to the case.

Lily shook her head, averting her thoughts from the rocky slope. Damage could be buried. She'd learned pain management techniques at a young age. Refined them by the time she turned twenty.

Disappointment hit like a tidal wave when the space behind the mirror turned out to be solid wood paneling, no pinpad, dial, keyhole or other anomaly in sight. Elation began to drain from her bloodstream, leaving exhaustion in its wake. Stretching to secure the fixture in its original position, her fingertips curled over the bottom of the mirror.

They landed on a tiny cubby hollowed from the inside section of the frame. A thin capsule the size of her pinky tumbled out when she wiggled her fingers inside the space.

She caught a USB drive in the center of her palm before it could smack the ground. For the space of several racing heartbeats, she stared at the device, unable to believe her luck. A grin spread across her face, distorted in the beveled edge of the mirror, as she resealed the hiding spot.

A flicker of movement in the space behind her stopped her dead.

Morselli's chuckle sent ice down her spine. "Oh, this is going to be the most fun I've had in years."

It took another precious second for her to realize he hadn't spoken directly to her.

He wandered from the office door deeper into the room next door. Whether on the phone or conversing with someone accompanying him, she couldn't tell. And she didn't wait to find out.

Lily bolted for her escape route. She'd barely ducked behind the curtain when the clink of glasses on the sleek bar assured her the monster had joined her in his office. Searching her memory, she couldn't be sure the door to the passage had opened silently.

Before she could decide to risk it, Morselli wandered nearer. He plopped into his executive chair, kicking his feet up onto the surface of his desk. Reclined, he balanced his highball glass on his paunch. If he turned his head a fraction more he'd spot her in the shadows. Thank god for her dark red leather, which blended as well as could be hoped with the dreadful curtains.

"Are you sure you're willing to do what it takes to earn more of the drug? I can't say I blame you. The spectacle your Mistress made on her knees last night would be enough to tempt most men. Too bad you can't get her there without chemicals. They don't come cheap."

Jeremy! It had to be him. Could he really plan to drug her again? Maybe after today. He had to know she wouldn't bend for him willingly ever again. Still, some sliver of her heart prayed for a mistake. Some crazy explanation.

"Once she's mine, I'll have her daddy's money to spare. No problems there, friend." Jeremy's sleazy tone cut her to the bone.

Too bad for him, she'd spent the bulk of her share of the Buchanan fortune in aid packages for the women she'd rescued earlier in the year and the hefty fees she'd earned as a Mistress on supplying allied buyers cash to purchase freedom for others.

Lily grasped for rage. She tried to pull indignation around her like a shield as she had so often before. This time when she pumped the well, all she surfaced was misery and desolation. She couldn't fight on her own anymore.

That hadn't been a lie.

A tiny gasp escaped her throat.

"What was that?" Morselli's feet clomped to the floor.

Her eyes widened as her fingers curled in the starchy fabric abrading them. She prayed the end came quickly though she couldn't imagine fate helping her out now when it never had before.

CHAPTER NINETEEN

Jeremy bolted for the window, attempting to appear calm when his guts quaked like a mountain of green Jell-O. The squeak had become familiar to him sometime around three am when he'd slid his cock into the tightest, hottest pussy he'd ever had and fucked his way to nirvana.

How could she believe it'd been nothing more than carnal satisfaction?

Oh, maybe because she'd been drugged. Add to that the fact no one had ever earned her trust in her entire life. Of course she'd expect him to deceive her at the first opportunity. He couldn't wait to prove her wrong.

To do that, they both had to make it out of here in one piece.

He stepped between Morselli and the curtains Ryan had frantically explained concealed a tangle of paths riddling the compound. Every cell in his being screamed for him to peek in Lily's direction and reassure her. Instead, he concentrated on the landscape outside the window.

"Must have been one of those birds." He motioned toward the pond with his untouched drink. Like he'd ingest anything this loser handed him. "What are they? Herons?"

"Yeah." Morselli grabbed a set of binoculars off a pile of junk near his desk. "They're loud as shit sometimes. Maybe I'll take a little target practice later."

Jeremy reined in the urge to punch the asshole. Satisfying as it might be, it wouldn't serve his purpose. He glanced toward a display case overflowing with antique guns on the far wall, opposite Lily's hiding spot. "Looks like you have a sweet collection over there."

"*Sweet.*" Morselli laughed so hard he burst into a coughing fit.

From the cover of his hip, Jeremy waved his fingers toward the wall. *Run, Lily.*

He slapped his host on the back hard enough to inspire another round of giant exhalations then laughed as loud as he could justify as reasonable. "Drink much?"

Fuckwad. He appended the insult in his mind, but he couldn't restrain himself from stealing a glimpse of the gently swaying curtain. A slice of light hung behind it where only shadows had lingered moments before.

Morselli swiped at his mouth with the sleeve of a silk shirt that probably cost as much as the Chief made in a month. "What kind of pussy says sweet, anyway?"

The kind that just snuck his woman from your grubby clutches. Jeremy grinned and shrugged, wondering how much longer he'd have to endure the slimy bastard before he could reunite with Lily.

Even more difficult to predict was whether he'd squeeze her in half or turn her ass bright red first.

***

Jeremy marched toward his quarters, attempting to maintain a sedate pace while dreading what he would find inside. Would she be there?

She had to be there.

Please God, let her be there.

The instant Matt and Clint came into sight, his heart plummeted. Dread etched deep grooves around their eyes and mouths.

"JRad. I'm sorry, man." Clint shook his head.

He threw his hand out, skimming it over the wall to keep from crashing as he staggered the last ten feet toward his rooms. "She didn't come home?"

"Not willingly." Matt's hedging ignited a spark of hope. "Ryan called off the 10-57 when she showed up in her office."

"Oh, shit." He clutched his chest. Relief weakened his knees. Matt's arm slung around his shoulders for the instant it took to regain his balance. He waved toward the partners. "So what's with the angst?"

"Like I said, she didn't seem to appreciate how upset you were when you realized she'd taken off on her own." Clint ducked his head. "She fought us. I didn't have a choice. To bring her back here—"

"We had to tie her up and force her, carry her, kicking and screaming." Matt flinched when Jeremy shifted out of his grasp.

"What kind of dickhead do you think I am?" He glared at his friends. "You kept her safe no matter what the fool tried to do to herself. Hell, probably looks good for Morselli on the cameras anyway. I'm not going to beat you up for doing as I asked."

"You could try." Clint couldn't help the knee-jerk reaction. The men in blue talked shit on a fairly constant basis. In some twisted way, the familiar taunting lightened Jeremy's load.

Muffled shouts leaked into the hallway.

"Uh, she's still pretty pissed," Matt warned.

"That makes two of us." Jeremy's enduring terror vaporized into a cloud of steaming anger. What if he hadn't blocked the hacker and they realized she'd fought on their side for months, if not years? What if he hadn't intercepted Morselli on the way to his office? What if the fucker hadn't been half-sloshed in the middle of the afternoon? What if the evil bastard had turned one instant sooner and caught Lily behind the curtains?

Clint groaned. "And I might not be able to have kids. She speared me with one of those hot-as-hell heels."

"Okay, that part was pretty classic." Matt chuckled. "But someone's going to have to smooth things over with her staff or they'll riot. Lucas and Steve will need backup pretty soon. She has a lot of guys rooting for her. You better fix things quick so she can order them to stand down."

"Or take her back." Clint looked as though he'd drunk a swig of bitter beer.

"If she's changed her mind..." Jeremy scratched the prickle of his beard. "If she isn't the woman I thought, I'll let her go. We'll figure something out. Either we'll lock them in safely or ship them out before someone really gets hurt."

The bitch of it was he already had. If Lily had lied to him—if she'd run the moment his back was turned—she couldn't be the woman he'd fallen hard for.

Damn it.

He stormed into his apartment and slammed the door behind him. The vase gracing the nearby table rattled. If he could have done it twice as hard he would have when the sight of his disobedient lover, trussed and gagged in the middle of his bed, inflated his cock from soft to full erection in a heartbeat.

The sway of her ass as she wriggled against the silky sheets launched him beyond sane reasoning straight into raw reaction. He leapt onto the bed, blanketing her struggling form with his, smothering her attempts at escape.

"Oh no you don't." He pinned her, face down, to the mattress. "You wormed away from me once. Not again."

Despite the gravelly tone of his voice, she didn't seem deterred. If anything, she fought harder, bucking like a world-class bronco beneath him. He squelched her revolt without mercy.

Unfortunately, the full-body tackle left his hard-on nestled in the valley of her ass.

Shrill shrieks ebbed into moans. Lily quit fighting.

"Careful, darling," he growled into her ear. "Don't mistake my lust for leniency. You better have a fantastic reason for skipping out on me."

He flipped her over, sinking over her again.

Icy blue eyes met his, unblinking.

"Tell me why you did it." He tugged the cloth from between her lips onto her chin, and left it in case he needed to replace it quickly. If she spouted one single lie that had his heart yearning to make poor decisions, he'd silence her.

Sharp teeth sank into his finger.

"Son of a bitch." He turned her again. The crack of his hand on her leather-coated ass startled them both. He'd bet the noise far outweighed any sting that penetrated to her tight cheeks. Rolling on top of her, he settled in, his legs spread on either side of her bound ankles and knees. Trussed, her hands fisted in the small of her back. They formed two small rocks beneath his abs.

"Why, Lily? Why didn't you wait for me?" He buried his face in her hair, grateful despite her betrayal to have her close. Safe.

"Fuck you," she snarled. "Don't play the injured party. You had to know I would run if I could."

Suspicion had infiltrated his mind on the long walk from Morselli's office. It couldn't be, could it? "Do you want Sex Offender for yourself? All this time...have you been waiting for a chance to cut in on the action?"

With one side of her face mashed against the mattress, she stared at him from the corner of her pretty eyes as though he'd lost his mind.

"Is that what this is really about, Lily? Are you trying to one-up me for information?"

"Fuck no. And I heard your buy from Morselli. As if it's not bad enough you conned me into giving it up willingly." All the fight leeched from her body. "Now you'll take me by force."

Jeremy struggled to maintain his fury when she played possum. The appreciative Dom inside him ached to cuddle her close and relish her yielding. She would anticipate his triggers better than anyone. She could turn his instincts against him.

"Quit playing games! You know that was bullshit. I had to do something to keep your ass out of the fire. I had to think of a reason to show up there. *Alone.*" He tried to ignore her flinch when he barked in her face. "Don't you fucking realize how close you came to ending it all? For you and every person you claim to care about."

Jeremy didn't bother spelling it out. He'd counted himself among those ranks for a little while. *Dumbass.*

"I'm not the one who broke my promise." Fragmented speech could have resulted from true emotion or his bulk, which squished the breath from her lungs.

Moving now would be impossible in either case. "You didn't? Running off by yourself without taking a single person for backup? What the hell was so important you couldn't wait thirty more minutes for me to take care of the cyber attack?"

"What—"

"Not a great strategy in any case. You could have roped me into it with you and still screwed me over afterward. I would have been blinded by the stars in my eyes. At least I would have protected you while you snuck around there like James fucking Bond. Or maybe Austin Powers is more like it."

"*You* abandoned *me.*" She glared at him through slitted eyes. Sharp claws pinched his stomach. "Don't try to turn this around."

"Shit." He hissed at the sting of the slices she'd raked across his six-pack. How sick did it make him that the burn steeled his cock further? "Would you rather they had dug around in my files? Maybe I should have allowed them to poke through all the pictures I've collected of you? All the testimonials and evidence I've hoarded to fireproof your ungrateful ass when the shit hits the fan?"

"I'm confused," she whispered. Eyelashes swiped her cheek as she blinked furiously. "What are you saying?"

"That even though you played me like a fool, I'd still never stand for anyone to put you away. Because despite whatever fucking shenanigans you pulled today, I don't believe for one second you're in this for the drug. So tell me. *Now.*" He shook her. "Why the hell didn't you wait for me to handle shit so we could visit Morselli together?"

"I didn't know there was shit to handle other than him. Steve told me you were gone. That you'd ordered them to hold me until you came back. A prisoner in my own fucking space."

Oh, shit. He had. But not without cause. Not to sneak off and do exactly what he'd promised her he wouldn't. Even, still..."You believed them? Over me? You didn't ask more questions? Didn't demand the details? Come on, Lily."

"I... No, I didn't."

"You assumed the worst?" The swirling ball of anger, terror and loss occupying the pit of his stomach shifted, finding a new outlet. "You think I'm like every other man in your life? That no matter what I swore to you when I looked into those sexy blue eyes, I'd lied?"

"Yes." Her bottom lip quivered.

Through a monumental test of willpower, he resisted kissing the flushed pink curve of her mouth. If he cracked now they might never recover.

"You called me Master, but you didn't mean it." He released her, rising to his knees as he angled toward the

271

edge of the bed. "You took back your gift. Your faith in me."

"Wait!" She rolled as best she could to maintain eye contact. "Don't leave."

"You did."

"So did you." Some of her vigor returned. Fury painted her cheeks. It was the tiny indentations her teeth pressed into her lip that did him in.

He slumped to the mattress, cradling his head between his hands. If he expected her to believe in him, he had to earn her trust. Over time. Not in one crazy, if intense, day. How could he blame her for wavering when every important person in her life had conned her? Not all of the blame could be laid at her feet.

It had cost her to reach out and call him back. Torn, ragged breaths bordering on sobs pummeled his hunched shoulders. Ego they had in spades.

Riding the line between equity and passion, he considered what Gunther might advise if his mentor had watched their situation unfold. Despite Lily's contribution to the fiasco, it was Jeremy's duty to protect her, not just physically but emotionally too. Clearly he'd earned a ginormous fail on that front.

"I let you down today, Lily." He rotated ninety degrees, shoving off straight-locked arms until his shoulders met the headboard. "You're right. I should have spoken to you personally before leaving, no matter the emergency."

"I was in the middle of—"

"That's not the point. I should have realized the conclusions you'd leap to." He used the rope binding her to tug her around until her head rested on his lap. The tip of his finger seemed enormous when it traced her meticulously arched brow. "We're just out of the gate, you and I. In five years, I hope it won't matter as much. You'll learn to rely on me as much as I will on you."

"Five years?" The last of her stony resistance melted.

"Okay, maybe after ten you'll realize I'm not going anywhere. I'm sorry to break this to you..." Rapt attention focused on his face as he teased her. "You're stuck with me."

"You were really coming right back?" Tears pooled, unshed, in her eyes.

"If for whatever reason we're ever separated, I swear I will always come back to you. For you. Without fail."

"I'm sor—"

He laid his hand lightly across her mouth.

"Not necessary." A slow, devious smile spread across his lips. He wrestled the excitement out of his tone, attempting a nonchalant offer. "I was a bad Master. Would you like to take my spanking for me?"

"If you'll add my strokes to the tally, sir." The swell of her breasts drew his attention. Lamplight glimmered off her chest, which rose and fell quicker and quicker.

"Will the pain ease your guilty conscience?"

"Yes, sir."

"Do you understand that if I give you this punishment, the rest disappears?" He circled her mouth with one finger, pleased when she opened and drew it inside. "We'll erase today from our memories and start over. Without betrayals. Without doubt."

"Please," she whispered.

The tiny supplication affected him like a gunshot. A flurry of motion had her bindings unknotted at record speed. She didn't attempt to move from where he situated her.

"Please what?"

"Please lay your palm on my ass. Burn away all the pain and fear we caused each other today and leave only the heat behind. Spank me. Please, Master Jeremy."

A roar built behind his sternum and his knees went weak. Her supplication rushed to his head faster and more potent than the expensive bottle of Merlot the men in blue had pitched in to buy for his birthday last year. "I'd be honored to."

He bent at the waist to cover her mouth with his. The caress of his lips started slow. It quickly built from tender nudges and gentle licks until they ate at each other. When it became a matter of lifting his head for oxygen or passing out and crushing her, he was surprised to find himself already on his feet beside the bed.

"Bare." He growled. "I need you naked. Now."

She held her hands out to him, and he stripped off first one than the other of her gloves. The soft skin at her wrists bore purple ligature marks from where she'd thrashed in her bonds. He pressed a light kiss to each one, liking the pretty color on her. She wore it well.

"Give me more." Her moan drew his heavy-lidded gaze to her wide eyes. "Something to remind me of you—of this—when you're not beside me."

"You'll always be imprinted on my heart, Lily. I'll take you everywhere I go as part of me." Next he unbuckled her boots.

Some preferred to rip the paper from a gift instead of meticulously unwrapping it. Less fuss and more of the good stuff. Anticipation was more his style. He delighted in every lace he untied and every zipper he released. Pale porcelain skin peeked between the components of her outfit, driving him insane. The only good news was that she was so engrossed in his touch she didn't seem to notice how he toed the edge of his control.

He didn't dare remove his clothes. If he eliminated the last barrier between them, he'd forget all about her punishment and fuse them with one desperate lunge. Forced abstinence sounded pretty hellacious to him.

Accepting his own punishment for disappointing her earlier, he tugged the leather pants off her shapely legs.

Lily wiggled, lifting her hips to aid him.

With her ass completely exposed, he could have flipped her over and laid his hand to her naked flesh. Except she still wore the top of her suit and he couldn't stand to have an inch of her veiled from his view. He rolled the pliant material from her, wondering at the all-over hug it had wrapped her in.

"You like wearing these...things." He considered the latex version she'd showcased at Black Lily or the corsets he'd spotted her in when he hid in the shadows on Main, watching over her as she walked through deserted streets to her club, when he could manage it. "The constriction, the structure, the slight discomfort. You get off on it, don't you?"

"Mmm..." She purred as her breasts were released from the confines of her outfit. "Yes, sir. Right now I like *not* wearing them more."

"Same here." He plumped her surprisingly stacked chest in his palms. "You're gorgeous, Lily."

"I'm glad I make you happy."

"You have no idea how much." He plucked her from the bed. A wry grin tipped up the corners of his mouth when she yelped, unused to someone manhandling her. With two or three giant strides, he carried her to a large leather chair. The low, arched arms made it perfect for what he had in store.

Jeremy sat, turning her until she stretched facedown over his lap with her legs extended to his right and her chest supported by the elegant sweep of the chair on his left.

"Comfortable?"

"No, sir." Her thighs and ass flexed as she squirmed. "Too empty and I want the release you promised. I need you to replace all my doubts with something hot. Please."

His cock nearly destroyed his favorite pair of jeans. She fit over his lap as though she'd been made especially for him. Maybe she had.

He expanded his massage of her ass, rubbing his hands in broad circles up her back until he reached her thick braid, which dangled down to the ground. The silky mass passed through his fingers as he lifted it. When he unwound the elastic at the base of the long tail, she stirred.

"Even this, so tightly arranged. You couldn't stand to let one single part of you free, could you?" He released the woven plaits one fold at a time until a lush mane of soft waves tumbled across her shapely back. The softness pillowed his left forearm when he lowered it across her shoulder blades, pinning her in place. "Count them, Lily."

"Yes, sir." Her affirmation took the form of a keening whimper.

Music to his ears. Almost as good as her cries of sensual pain would be. "Relax."

"Yes, s—"

Jeremy didn't wait for her to finish before connecting with the firm muscles of her pert ass. The adorable jiggle that resulted mesmerized him nearly as much as the pink outline of his fingers that developed.

The only sound she made was a sharp inhalation. To her credit, she stayed still as a statue. Accepting—no, welcoming—all he chose to impart. He soothed the impact area.

"Forgetting something?"

"One." She whispered, "Thank you, Master. Please, may I have another?"

"You'll have plenty more before we're through. Don't make me remind you again."

This time he spanked her harder.

"T-two."

The smack of his palm on her lush curves rang through the room again and again. He half-expected Matt and Clint to ram through the door and rush to his damsel's rescue. To their credit, they didn't intervene. They probably still couldn't fully appreciate his lifestyle choices, but they trusted him not to hurt Lily. Or any innocent for that matter.

Escalating numbers accompanied his steady barrage of rough touches. At a dozen, she began to struggle with focus. By fourteen she double counted.

Jeremy granted an intermission as he soothed the pain with kneading pressure. If she had been a beginner, he would have stopped there. He knew better than to quit early on her. "Five more. Harder ones. A spank for every minute I suffered, wondering if you were okay, while I tracked Morselli to his office."

"May I have another on your behalf for the knot in my guts when Steve told me you'd caged me in?" Her teeth chattered. "The hardest of all. Please. Take the pain away."

"Feed it to the fire." He aimed carefully then swatted her with enough force to set her legs kicking as she struggled against his arm for the first time.

"Fifteen."

"Such a good girl." The next spank landed on her opposite cheek, balancing out the rose shading.

"Oh, shit. Yes." She moaned. "Sixteen."

He held her tighter, containing her squirming, which would have dumped her onto the floor had he not cradled her close.

"Seventeen."

The smell of her arousal hit him a dozen times stronger than the careful force he applied to her ass. He couldn't wait to reward her for her supplication and beautiful suffering. After they expunged the last of the horror they'd inflicted on each other.

"Eighteen."

"It's okay to cry, Lily. You were scared. Alone. Let it out." She never would have released the pent-up emotion if he hadn't provided her with a justifiable outlet. Her wrenching sobs broke his heart, driving him to end her agony. "Never again. I'm here. Do you feel me?"

Tingles spread across his hand when it connected with her radiant ass. He considered stopping short. Swallowing hard, he annealed his heart. She needed this.

"N-nineteen."

He rubbed his target, aligning his palm just at the base curve where her thighs swelled into her ideal ass. The classic placement. "This one's for me. It's going to sting. It's going to hurt. And then it'll all be over. Behind us. Harness the pain. Push it outside of you."

"Twenty," she screamed.

Jeremy shifted, intending to smother her with affection while buried in the deep pile of pillows and blankets on the enormous bed, his favorite thing about the haven they'd created behind enemy lines. She surprised him again when she wrenched off his lap, kneeling on the floor between his spread legs.

He automatically cupped her tear-stained cheek in his palm when she scooted closer, resting her head on his thigh. The stark splendor of her cascade of midnight hair against pale skin was only outshone by the bright red splash of her parted lips and the impossible blue of her eyes. A single tear clung to her lashes like a precious diamond.

"Lily—" A lump formed in his throat, preventing him from sharing the awe in his heart.

"Let me." She lifted her hand to the swell of his cock, tracing the bold line it made from his groin to his hip. "Please, Master."

He couldn't deny his own need for release—a channel for the overwhelming relief following his adrenaline high. Besides, he hoped to show her what he seemed incapable of putting into words. Neither of them could deny how desperately he needed her or how much her submission appealed to him when she unbuttoned his pants and his ultra-hard cock unknitted a solid inch of the zipper constraining him.

"Yes." He ripped the rest of the closure open then guided her head toward his erection. Had he ever been this hard in his life? He doubted it.

When she would have swallowed him whole, he stopped her short and painted the bead of precome decorating his tip across her sinful mouth, enhancing the shine of her lips. "Lick it off."

The sight of her nimble pink tongue swiping his taste from soft curves nearly had him shooting the rest of the fluid making his balls ache across her gorgeous face. She gripped his shaft, pressing hard at the base, returning some semblance of control. God damn, sex with her could never compare to the pale imitation of passion he'd settled for post-Karen.

So in step, they fed off each other.

A moan vibrated around his cock when he inserted it between her slick lips. Without direction, she began to blow him as though the act soothed her as much as it incited rapture in him. She hummed, her cheeks going concave as she suckled his thick shaft.

"Fuck." He buried both hands in her hair, guiding her head in the rhythm he preferred. Scooting his ass to the very edge of the chair, he provided her more room to work. With each pass she consumed more of him until her mouth hugged his full length. The steady clench of her throat around the tip of his cock had him seeing spots. Whoever had taught her that trick was dangerous.

Even if he could have prolonged his ecstasy, he would not have. Her generosity was enough to please him for the next decade. Rewarding her would be twice as fun as the epic orgasm about to crash through him.

"Drink it, Lily," he growled when the first strike of pleasure drew his sac tight to his body. "All of it. Every drop for you."

He waited long enough for her to stare up into his eyes before releasing his tenuous hold on the rapture she inspired. Without breaking her gaze, he spurted into her greedy mouth, loving the flex of her throat as she ingested every bit of the offering he had to give her.

"Yes." Through the height of the storm, he made sure he didn't squeeze her too tight. "Lily. Goddamn, perfect."

CHAPTER TWENTY

Come still dribbled from Jeremy's twitching cock when he lurched to his feet, whisking Lily into his arms. She wrapped her legs around his waist, clinging to him like a baby koala as he kicked off his jeans and socks. Within two seconds flat, he lowered them to the bed, covering her mouth with his.

She sighed when her ass met the cool, satiny material. He inhaled the gasp, consuming all her pain and transforming it into something beautiful. Tears pricked her eyes once more. Bliss threatened to block out important realities in favor of keeping her locked in their idyllic fantasy. As much as she longed to be swept away, too much depended on the success of their mission.

Lily sniffled before whispering, "Master Jeremy."

"Hmm?" He tucked her hair behind her ear.

How could she have forgotten the most important part of her ill-fated adventure? "It wasn't all for nothing."

"What?" He levered onto his elbows. His hand stalled in its soothing rub over her flaming cheeks.

"I found something in Morselli's office."

"You did?" Jeremy sat up, hauling her into his lap.

She curled against his chest, uncaring how weak it made her to indulge in the security he provided. After the craziness of the day—hell, the whole year—she relished the chance to soak in his strength.

Hugging her tight suited him too if his sigh gave any indication.

"Yes. A thumb drive, hidden behind the mirror. I stole it." A thought hit her suddenly, tensing all her muscles at once. "What if he notices it's gone?"

"One step at a time." Jeremy rocked her in a lulling sway when she grew more agitated. "Let me grab it so we can check it out."

He leaned toward the floor, reaching for her abandoned outfit.

A light touch on his forearm halted him. Confidence had never deserted her before. This time she cared a bit too much about what he'd think of the drastic measures she'd taken. "Look, that thing doesn't exactly have pockets."

"So where'd you stash the drive, Lily?" He cocked his head as he attempted to decipher her hesitation.

"Uh…"

"You didn't." He chuckled.

"I might have." She blushed. When was the last time that had happened? Maybe when she was a kid and bullies had shamed her with explicit descriptions of the services her mother traded for her next drink. "The suit is skintight. I couldn't risk someone spotting the bulge if they stopped me in the hallway. God only knows what's on that drive. If it fell into the wrong hands it could spell disaster."

Jeremy gritted his teeth as though he imagined her stalking along the corridors alone, where anyone could have crossed paths with her. "And you haven't…retrieved it?"

"When do you think I might have had a chance to do that?" She focused on the burn in her ass instead of the acid that had eaten at her as the cops bound her then threw her over their shoulder like a bag of potatoes. "Clint pounced on me the minute I stepped inside. I had to call Ben and Ryan off before their standoff deteriorated into a brawl."

"Good to know. I'll have to thank him later," Jeremy grumbled. "And watch your tone unless you want another dozen swats."

"Don't judge me."

"Shit. I'm not." He drew an X over his heart then kissed her softly. A connection sparked between them brighter than ever. "Swear."

"I've done whatever it takes to survive for more than a decade. Why stop now?" Unless…" She bit her lip. "Do you think I ruined it?"

"Nah. If you'd swallowed it, stomach acid could have been a problem. A solid state drive like that can resist moisture no problem."

"I'm pretty wet." She buried her face against his pecs. Damn him for turning her on with his barbaric display. His compassion had affected her through and through. She parted her lips and drew his nipple ring between her teeth, flicking her tongue over the fascinating mix of jewelry and warm man.

"Hmm, really?" He glided two fingers along her arm to her hip then inward. "Enjoyed your spanking, did you?"

"Yes, sir." The pressure of his digits had her shifting her legs, dying for his touch on her mound, which felt thick and heavy with the lust he inspired.

Her lips meandered upward, over his collarbone to the base of his neck. Instead of shutting her down, he lifted his chin, granting her access to the vulnerable pulse tripping there. For a man so ingrained with dominant instincts, it was a privilege he could not have given to many. Gratitude swamped her, leaving her utterly at his mercy.

How did he always make it so easy for her to relinquish control?

"That's right. Just like that." One of his hands clenched on her hip when she melted all over again. The other continued to tease her, plying her with more finesse than she could have mustered after years of self-pleasure. "You concentrate on enjoying my attention. I'll take care of the rest."

The room flipped around them as he settled her on her back. A mountain of pillows cushioned her, propping her torso so she didn't miss a second of the show he put on as he nestled between her legs.

Lily hoped he'd meant what he said about moisture not damaging the drive because the fucking thing had to be saturated by the time he wandered from her lips, down her neck, taking a leisurely break around her chest to lave first one breast than the other with bold, open-mouthed kisses.

No objections followed her burying her fingers in his thick, silky hair. Could he comprehend she didn't intend to direct him, only to glean another tactile sensation from the menu of options his body offered? She relished the strands tickling the juncture of her fingers until he continued his journey down her ribs and across her belly. He worshipped every inch of her between there and the drastically trimmed patch of fuzz decorating her pussy.

"Someday I'll have you completely bald. You'll look even tastier with your juices glazing you here, tempting me to devour you." His broad shoulders looked gargantuan as they wedged between her thighs. He didn't hesitate before burying his face against the slick folds of her lips. A moan buffeted the puffy tissue, so primed for contact she nearly came on the spot.

He paused long enough to grin up at her, curving one arm beneath her thigh then around her waist to fondle her breast. Locked to him, she could only shiver in his grasp. He descended once more. "You're delicious, Lily. In every way."

Panic rose in her chest, forcing a whimper from her throat when he flicked the tip of his tongue in the neighborhood of her clit. Without direct stimulation, she should have no trouble collecting herself. Still, she hovered on the edge of orgasm. The tingle across her ass, his possessive grasp, the sexy light in his eyes—all of it combined to destroy her legendary restraint.

"Shh... You're fine. No need to deprive yourself. This isn't some sex diet. You have my permission to come as often as you can." He growled, "I can't wait to see it. Hear it. Feel it."

"The drive—"

"My concern, not yours." He nipped her inner thigh.

Oh my God, so *not helpful.*

"Don't worry." A grin spread over his superfine lips. "I'll get it back."

Regardless of his instructions, she would not have been able to suppress the first bloom of pleasure that washed over her when he slipped two long fingers inside her channel while returning his mouth to the apex of her slit.

Shallow strokes opened the entrance to her pussy. A flight of fancy had her imagining she could actually sense the tiny drive lodged inside her tensing channel. Probably, his fingers provided the mass she hugged as a miniature quake rumbled through her.

"Really," he shook his head in mock disapproval. The motion slid his mouth back and forth across her clit, enhancing the tremors. "You can do so much better than that."

"Fuck you." She laughed through the final remnants of pleasure. When was the last time she'd had fun with a man in bed? She couldn't remember because it had never happened before. Not this deep melding of equals.

"Maybe later. If you're especially good." He spread his fingers inside her. "Are you sore?"

"A little." Lying would be ridiculous. "And I sort of like it."

285

"You enjoyed being stretched yesterday, didn't you?" He probed deeper on his lascivious search and rescue mission, careful to spread her as he progressed.

She hadn't exactly shoved the thing to the moon. His meticulous approach reassured her he wouldn't knock the drive deeper. Relaxing, her pussy accommodated the outward spread of his fingers, which widened her by gentle degrees.

"Answer me." He trapped her clit between his teeth, applying the barest of pressure with the sharp edges.

Think. Stretched? "Hell, yes. It burned. So good."

"When I watched Matt's cock plow into you and your pussy accommodated him," he growled. "It made me twice as hard. I forget how little you are sometimes. How young."

"I can handle you."

"I'm pretty sure I can say the same." His grimace turned into a grin. "Guess what I found?"

"I hope it's a way out of this mess."

"Me too, Lily." Steadily, as though playing a game of erotic operation, he withdrew the innocuous plastic capsule. When it cleared her body, he pinned her with a blazing stare. "Don't move. Not one inch or you'll have your first serious flogging from me. I mean it. I'll be right back."

If he knew how much his threat tempted her, he might have picked something else to ensure her obedience.

Water splashed softly from the bathroom. When he returned, he surprised her by laying the device beside one of his computers and focusing on her without investigating the contents. His fluid pounce onto the bed brought his face within inches of hers. "Are you up for an adventure? As usual, you've given me a very naughty idea."

The gleam of his molten gold eyes had her breath hitching in her chest.

"What did I do? I'm just lying here." She battled the weight of her heavy lids when he petted her abdomen.

"You're looking sinfully sexy, reminding me of how amazing you were last night. I want to fill you like Matt did. More than. Until all you can feel is me. Inside you. Always."

That made two of them.

"How..." Though he had plenty enough to satisfy her, he couldn't stack up against Matt's all-over bulk. She much preferred Jeremy's long, cut lines to the thickness of his friend.

Before she even had the question out, he returned his hand to her pussy. This time he invaded with three fingers on the initial penetration. He slipped further inside, aided by the copious lubrication his touch generated.

"More, please." She craved release.

"Exactly. Much more. I'm going to fist you, Lily."

His blatant promise caught her off-guard. She sputtered.

"Surely, you've done it plenty." His rasp did funny things to her stomach. "I saw the pictures of you with Malcolm, remember?"

"Yes." The rush of power accompanying such a complete possession had thrilled both her and her slaves. Fragments of inflaming memories zipped through her mind—the snap of a latex glove, cool gel coating her hand, grunts leading to moans and the mess created by her submissives' explosive orgasms. "But my hand is half the size of yours and they're bigger. It's way easier for them."

"Oh, I don't know." Jeremy pressed soft kisses to her pussy. At her whimper, he snuck his pinky inside her too. "You're engineered for this. My hand is a hell of a lot smaller than a baby."

Shallow breaths had her breasts bobbing, stealing his attention for a few seconds.

"You're going to try for me." It wasn't a question. The iron in his tone brooked no argument.

Truthfully, she didn't attempt to rebel. Why fight when the idea alone had her creaming, easing his passage deeper into her pussy?

"You have to trust me. I won't push you further than you can go." Between gentle reassurances, he lapped at her pussy, working toward her clit. "You're burning my hand. So soft. Sweet."

She sighed when he withdrew and sampled some of her arousal.

The unmistakable snick of a bottle of lube opening drew her gaze to his other hand. He drizzled the slippery substance over her pussy before slathering his hand and wrist. "As wet as you are, it'll take more to ease inside."

"Show me." A switch flipped her instincts into overdrive. She reached for him, but he stayed the course, reinserting his four fingers and wedging them until he encountered the resistance of her body, somewhere around his second set of knuckles.

"Nice and slow, Lily." He sucked lightly on her clit. "This could take a while. Lay back. Enjoy my present to you."

"Your wrist isn't much bigger than Matt's cock. Do it faster." She couldn't still her hips, which lifted to meet his steady pushing. The wedge of his hand gradually widened her, permitting more of his fingers to impale her.

"It's not my wrist that's the problem, it's my knuckles. You know the thumb is the hardest part. After that, you'll suck me right in." He pinned her to the bed with his free arm, highlighting the elevated sensation on her ass.

"Have you done this before?" Lily panted at the hard-core stimulation he delivered. He stroked her from the inside, persuading her muscles to relax and absorb more of him.

"Personally, no," he murmured against her mound. Vibrations enhanced his slow assault. "I observed one of Gunther's sessions during my training, though. The woman he fisted came so hard she passed out. Even unconscious, she shattered again when he withdrew."

"I'm not surprised. The thought of you, so deep inside me..." She shuddered.

"I remember the look on her face when she woke up. How she and Gunter were always closer than some of his other subs. I want that with you, Lily. Another bond." His tongue wriggled around her clit, tensing her muscles in a counterproductive spasm. "That's right. Why don't you come on me? Get rid of some of this extra tension. Go ahead."

Permission spurred her higher. Spreading digits trapped sensitive nerves against her pubic bone. Pinched flesh clamped around him, squeezing him tight. Sparkles danced behind her scrunched lids as she embraced the flare of arousal and nurtured it until it flared out of control. It consumed her, flashing over her entire being like a rag doused in gasoline finally exposed to flame.

"Master!" She flailed in his direction as sensation overwhelmed her. Fingers threaded through hers, holding her hand during the storm of ecstasy that rained through her body.

Jeremy pumped into her, maximizing each flex and release to enhance her experience and burrow deeper in her welcoming body.

"Thank you, thank you." She didn't realize she chanted it again and again until he paused his suckling to accept her gratitude.

"It's always my pleasure." His thumb took up where his mouth left off. It glided around her clit, desensitizing the engorged bundle of nerves while he levered over her for a long, drugging kiss.

Sweetness flavored his mouth, merging with his usual spicy tang. She drew on his tongue, craving his possession in every part of her capable of hosting him. For long minutes, they exchanged heated licks and nips. When he drew her bottom lip between his and nibbled, she began to emerge from the sensual fog he'd generated.

"Most of your hand is in me?" She slid her fingers between their torsos to feel for herself. Circling his slick wrist, she worked past the heel of his hand. Not much farther and she encountered her own stretched tissue. He cupped her pussy in the juncture of his hand and thumb, the devious digit manipulating her into a renewed burst of pleasure.

"Yeah." He seemed a little out of breath himself. "You're so silky. Warm. Can you take more?"

"Yes, sir."

The snarl he made as he dipped lower, lavishing bold attention on her chest, might have frightened her if she didn't share his experience. How many times had she reveled in the surrender of a man who begged for her to use his body?

Though she'd appreciated their sacrifices, she hadn't fully realized how much she might have given in return. If he didn't take her higher she might dissolve into an unsatisfied puddle. On the brink of a major breakthrough, she couldn't turn back.

Jeremy thrilled her with undiluted lust. He laved her nipple, alternating harsh bites with tender swipes of his tongue.

"Please. More." She trembled beneath him. "I need more."

He responded like lightning to her desperate petition. Sitting on his heels between her legs, he folded his thumb behind his fingers until his hand resembled a duck's bill. The ideal formation made his fist as narrow as possible. He snatched the bottle of lube with his left hand and held it out to her. "Open it."

She lurched forward, flipping the cap up with her teeth.

"So eager?" Crooning platitudes followed as he doused the exposed portions of his right hand with more lube. Coupled with steady pressure, he initiated a twisting of his wrist that insinuated him a fraction of an inch deeper with each motion. "It's probably going to hurt, Lily. Deep breaths now."

"Ahh." She couldn't manage more than that. The wedge of his hand spread her wider with every passing second. It wasn't exactly painful, but it sure as hell burned. So good.

Driven by the motion of his arm and the heartbeat pulsing through his veined shaft, his stiff cock waved.

She licked her lips.

"I'd rather fuck you, though I may take you up on that again later." He grimaced. "If I don't shoot the second my fist is buried inside you."

"You'll probably need something tighter than my pussy after this." She angled her head away. Her heart hurt when she considered she might not have what it took to satisfy him.

"You know it doesn't work that way." He slapped her inner thigh hard enough to claim her undivided attention. "Don't forget all you've studied just because this is you and me. Your pussy is elastic. Plenty tight even minutes after fisting. And even if it wasn't...there's always your ass. I haven't taken all of you yet, Lily. But I will. Count on that."

The jerk of her hips embedded him a tiny bit deeper.

They both moaned.

"In fact, the time I told you about." He groaned as he increased the pressure on her muscles. "Gunther fucked his sub in the ass while he fisted her."

"If it pleases you—"

"Not today." He stroked himself a few times before resuming his position on his belly between her legs. After arranging his package, he used his fingers to test her pussy where it smothered his hand. "Maybe next time. If you're a good girl."

"I promise." A yelp escaped when he pushed a little too hard and pain shot up her spine.

In an instant, he backed off. "We might need more than one session to do this right, Lily. I won't rush you."

"No!" She grabbed his forearm and dug in her nails to keep him from retreating.

"Excuse me?" He froze. Instincts wrestled for control over his paralyzed features.

With a concentrated effort, she lowered her hands to the sheets, digging them into the rich material to keep her grounded. "Please. Don't leave me."

Jeremy closed his eyes as though praying for strength. When he opened them, she gasped at the raw hunger she glimpsed. "I told you. I won't ever do that again. I'm part of you."

"Make it true." She begged from her heart. "I can take it. So close. Please fill me, enter me, make me yours. I trust you to take care of me. And right now this is what I need."

"Yes, right on the brink. My knuckles are resting at your entrance." He cursed. "Fuck. Bear down, Lily. Take a deep breath then let it out long and slow. On three."

He dropped his head long enough to surround her clit with his wicked mouth and ply the sensitive organ with tricks she'd never even imagined before. Combined with his hand—lodged in her pussy—and the desire radiating from him, he had her poised on the brink of another orgasm in record time.

"One." He continued the twisting of his wrist, nestling his knuckles as close to the ring of muscles guarding her entrance as possible.

"Two." Pressure built both inside and out when he looked straight into her eyes and smiled.

"Three." She said it for him.

"Yes." He pushed through the last of her resistance. "Three."

Lily's eyes rolled. Her hips arched off the mattress and she released a keening wail. Not only because of the stab of pain. God, it stung. But also because the overwhelming physical sensations allowed her to surrender completely to the emotional firestorm raging through her heart and soul.

Reality smacked her as his fingers naturally curled into a fist inside her. She never would have allowed anyone except her soul mate to invade her so completely. It wasn't a matter of permission so much as acceptance. He owned her.

"You were made for me," he voiced her thoughts.

Lily wrapped her legs around his shoulders, pulling him closer. Speech eluded her. Instead, she allowed him to do all the talking. He whispered endless promises in the artificial dusk of their little world. Things she had never dared to hope for from a lover.

Discomfort faded. Pure happiness replaced unease.

"That's right, Lily." He peppered kisses over her mound, belly and thighs. "I'm inside you. Part of you. Just like you're branded on me. Since the first moment I saw you I knew. You were meant to be mine."

His fingers unfurled a little.

The internal massage sent a shock wave of pleasure bursting out toward her fingers and toes. "Yes. Yes. Please."

Managing more than monosyllabic feedback was beyond her capabilities.

He pumped his fist forward then back in tiny jabs. The barest motion triggered a riot of sensation. Fingers splayed, she slapped the bed. Her heels dug into his back. Whether it was his fist or his heart triggering her rapid climb toward bliss, she couldn't say.

"Fuck, yes," he growled before he lowered his mouth to manipulate her clit. "I can feel your pussy rippling around my hand. Come for me, Lily."

Her toes curled, and her breath caught in her chest.

Jeremy rocked inside her as he devoured her pussy. The combination of his bold stuffing and his gentle worship tipped her over the edge. Rainbows bloomed behind her scrunched eyelids. Her pussy spasmed around him. Though spread enough she could barely clench, she didn't need to grip much to smother him with her passion.

When she would have descended on the far side of rapture, he chuckled against her sopping flesh. "Oh no you don't. You have more to give. More to take."

The rotation of his wrist added another dimension to the power of his shallow yet mighty thrusts. He drew a figure eight with his fist inside her, filling her to overflowing. The addictive pressure had her seeking the next crest before she'd fully dropped into the valley of the waves battering her.

Another climax stole her breath, making her gasp and shout. She clamped around him, losing track of time and space. All she knew was he had control, he wouldn't abandon her and that she could trust him. Those were the only things that mattered.

Lily soared.

She wrung every drop of pleasure from his touch. When she laid shuddering, teeth chattering in the wake of his awesome present, he finally relented.

"Very good. Such a sweet girl." He hypnotized her with his praise. "Time to let go, Lily."

She thrashed her head on the pillows, her hair tangling around her. "Nooo."

"Sorry, you have to. Just for now. We'll try it again someday. I promise." He brushed the stray strands from her sweat-slicked brow. "Remember, I'm always with you. This won't change a thing."

How wrong he was. It had altered absolutely everything.

Lily wasn't proud of the noise she made when he began to slide from her sopping pussy. A blended yell, groan and protest ricocheted around them. Pressure built to a small pain that couldn't match the sense of loss swamping her as his hand squeezed from her body.

He lunged for the nightstand and the towel he'd staged there. Even that meager distance was too much for her system, which operated on raw, primal levels after being deconstructed by his mastery. Tears leaked from her eyes and sobs bubbled up.

Jeremy surrounded her as soon as he finished drying his arm.

The mighty attempt she made to contain her emotions failed. Another hiccup slipped past her guard.

"It's okay to cry." He showered her with care and attention. Rubbing her back, he nestled her against his chest and began to rock her softly. "You've stood alone so long. No more. Never again. You don't have to hide from me or yourself. Just be, Lily. Feel. It's all right. You're safe."

"I wish I could repay you." She had nothing left to give.

"Look at me." He nudged her jaw until the blaze of his stare filled her vision. "You have. A million times over. No one's ever given me anything as special as you just did. I'll treasure that experience until the day I die."

"You're still hard." She nibbled her lip. "I didn't take care of you."

"I'll let you know when I require you to service me." He nuzzled her nose. "Being with you, holding you, is all the satisfaction I need right now."

She doubted that was true. The idea of him jerking off in the bathroom after she fell asleep bruised her heart. It didn't seem fair after all he'd done to guarantee her pleasure.

"Remember your lessons." He pressed his palm over the sore spot on her ass where he'd landed his final, stinging spank. "Would I lie to you?"

The handsome lines of his face blurred behind another curtain of tears. She'd nearly slipped into her old thinking. "No, Master. You wouldn't. I'm sorry."

"Don't worry, wildcat." He rubbed his chin over the crown of her head. "I'm going to have lots of fun taming you. I don't expect a lifetime of disappointments to evaporate in one day. For now, why don't you rest for a little while?"

Sleep sounded divine. After hitting emotional bottom then crashing through the ceiling of her preconceived limits, she didn't have a lot of energy left to spare.

"I've got you, Lily."

A smile tipped up the corners of her mouth as her eyes drifted shut. "I know."

The last thing she heard before dozing off was his whisper, "Sweet dreams."

CHAPTER TWENTY-ONE

The rumble of curses falling from the trio of cops crescendoed until Matt howled, "Son of a bitch!"

"Shh." Jeremy knocked his elbow into the overgrown oaf although he wholeheartedly agreed with the sentiment.

"Too late," Lily mumbled from the bed.

He pivoted from the monitor they huddled around in time to watch her sit up. She pressed the rumpled sheet to her chest with one hand. The other scrubbed her eyes while she yawned and stretched like a sleepy kitten.

As quick as that, he had to shift the bulge forming in his jeans.

"I'm awake."

So was his cock after taking in her adorably mussed hair and the well-fucked pout of her slightly swollen lips. He unbuttoned his pants, thankful neither of his friends could pry their stares from the gorgeous woman lounging in his bed.

"Sorry, Lily." Matt winced.

"After you stood by and let Clint manhandle me, this is the least you should be apologizing for, asshole." The gentle smile accompanying her harsh dress down remediated some of the bite.

"C'mon, JRad." Clint huffed as though he were actually offended. "You're not going to let your girl talk to us like that, are you?"

"Absolutely." He hoped she could read his approval in his smile. "As long as she kneels for me, the rest of you are on your own."

Their jaws dropped when she climbed from the enormous mattress, unconcerned with her nudity. Thank God Jeremy's earlier explorations hadn't damaged her no-holds-barred sensibilities.

Lily stuck to her guns. Slinking over to them, she propped one hand on her hip. "I'll forgive you both if you join my harem for a day. Beg nicely and I'll consider your newbie status."

Respect flared in Jeremy's chest at her brazen sexuality. A soul-deep laugh overcame the remnants of worry their strategizing and the results of his hacking had planted in his mind.

His friends exchanged nervous glances as if unable to tell she was joking. Mostly. They flip-flopped between avoiding gazing below her shoulders and meeting her fierce stare. Adorable yet formidable, she kept them off balance with her extended silence. Hell, it wasn't like the cops hadn't fucked her the night before.

Lily toyed with them because she had to know as well as he did, the other men had only been his agents. He'd directed their attraction to bolster her pleasure and relied on their loyalty to keep her safe. She had a million times more experience with mind games than either of his friends and she didn't hesitate when it came to exacting a bit of revenge.

"Or..." She drew a meandering path down Clint's chest. "You could perform a little right here in the comfort of our private quarters. I think a simple kiss might do the trick."

"You got it." The younger cop fell right into her trap. "A kiss I can do."

"Fantastic." She beamed up at him. "Matt, get over here."

"What?" The muscle-bound giant looked at him for help. "JRad?"

"This is between you and her." He chuckled. Observing her craftiness would never get old.

"I have a thing for watching my guys touch." She shrugged, distracting them with the bounce of her luscious tits. "Give each other one tiny peck—on the lips—and I'll consider it bygones. Who knows, you might like it."

Lily had bitten off more than she could chew this time. Jeremy had worked closely with the men for years and they'd never once given any indication of bisexual tendencies. However, instead of the objections JRad expected, Clint shrugged.

"Fuck it. I've done crazier shit on dares." He wrapped his hand around Matt's beefy neck and yanked. Such an artless move couldn't have forced the larger man if he hadn't been willing. Their stares clashed for a fraction of a second before Clint laid a perfunctory smack on his partner's mouth.

"Lovely." She patted each of the men on their abdomens, which rose and fell more quickly than usual. "I caught your fascinated stares at Ryan and Ben when they pleasured me while Jeremy fucked me last night. Feel free to discuss amongst yourselves later. I'll be giving Jambrea a call soon. I think I have some terrific advice for her."

"We're totally screwed." Matt smacked his forehead.

"Pretty much." Jeremy laughed out loud then winked at Lily. "Jesus, you're hot when you're devious."

"Mind if I take a shower?" She bowed her head as she stood, feet spread, hands clasped behind her back. The subtle shift might not have been noticeable to Matt and Clint. Jeremy sure as hell cherished her submissive pose.

"Go ahead. Make it quick, though." He glanced at the thick leather cuff supporting his square watch face.

"There are a few things we need to discuss before we figure out how to plant this drive, minus the data, back in Morselli's office. You should hear it. Weigh in on our plans."

"Ten minutes tops." She thrilled him by leaning in. Considering her bare feet, their faces were level as he sat and she stood, presenting her an opportunity to kiss his stubbly cheek.

At the last moment, he angled his jaw so she caught him on the mouth instead. He tried to keep their encounter fun. When she parted her lips, he staked his claim.

Clint's cleared throat made it clear he'd failed.

"Clock's ticking. Nine and a half minutes. You'll earn a stroke with my belt for every ten seconds you're late. I don't like to be kept waiting."

"Yes, sir."

None of the three men spoke as she sauntered into the bathroom.

"JRad, was that your handprint on her ass?" Clint swallowed hard.

"It sure as hell better not be anyone else's."

"I'm not going to claim I get how everything works between you." Matt surprised him by tackling the potentially awkward subject head-on. "But I can tell you're happy. Like really...in a way I stopped expecting to see from you. I'm glad she helped you find what you were missing."

"What he said." Clint nodded at the other man. "Don't fuck this up."

"Not planning on it." He sighed. "One thing at a time. Let's finish this first, huh?"

"Yeah. I still can't believe you cracked that password. I wish we could bounce this off Mason, Ty and Razor." Matt paced the marble floor. "It feels odd not having them at our backs."

"They're probably doing their best to hold off Agent Sterns." Jeremy assessed the various clues swirling around them, trying to assemble the bigger picture of Morselli, the Scientist and Sex Offender. Something didn't quite add up. He just hadn't figured out what it was yet. Without their three homebound teammates, they didn't have as many theories to test. "We'll ask Ryan to smuggle this into Morselli's office. I'll come back here, keep working on the formula. I might be able to build a query that attempts every combination. I don't know how we'll know which one's the right one. It's the only thing I can think of though."

Long before her deadline, Lily emerged from the bathroom in a cloud of steam. She sported a thin, fuzzy robe. "You don't mind, do you?"

"Normally, yes. I prefer you nude." He situated her on his lap, cradling her close. "For now, we have other problems."

"What was on the drive?" She peeked at his computer screen, tilting her head first one way then the other. "Is that what I think it is?"

"Do you think it's the chemical formula for some derivative of amphetamine in the entactogen family?"

"I have no idea what you just said." She squirmed on his lap. "But I do find nerds incredibly sexy."

"Good to know. Though I prefer to think of myself as a geek." He permitted himself a tiny taste of her smile before getting down to business. "Entactogens are the group of drugs ecstasy belongs to. They fuck with your serotonin levels for the most part. It seems like Sex Offender uses X as a base then twists it even more. The key is whatever's going on here."

He pointed to a blank spot in the structure.

"One of those doo-dads is missing, right?" She wiggled her finger toward the honeycombed lines of the molecular drawing.

"At least one. Maybe more." He clenched his fingers on her hip. "It's hard to say for sure. I'm guessing the gap is the reason The Scientist is spending time in Morselli's dungeon instead of swimming with the fishes."

"Do people really do that?"

"What? Murder their opposition?" He raised his eyebrows at her. Considering the lengths her father had gone to, she should have no doubt of the stakes.

"No, I meant the cement shoes thing. Seems a little old-fashioned."

"Figure of speech." Matt rolled his eyes.

"I wouldn't put anything past people after all the shit I've seen on the job." Clint would have spun away except Lily reached out and laid a hand on his arm.

"Stay." She laced her fingers with his.

"Thanks." He kissed her knuckles, not letting go.

Jeremy stared, in awe of her ability to read people. She had real talents you couldn't train. No, she'd been born with this aptitude. Her empathy turned him on as much as the curves beneath his palms.

"Maybe this is good news." Lily peeked up at him from beneath thick lashes. "If The Scientist isn't sharing and Morselli can't figure it out either, then the whole thing will go away. Morselli isn't patient. If The Scientist doesn't crack soon, he'll kill the bastard."

"She has a point." Matt nodded.

"If not them, someone will figure this out. There are notes. Lab techs. *Someone* knows." Jeremy groaned. "It's not that easy."

"Ryan told me his sister was hired by Morselli. To do research. She didn't know anything. They're kept in the dark. Only managing their little piece of the pie." Lily shared Ellie's story. The collateral their suspect had kept the submissive man in line with had them all fired up. "I know. And it gets worse. He has Ben's sister and his seven-year-old niece, too. We have to find them...if Morselli hasn't already gotten rid of them."

"Damn, this thing is spiraling." Clint smacked his palm on his thigh. "Too many objectives. We'd do better to divide and conquer."

Jeremy looked at the woman he held. She didn't object. Trust sparkled from her deep blue eyes. As much as he longed to lock her up somewhere far from danger, he couldn't risk damaging her faith by making the wrong call. So new, fresh, it wouldn't take much to wither her conviction. "No. Lily stays with me. Priorities are replacing this drive and locating The Scientist. She and I will hunt him. If Morselli spots us on his surveillance we can always claim to be checking out the facilities. From what we have so far, I assume he expects me to torture the man anyway. When I went up there before—" Lily massaged his chest over his pounding heart, "—I had to think of some reason for my visit. I told him Lily was addicted to SO. He offered a job he would pay handsomely for me to take care of and counted on me not asking too many questions up front. In the meantime, he gave me that. In his mind, I'm on the hook."

Matt stared at the vial next to the computer equipment. So unassuming, it cloaked the deadly hazard bottled inside. "Agent Sterns will be glad for the sample. You didn't hear him the other day, ranting and raving about it. We can run it out to Mason so he can coordinate work on the formula. If we figure out what's missing, we could identify some of the component compounds. By tracking bulk purchases of the supplies, we can try to locate the production facility."

"Good idea." Jeremy nodded. "In the meantime, Lily and I will snoop around for The Scientist."

"I wish you would wait for us to get back." Matt frowned.

"What time is it anyway?" Lily had lost all her bearings.

"Two-fifteen." Clint stifled a yawn.

"In the morning?" She ran through the day in her mind. Waking up in Jeremy's arms seemed like a million years ago and yet it was hard to believe almost an entire day had passed. "Damn."

"We can't afford to sit around any longer." Jeremy shook his head. "Things are changing. I can feel it."

"Fine. Then take Ryan and Ben with you." Clint glanced at his partner.

"Yeah, that would make me feel a little better anyway."

"We need them to return the drive to Morselli's office. Staff are used to them roaming those halls, especially near his private quarters. No one will question them." Jeremy argued against it.

"Damn it." Clint turned toward Lily. "Lucas will watch your back. Steve can handle your guys. Hell, most of them could kick some serious ass if necessary. They don't need both of their handlers for the time you'll be away."

She peeked up at Jeremy. "What do you think?"

"They're right. I'll be more comfortable if you have another set of friendly eyes on you." He stroked her cheek. "Not because I think you can't take care of yourself. But because I don't know what I would do if something happened to you. Okay?"

"Yes, sir." She leaned into his touch.

"Verify Sterns has warrants and is standing by to raid." Jeremy rose, setting Lily on the floor. "If we find what we're looking for, today could be the day."

"I hope you're right, JRad." Matt clapped him on the shoulder.

He snatched the vial off the desk and handed it to Clint. "Be careful."

"We're not the ones heading deeper into this mess." The men bumped his outstretched fist then took turns hugging Lily.

"Tell Izzy I love her," she whispered to Matt.

"You can tell her yourself as soon as this is over." He reached out as though to rumple her hair, but stopped short when he caught her do-you-want-to-keep-those-fingers glare.

"Right." He chuckled. "Later."

Jeremy wondered what the hell was wrong with him. He cataloged Lily's tight black jeans and matching lace tank along with her flat-bottomed shit-kickers and missed her usual racy Mistress gear.

"What?" She swiped a hand over the triple strand of onyx beads draped over her fair décolletage then down her chest and flat belly.

He would have paid a million dollars to lick the same path.

"Do I have something on me?"

"No." He twined their fingers as they followed Ben's scribbled directions toward the holding cells. "It's nothing."

Without the drastic heels she preferred enhancing the shape of her legs, most of her wicked curves were hidden. The solid six inches she'd lost in height didn't help him forget how easy it would be for someone to hurt her either.

"You're tense." Her thumb caressed his knuckles. "Jumpy. What's your gut telling you?"

"I don't know." Jeremy cursed. "For the first time I understand how fucked up Razor was when he lost his edge. He doubted himself constantly. It's like living with a false alarm ringing nonstop in my brain because I want you as far away from this as possible. Having you here screws with magnetic north. Instead of honing in on the right path I feel like I could chase my tail for hours."

"I'll go." The line of her tight lips went white on the fringes when she pursed them.

"What?"

"After this little stroll." She glanced at him from the corner of her eye. "You have your scrambler on?"

"Yeah, but—"

"Tell Morselli I freaked about Sex Offender. That I don't want to end up like Malcolm or my father. It's bothering me to have the guys in danger. They didn't ask for this, and it's worse than I anticipated. On top of that... I'm a distraction to you."

"No shit." Lucas muttered from where he trailed a pace behind them.

Jeremy glared at the other task force member. "I didn't say that to pull a guilt trip."

"I know." She slung her arm around his waist. "If you had I wouldn't be offering."

A shriek rang off the walls around them.

"What the...?"

Jeremy didn't stick around to answer Lucas's question. Instead he grabbed Lily's hand and took off at a run in the direction of the wail. Lily sprinted, impressing him with her speed. They barreled down a staircase then into a stone-lined foyer. Three passages led out of the junction. Torches flickered on the wall, lending to the dungeon's atmosphere.

No doubt intended to be serious, the surreal decor reminded him of a cheesy film set in a way Black Lily and Gunther's Club never had. They didn't need to consult Ben's map when another howl bounced through the space. The three of them ran shoulder to shoulder in the wide alley.

Walls became bars before long. Malnourished prisoners huddled on bunks while some, more alert, pressed against their cages for any hint of the action. Maybe they sought advance warning of impending danger. Whispers rushed along from captive to captive faster than the trio could sprint.

Jeremy counted as they passed. He lost track of the blend of addicts and Sex Offender waste products somewhere after two hundred ruined lives. With every stride, the audible pain grew louder until moans and cries formed an insistent cacophony.

"The gate!" Captives shouted at them as they ran. Distress from individuals blurred into a single message as they streaked by, "It's closing. They'll all be trapped inside with him. Someone open the gate."

Illumination ringed the bend in the hallway ahead. Dread coalesced in Jeremy's gut as a sinking suspicion developed. Could this be the pit Morselli had showed him from their lofty perch while slaves were prepared for last weekend's auction?

Sure enough, when they rounded the final corner, the stark white surfaces of the chamber loomed in front of them. Only today, it was clear The Scientist's temporary laboratory had been constructed here. Mobile stations made it easy to roll away the evidence when guests arrived.

A woven steel lattice descended, blocking escape for the herd of men and women wearing white lab coats, while preserving the view. They had been corralled into the far corner of the space. The captive audience had ringside seats to The Scientist's epic meltdown.

A tall, thin man—he might have been handsome once—he thundered from his perch on top of a stainless steel preparation table. "None of you will reveal my secrets. I developed this masterpiece. It's mine. Not to be stolen by a moron, who lucked into the drug. If Morselli thinks I'll work for his prosperity like a common laborer, he's crazy."

You would know all about that.

The psycho drew another shriek from the crowd as he launched a beaker at the floor in front of them. A trapped technician dove for the glassware. It shattered before he could reach the drug-filled bomb. The miss meant he was the first of many to inhale a lethal dose of Sex Offender.

At least his suffering would be relatively quick.

Spurred to motion, Jeremy, Lily and Lucas stormed the gate. It had already covered most of the entrance and descended from mid-thigh to knee height as they surveyed the scene. Lucas grabbed hold at the same time Jeremy did. They wrapped their fingers around the grate and heaved.

Fuck! Jeremy yanked his hands back, shaking the sting from his digits. All the effort had netted them were sliced fingers.

Welling blood, Lucas's hands must have grown as slick as Jeremy's. The man crouched anyway, having more success in slowing the narrowing gap by counteracting the pressure from the bottom of the portcullis. Still, it continued to close. Tendons in his neck strained.

"Jeremy," Lily shouted. She pointed to a box on the wall. "Over there."

He raced to the pinpad, leaving them to battle the inevitable. In matters of brain versus brawn, he opted for the intelligent method every time. The faceplate popped off with a hint of pressure. Using his jeans to swipe most of the blood off his hand, he traced wires to their sources. He wasn't going to make it in time.

"Lucas!" Lily's scream drew Jeremy's stare like the world's strongest magnet.

The man's grip had slipped. He toppled off balance. The gate dropped a solid foot in one instant, crushing Lucas's knee beneath the weight. His roar didn't faze The Scientist. The insane bastard continued to rain Sex Offender on the staff, who had unknowingly helped to create and distribute the vile substance.

Chaos consumed the world.

Too far away to help, Jeremy yelled, "Noooo!"

He couldn't make it to his teammate or the woman he'd claimed before she risked her life to save Lucas from amputation.

His heart stopped in his chest when Lily dropped to her belly. Thinner than Lucas's thigh, she slithered beneath the gate, which threatened to bisect her vulnerable body.

"Don't do this." Lucas growled through gritted teeth and the pain that had to be rampaging through his receptors. "You'll be trapped."

"Jeremy will open it again. It's just for a minute." Her shoulders flattened out as she stared straight into Lucas's eyes. Jeremy had seen her wear similar determination when she whipped her slave at Black Lily. "I'm sorry, this is going to hurt."

"Lily!" Jeremy's cry didn't matter.

Lucas yanked up on the barrier as Lily shoved his leg through to the outside. Agony forced Lucas to abandon his grip. The gate clanged shut. With Lily on the wrong side.

"One puny pinpad is a walk in the park for you." She stared straight into Jeremy's eyes and smiled. "I'm going to find Ellie."

"Stay and we'll search as soon as I fix this." Even as he issued the command he knew it would be too late. Frenzied men and women tore at clothes—theirs and their neighbor's—in the ruckus, which drowned out everything else, even Lucas's brutal curses. People would be raped, trampled or maimed beyond recognition if they didn't overdose on the vapor dispersing in a noxious cloud around them.

"You're too honorable to sacrifice someone else's safety for your own." Lily blew him a kiss. "Don't ask me to lower my standards. You wouldn't respect me for it later. Besides, I took the antidote less than twenty-four hours ago. I should be covered, right?"

"Son of a bitch." He rushed to the steel separating them and poked his fingers through. "I don't know, Lily. Maybe. I'll have this thing open in three minutes or less.

Get your pretty ass back here by then or I'm coming in, drug be damned."

"Yes, Master." She kissed his knuckles then tugged the hem of her shirt up over her mouth, baring her abdomen.

Jeremy hoped the men and women under the influence of Sex Offender didn't catch a glimpse of her stunning physique and try for a taste of their own. Tearing his gaze from her progress across the stadium floor, he flew to the access panel and employed the tricks Gunther had taught him so long ago to compartmentalize his mind and focus despite the distractions swirling around him like a typhoon.

Failing Lily was not an option.

CHAPTER TWENTY-TWO

L ily decided stealth had flown out the window as a viable option the instant four men noticed her alone and charged. She grabbed a hose off a nearby table of supplies and swung experimentally. The resulting whistle reminded her of her favorite bullwhip. She could do this.

If the drug amplified sensual caresses, she bet it also multiplied painful stimuli.

She didn't hedge when she aimed carefully and swung full force at the man approaching. Deterring him from the start was her only hope. He screamed then retreated—nursing the fiery mark she'd left across his cheek. The three others with him decided their fallen pal would serve them better than her and dove on his writhing carcass.

"Oh God, I'm sorry." She couldn't watch as they forced themselves on her would-be attacker. Despite his grunts and groans she couldn't call his participation consensual when The Scientist had stolen his inhibitions.

The ratio of men to women in the frenetic crowd made her search a little easier. Most of the lab assistants deteriorated into jumbled piles of limbs comprised of masculine parts. She climbed on top of a supply chest to survey the crowd. Though no guarantee, her gaze naturally honed in on the two or three blond manes dotting the room.

Ryan's extra-fair features supplied her only clue to his sister's appearance.

Lily hunched low to the ground as she made a beeline for the nearest candidate. The woman bounced on top of a twiggy guy hard enough Lily feared the tech might permanently injure him. Her bloodshot eyes and the visible pulse slamming in her neck didn't bode well for the stability of her vital signs.

"Ellie!" Lily shouted at the woman, but she didn't blink. The patch on her lab coat proclaimed her *Julia* instead.

Lily moved on. She scrambled around five or six unmoving bodies near the impact site of one of the Sex Offender bombs. The faint odor of lingering chemicals assaulted her. Determined to resist their lure, she braced herself for the overwhelming urge to fuck. Except the craving for rough touches never materialized.

Thank you, Jambrea.

Lily called out as she ran past any of the women. "Ellie!"

The holler drew unwanted attention. She managed to evade grasping hands by staying on the fringes of the atrocity. Interspersed with fucking bodies, she saw more than one person in mortal distress. Several grabbed their chests and keeled over before being swarmed by others eager to slake their need. Their bodies couldn't endure the racing of their hearts or the hyperthermia that would cook their brains.

How many of the lab workers would survive this horror? How many would wish they hadn't?

Lily glanced toward the entrance. Completely separated from it by the mass of addled people, it remained firmly shut. Jeremy would come through, she had no doubts. But the moment the gate opened, she would have to flee—Ellie or no Ellie. She wouldn't risk Jeremy coming after her only to become another senseless victim.

She raced for the last blond in the room. "Ellie!"

The woman ignored her. Dazed, she stared as a man fucked her pussy, another pounded her tits and a third filled her mouth. As Lily approached, she realized the woman was too old to be Ryan's little sister. Damn it, no.

"Ellie!" She pivoted and screamed into the throng.

"Help me." A faint response caused Lily to hold her breath, afraid to risk a peep that could obscure the thready entreaty.

"Ellie?"

"Here. Ahhh." The young woman moaned, deep and guttural. Whether in pain or pleasure, Lily couldn't say for sure.

She took two giant steps toward the thin girl buried beneath a pile of feverish men. Lily hadn't even seen her on the first pass, so many bodies engulfed her.

The whiz of Lily's improvised weapon zinged through the air as she advanced, swirling it over her head. Prepared to battle, she didn't notice the man hovering on the desk beside her until he jumped into her path.

The Scientist.

She allowed him to stumble closer, laughing manically. Foam gathered at the corners of his chapped lips. He'd inhaled too much. It wouldn't be long before his heart exploded in his chest. Either that or his own creations would destroy him.

"You." A long line of drool stretched to his shirt.

The dazed victims pairing off and fucking each other senseless blurred in the background, as close to a real life zombie apocalypse as Lily could imagine. Worse considering none of the impacted humans attempted to fight the drug mutating their natural tendencies as surely as some sci-fi virus.

"You were supposed to be mine." He lunged faster than she would have believed possible. The drug hadn't stolen all of his coordination. His ragged yellow

313

fingernails scraped across the exposed skin of her chest, snapping the necklace she wore.

Beads bounced in every direction.

"No, fuckwad." She refused to be cowed. If she died here, at least she'd make sure he suffered at the end. "It was my sister, Isabella, you tried to buy and rape. She was a virgin and you didn't give a shit. How many other innocents have you destroyed?"

"Maybe just one more..." Zealous light entered his eyes as he stalked closer.

"I'm no innocent." Instead of backpedaling, she ran forward and slammed her knee into his groin. "That's for Izzy."

He doubled over, grasping his crotch.

"And this is for me." Lily channeled the mixed martial artist she'd traded tutoring for topping close to ten years ago—after the first time one of her father's associates attempted to force himself on her. The Scientist became all of the slimy motherfuckers she'd been exposed to in her lifetime all in one. Before she realized it, her foot had launched into a roundhouse kick. She heard the crack of his jaw when her boot connected with his face.

The Scientist flew backward. Blood and something that looked like a tooth spurted from his mouth. He smacked his head on the corner of the desk. The ragdoll flop of his body as it crashed to the floor ensured he'd been knocked unconscious...or worse. A nearby cluster of men stopped tearing at each other long enough to descend on the fresh meat.

Lily gagged when one humped the limp man, pinning his body to the industrial linoleum while another yanked The Scientist's head toward his exposed hard-on. The sick pop that resulted left no question they'd broken the evil bastard's neck.

That didn't stop them from ravaging his lifeless body.

From the epicenter of anarchy, pandemonium raged around her.

Shock paralyzed her.

"Lily!"

She peered over her shoulder. The gate rose steadily. Jeremy ducked beneath it before it rose waist-high.

"Stay back." She waved him off. "Sex Offender. It's still in the air. It's strong."

He slowed, watching cautiously.

Lily closed her eyes for a fraction of a second then screamed, making as much noise as she could. Along with her battle cry, she lashed out with the segment of tubing, whacking a half-dozen men from the crumpled form on the floor. Ellie no longer fought them. Instead, she gazed with blank eyes at the avenger blazing toward her.

"Move," Lily yelled, holding the guys at bay as best she could. Sooner or later, one of them would snag her feeble weapon. "Now. Go!"

If she could save only one of the unfortunate people here today, she wanted it to be this one. She had to do some good.

"Ellie. Get up." Lily grabbed her arm and dragged the woman. She couldn't do much while staving off the pack. "Ryan needs you to move. Now."

"Ryan?" The girl blinked. A trickle of blood leaked from her eye. If Lily couldn't smuggle her to safety soon, she wouldn't survive. She might not anyway.

"Yes. Ryan." She stared straight at the girl and told the truth. "He needs you. Run."

Ellie scrambled to her feet. Clumsy and uneven, her strides carried her toward Jeremy, away from the disaster they left behind. Lily turned and paced her, throwing one arm around Ellie's waist. Jeremy met them halfway. He mirrored her supporting grasp and half-carried Ryan's sister from the chamber.

The instant they cleared the gate he stabbed a code into the reconstructed pinpad.

Metal creaked and groaned as it separated them from the Sex Offender targets.

Jeremy released a giant sigh, either because he'd held his breath while he dipped into the contaminated area or because he relished their safety. Probably both.

"Help me." Ellie collapsed at their feet. She swiped at her own skin. "It hurts. Please, please, do something."

Despite the awkward angle of his leg, Lucas didn't hesitate to comfort the woman they'd rescued. He whipped his shirt off a spectacular set of muscles and covered her perky breasts, bared by her tattered clothes.

"Leave me behind." Lucas dusted Ellie's bangs from her eyes. She lurched upward and attempted to grind against him. "She needs help quickly. I'll only slow you down."

"We're not abandoning anyone." Jeremy grasped Lucas's arm. He hauled the other man upright, bracing his bad side. "Don't pass out on me and we'll be okay."

Lily nodded at her lover, grateful he trusted her so completely. She took a deep breath, cleared her mind and embraced the motivational faculties she'd developed her entire adult life. "Come on, Ellie. We're going to see Ryan. He'll help you. He'll make it stop hurting, right?"

"Ryan." The girl probably didn't even notice the tears streaming down her face. "He'll fix me. He always does."

Minimizing skin to skin contact for Ellie's sake, Lily helped the tech to her feet. She spoke gentle, calming nonsense the entire scramble to the wing housing her harem. What had taken five minutes at most to traverse the first time took at least three times as long on the return journey. Sweat poured down Lucas's back. He never once complained.

When Ryan's name began to lose its effectiveness in keeping Ellie alert, Lily changed tactics. "Tell me what you did for The Scientist?"

"Bonding."

"What does that mean?" The string of technobabble that followed might have meant something to Jeremy. It didn't to Lily.

"Do you know the molecular structure of the compound you were working on?" She tried a few times to cut through the fog growing thicker in the woman's bloodshot eyes.

"Dimethoxy, dimethoxy, dimethoxy." Ellie chanted it over and over.

"Jeremy, was that part of the drawing?"

"No." He peered over his shoulder. "But it could fit. What are the odds?"

"Pretty good I bet." Intuition reared up. They'd found the missing link.

Ellie began to whimper and shudders wracked her. Lily wondered if walking alone might be causing the woman to come involuntarily. Ellie impressed Lily as she fought the debilitating arousal by chanting her brother's name over and over to survive the betrayal of her body.

"She's not going to make it much farther." Lily whispered to the men in the lead.

"Almost there, sweetheart." Jeremy glanced over his shoulder, his eyes dark with fury and pain. "Hang on. You've got this."

But she didn't.

Ellie collapsed and nothing Lily said or did could make her move again. Lily attempted to lift the woman. Every time she touched Ellie, the girl thrashed and groaned.

"Ryan!" Jeremy bellowed despite the risk.

Not more than five seconds later, the man appeared at her side. He skidded to a halt, crashing to his knees. "Ellie. Oh, God. What have they done to you?"

"Ry?"

"Yeah, it's me." He jerked his hand back when his comforting touch made her flinch and cry harder. "You're going to be okay."

"Love you."

Ryan returned the sentiment. His sister didn't hear. She'd already blacked out. At least Lily hoped she'd escaped to unconsciousness and not something worse. He scooped his sister into his arms and dashed, overtaking Jeremy and Lucas, who'd continued their steady march toward shelter.

Lily brought up the rear, shutting the door to the hallway firmly behind them once they all trundled inside her office. "Move the dresser in front of the passage. No one gets in."

Ben, Cameron and several other slaves rushed to obey.

"Hurry, Ive." She waved over one of her assistants and rattled off a string of orders. "Bathe her in cold water then hook her to one of the fucking machines. We won't be able to administer the antidote for at least an hour or two. She can't sleep through this. It'll wake her up, burn her alive, if we don't get it under control."

Ryan stared at her like she'd gone crazy.

"The Scientist dosed her with Sex Offender. A bunch of it. More than what I took last night for sure."

"I'll kill him." Ryan snarled as he headed for the makeshift barrier. Lily didn't doubt he'd rip it to shreds if she didn't prevent him from leaving.

"Too late." She swallowed bile. "I did it for you."

"Oh, fuck." Jeremy bustled her into the far corner of her office, stealing as much privacy as the space could afford. "Are you okay?"

"Numb, mostly." She dropped her head against his chest. "I have to stay calm for my guys and my staff. I can't think about it now. Later...maybe we can talk it through."

"Damn straight." He kissed her brow. "Of course we will. You're doing great."

She adored him for putting his back to the room. No one could intrude with his broad shoulders shielding her from losing face. Not that any of her chosen family would respect her less for temporary weakness in the face of such horror.

"This is crazy, Lily. We have what we came for." Jeremy squeezed her hand. "Round everyone up. Let's get the hell out. There were too many eyes. Morselli will know soon, if he doesn't already, about our interference."

She nodded.

"I'm calling Mason." Jeremy checked his watch for the thousandth time. "Matt and Clint should have been back by now. Something's not right. He'll figure out a way to cover our extraction."

Lily winced when Jeremy daubed a drop of blood from her split lip. How had that happened?

"Take care of your guys. The assistants. Lucas and Ellie. I'll gather my equipment, make the call and be knocking down your door in fifteen minutes tops." He took her shoulders in a light grip. "I promise. I'm coming right back for you."

"I know." She didn't hesitate one instant before surrounding his wrists with her fingers.

He sighed as he took in the ripped nails tipping her hands. "Be ready to run."

"Yes, sir."

***

"Agent Sterns says it's not enough." Mason bit off the bad news.

Jeremy kicked over the chair he'd spanked Lily in the day before. "What the fuck else does he want? A sworn confession?"

"He wants the entire formula—"

319

"Which I'm ninety-nine percent sure we found." Jeremy refused to spread it over the unsecured phone. If he had the answer, it had to stay secret. Or everything they'd worked for would be for shit.

"—and a link to put Morselli away for life."

"Lily swiped the fucking drive from his office. The Scientist took out himself and most of his staff to avoid the fucker." He yanked on his hair. "The witness we rescued could be next. She wasn't in great shape when I left. How many more have to suffer? Die?"

"I agree with you, JRad." Mason cursed. "Your dickhead boss is arguing it's all circumstantial. He's lobbying for you to stay undercover until you locate the production facility."

"They only need probable cause to raid and discover the rest. You know it as well as I do."

"Yeah." His friend sighed. "I'm liking this less and less by the minute. The hair on my arm is standing straight up."

"Yours and mine both."

"Go grab your girl." Mason panted as though he were running. "We're on our way. We'll be right there to pull you out."

"Thanks." Jeremy punched the end button on his phone and shoved the device in his jeans pocket. He ducked beneath the strap of his duffle and made sure the items he'd left behind could be sacrificed.

As he flew along the corridors, he ran through a checklist starting with transportation for the wounded to potential weapons they could scrounge. No amount of mental war-gaming could have prepared him for what he found when he returned to Lily's quarters.

The door swung half off its hinges.

Steve swam in a pool of his own congealing blood. A bullet had torn a ragged hole in his chest. Jeremy paused to close the cloudy, wide-open eyes of his fallen teammate. He said a quick prayer before lurching to his feet and sprinting for Lily's temporary office.

He had to dodge a vase swung at his head when he blasted inside, unannounced.

"It's me, guys." *Jesus.*

"Master Jeremy." Ryan hovered beside his sister, blocking her from the entrance. Tears filled his eyes. His throat flexed when he swallowed hard. "Morselli took Lily. There was nothing we could do. She ordered us to stand aside—traded her life for ours. It's not fair. It's not right. She's the best of us."

Jeremy didn't hang around to ask useless questions or place blame on victims. Only one man was responsible for this.

Morselli would pay.

***

Lily dangled from her bound wrists. The rough rope wrapped around them cut into her pulse point, making her ultra-aware of her pounding heartbeat. Her fingers had gone numb almost instantly. The weight Morselli tethered to her chained ankles guaranteed it.

Pressure threatened to tear her joints apart. Her toes dangled in tepid water. Machines whirred nearby. She had no doubt the tangled mass of tubes and containers surrounding them housed Sex Offender in various stages of the cooking process. The enormous steel and glass-paneled vat she hovered over fed a plethora of pipes leading toward the production facility.

If her captor expected the constant discomfort—or the threat of being left to drown—to convince her to spill Jeremy's secrets, he had another thing coming. She could hold out against physical pain indefinitely. Her father had made sure of it.

"You might as well start using that." She angled her chin toward the long whip Morselli held. "Would you like a lesson first? I'm fairly sure your technique will be crude at best."

"Dumb bitch. I can't figure out why he still wants you. Once, for the hell of it... Why not?" Morselli grinned. "I would have broken you. After that, what's the point?"

"You could've tried." She'd die before she begged for his mercy.

"Feisty." He tsked. "Not really my thing."

He was quick. Lily would give him that. Telegraphing his intent highlighted his rookie status, though. She had plenty of time to counteract her ingrained tensing and prepare to absorb the blow. Sting radiated outward. She harnessed the burst of energy and banked it to help her withstand the next lash and the next.

Unlike a skilled, caring Master, Morselli considered nothing about her as he sliced through her thin tank and scored the flesh beneath. "Tell me who he's working for."

Lily didn't bother to respond. She focused on isolating the portion of her brain influenced by pain and diverted her mind to pleasurable stimuli—the color of Jeremy's eyes, the exquisite patterns of the inked art highlighting his cut body and the sensual purr her name turned into when he murmured it while he buried himself inside her.

"Damn you." Morselli increased the frequency and strength of his swings as she began to spin beneath the force of his blows.

She had always enjoyed having her back flogged. What this bastard did to her had nothing on sensual experiences, but it wasn't the first time someone had tested her limits. Habits sprang to life as she channeled the agony into something constructive. She pictured a day when all she'd lived through—every ounce of pain—paid dividends.

Jeremy would come for her. He'd promised he would. A man of his veracity would never violate an oath.

Especially not one he'd sworn to a woman he felt affection toward.

How much did he care? Enough to build something that would outlast his investigation?

A sliver of doubt crept in, opening her heart to the suffering Morselli attempted to inflict.

"I'll stop." The creep peddled false hope. "If you tell me. Is it Gunther trying to steal my secrets? Or is our dear Jeremy flying solo? Has he promised to share his empire with you?"

Lily stared him straight in the eye when she spit in the direction of the steel-grate platform he perched on.

"Not very ladylike. What would your Master think?" Morselli snapped the whip across her breasts this time. Though she withheld her scream, she couldn't prevent herself from assessing the damage. Blood oozed from the crest of a nasty welt already rising on her fair skin.

Despite her best intentions, the room, the universe, narrowed to one evil bastard. She bit her lips to keep from uttering a single peep. Nature granted no quarter. She couldn't battle the debilitating fog stealing her consciousness.

"Do you really think he'll cut you in on the action?" Another strike, this time to her calves. "No way in hell. Why should he?"

It didn't surprise her that Morselli couldn't comprehend the true reason for her silence.

In a kinder, more controlled environment, she'd facilitated extreme pain. Those subjects who'd begged for it often described a communion with their innermost essence following those episodes. They experienced a meditative high that could become addictive.

Surrounded by the brilliance of pure emotion, she admitted the reason she'd never reveal Jeremy's affiliation with justice. In a surreal, otherworldly place— far above the pedestrian plane she usually inhabited—a million disparate hopes and fears crystalized.

She loved him. Was *in love* with him.

"Fine. Bitch. Have it your way." Morselli ramped up his brutal attack.

With every new jolt of agony, she railed against the encroaching darkness, which threatened to consume her.

A stray swing of the savage instrument wrapped around her hip and picked up speed. The tip went supersonic and split open her inner thigh. Mercifully, the excruciating pain overflowed her mental strongholds and shut down her system.

The world went black.

***

Cold.

That's all she could think.

Until millions of razors attacked her. Her eyes flew open and panic spread when she realized the maroon stains floating before her meant Morselli had dunked her in the tank. Thank God he'd left her mouth and nose above the water line. With her weighted feet and bound hands, she'd never escape.

Master Jeremy, where are you?

A jerk nearly ripped her shoulders from their sockets. She gasped as panic replaced searing pain. Was she falling? Or rising? She couldn't tell.

"Welcome back." Morselli crouched at the edge of the vat, meeting her stare.

If only she could take him with her, she'd gladly sacrifice her life to rid the world of his malignant presence.

"F-fuck you." Her teeth chattered despite her best efforts at calm.

"Last chance." He snarled. "I don't have time for this shit. If you won't tell me who the two of you are teamed up with, I'll make sure you don't blab to anyone else about what you've seen. I'm not exactly a patient man."

"No shit." She glanced toward the door, expecting to see the silhouette of her sexy-as-sin cop.

Nothing.

"Burn in hell." She didn't flinch when he threw a lever. The entire hook suspending her separated from the chain. Somehow it missed bashing in her head and ending things immediately. Whether that was a blessing or a curse, she couldn't say.

Bubbles rose around her, whizzing skyward as she sank. The weight between her feet clanged into the bottom of the tank. She supposed that's what she got for making fun of cement shoes. Awkward angles paired with the slimy surface beneath her feet, guaranteeing she wrenched her ankle.

Still, she didn't thrash. Lily preserved her breath as best she could.

Jeremy *would* come for her. He'd promised.

Unless Morselli had already done something to him...

No.

She calmed the immediate jolt of despair causing her to wriggle against her bindings.

If only she could see him again she wouldn't hesitate another minute to share what she'd suspected for months and had given herself permission to admit when the lightning of Morselli's whip had smote all her false pretenses.

Lily would shout her love for Jeremy from the rooftop if she had the chance.

She held hope even as her lungs screamed for oxygen.

And screamed more.

And more.

The final wisps of air disintegrated into her bloodstream as memories flashed before her eyes. She comforted herself by imagining Jeremy supported her in the bathtub and any second now he'd raise her up.

Because that's what the man she trusted would do.

The friend who'd comforted her at Malcolm's funeral and in the hospital afterward, the champion who'd fought for innocent victims by her side, the Master who'd shared his taming touch on stage in this hellhole and the soul mate who'd demonstrated complete possession of her being.

Her lungs shriveled as she forced her instincts into remission. Aspirating a huge swig of water would end her battle.

He was coming.

He would save her.

The fringes of her vision dimmed once more. True gaspers chased the euphoria lifting her spirit higher with each passing moment. So high, she thought she imagined a distorted version of Jeremy's voice and his face just outside of her reach. Close enough to her final wish, she figured there was no better way to spend her last instant on Earth than to tell the illusion what she wished she'd shared with her Master.

"I love you."

Chapter Twenty-Three

Jeremy charged between a pair of stainless-steel silos. He didn't have to pause to figure out he'd stumbled into the belly of the beast. All around him Sex Offender oozed through enclosed, large-scale production equipment.

Mother fucker.

Didn't it figure he'd breached the inner sanctum exactly when it no longer ranked as his top priority? He'd lost precious time searching for Morselli on the surveillance cameras he hadn't been able to access before without leaving a trace. He no longer gave a shit about avoiding detection. Racing around hunks of metal, he searched for the two large holding tanks he'd spotted on the live feeds.

There. Except the spot where Lily had hung, enduring the cruel lash of Morselli's whip, no longer supported her.

Jeremy glanced around. He scanned the floor for footprints. Fresh paint on concrete had ensured none lingered. Rounding the corner, he tripped when he caught sight of Lily, submerged in a water storage tank. The slight blue hue to the liquid painted her face with an unhealthy cast. She thrashed in her bindings, clawing at the rope around her legs.

"Lily!"

"I'm sorry about that, *Detective*." Morselli stepped from the shadows, a gun aimed point-blank at Jeremy's heart. "I have to admit, I'm a little disappointed. You had me convinced you were a player. A worthy opponent, not a pathetic cop who's dumb enough to speak openly over an unsecured phone line."

"Get her out!" He snarled despite the danger to himself.

"Or what, you'll turn over all the evidence you've compiled?" Morselli's cackle proved he'd flipped over the line from functioning despot to full-on psycho. "You've already done that, haven't you?"

"Fuck yes." Jeremy struggled to win their game. If he had any chance to save Lily, this was it. Standing there, negotiating, when he needed to rush to her aid killed a part of him as surely as if Morselli had blown him away. If he didn't live up to his promises to Lily—to always come back for her, to keep her safe—the man might as well pull the trigger. "But a jury might be more lenient if you free her."

"I think I'd rather take my chances." Morselli chuckled. "Maybe you'll kill me yourself and save me the trouble of a brutal prison murder. I'm not the kind of man to rot under someone else's reign. I make my own rules. I won't go to jail."

"Too much a coward to do the honors yourself?" Jeremy raised an eyebrow. "Go ahead. Take the easy road."

"I'd rather reunite you with your pet Mistress if you don't mind." Morselli's knuckle turned white on the trigger.

Lily, I'm sorry.

And then Morselli's wide, joker smirk dissolved into a chunky red and grey sauce.

The bang of the gunshot didn't register on Jeremy until the husk that used to be Tony Morselli hit the floor.

Razor raced to his side. "Holy shit, JRad. He was going to do it. Are you okay?"

When Jeremy did a double-take toward the doorway, Mason stood with his gun still leveled in a double-handed grip. Tyler pressed his forearm over the other man's wrists, lowering his weapon. He smothered his lover in a one-armed hug.

Their blatant affection triggered the defrosting of Jeremy's brain.

"Lily!"

"What the—" Razor gawked at him as though he'd lost his marbles when he bolted toward the tank.

Struggles over, she floated at the extremes of her bonds. The peaceful look on her face terrified him. His heart stopped in his chest when she moved a tiny bit. She smiled and mouthed something he swore looked like, *I love you.*

Spasms racked her body. Her hair billowed around her like a dark cloud in a violent summer storm. Though it seemed like an eternity, she went lax in a matter of moments. Deathly still.

No! Not again!

He refused to be too late for her.

A metal cabinet seemed light as a feather as he hefted it above his head and smashed it against the glass panel. A clang reverberated around them when the fixture tumbled to the floor. It hadn't shattered the industrial thickness.

"Mason, I need your—"

A *crack* winged around the room. The thin white line on the tank spider-webbed across the surface until dozens of flaws developed.

"JRad! Move!" Razor shouted to him as water and glass gushed from the weakened pane.

The tsunami slammed into Jeremy, washing him a dozen feet from where he'd started. He scrambled toward the gaping hole in the container when Lily poured from the opening. A weight anchored her to the base of the tank.

"Need a knife." He shook his head, sending a spray of water from his face and hair.

Tyler leapt over the debris and hacked at the soggy rope with a small yet effective pocketknife. As soon as Ty cut her loose, Jeremy dragged her onto a clear section of the floor. He deposited her gently, tipped back her head and began CPR.

His brothers stood in a semicircle around the macabre scene. As though he floated outside his body, he noticed every detail of the nightmare while he worked on the woman who'd given him everything. Including her trust.

Razor folded his hands and prayed while Tyler made quick work of the cords binding her arms. Mason hauled out his cell and called someone, probably Lacey, to send an ambulance.

Jeremy willed Lily to breathe—pleaded for her heart to pump. Instead, her face blurred and merged with Karen's. The awful color of Lily's skin resembled the hue his ex-girlfriend's had taken on when she'd sprawled lifeless on the floor of her shitty apartment.

He redoubled his resuscitation efforts.

"JRad." Tyler laid his hand on Jeremy's shoulder. "That's enough. She's gone."

"No! I told her I was coming back. I promised."

"She knew." Mason wrapped his arm around Jeremy's chest and tugged him backward. "I saw the look on her face. She knew."

"Don't make me deck you." Jeremy wrenched loose and tried again.

More pumps.

More breaths.

More begging to every power in the galaxy.

"It's over." Razor crouched beside him. "I'm so fucking sorry."

"Lily." He buried his head against her chest and gathered her body into his arms. "I love you too."

CHAPTER TWENTY-FOUR

"**A**gent Sterns." Jeremy forced himself to stand despite wobbly legs. He teetered from the body on the floor. The grotesque lump beneath the canvas tarp resembled the woman who'd stolen his heart in no shape or fashion. Still, he had to force himself to tear his watery gaze away in order to meet his superior officer across the litter of rubble.

He scrubbed his cheeks as though the evidence of his desolation could be wiped clean so easily. Soggy clothes barely registered on his dazed brain. He had to concentrate on making it through the next hour, the next minute. Otherwise Lily's suffering might be for nothing.

Shivers racked his body. "Thanks for coming. Things turned into a giant cluster."

"You can say that again." The agent edged closer, not paying full attention to Jeremy as he scoped out the facility, the shrouded form—Jeremy couldn't bear to think of it as the woman who'd filled his arms with laughter and heat—and the smeared remains of Tony Morselli. "You were smart to call me in. Alone. I can help. We'll keep this quiet."

"Thank you, sir. I never meant for it to go this far." He groaned then attempted to choke out some explanation. "If the public sees this… It looks bad. On Lily. She didn't deserve—"

"You're a cop, son. Problem number one, I gave you instructions. A mission. Your hard-on for some expendable bondage Barbie shouldn't have rated in our investigation." Agent Sterns came awfully close to having his heart ripped from his chest with Jeremy's bare hand.

Screw his career. It had probably breathed its last gasp along with the woman he'd never have chosen to leave behind. He refused to hear anyone, especially this man, insult her.

Not right then, not ever.

"She was *not* a prostitute." Jeremy gnashed his teeth as the bastard approached the tarp and stared down at the carnage there. The angle of Jeremy's torso prevented the asshole from attempting to touch her or even look at her.

"Whatever you want to call it." Agent Sterns shrugged. "I'll have to call in favors to pass you through board review after this fiasco. If I'm gonna go to all this trouble for you, I have to know I can count on you next time. No matter what I ask. Maybe if you'd done less fucking and more undercover work, you might have some idea of the final component of the drug."

Jeremy didn't really give a shit about *next time*. He couldn't stomach anymore of this bullshit. He had to end the game, break free of the lies. Time to cut to the chase. "I know the whole formula."

Sterns stopped dead in his tracks. "What? Why the fuck didn't you say so?"

"It didn't seem important anymore." Jeremy gnashed his teeth as he remembered how Lily had thrashed as she drowned in the storage tank. His guts cramped.

Agent Sterns laid an arm on Jeremy's shoulders.

Jeremy didn't think he imagined the tremor there.

"You know, you're right. I've been insensitive. You had feelings for this woman. Let me help. Share your burden with me and I'll make sure the trial proceeds as it should. You can stay out of it and nurse your grief."

Jeremy chewed his lip. Detachment pervaded his mind despite instincts screaming at him to think. To react. All he hungered for was an end to the madness.

"We have the production facility. The chemical construction is the last thing we'd need. If you're able to button up the case, I'm sure the department will overlook the tragic repercussions of decisions made in the line of duty. Sacrifices are often necessary for the greater good." Sterns nudged the body beneath the cover with the toe of his boot before Jeremy could stop him.

"Seems extreme to prove Morselli was the ringleader." Jeremy shrugged. "What does it matter anymore? The man is dead. We're shutting down the premises and no one but me knows the formula. Why not let it die here?"

"Too many people know about Sex Offender." Sterns shook his head vigorously like a dog after a bath. "Someone will figure it out. If we have the formula we can take countermeasures. Bolster the antidote, monitor key supplies..."

"I see your point." Jeremy had to agree since he'd argued the same points earlier. "Diethanolamine."

No sooner had the information passed his tight lips than Agent Sterns drew his service weapon and aimed it dead center on Jeremy's forehead. "Thank you, Detective."

"So it's like this, huh?" Jeremy didn't bother to react. Instead, he stared down the cold steel barrel and into the eyes of Judas.

"Don't worry. I'll put you out of your misery." Sterns cracked a smile that revealed his crooked, yellow teeth. "Couldn't have planned it better, really. The reports will be easy to fabricate. Plagued by guilt over failing your lover and killing a man, you take your own life. Tragic. At least you'll probably be honored as a martyr."

"Could be worse." Without Lily, he would have nothing to lose.

"Yeah, you could be spending life behind bars for betraying everything you ever stood for." Matt smothered Sterns in a bear hug. The cop could be scarily quiet for someone his size.

Clint swooped in to steal the agent's gun and knock his knees out from beneath him before the fucker realized what had happened. In the blink of an eye, the agent knelt with his hands cuffed behind his back.

The men in blue dashed from their hiding spots. They surrounded the traitor who'd disgraced all they upheld. If looks could kill, Sterns would have been rotting in hell with Morselli.

"You think you're so fucking smart? Take me away. It doesn't matter. I have the information I need. Something with this kind of potential can't be stopped by steel bars."

"You really think I'd give you the key? How stupid do you think I am?" Jeremy imagined pummeling the asshole, maybe landing a few solid kicks to his ribs. Instead, he crossed his arms over his chest and glared.

Sterns shrank away, whimpering.

"Dumbass." Jeremy shook his head. "I can't believe it took this long to map your trail of lies. I should have seen it sooner. Sure, you rated the occasional hand-slap for tampering, tainting evidence or skirting space between black and white, but you were smart about hiding your addictions. I'll give you that."

"No one understands. Until they try it. You could have been one of the few. The power, the stamina, the drive..." Obsession flashed in Sterns's eyes. "I could have had it as often as I wanted. No more tiny samples from the evidence locker."

Oh shit. Jeremy wondered how he could have missed the signs. The investigation had moved too slowly. All those delays. Not to facilitate proper substantiation. No, more like time to ensure the cooking operations had been restored. Mother fucking Sex Offender. "I don't need drugs for a free pass. You could have earned those things from a true partner."

"Like your dead bitch?"

Jeremy growled. He whipped the tarp off the figure on the floor.

Lily's faint smile expanded as she sat up, slow but steady. She held the sleek digital recorder he'd equipped her with. "I could hear him crystal clear once you lured him closer. It's all here. Every bit of the confession you need to put him away for life."

"All I care about is you." Jeremy settled to the floor, welcoming her into his arms. "That's enough. You're done. We're going to the hospital right fucking now. You need to be examined. So long. God, you stopped breathing forever."

Lily snuggled into his chest and patted the muscle above his stuttering heart. "I'm okay, Jeremy. I promise."

"I'm not sure I am." He pretended not to notice his fellow cops forming a barrier between him and the corrupt agent. They shuttered him from sight, granting him as much privacy and protection as they could.

"We will be okay." Her eyelids fluttered closed. "It's finally over."

EPILOGUE

Jeremy sat beside Lily on a stone bench at the top of the hill in their friends' backyard. Wildflowers rioted in colors ranging from white to yellow to pink to blue. Crisp air rolling off the lake in the distance puffed his lungs full of peace and tranquility.

Below them, their ever-growing family celebrated Mason, Tyler and Lacey's garden wedding. Matt and Clint shared a table with Jambrea, falling all over themselves to be next in line to bring her a drink or another slice of cake. Lucas lingered nearby in his wheelchair. Ellie surprised Jeremy by keeping the brooding soldier, who'd been honorably discharged from a no-name Special Forces group once the extent of his injury had become clear, company.

Ryan hovered nearby, sharing occasional laughs with Ben and Gunther. Little Julie frolicked in the long grass. Despite the loss of her mother, she seemed to be hanging in as best as could be expected. The intimate gathering of a few other friends including Zina, Rhonda, Dr. Joy and Mama Rose overflowed with smiles. They created good memories to replace some of the terrifying ones they'd lived through in the past year. Camera flashes dotted the dimming evening.

Razor swung Isabella in a circle while executing some fancy move on the cobblestone patio they'd transformed into a dance floor. Their puppy barked and jumped for the ribbon dangling from Izzy's light and airy dress. They laughed and scooped the adorable mutt between them.

"They'll make great parents one day." He hadn't meant to speak out loud.

Lily hummed and snuggled closer. Her silence lingered a little too long.

"What?" He tipped her chin up and studied her eyes. The electric blue—the most beautiful color in the world—would never dull in his esteem.

"It's a secret."

"I'm good at keeping my mouth shut." He frowned. "Besides, we don't have any of those from each other, do we?"

"Of course not." She kissed his palm then whispered, though no one else was near enough to overhear. "Isabella is pregnant."

"What?" He sounded like a broken record. Damn, he'd have thought he'd be one of the first to find out. "The kid didn't say anything to me."

"He doesn't know yet." Lily smirked up at him. "Izzy told me when I found her in the bathroom last week. She knew it was the only way to keep me from ratting her out about being sick. She didn't want to steal any of the wedding thunder."

"No shit." Jeremy grinned. "Were they trying..."

"No, but she said they're ready. They've talked about family. Marriage. She's going to tell him tonight." She smiled. "So it looks like you're going to be an honorary uncle."

The joy in her gaze hit him like a ton of bricks. He couldn't stay quiet a moment longer. "What if I want to be an official uncle?"

"What?" It was her turn to be surprised.

Jeremy liked this side of the game a lot better. "I love you, Lily. There will never be anyone else for me. I know this is all new and fresh, but I'm sure."

He dropped down on one knee and took her hand in his.

"Are you...?"

"Yeah." He withdrew a red satin pouch from his pocket. "I saw this the other day when I went with Razor to buy a ring for Izzy."

He laughed out loud. "He's not the only one who'll be getting the surprise of a lifetime tonight, huh?"

"She'll be so happy." Tears welled in Lily's eyes.

"And you? I know how important family is to you." He kissed her knuckles before lining up a platinum and diamond ring, shaped like two calla lilies entwined, at the end of her finger. "It would be my honor to share the rest of my life with you. I promise I'll do my best to make you happy every day. Will you marry me?"

"Yes," she sobbed as he slid the band on her finger. A perfect fit. "I love you, Master Jeremy."

He cleared his throat. "About that..."

Her eyes bugged when he tipped the bag upside down and a matching necklace dropped into his palm. The thick chain formed a solid rope dotted with more lilies and subtle yet handsome stones.

"Do you like it?" He studied her reaction as she ran her fingertip along the length he held out to her.

"It's gorgeous." She stared into his eyes, her fingers trembling in his.

"Not even close to how spectacular you are. As what we have together is." He had practiced this speech for weeks, never finding exactly the right words to express himself. Here, with her, it came easily. Natural. Just like always. "I want you to be my wife. More, I want you to belong to me. Accept my collar, my promises and my love. Lily, I know how much I'm asking of you, and I swear I'll earn every bit of your devotion. Please, give me everything."

"I already have." She bowed her neck so he could fasten the collar around the slender column. "I'm yours. Always."

"And I'm yours." He smothered her in his arms. The shift in their weight as she leaned in knocked him off balance.

They laughed as they tumbled to the long grass. He pillowed her descent on his chest before rolling her beneath him. "One last thing—"

"There's nothing else. I have everything that matters." She gazed up at him, touching her fingertips to his cheek.

"Let's just say, I'm glad you didn't turn me down." He grinned as he shucked his sport coat then unbuttoned his dress shirt. When he'd made it about halfway, she gasped.

"Is that real?" She dropped her hand, lightly tracing the pattern through the clear saran bandage holding the healing gel against his new tattoo.

"Fuck, yes." He laughed. "Permanent. Just like us."

Lily laid a kiss beside the bouquet of lilies tattooed over his heart. "Forever."

"Starting right now." He couldn't help himself. His hand slid up her thigh beneath the flirty skirt Lacey and Izzy had convinced her to wear. Pausing briefly, he soothed the healing mark on her thigh. It would scar. But it wouldn't mar her beauty. The evidence of her strength only made him love her more. When he reached her pussy he hissed. "No panties? You naughty girl."

"Maybe you should spank me." She wiggled her eyebrows.

"Later," he growled against her lips as he unfastened his pants. "Right now I want to love you. Sweet and slow."

"Another first?" She massaged his scalp as she kissed him with lingering swipes of her lips. She tasted like icing from the wedding cake.

Yum. "Yeah, but not a last."

A soft moan escaped her when he pushed inside her pussy with gradual shifts of his hips. The sound of birds chipping, the wind in the flowers and their friends laughing in the distance accompanied their gentle mating and the only variety of love that mattered.

The forever kind.

WHAT HAPPENS TO JAMBREA,
MATT & CLINT AND THE REST
OF THE MEN IN BLUE?

SPREAD
YOUR
WINGS

MEN IN
BLUE

JAYNE RYLON

NEW YORK TIMES BESTSELLING AUTHOR

Waiting. Watching.

Jambrea was patient long enough. After nearly ten years pining over a man with whom she'd spent a single night, her job set her on a collision course with two sexy cops who turned her head...and ignited her passion.

More agonizing. Debating.

When it became clear that Matt and Clint would never admit to the bisexual attraction making an equilateral relationship possible, she couldn't choose a favorite. So she had to turn away and move her life forward—without them. Jambrea approaches Mistress Lily and Master Jeremy to arrange a wild night at their sex club—never expecting her friends would pull a bait and switch.

Time's up.

Just when happily ever after dangles within reach, it becomes clear someone has Jambrea in their crosshairs. Is it one of her lovers' old cases coming back to haunt them, or a ghost from her military past? One thing's for certain. Now that they've made the leap, they'd better learn to soar...or they'll all crash together.

Warning: The Men in Blue have handcuffs and they're not afraid to use them. On their woman, or each other. Be naughty, if you must. Maybe they'll come for you next!

AN EXCERPT FROM SPREAD YOUR WINGS, MEN IN BLUE, BOOK 4

"Hey, Jambs, come on," Izzy shouted to her from the dance floor, waving to their group. The couples had split up a bit now that something other than endless love songs bleated from the speakers. All too eager to leave her dates, Jambrea shot to her feet.

Clint braced her when she teetered. Damn heels. She smacked his overly familiar hand before it could work any of its hornifying magic. Enough with the pheromones already.

Then she sauntered onto the floor in time to the beat and tried to burn off a little of the buzz she might have underestimated. Lost in the music and revelry, surrounded by friends, she forgot about some of her angst. Until Lacey leaned in and whisper-shouted, "Matt and Clint are about to choke on their tongues over there. Show me some hip shimmies!"

Screw them. Why not?

Jambrea obliged.

It wasn't long before Lacey's face lit up. "Incoming."

"What?" Jambrea peeked over her shoulder. Sure enough, the two men she'd obsessed over for the past year or so stalked closer. She whipped her head back around toward her friends. "They don't dance."

"Maybe they will for you." Izzy grinned as she ground her backside against her fiancé, who wrapped his arms protectively around her and the child she carried.

"I doubt it." Jambrea refused to let them ruin her fun though. If anything, she redoubled the swivel of her ass and dug into the groove of the beat.

And then there were hands on her waist, turning her. From the way her captor's thumbs nearly touched in the base of her spine, they could only belong to Matt. He tucked her close to the furnace of his body and rocked in a basic side-to-side step, mostly in time to the music. She closed her eyes and settled against him.

"Hey, mind if I cut in?" Clint asked.

Jambrea blinked when he reached out, cupping her ribs in his palms. Four hands on her at once nearly short-circuited her brain.

"Actually, I do," Matt growled.

"Too bad." The other man wasn't retreating. Instead he pressed closer, flanking her with their gyrating bodies. Her breasts brushed his chest as she undulated, caught between rubbing herself on one or the other. Or both, after Clint took another half-step in.

Instinctively, she wrapped one arm around his neck while the other reached behind her to palm Matt's ass. Her head fell back, resting on his chest. Clint leaned in and took a taste of her exposed neck. When someone whistled, they all jolted. What the hell was happening? Where were they again?

Oh, right. The reception. Jambrea shook her head, clearing the blazing desire from her mind as best she could. Unfortunately that only made the dance floor rock like the deck of a ship. Uh oh.

"I've got you," Matt rumbled in her ear.

"No, we've got you," Clint corrected.

For a few minutes, she stopped fighting and pretended that they meant it like it sounded. It was the best one-hundred-and-twenty seconds of the year so far. Then the song ended and the DJ announced the final dance. A ballad.

"We're getting the hell out of here," Matt proclaimed.

The guys corralled her toward the guests of honor. They exchanged congratulations one more time.

"Have a good night." Lily's sly grin didn't allow any room for misinterpretation.

Before Jambrea could respond, her dates whisked her to Matt's waiting black chariot. Clint didn't bother to boost her into the truck. This time he encircled her waist and lifted her onto the seat as though she weighed nothing at all.

"What were you trying to prove out there?" Matt rubbed his jaw. "Every single guy in the room was drooling over you. You've had too much to drink to be advertising like that."

So they hadn't rushed her home to sample the wares she'd been hawking? No, they'd just planned to block any other interested man. The wave of disappointment that hit her made her feel sick. Fortunately, she only lived a few blocks away.

They spent the entirety of the ride in silence.

The teeter-totter they'd been balancing precariously on slipped from its fulcrum. She couldn't take another minute of the erratic highs and lows, and especially not these weird, forced, blah middle points. No more.

Despite her protests, they insisted on walking her to her apartment. Granted, she lived in a relatively crappy neighborhood that had deteriorated bit by bit since she'd moved in nearly a decade ago, but she'd never had issues before. Her pair of cops were more dangerous to her than random thugs.

When they held the door, she couldn't help making one last bid for what she felt slipping through her fingers. It was now or never.

"You know, I didn't even see any other guys at the reception tonight. What do I have to do to make you like me?" She rubbed against Matt, uncaring about how pathetic she looked or how much she'd hate herself in the morning.

"Son of a bitch. I do like you. Too much." He stared at her in horror as they squeezed together into her apartment, Clint close on their heels.

He groaned in the background. She spun on him. "Come on, tell me. What'd I do wrong? How did I screw things up? Am I supposed to pick one of you? Is that what this is? Some stupid male contest? Was it because I kissed you both? Was that some kind of test? Did I fail?"

"Jambi, no." Matt spun her around again. The world tilted and she wondered when the last time was that she'd been so hammered. "You've got this all wrong."

"Then why? Tell me what I did!" She couldn't believe that she raised her voice, but it felt good to finally let off some steam so she kept ranting. "One minute you were sucking my face off and the next time I saw you, you wouldn't even look me in the damn eye."

"It wasn't because of you. It's...us," Clint admitted as he and Matt exchanged a worried glance. Good, let them be afraid. They could share the sour stomach that had been rotting her from the inside since the fallout of that single reckless, yet addicting, moment became apparent.

She waited, but they didn't elaborate. "Really, that's the best you can do? Some talk. 'It's not you, it's me' never convinced anyone."

"Maybe this isn't the best time..." Clint hedged.

"It's never going to be the right occasion. It's been months already. You're cowards, both of you. I never would have guessed it before. Go home, jerks!" She wrenched off her shoe, then threw it at Clint, catching him in the gut. His oomph held a note of surprise. "You're not going to do this to me anymore. I'm tired of waiting, hoping, for something that's never going to happen. If you won't be honest with yourselves, at least be upfront with me. Tell me you don't want me. Say it."

"Jambi, you're dr—" Matt cut off when she swung her furious glare toward him instead.

"No. Forget it. Shut up." She flapped her arms, not caring that she'd lost her temper for the first time...maybe ever. Irrational fury barred them from conjuring some ridiculous explanation that would steal her thunder. "No more excuses."

"I don't think it's smart to leave you like this." Clint looked to his partner for backup.

"I'd rather be alone than babysat by you two. Unless you plan to come to bed with me, get out." She yanked the hem of her dress over her head and launched the gossamer sheath against the wall. It slithered to the floor and lay crumpled.

One of the guys, or maybe both, cursed as they took in her silk lingerie. It only made her feel stupider that she'd pretended even for an instant that she'd get to display it in far more favorable circumstances tonight. When would she learn that just because she hoped something would happen, that didn't mean it would?

She kicked off her remaining shoe, enjoying the clunk it made as it joined her dress, then stormed into her bedroom. Alone.

ABOUT THE AUTHOR

Jayne Rylon is a *New York Times* and *USA Today* bestselling author. She received the 2011 RomanticTimes Reviewers' Choice Award for Best Indie Erotic Romance.

Her stories used to begin as daydreams in seemingly endless business meetings, but now she is a full-time author, who employs the skills she learned from her straight-laced corporate existence in the business of writing. She lives in Ohio with two cats and her husband, the infamous Mr. Rylon.

When she can escape her purple office, Jayne loves to travel the world, SCUBA dive, take pictures, avoid speeding tickets in her beloved Sky and—of course—read.

62843315R00199

Made in the USA
Lexington, KY
19 April 2017